A MIXTURE
OF MADNESS

BOOK II OF
THE BOW OF HEAVEN

A NOVEL OF ANCIENT ROME

BY

ANDREW LEVKOFF

ISBN-10: 0983910154
ISBN-13: 978-0-9839101-5-2

cover illustration / design by Lynnette Shelley
www.lynnetteshelley.com

for Allison and Stephany

• • •

"No excellent soul is exempt from a mixture of madness."
- *Aristotle*

• • •

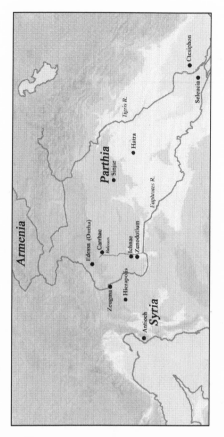

Illustration credits

Map: Christopher Jones, riversfromeden.wordpress.com, with additions by Andrew Levkoff

Part I: Coming Home, *Landscape with the Ashes of Phocion*, Nicholas Poussin, 1648

If you would like to see more maps from the period, please go to andrewlevkoff.com/maps2.

Bob & Di —

Save this,
some day it
may be worth
the paper it's
written on!

You guys are
the best!

[signature]

PREFACE

55 – 54 BCE - WINTER, ON THE MARCH

Year of the consulship of
Gnaeus Pompeius Magnus and Marcus Licinius Crassus

"**B**ona Dea! What was that?!" Legionary Flavius Betto sat up, shoving Drusus Malchus awake. Betto, whose tent-mates called him Muris, the mouse, set to work upon a hangnail as if he were breaking his fast.

"It was a scream," Malchus said, yawning and stretching. "You're a soldier. We're at war. You'll hear lots of screaming. Go back to sleep." The four other soldiers in the tent agreed with short, vehement curses. The Celt threw a bronze mess cup at Betto but hit Malchus. Betto was lucky the two remaining members of their *contubernium,* the brothers Broccus, were on guard duty.

Malchus casually tossed the cup back toward its owner. He was philosophical about these things. People were often throwing things at Betto, and his friend Malchus, being so much the greater target, took his share of unintentional abuse. He was the only man in his *century* who could not wear standard issue. It would be unfair to call him fat, and more unkind than unwise. Hostus Broccus had once said that if they were ever shipwrecked

1

together, they could make a raft of his body and a sail from his tunic. Hearing this, Tarautus Broccus had pressed a finger to one broad nostril, leaned over and emptied the other with a sharp exhale. Broccus had wiped his face on his tunic, then said he'd rather swim for it than lie on Malchus' naked chest. Drusus had laughed along with everyone else.

"It wasn't a scream," Betto argued. "It sounded more like…like the moaning of my Aunt Iunia."

"You told me she died from eating bad mullet year before last."

"My point exactly." Betto began to reach for the tent flap, then thought better of it.

"It was a scream," Malchus muttered, knowing this was an argument he would not win. He pulled his brown wool *sagum* all the way up over his head, wondering if he could fall back asleep before the next sentence was uttered.

"How could it be a scream?" Betto asked the woolen lump that was his best friend. "Have you looked outside? We're in *Roman* Syria, not Ctesiphon. The fighting hasn't started yet."

"It will if you don't shut up!" said the Etruscan.

"That's it. I'm wide awake now," Malchus grumbled. He threw off his cloak, leaned forward and peered through the tent flap. "The blessed *cornu* will blow within the hour anyway."

"It's another omen, I know it," warned Betto, peering over Malchus' shoulder.

"Oh, here we go again," said someone else.

"You think I'm joking?" Betto said. "Tell me, how did Malchus and I come to join you fine fellows? I'll tell you how." Someone muttered "again," but Betto plowed ahead. "Because the six other legionaries we shipped out with drowned, that's how! Remember the men who stood on the *rostra* with us in Brundisium? Well now they're DEAD!"

"And here *you* are in the first *century* of the first *cohort* of Legion I *Columba*," said the Celt, throwing his tunic over his head.

The Etruscan muttered, "Columba. Why name an army after a bird of peace? The Dove Army — about as threatening as a kiss on the cheek."

"Ever have 30,000 doves shit on you?" Malchus asked.

The Celt continued unperturbed, "Under whose standard march the best legionaries Marcus Crassus' *sesterces* can buy. So I suggest you start acting like it."

"It's been almost five months, Flavius," Malchus said. "You need to let it go. You're driving everyone crazy."

"You don't understand," Betto persisted. "Thousands of men drowned. I don't suppose you call that a *good* omen, do you?"

"Think on it, my superstitious friend," Malchus said, "there is a reason the gods gave you a mouth that closes and ears that don't." This got a laugh from the others, who had now resigned themselves to being well awake by the time Diana's Hymn sounded.

"Scoff if you want," Betto said. "But between the tribune's curse and the ill wind that took our brothers, I'd say someone in the command tent isn't praying hard enough."

A voice in the dark said, "The proper sacrifices were made to Neptune and Tempestates. The legion's augur confirmed our crossing at that inopportune time has been absolved. There's an end to it."

"There's an end to it, all right," Betto groused. "If by 'it' you mean us." He joined the others and started dressing. At least his pre-dawn nerves, Malchus told him cheerfully, would enable them to beat the morning rush to the latrine.

•••

"This is not the way. We're in the wrong wing! Give me that!" I seize the torch from the slave. "See my atriensis *in the morning and instruct him to flog you. Ask for Alexander. Now be gone!" Athena, protect me – not here again. Not again, I beg you.*

I point the sputtering torch down a dark hallway and see that it is too short to be my own. In the dark, they all look alike. The spirits of a house come alive at night. Torchlight sets them free. Too many columns. Too many shadows. No one about. Even the slaves are abed. I'm drunk. How can I be drunk and dreaming?

Luca.

They say the entrance to Hades is at Avernus, but for me it lies here, somewhere in this house. No matter where I walk, in the end, the torture of the pit awaits me. I'm so tired. If I could but sleep a dreamless sleep. Come nightmare, do thy worst and let me rest. I hurry now past columns that throw grasping shadow arms. There is the garden atrium, rain splashing into the impluvium and blowing spray in gusts over the slick tile floor. I slip on a wet spot and fall to my knees. The torch skids, hits a clay planter head-on and goes out with a hiss and a small explosion of sparks.

That is the sign. I am close now. I get to my feet and grope along the walls until finally, I hear a woman's voice, low and urgent. It doesn't sound like my wife. More words, then a grunt as if someone has been struck. I draw my pugio *from its scabbard for the hundredth time, swearing that this time I will plunge it into the traitor's neck. I make my way down the hall, past two empty cubiculae. I squint at a wall painting, recognize the image of Orpheus and Eurydice, the viper curled around her ankle. Now it comes.*

Knowledge spurs me not to greater speed, but turns my feet to stone. They scrape on the stone floor as I drag myself forward, my mind silently screaming, 'Awaken! Awaken!'

The cubiculum has no door, and the heavy drapes that separate it from the hallway are partially drawn. I peer past the curtains. The room is dark, and I can hear more than I can see. The rhythmic grunts of the man in the room are occasionally echoed by a woman's groan, whether in pain or pleasure I cannot tell. There is also the intermittently rhythmic thump of a chest of drawers as it is knocked up against a wall.

Forms begin to be discernible out of the murk. Two bodies face the wall, leaning over the waist high wooden chest. A man whose head is turned away from the doorway has his tunic pulled up above his waist and stuffed into his belt. His pale, exposed buttocks moves in a short arc, up and down, like comic moons unsure whether to rise or set. I can see the prominent bald spot on the back of Caesar's head as he hunches over my wife's right shoulder.

"Haste, Julius," she says, "or my husband will discover how boring you are." Her last word turns into a grunt as Caesar responds with a vicious thrust that practically lifts Tertulla off her feet. I gag as I always do. Does she mock him, or encourage him? I can never tell. The left shoulder of her tunic is torn. Did she struggle? Or is this more evidence of their ardor? I know as I follow the slender line of her bare arms, up to her shaking shoulders, past her neck and the ringlets of hair that half obscure her cheeks, that whenever I force myself to gaze just a little higher, I will find that she is looking straight into my eyes.

5

Now Crassus, now! Here in the instant of recognition, in the one moment when all the gods call out for decisiveness, for retribution, this is the moment for action! I feel the knife in my hand, but I cannot move a muscle. She has pinned me like an insect; though the light is still very dim, I know she sees me standing here. Is that a look of terror that passes over her face at the sight of me. Too soon, whatever was there is replaced by an expression of unbearable sorrow.

The meeting of our eyes is far more terrible than the sight of her rutting. Move, Crassus, move! The longer I stand here, the more my shame grows. The longer I delay, the more shards of me fall away and shatter. Quiet! or they will hear. Look away, Tertulla, set me free to act, but she holds me fast with the saddest gaze in all the world.

Cold sweat pools around the hilt of my dagger till I feel it will slip from my fingers. Something new in this recurring nightmare! With immense effort, I can raise the blade till the iron comes between my lady's eyes and mine. The spell is broken. Now to act! Quickly, choose one of three fates and end these night terrors. Slip it beneath my own breastbone or, if Tertulla be untrue, then this long knife should pass full through her slender throat. No, no blood shall stain her fair neck with crimson, not by my hand. It must be Caesar then, whose pulsing artery cries out for severing. The man I'd thought my friend is turned the other way; he cannot see me, his mind fixed as it always is, on conquest.

Tertulla makes a small, frantic gesture. She shakes her head in a clear imprecation for me to do nothing. Her eyes widen and only because of thirty years' intimacy with that face, could I see she wants me to slip away, to depart – to continue to do what I have done since the moment I had come upon them – nothing.

So, there is to be no peace. Nothing changes. Does she save me, or spurn me? Knowing that my mind will now crack like an egg only makes the coming agony worse. In my chest, there lies a thick knot of rope where my heart had but a moment ago beat; now it tightens, tightens. I know I will obey her. Even in betrayal, it is a reflex of love I cannot abandon. And the core of me, already broken in two, finds it can shatter into even smaller pieces. I take one step back and let the curtain come between my eyes and hers, between a joyous past and an empty future.

When I am all alone again in the dark, I scream.

PROLOG

19 BCE - SPRING, SIPHNOS, GREECE

Year of the consulship of
Quintus Lucretius Vespillo and Gaius Sentius Saturninus

I forgave him.
Perhaps that is my failing.

•••

My head jerks off the table and once more I take up my pen. Why must the old succumb to so many naps? We begin as babies and end the same; but the dreams of the very young are free from torment. I have lived too long and seen too much to be at peace. Sleep is not the refuge it once was.

I see a man on a skittish horse, but memories of dreams do not hold up well in the light — the fragment is frail and fleeting. I think of Crassus, and how I used to calm him from his recurring night terrors.

Melyaket pads quietly onto the patio, sits on the balustrade, one foot on the floor, the other dangling. His strange attire no longer startles: today he wears a pale green, belted shirt with a wide band of embroidery along the edges and the wrists of its odd, long sleeves; a plain leather vest and the *sherwal* of his land, baggy trousers tied at the ankles. I ignore him until a cloying, acrid smell wrinkles my nostrils. "Must you do that here? " I ask him. He is waxing his bow with what smells like rancid goat fat. I glance up and notice for the first time that grey has begun to cajole a place in amongst the thick tangle of his short, black curls. He tells me he must leave, an announcement I have anticipated yet quietly disregarded. I think how sad his absence will make me. He laughs and I realize I have spoken my thought aloud. "I thought you'd be happy to be rid of me," he says.

"Let us say your departure will give slightly more pain than your arrival. When will you go?"

"At sunrise."

"Then waste no more time with an old man. Go, prepare yourself," I say. Melyaket reminds me that there is real work yet to do; he cannot sit like me, day in and day out, doing nothing but admiring the sea.

A man of astonishingly fleet reflexes, which in my case are hilariously nonessential, Melyaket has taken a step backward before the thought to strike him has reached the muscles in my arm. Intention finally pairs with action, and my walking stick swings ineffectually past him. "You think this is nothing?!" I cry hoarsely, pointing a shaky finger toward the stacked tins stuffed with completed parchments. Melyaket smiles, lays his bow against the railing and wipes his hands on a rag. He pads behind me, grips me with strong fingers and kneads the stiffness from my shoulders.

"You're a good boy," I say, mollified. I reach up to pat his hand.

"And you are an alarmingly old man," he says. After awhile he circles round and drops to his knees before my chair, his necklace of polished blue stones clinking. Sitting on his heels, he says, "Try not to die while I'm gone." His eyes speak in silence what words would cheapen.

"Try not to get killed before you return," I reply.

Melyaket smiles the smile of faith. "By the grace of Melek Ta'us, we will see each other again."

"Hmmph. You and your Peacock Angel."

"Do you think we have come all this way by accident?"

"What I think about it is as irrelevant as your faith. Then, we were there; now, we are here. Go, live your life, what's left of it."

"Wait and see. With Her blessing, I shall bring company when I return."

I glance up at him, my eyes two stones. "He is dead."

"You do not know that for certain."

"Then I am dead, to him. Don't waste your time."

As he so often does, Melyaket ignores my words. "How about one more foot massage before the midday meal?" He reaches into one of the bottomless pockets of his trousers and wags a small vial of oil before my eyes.

"If your hands are dry, just say so," I answer, bending to remove my sandals.

"You are a gnarled old walnut tree, aren't you." He warms a few drops of oil in his hands. Then he looks at me with that way he has. I hate that look. "Camel," he says.

I stare him down, but it's no use. Before his hands touch my grateful heels, I start to smile. And then we laugh.

•••

The scrolls of the first part of my tale are on their way to Alexandria, and Melyaket has left to find whatever destiny awaits him. Both are dear to me and I pray that each may find their way. Neither is a certainty. Was it chance, prowess, or the goddess Melek Ta'us who had protected him through all his years? If this Peacock Angel be everything Melyaket claims, may she watch over him and return him safely. And while I am asking for miracles, may she and any other gods who are eavesdropping on an old man's thoughts watch over me as well, so that if and when Melyaket returns at last, he does not find me feeding the vegetables in the garden, and I do not mean from a bag of manure.

My writings are as safe as I could make them: a friend at the *Serapeum* will see to their copying and distribution. To publish the work in Rome would be to invite the ire and censorship of mighty Augustus, who not only styles himself Caesar, but *divi filius,* son of the divine one, Julius Caesar himself.

Octavian's great-uncle was no god, no matter what accolades the senate may have heaped upon him. Julius Caesar invaded our home to filch advantage from a counterfeit friendship, looked down upon his benefactor as if my master's generosity were an amusing imperfection in character, and most heinous of all, Caesar sought to cement his own political advantage through my mistress by assaulting her and using the rape as political blackmail. I would wipe the horror of that night from my mind, but it will not go. It remains as fresh and vile as the stink of Melyaket's goat fat.

•••

Years ago, letters from Rome described the political ascendancy of Gaius Julius Caesar. I still have them. At the time, I told myself an ailing empire had finally fitted to its neck a cunning, ruthless head to match its foul and corrupt body. I cannot deny that my gratification was palpable when word reached us here on our tiny island refuge, almost a decade after Crassus had sailed from Brundisium to meet his own fate, that with a frenzy of daggers, the gods had granted Caesar's wish for an "unexpected death. "

Calmly, Alexandros, calmly; you are too brittle to allow yourself to be cracked by immoderate indignation. At whom would you direct it, and to what effect? You must husband your strength if you are to have any hope of achieving your own modest purpose. Righteous choler is such a taxing emotion. Indeed, at my age, it takes some bit of wind to rise or sit, hence I am resolved to stay where I am put. No, hatred is a coin best spent by vigorous, ambitious youth.

Harken to me now; I am composed.

PART I

HOME

Andrew Levkoff

CHAPTER 1

56 BCE - SUMMER, ROME

Year of the consulship of
Cn. Cornelius Lentulus Marcellinus and L. Marcius Philippus

It was a bad day for Livia's homecoming. We had just returned to Rome from Luca; nerves were frayed and twisted like an unkempt braid. Though Crassus had been assured of a five-year term as governor of Syria, he was sullen and the mood of the *familia* was more funereal than festive. Normally, I would have helped him through his discontent with dialogue and philosophical diversions, but not today. I occupied myself instead by making a distracted attempt to teach my new assistant to balance the monthly grain accounts; my distraction was total — I was as breathless and as jumpy as a fish in a net. That evening I discovered the man had done a superlative job without any help from me. I was soon to learn why Crassus had foisted this freedman upon me. There were two reasons, one more disturbing than the next. But we shall come to that.

Pacing back and forth through the atrium, then out past the guards to scour the street for any sign of her, I thought about one of the last times Livia and I had been together, almost six years earlier. Another unhappy day.

15

•••

The true and lasting punishment from being whipped comes not with the stinging agony of your flesh being stripped from your back. Though you think it never will, that pain fades. Not so the humiliation you are meant to carry with you ever after. These Romans have had centuries to refine the art of encouraging submission. The true penance of a good scourging is writ with a dye more indelible than the knots of twisted rope that crawl beneath your tunic. Those scars that tug and itch with every bend or stretch are proof that you have been separated forever and always to live amongst that class of creature which welcomes those rebellious individuals of their breeds – horses, oxen, dogs and other unmanageable examples that are not fully domesticated. In my case, I was moronically proud to claim that I was not a very good example of Roman subjugation, for both Crassus and I knew, even as he cracked the *lorum* into my flesh, that faced with the same circumstance, I would repeat the "offense." Did this make me a bad slave? Or Crassus a lenient owner? Neither one of us paid heed to the strict rules of Roman society — as a slave, I should never have laid hands on Julius Caesar, *praetor* and *pontifex maximus,* and because I did, Crassus should have had me crucified, and yet he spared me.

But you see, this whipping had very little to do with punishment, and almost everything to do with love. No, I have not lost what little remains of my senses. When Caesar assaulted Livia, meaning to defile her, it was either love or madness that spurred me to break his hold, punch him in the face and knock him to the ground. (Truthfully, he fell back onto a couch, but the affront was the same; I might as well have thrust a knife into him.) In the crystal sanity of that moment I was certain beyond any doubt that my love for Livia was genuine and pure. How? Because I knew the next day I would be dead. I was surprised and proud, with only a smidgeon of regret to discover I could count myself among the very few who could say they were willing to die for love. And prove it. At least my 8,791 days as a slave would finally come to an end.

Crassus had no choice but to set an example. A slave assaulting a noble must be dealt with swiftly and brutally. The consequences must be a merciless warning to others, severe and shocking, so that news of the horror of it travels far and wide. Even more so in our case, since we were summering at Baiae, over 100 miles from Rome. That is how I am certain that Marcus Licinius Crassus, the same general Crassus who revived the dormant, lethal discipline of *decimation* and subjected an entire *cohort* to it for fleeing the field of battle in the war against Spartacus, the heart of that same hard man bore some kind of love for me. Here is how he demonstrated it: he threw Caesar from his home and chose the whip for me rather than the cross. Granted, it was a peculiar display of affection, but affection nonetheless. Did I love him for it in return? No, but Pan's hoof, he knew me too well. In truth, I did not want to die, and I had no choice but to be *grateful* to my master that the kiss of the *lorum* was all that I suffered. That tickled him, no doubt. I took solace in the knowledge that though he would never treat me as an equal, he often treated me as a man. For a Roman slave, that was something.

By the way, if your predilection for lurid details has not been satisfied by this abbreviated version of these gruesome goings on, and you slaver for the original and more explicit accounting, the Serapeum will have copies of the first set of scrolls of this sad chronicle. Providing that ancient temple and repository of knowledge still stands.

Just before my sentence was carried out, Livia ran up to me and kissed me briefly on the mouth, her eyes shimmering. She also called me stupid, which stirred as much hope in my breast as her caress. Unfortunately, there shortly came proof that doused that anemic, yet emboldened flame: before I had risen from my sick bed after my ordeal, I discovered she was gone, and without a word of parting! *Dominus* had allowed her, at the last moment, to accompany Baltus, the pompous but competent *medicus* who had treated my wounds, along with a dozen men and several women from our own fledgling clinic and medical school to travel to the House of Life in Memphis to learn all they could of that ancient civilization's healing art. Livia, it seemed, had been granted permission to set aside her duties as seamstress to follow in the footsteps of her disgraced mother. She intended to become a healer. The excruciating irony of this tale is that with Crassus' blessing and funding, it was I who had established our school of medicine, of which there were almost none in plague-ridden Rome, ravaged as it was by the rose-spotted fever and again every summer by the rage of the Dog Star.[*]

I learned of her departure three days into my recuperation. They had kept me drugged with opium-laced wine to keep me still and on my stomach. When I came to my senses, I found lady Tertulla by my side with Baltus' replacement standing close by, a florid and

---

[*] *(Editor's note: typhoid fever and malaria, respectively. See Glossary.)*

overheated physician who annoyed me by rocking back and forth on the balls of his feet, keeping his less than immaculate fingers interlaced over his belly.

"*Domina*," I croaked. Crassus' wife, then thirty-eight, was almost as lovely a first vision upon waking as Livia would have been. Her dark curls were laced with periwinkles, the same color as her *peplos*, which was o'er-draped by a white *palla* of such fine material it appeared as if she sat in a cloud. She smelled of verbena.

Tertulla took my hand and said, "My fine, brave fool. Is there much pain?"

"Where is Livia, *domina*?

"I am so sorry this happened." Romans tend to crush conversation with the wide wheels of their own thoughts. "You know my husband had no choice in this matter?"

"I am thankful for his lenience."

"You acted exactly as I would have done, Alexander, and more bravely, too. Would that I had been there in your stead." She laid a gentle hand on my blanketed shoulder. "The repercussions," she said, glancing down the length of my back, "would have been contained. Caesar is a disgrace. Politics makes his presence necessary, but I will do all I can to keep him from our home in the future. Of course we can never admit it publicly, but *dominus* and I will always be in your debt for protecting one of our *familia*."

"It was very good of you to be here upon my waking, my lady, but I should very much like to speak with Livia."

"She sat by you, in this very chair, day and night."

"Might you summon her, my lady?"

"She's gone," the fat doctor interrupted.

"Gaius Flavius!" Tertulla snapped.

"Gone? What do you mean, gone? Gone where?"

"You need to rest," they both said at the same time. Flavius wiped his brow with a hairless forearm.

I forced myself to a sitting position, buds of perspiration blooming almost as rapidly upon me as they grew upon the good doctor. Tertulla said, "*Dominus* asked to see you when you were well, but don't tax yourself now. He will explain everything to you."

I asked forgiveness from my lady as I stood, sat down, then stood again, wincing as my wounds complained from far too many places. I steadied myself against the scrollwork of the couch's arm, breathing through my nose, lips pursed, refusing to take my eyes off *domina*. At last she relented and told me he was in the *tablinum*, nodding for Flavius to assist me. I shuffled through the house and as Tertulla had promised, found Marcus Licinius Crassus in his study. "You let her go!" I cried. "To Memphis!"

My owner looked up from his work.

"In Egypt!" I said.

Dominus asked Gaius Flavius in a voice which incontestable power had made soothing, almost seductive whenever he addressed those over whom that dominance was wielded, "Should he be up?" The doctor, standing nervously at my side, supporting me gingerly, glanced at the dressings on my back and shrugged, a gesture which would have him seeking new employment as soon as I was well enough to tend to the matter. I gripped the back of a chair for support and told Gaius Flavius to see to his other patients.

"You sent her to Egypt," I repeated when the healer had retreated to wherever it was he went to practice being inconspicuous.

"Calm yourself, Alexander. In fact, it was Livia who begged me to let her go."

"And you agreed to this?"

Crassus rose from behind his worktable and bade me walk with him in the peristyle. "Do you remember that first day when you were brought before general Sulla as a gift for me? It must be 25 years or more. You burned as hot as the eternal flame in the Temple of Delphic Apollo."

"Yes. As I recall, Sulla extinguished that flame and sacked the temple about the same time his soldiers seized me in Athens."

"He may have done, but that is irrelevant to my point, which is that you were in a frenzied state that only an arrow could subdue."

"Lucky for us someone had one handy. Can you stop her? I am begging you to bring her back."

"Hush. Look at you now. Time has softened your resolve to murder every Roman citizen in his bed. One might even say that after all this time, you are content."

"I live only to serve."

"If only that were true." Crassus sighed. "But then, a *gladius* would be worthless with a dull and blunted edge."

"It may not be too late, *dominus.*"

"You are the penultimate proof, my old friend." My look was blank, peppered by twitches of frustration. "To test my intellect," he explained, "I understand that those who surround me must also test my patience. But once again you have steered me from my intended harbor."

"Your point is clear, *dominus.* Give her time, give her time. I have given her twenty years! We fell in love, barely more than children, but then her mother murdered Tessa. When I proved it so, the light in Livia's eyes turned to ash. For years, we toiled beneath your roof as strangers; I kept my distance, but my heart, once given, could not find its way home. I followed your advice. I waited. Waited, while

21

she formed a *contubernium* with that sculptor; waited as she buried him a year later. She was twenty-five. Afterwards, the years were kind to me; Livia did as you predicted, her regard softened and we became friends once more. But it was not until now that I dared hope she felt something more. And she is gone." I sagged, unable to bear the weight of Roman will that pressed in upon me.

Crassus held my shoulders as gently as he could. "She will return, my friend. I promised her that if she studied hard and proved herself able, she could assume her mother's duties in the clinic."

"Why did she go?" I whispered. "Why now?"

"Perhaps the answer lies in here, my lovesick *atriensis*. Go, read it in private, then return to me before the fourth hour. The senate is still spluttering about Catiline's surviving supporters, and I promised the conscript fathers I would appear by lunchtime to hear more of Cicero's pathetic attempt to ingratiate himself with the senate after his exile. I'd sooner bite the head off an uncooked mouse, but there it is."

Crassus handed me the letter; I tripped three times in my gangly haste to find the privacy of my rooms.

•••

To Alexander, House of M. Licinius Crassus
Rome, Quintilis
I have much to say to you and hardly know where to begin. First and above all others: do not expect my gratitude for your foolhardiness. Why would you risk everything for me? Someone with the right to stop Caesar probably would have come along, and if not, who are we to resist? What if he had asked *dominus* for permission and it had been granted? Would you have tried to save me then? Whether he raped me or let me go—these

things are both of a kind, the same side of the same coin. We are nothing. You less than I, had your intervention gotten you killed. I do not want you to be my hero.

It is late and I am tired. I would feed what I have written to the brazier and start again had I more time and parchment. You are brave and kind, Alexandros. You are also a fool, but maybe I have been one as well. I know you expect no words of gratitude, but you shall have them anyway. I could not bring myself to wake you, and they will not hold the ship. I must leave for Ostia before dawn. Thank you for rescuing me.

I think that maybe I can say what I am about to say, even after all this time, because I am leaving and must write my feelings down rather than speak them to your face. You see, I am a coward as well as a fool, and will not risk the lash of your remonstrations. After Sabina was sent away I could not approach you, first from anger, then from sorrow, and finally from shame. The more time that passed, the easier it was to let it go. To let us go.

I ask your forgiveness. I was so young when we fell in love—barely seventeen, and then came the awful business with my mother. I despised and blamed you when *dominus* sent her to the mines for killing poor Tessa. I hated you for proving her guilt. But here is the truth I have never spoken till now: Sabina was a murderer. Not you. You did what you always do: you chose the right over the good. She did an awful thing, a crime to be punished and reviled. But I could not bring myself to lay those loathsome feelings upon my own mother. So I draped them over you, and poisoned everything that was ever good between us.

I must speak to you of Lykos. Sabina was gone, I had turned my heart against you, and I had no one. I was miserable, and Lykos was kind. It is unbearably sad that he came to such a terrible end, but the truth is, I hated myself for never being able to fully return the feelings he had for me. I could love no one in those days. It is a terrible thing to say, but when he died, part of me was relieved. And something else. It was my time with Lykos that showed me that my love for you *was* real. And that I care for you still.

I need to get away from here, from this house, from the memories and the pain. Bless *domina* and *dominus* for allowing me to make this choice. I need to find myself again. Sitting by you while you slept reminded me of the first time I saw you — shot by one of Sulla's archers all those years ago. If you would only learn to keep your mouth shut your health would drastically improve! See — I am learning to smile again. When I return, I hope to be a new person, with new purpose and new hope.

It is almost dawn, and I have yet to pack. Wish me well. Write. I promise to reply with speed. Livia

•••

I read the letter over and over again, sitting on the edge of my *lectus*. When I finally dropped the scroll to the floor, I had practically committed it to memory. I thought about the years she would be away. Then, for the longest while, I sat very still, my head in my hands, and tried with a shaking will to think of absolutely nothing at all.

•••

That was six years ago. And now the carriages which carried her and the others were pulling up to the gates. *Domina* had allowed a small crowd to assemble in welcome. I stood on the curb, but as the *familia* pressed forward around me, suddenly I turned and pushed my way through the throng, walking briskly back into the house. In my *tablinum*, I could hear the sounds of welcome and celebration coming from the atrium. I stayed where I was.

An hour later she found me, announcing her arrival with the cheerful, maddening whistle that had been her habit ever since she was a child. The tune has always been unrecognizable, but hearing it once again for the first time in such a long time made my back ache and my stomach tighten. The song stopped as she entered my office. She pulled a chair up to the opposite side of my table and lowered herself into it without every taking her eyes off mine. She was dressed as I remembered her, except the belt cinching her plain linen tunic was made of a double strand of green malachite beads. Her dark red hair was cut in the Egyptian style—draped in front down either side of her neck to cover her breasts, short bangs hiding half her forehead.

"You look well," I said. "What's that on your eyes?" Livia's eyelids were brushed with a powder the same color as her belt.

"You never wrote."

"No. You never gave me the chance to talk you out of going. The only thing I could think to write was, 'come home.'"

"That would have been something."

I stared at her, sure that my heart was beating hard enough to make my tunic visibly pulse with its rhythm. "So, you're a doctor now?" She nodded. "Most physicians I know don't smell as…fresh."

"It's a perfume made from cardamom and myrrh. Good for keeping the flies away. Is that grey in your hair?"

"A little. Still mostly blond, but Crassus manages to whiten a strand or two each week. Doesn't matter—I'll be bald in a year or two. I understand Baltus did not return."

She shook her head. "Went for a swim in the Nile and never came back."

"You don't look as if his passing was mourned." Livia shook her head while pursing her lips, a mischievous expression. "I never knew him well, but thought him competent. Well, that's a shame, then."

"Pity."

We looked at each other. "He did love a good soaking, though," I tried.

"Scrubbed himself pink, he would."

"Not his color now, I should think."

"Greenish brown, I'd guess. A better match for his eyes, if he kept them."

"I'd rather not imagine."

"Bloated before he went in," she persisted. "More so now."

"Come now. A learned man. He'll be missed, surely."

"Not by me," she said. I cocked an eyebrow. "Nothing was worth studying unless he discovered it first."

"Trying his hand at ichthyology now, is he?"

"He guessed I was about to develop an interest."

"And took the plunge to beat you to it."

"Now the fish are trying his ... hand."

"You *are* delightful, aren't you."

Livia stretched, long and luxuriously. "It feels good to be back in the *familia*."

"You've been away too long. The fault is mine and I feel awful."

"No you don't."

"No, I don't." *Bless you, Baltus. May the gods forgive us. Thank you for putting us at our ease. Tonight I'll make an offering in your honor.* "Wine?" I said, reaching for the *amphora*.

"Can't. *Dominus* told me to get you an inventory of what I'd need for the clinic by supper."

"Did he now? Who appointed you the new *medicus*? You didn't even know you wanted to apprentice the day before you left."

"*Dominus* promised it to me. Besides, I'm smarter than any of the rest."

"I see. Well, I suppose then, you'd better pick your staff and let me know who needs to be reassigned."

"Yes, my lord."

"Don't start that again."

She laid a list on the table between us. I smirked. "Confident as ever, I see. Just like your mother." *Curse me for a fool. Oh, to have a brain that operates faster than my mouth.*

"As ever," Livia said, her lively tone gone serious. "How goes it here? Everyone seemed a little, I don't know, tense."

"It's not good," I said, lowering my voice, even though I knew Crassus was not in his *tablinum*, adjacent to mine. "I'll tell you later. You must be tired."

"Don't tell me what I must be," she said with a curl of her lip.

"Gods, it's good to have you home," I said before I could stop myself.

Livia stood, and I rose with her, deciding not to upend the table between us so I could crush her in my arms. I probably couldn't have lifted it anyway, at least not without her help.

CHAPTER II

56 BCE - FALL, ROME

Year of the consulship of
Cn. Cornelius Lentulus Marcellinus and L. Marcius Philippus

O ur home was not the same after Luca. Rumors of what had happened there spread like weeds. It was my task to uproot and dispose of them wherever I found them, but for every one culled, three more would sprout. How could it be otherwise, for it is one of the rare joys peculiar to those who serve to conjure outlandish stories regarding their masters. If our lives are destined to be plain, at least we may pilfer a little color, however impermanent, by rubbing up against our betters.

In the slaves' quarters it was whispered that Pompeius Magnus, our master's lifelong rival, had tried to poison *dominus*. *Dominus* had slept with a dining room slave. *Domina* had found a lover in the stables. Caesar had broken with *dominus*. Crassus had slept with Caesar. Each tale was more preposterous than the last. Yet every now and then I would be forced to laughingly dismiss a rumor that was not gossip at all, but a stab that cut sickening close to the truth. Caesar had had, or was still having an affair with my lady. *Dominus* was either impotent, ignorant, or plotting his revenge.

Here is the truth. At Luca, at a gathering of vultures dressed as senators come to pick and tear at the choicest bits of Rome, Julius Caesar raped my lady Tertulla. No good can be born from the coupling of lasciviousness and political ambition, and Caesar fairly bubbled with both. Caesar had called the meeting at Luca because the deteriorating situation in Rome threatened his own political future. Crassus and Pompeius had to stand for *consul* for a second time to protect the interests of all three, but Caesar's most of all.

Crassus saw no need to put himself through the frustration of another term with Pompeius. He needed neither the prestige nor the aggravation. When Caesar saw Crassus' commitment wavering, he knew his campaign in Gaul and his plans for dominion over Britannia and Germania were in jeopardy. My lord Crassus had confided to Caesar that he always harkened to the advice of his wife. Assaulting her was his craven insurance that, as always, Caesar would get what he wanted. If she did not convince her husband to take the consulship and thus, with his tremendous influence, push through the law that would extend Caesar's command another five years, Caesar would make public her "transgression." One more scandal would hardly stain his own reputation: he was already known as a defiler of both men and women. But the house of Crassus was one of the most dignified and respected in Rome. If Tertulla failed to convince her husband to seek the consulship, Caesar would see them in disgrace, destroy her marriage and topple her husband's life's work.

What the villain did not know was that there was a witness to his crime. Crassus himself, exhausted and full of too much wine, came upon them in the dark. To his eternal shame, my master did not act, even when Tertulla's stricken gaze met his own. Fearing for her husband's life, Tertulla begged him to withdraw with a silent plea. Caesar would surely have been the victor in a physical contest with the much older man. Unseen, Crassus slipped back into the shadows, rage and shame growing with each step. Their marriage almost ended the next day, but Tertulla convinced him that what he had witnessed was not infidelity, but rape. From that day forward, Marcus Crassus was filled with but one thought: to avenge himself upon Gaius Julius Caesar.

•••

We went about our business quickly, heads bowed, avoiding eye contact, speaking little, as if a stiff, winter wind blew through the halls. One evening, not many weeks after their return, as *dominus* and *domina* were taking their couches in the dining room, Eirene, who had been with us since the old days, set a bowl of pomegranates down too quickly, dislodging two pieces of fruit. They rolled off the table and one overripe globe burst upon the floor. Tertulla blinked, keeping her eyes shut an instant longer than was natural. Everyone froze, as if the dear serving woman had shattered one of the family death masks. My new assistant, Lucius Curio, shouted Eirene's name just as you might bellow at a dog who had defecated on the masters' bed. I thought the poor woman's feet had left the ground, she started so.

Before Eirene could get an apology from her quivering lips or her knees to the floor to begin cleaning, Crassus had reached down and just calm as you please, scooped up some of the pulpy mess. He leaned over his couch and smeared a dripping handful of fruit across his mouth. Looking like he'd taken a sword thrust through the mouth, he chewed thoughtfully. We were all mesmerized by this performance, including my lady. At last, I gestured to a dining room attendant who handed *dominus* a towel. Wiping his face and hands slowly and deliberately, Crassus said, "That was perfect, Eirene. See if you can find me another as ripe as this and I shall ravish it in the more traditional manner." Most of the *familia* thought the master's humor mollifying, but I winced at his choice of words. A moment later Tertulla rose, and crying quietly, fled the *triclinium*. Crassus cursed softly and quickly followed, leaving us to clear and preserve the untouched platters in brittle silence.

I asked Curio to walk with me and found an empty room lit by a single lamp. "Lucius," I said, "how are you settling in?"

"My quarters are exceedingly adequate," Curio sniffed, examining his perfectly manicured nails. "Does that amuse you?" he asked, depressing an errant cuticle on his thumb with the nail of a forefinger.

"No, not at all. I smile only because you remind me of myself when I first came to this house."

"Why is that, Alexandros?" he asked, studying his hands, "What affectation of personality do you find we have in common?"

"Honestly, the one that comes to mind at the moment is insubordination. Lucius, I am obligated to give you a word of kind advice."

"Then I must be obligated to give heed."

"Please begin to do so," I said in as even a tone as I could manage, "by looking at me when I am addressing you." Lucius Calpurnius Curio raised his gaze and smiled benignly at me. His eyes, grey or pale blue depending on how the light hit them, were now steely and devoid of color. The bridge of his nose was broad, and I found my focus flicking back and forth between his own unmoving stare. In an instant I felt that I was the one being scrutinized and deconstructed, like a heap of Lucretius' elemental 'atoms.' I cleared my throat and pressed on. "I am aware that when you served Lucius Calpurnius Piso our positions were of equal rank. I am sensitive to the difficulty this must pose for you now, working in a much greater house."

Without taking his eyes off mine, and with a look that suggested complete attention to my every syllable, as I spoke, Curio braced the lowest joint of the middle finger of his left hand between the thumb and forefinger of his right; with a smooth, round motion he pulled up upon it until there was an audible crack. He kept at this with his other fingers until I finally had to ask him to stop.

"Lucius, I am unaware of any offence done to you as a result of my behavior, but if any such blunder exists, I humbly apologize." Curio's open face, slightly raised eyebrows and half smile was the perfect engineering of flesh and bone to make me feel as foolish as possible for even suggesting such a thing. "All right, we've both work to do. Let's get down to it, shall we?" I said. "Until I give you leave to do otherwise, when we are both present among the staff, it is not your place to chastise any servant not directly under your purview. I am speaking of your treatment of Eirene. And when I am not present, Lucius, learn from *dominus*. Be gentle, be lenient, be understanding. Our master did not cultivate the largest, most skilled, educated army of servants in Rome by being feared. The Palatine estate may be served by hundreds, but we are all still *familia*. I want you to be a part of it. Is that understood?

"You have my solemn word that I will follow your instructions to the best of my abilities."

"Good. Very good. One last thing. You have been with us almost two months. I would like two lists from you in my office by the end of the week: one — any physical items or training which you feel you lack in order to perform you current list of responsibilities to your highest capabilities; and any personal grievances or issues that you and I need to address in order to have the best possible working relationship for the benefit of the house we now both serve. You may go."

I never received either list, and to my discredit, I never asked for them again.

•••

After the incident with the pomegranate, a change came over our lady. She refused to keep to her room, dressing with desperate elegance after fretting over each detail of her makeup and attire. She threw frequent and elaborate dinner parties, arranged poetry readings and plays in the atrium; one night she amazed her guests by unveiling a caged tiger from Asia Minor for their inspection. Alone, though, those who knew her well would note she spent more time before our household gods, lighting incense, sprinkling salt over fresh barley cakes, murmuring prayers with an urgency she had never demonstrated before.

Crassus was courteous, soft-spoken and as solicitous as always. He never failed to take his wife's hand as they walked through the house; he brought her little trinkets and made sure to compliment her on her hair or a menu

33

she had prepared. But his voice was just a little too loud, her gaiety a little too forced. The genuine affection of decades, a vase of subtle and delicate craftsmanship, had cracked and chipped. We watched as our lord and lady toiled to glue each tiny fragment to the whole with kindhearted routine and time-worn habit. Every one of us prayed that they would succeed at their task, and that when their work was done, no one would be able to see the imperfections. We prayed, because we knew better than to hope.

In Junius, having been at home less than two months, we fled the city, a month earlier than most, taking refuge in our Baiaen villa to escape not only the heat, but the extravagant parties that preceded the aristocracy's departure just after the elections were announced in Quintilis. So it was that my lord made himself unavailable to stand for *consul* as he had agreed with Caesar. Pompeius, too, was absent, having sailed for Sardinia, Sicily and Africa to negotiate the purchase of desperately needed grain to feed the 300,000 mouths of Romans citizens who depended on the state to sustain them.

We tarried in Baiae and did not return to the city until October. Livia stayed behind, asking and receiving permission from Crassus to remain in Rome over the summer. The city suffered its worst bouts of illness in the heat and humidity of the season; my brave healer would do what she could in our master's clinic, opening its doors to all, with his blessing. Crassus left both guards and provisions to feed and heal the sick, and though his name was imprinted on every sack of grain and every *ampulla* of medicine, I cannot believe his sole motive was selfish.

Fate had just returned Livia to me and now, laughing, was dragging me away from her again. Oh, it must have been great fun for the immortals to play this foolish game of hide and seek, concealing Livia from me, then allowing me to find her, then pulling her away again. Thus it had been ever since we had met, she as a child, me newborn to the house of Crassus. I pined for her when we were apart, and wept when we were reunited. Since that first kiss under the statue of Apollo in the garden of Crassus, a memory twenty years old yet fresh as a new-picked flower, I was no longer master of the heart that beat inside my own breast, but slave to a desire postponed and never satisfied.

Oh, for the love of reason! Surely you who read these scrolls must agree this kind of hand-wringing whining is utter drivel. Can love and wisdom coexist? Do not think it for an instant. It is widely known that Aristotle defined love as "the composition of a single soul inhabiting two bodies." First of all, he was talking about friendship, and second, I have it on good authority that at the time he uttered those words, he was falling down drunk.

One has to be at least as ancient as I am now to see that if you try to make sense of life, if you look for patterns and meaning, not only are you bound to be disappointed, you are likely to waste a good deal of precious time.

•••

As we neared the city late in the day, the tombs of the wealthy sprang up like mushrooms on either side of the Via Appia, each vying for prominence, crowding up against each other until the left side of the road succumbed to the shadows of these tall and lavish castles of the dead. A bulwark of beggars, arms waving like undersea flora in the tide of our passing, hugged the curb on the opposite side, still awash in the warming sun. Only those few creatures too sluggish of thought or foot were left almost unseen in the gloom.

Riding at my place just behind *dominus*, I was applying needless energy with helpless gusto worrying over something over which I had no control. As you may imagine, this was a pastime I visited with zealous frequency. Presently, I was ticking off the preparations Curio would have had to oversee and complete within the hour to adequately, which is to say, perfectly prepare for our homecoming. Had the furniture been cleaned? Had the masks of the ancestors been dusted? Was the house warm enough? What about supper? Had the gardens been pruned? Were there fresh flowers in every room? Had the house gods received their offerings? The list went on and on until even I began to tire of my finikin disquiet. Why should I fret? Lucius was a younger version of myself; left to maintain our Roman residence while we sought the cooler breezes of Baiae, I knew I would find everything in pristine order. Which is precisely when a more insidious thought crept in to harass my better self. Wouldn't I love to find just one small thing with which to find fault: a lamp wick untrimmed, a corner not swept, a pillow not plumped, *something* to chide the ever-flawless Lucius Calpurnius Curio? Of course I wouldn't.

I diverted my mind's energies to screwing tight the taps on my mind's caustic, leaky faucet and concentrated instead on nothing at all. I had only a moment's rest from myself when, from her *raeda*, lady Tertulla leaned out a window and called the procession to a halt. Being closest to her carriage, I leapt off Apollo, my dark brown bay, and inquired how I might assist her. "Follow me," she said, opening the door and stepping down onto the road. Immediately surrounded by a troop of guards, she brushed them aside and headed for the shadowed curb. Only Crassus seemed unperturbed. He did not know what she was up to, but was not about to come between her will and her objective. His six senate-appointed *lictors* crowded about him, their eyes busy.

Tertulla approached a boy who looked no more than twelve (I later learned his small frame had suffered in this world for fifteen years). He was wrapped in rags, sitting on the curb with an empty begging bowl between his legs. His hair looked as if it had never been cut, or washed. Something about his eyes was off and unsettling—they were too far apart and their focus lagged behind whatever drew their attention. In addition, his head struck me as too large for his frail shoulders. These defects, however, faded to insignificance in the light of the boy's startling, beatific expression. He was looking up at us with the most innocent, guileless smile I had ever seen upon man or woman. He positively beamed, as if he had been sitting there waiting for this precise moment his entire life. The effect was multiplied by his outstretched arms: they did not seem so much a supplication for alms as an urgent wish to be picked up and held.

Then I saw his hands.

What I beheld was the result of no accident. Someone had deliberately cut off the majority of the poor child's fingers, leaving him with only the thumb and third finger of each hand. An involuntary shiver ran through me as I imagined the transformation in his trusting aspect when that mutilation was perpetrated. It had to have been deliberate—what kind of accident could leave such a perfect array of carnage?

Domina snapped me out of my morbid speculation. "That smile — I saw it from the carriage. I had to stop to behold this wonder."

From deeper within the shadows behind the boy, one of the guards dragged an older man. He was dressed no better than the lad, but unlike the boy, his grey, whiskered face was made of a clay that had long ago set into a resentful scowl.

"Put your arms down, fool," he growled at the child. The boy winced at the man's voice, slowly lowering his arms in unison without unlocking his elbows, as if he were setting down an invisible basket.

"Can you speak?" *domina* asked. "What is your name, child?"

"Hanno!" the boy shouted proudly, his head shaking for emphasis, his arms springing up again into the air.

"*Domina*," I whispered in her ear, "the boy is what we in Greece call an 'idiot.' He is malformed in both mind and body. Let me put a coin in his bowl so that we may depart." I dropped an *as*, then another into the wooden bowl and was taken aback by the boy's reaction. His attention, which had been riveted to the kind smile on my lady's face, whipped from her visage to mine; his jaw dropped, his eyes widened, and he yelped with what I was to learn was his unflappable state of ear-splitting enthusiasm. His squeal of gratitude, and now his outstretched arms were directly squarely at me. That others were witnessing a communication between myself and this unfortunate…well, I was discomfited. I thought to reply with a curt word of comfort or a nod of my head, but I could only stand with my hands at my sides, pinned by his idiot grin.

"Are you the father of this child?" Tertulla asked, her blue eyes narrowed ever so slightly. She had not yet condemned him, but she was close.

"I am not," he answered. His tone was enough to cause a second guard to take hold of his other arm. "But we took him in, and fed him, and kept him alive, which is more than most would have done."

"What do you mean, 'we took him in?'"

"My wife found him, in the woods near Norba. He'd been left for the wolves."

"Where is your wife?"

"Dead. Died birthing. Took the baby with her, too. Been two years now. 'Couldn't keep the farm up without her, so me and the boy moved to town."

"I see," Tertulla said. What she saw was much more than what this scrofulous miscreant was saying. Remembering my first days of enslavement, thrall to eight legionaries in the hidebound misery they called a tent, I wondered what else the child had suffered at his hands. "Despicable," she spat. "You couldn't find work, or maybe didn't even look. Why bother, when you had the child? Was not the poor boy sympathetic enough with all his fingers?"

"I done no such thing!" His eyes darted about, looking for an escape he would not find. "I never hurt him." His wild eyes told a different tale. The child could not help the subhuman condition of his birth; as distasteful as it was to look upon him, I might at least pity him. For his 'caretaker,' I felt nothing but revulsion.

At that moment, Crassus, mounted and glorious, came into the thick of us. Eurysaces (sired by Ajax, now put to pasture) bent his ink black head and to the delight of the boy nuzzled his cheek. One dumb creature recognizing another.

"What mischief are you up to, *columba*?" my lord asked.

Domina told him. Crassus thought a moment, then, from a height loftier than even that afforded by his horse, handed down his judgment. "You will accompany my men," he said, pointing at the boy's soon-to-be former caretaker. "Tomorrow, we will go to the courts and for the sum of 500 sesterces you will relinquish any and all claims upon this child…to me. Is that clear?"

"Really, *dominus*, is that necessary?" I said. "I'm sure we can find the boy a suitable home."

"I just did," Crassus said. "Clean him up. Tend to him. Make your mistress happy, *atriensis*." There was no brooking that tone.

Domina reached up and squeezed her husband's hand. A look passed between them, of gratitude and something more.

As the guards dispersed the crowd that had gathered, I sighed and held out my hand to the boy. He made to pick up his begging bowl. "Leave that," I snapped.

Using his thumb, he pointed to the coins and said, "Yours." To my surprise, his pronunciation of this difficult word was acceptable.

"No, yours. I'll keep them for you." I bent down to collect the money, then offered my free hand to him. He took it in both of his. The feel of those four bony hooks clinging to the soft meat of my palm made my bile rise. I helped him stand, and as soon as he got to his feet he threw his arms around me with such ferocity I was compelled to take a step backward to keep my balance. Oh, the stench! If I could not wriggle free of him, I would have to burn my tunic. I would most certainly incinerate his.

"Thank you, thank you, thank you," he kept repeating, his forehead pressed hard upon my chest. He might just as easily have been thanking me for holding his money as freeing him from that monster. I was clueless, and frankly too distraught to care.

Before getting back into her carriage, Tertulla laid her hand on my shoulder. "It will be all right. You'll see."

Waiting until the ironclad wheels of her carriage began to roll, the guards snickered. One said, "Look, Alexander has a new puppy."

After spearing them with one of my most well-honed glares, I told the boy, "Now, you must let go so that I may mount my horse." The rest of our procession had already started to move off. Once asked, he complied straightaway. *Now that's a welcome change.* I looked round for someone to help me mount. Because of my height, I could have flung myself up and into the saddle, but preferred to avoid such an unseemly display. This proved to be unnecessary, for looking down I saw that the boy had dropped to one knee and was offering to assist me. He had linked his four fingers in such a way that the backs of his thumbs and wrists provided the area of lift I required. Perhaps he would have some utility after all.

But not at this occupation. A few of the guards had lingered to watch; they laughed as my weight drove the slight child's hands almost to the ground before I hauled myself up by the pommels, legs swinging wildly. Not having the strength to drag myself up all the way, I dangled between heaven, earth and soldiers' mirth. Something solid met my soles; recognizing it for the boy's bent back, I pushed off as lightly as I could and pulled myself inelegantly into the saddle to the sound of enthusiastic applause.

"Get up, boy," I said. The child Hanno did. I was not surprised to see that in spite of the fact that I had knocked him down, his smile had remained intact. I felt obliged to add, "Thank you."

We walked on, Apollo instinctively slowing his pace for the benefit of the lad. My horse, it must be said, was more attentive than I, for it was only after we had restarted our journey that I looked down to see that the boy's oversized head was not his only irregularity. He walked with a pronounced limp, pushing off with his undersized left foot which he planted at ninety degrees to his right. The sight of this asymmetry distressed only those who witnessed it, for the boy had long ago adjusted his style of locomotion such that he was completely at ease with it. He rested his hand on my leg, frequently glancing up to bestow upon me his undiluted grin. If he wasn't irritating me with that look of gratitude, he was staring with unabashed wonder at every mundane sight we passed. Further proof of his insanity. Any being exhibiting such complete contentment with the world and his place in it must be lacking any true understanding of it.

I would like to be able to tell you that on that day my heart went out to the boy, but suffering the touch of his two fingers on my calf, all I could feel was another headache coming on.

•••

And that was how Hannibal came to be in our midst. Yes, I know, that was not his true name, but within a week the *familia* had changed it for him, from Hanno to Hannibal. It was inevitable. At least he and I had that in common. The difference was that as in most things, the boy perceived this as kind treatment. Hanno loved the change, skipping about the *domus* repeating his new name over and over again. I snagged him in the colonnade and holding hands, we walked back to my *tablinum*.

"Well, Hanno, we must find a way for you to earn your keep."

"I'm not Hanno. I'm Hannibal."

"But that is not your real name."

"It is my *new* name."

"Do you know it is possible to have two names? I have two, and one of them is a secret. Would you like to hear it?"

"Oh yes, please!"

"My secret name is Alexandros."

"I want a secret name, too!"

"Hmm. I wonder what it should be?"

The boy walked a few feet, his face crushed in concentration. "I can't *think* of any," he said, almost in tears.

"I know. What if we called your secret name Hanno? That would be easy to remember, wouldn't it?"

"Hanno! That's a good one!"

"That's it, then. Now, do you remember *my* secret name?"

"No."

"It's Alexandros. Can you say it?"

"I don't like it. I like Alexander."

"Yes, quite. As does everyone else in this wretched city."

CHAPTER III

56 BCE - FALL, ROME

Year of the consulship of
Cn. Cornelius Lentulus Marcellinus and L. Marcius Philippus

W hat was Hanno capable of doing which would keep him occupied and out of the way? I tried putting him to work with the fullers collecting urine; while he was used to the smell, the workmen were unused to and unforgiving of the constant spills. The garden was no better, because the peacocks chased him, and there were *bugs* out there! In the kitchen, he was underfoot, and cook sent him scampering back to me. Which was where he wanted to be in the first place, Athena knows why. In fact, he seemed happiest sitting at the foot of my work table in the *tablinum*, eager to accomplish whatever small errands I might demand of him.

Hanno had a keen sense of whether or not he was welcome in someone else's presence. In spite of lady Tertulla's warning that the boy was to be treated with respect and kindness, it was an old Roman custom, far from extinct, to treat such misfortunates as fools, good for a laugh; better yet, with a crowd present, to subject them to ridicule, scorn and derision. The larger the audience, the greater the abuse. Guilt and shame, when spread thinly among enough participants, may vanish altogether. I did not hold with maltreatment of any innocent, but I wish that *domina* and *dominus* had found some other way to help heal the brutal unkindness done to them by Caesar. They might feel noble as they passed the child on their way elsewhere, eliciting sunshine smiles with a treat or a coin, but the brunt of Hanno's care and feeding were foisted upon me. Have I told you that I do not like pets?

We cleaned him up, gave him a place to sleep and fresh clothes to wear, but when it came time to sit in the *tonsor's* chair, the shearing snick of Tulio's clippers sent him into a piteous hysteria. He thrust his hands beneath his armpits and swayed dangerously back and forth, moaning and hugging himself so tightly that later I discovered bruises on his sides. "Fine," I told him, "keep your hair. But next year, when you are sixteen and that fuzz on your face becomes visible, you *will* shave it off."

The effect was instantaneous. Off the chair he flew, piercing the puzzled but indifferent barber with a doleful eye. He was on me in an instant, showing his gratitude in a manner that was uniquely Hanno's: a painfully sincere hug with forehead pressed against my chest. If I did not embrace him in return, he would continue holding me until I did. In this, I was an apt pupil, learning on my own the added benefit of a few kind words and a gentle pat on his head. Tulio rummaged in his supplies and recovered a thin braid of leather which Hanno promptly refused. Exasperated, I had the barber give it to me and said, "We can't have you running around like a wild man. You're not a barbaric Briton, are you, boy?"

"No! I'm not."

"That's right, you're not, so let us at least arrange your hair so you won't be eating it along with your porridge." Hanno blew air from his compressed lips and nodded. I exhaled with relief, for I had no idea what I would have done had he refused. Thank the gods, he allowed me to tie back his plaits with the headband. I took a spare boar-bristle brush from Tulio and examined its narrow handle. "Tulio, when you have a moment, would you please build this up to make it easier for Hanno to hold?"

From that time on, Hanno's remarkable hair, though it hung half way down his back, was always restrained by that leather thong. He even learned to tie it up himself. And when he received his modified brush, one could almost always find it thrust through a loop in his belt, as dear a possession as any gladiator's sword. Watching him sit on the floor in my office, brushing away with ardent diligence, I caught myself smiling and quickly returned to my work.

In spite of myself, and the teachings of my school, I slowly warmed to the boy. The poor creatures who suffered from mental inferiority were known to Aristotle. He, unlike most of the illiterate and uneducated masses, did not share the belief that madness was either just punishment meted out by an irate god, or the result of demonic possession. Even his predecessor and teacher, Plato, believed that this sickness might at times be divinely inspired. Aristotle knew that those who suffered this affliction did so from physical causes, but the belief that mental health or disease is dependent upon moral virtue or vice persists. Hanno's parents, whoever they might have been, must not be faulted for their actions; in his *Politics*, Aristotle himself wrote, "as to the exposure and rearing of children, let there be a law that no deformed child shall live." If he would not suffer their existence, what audacity to question the great teacher's wisdom. Human perfection is the ideal; human imperfection, deformity of any kind, must by definition be less than human, mustn't it?

I put down my pen and studied the child as he pulled the entangled hairs from his brush and dropped them on the tiles. Hanno did not belong to me, yet he was nonetheless mine; *domina* had given me authority over him on her behalf. A slave's slave. I oversaw many in this way, but somehow Hanno was different. It seemed more poignant that in his case I ordered him about, slept in better quarters and ate better food (not that he would accept half the things he was offered). Just as Crassus lived a life beyond my reach. Did that mean I was entitled to look down upon Hanno as Crassus looked down upon me? *Dominus* would angrily deny that he did any such thing, but no matter how much slack he might pay out on my leash, the collar was still firmly bound about my neck. (I speak metaphorically, of course, although in other houses it was easy enough to find literal examples of tethering.)

Ironically, for most of us, being a slave was a mixture of shame but also of community—a gentle incentive to treat each other with civility, since there were plenty of others eager to remind us of our lowly station. Hanno did not know he was a slave, and if he did, he would hardly care. Why should he, when his prior life had offered no more freedom and far less cheer? I shifted in my chair, uncomfortable at the instinctive impulse to summarily exclude the child at my feet from the rest of our *familia*. At the sound, he looked up at me and smiled.

•••

In a few more moments, I was interrupted again. Lucius Curio, holding an armful of scrolls cleared his throat at the entrance to my office. I bid him enter and sit, sending Hanno to the kitchen for a sweet roll. As he squeezed past Curio, who made certain no part of either of them came in contact, Hanno asked for two. Two small ones, I told him, and off he went at lopsided speed, ignoring my shouted entreaty to slow down.

Lucius sat stiffly, feet flat on the floor. "How can you abide to have that *thing* scuttling about beneath your legs all day long?" I looked up to make certain no one was actually pinching his nose.

"Hanno is a member of the *familia*," I said.

"I mean really, why wasn't the poor creature left out in the woods as an infant?"

"He was."

"Then I am at a loss. It's not yours, is it?"

"Let's get on with those requisitions, shall we."

"Your productivity cannot help but be negatively impacted."

"Remember that when *domina* comes to you with a request you predict will negatively impact your productivity. Lay out your reasons and I am certain she will withdraw her application."

"The house should think of its reputation, then. Word is bound to get out."

"Have you no empathy whatsoever, then?"

"Empathy is a luxury for patricians, priests and women."

"I see. I'll bear that in mind should you ever incur the ire of the master."

Curio gave a short laugh, and I had to agree with him, there was little chance of that. "I for one, do not intend to have children," he said, curling his upper lip as he handed the first account across for my perusal and counter-signature. "The pleasure gained compared to the effort required appears paltry by comparison."

"You sound like your previous master, Lucius Calpurnius Piso, a staunch follower of Epicurus."

"*Former* master. You don't see a slave plaque hanging around *my* neck, do you?" Curio's eyes, grey or pale blue depending on the light, smiled benignly at me. Just now, they were cold and empty of color.

"Humble apologies. I misspoke. To be fair, you don't see one hanging about mine, either, do you?"

"No, and I won't, but that is of little consequence, since you are only *required* to don yours when you leave the grounds."

I could have shown him my slave plaque, unique in all the Roman world, but it was becoming clear that nothing I could do or say to this man would put me on an equal footing, so why bother? It was also dawning on me that the ground upon which he stood was no place where I wished to stand.

I held out my hand for another scroll. "You know, I've been meaning to ask you, why is it, since Lucius Piso has given you your freedom and you have taken his name as is the custom, that you are not his client and he your patron? What brings you to the house of Crassus?"

"Have you ever been to Macedonia? Piso's been governor there since his consulship, and every step since our departure has been a stride taken in the wrong direction. How I have longed for the art, the culture, the speeches from the *rostra*, the games, the baths, the forums. I've even missed the smell."

"You are a true Roman." Imagine the burning sarcasm I could not quite extinguish.

It went unremarked, for Curio was far more interested in the words about to come from his own lips than the two he watched, impatiently waiting for them to stop moving. "Piso is a man of his word. I was born into his house. He swore to my mother that on my 30th birthday he would give me my freedom, and this he did. A shame she did not live to see the day."

"I am sorry for your loss. And what of your father?"

"I did not know my father." A nerve unintentionally struck, Curio's voice failed to hide unmistakable shame. My mind began its inevitable calculations, and could not help but wonder how close senator Piso and Curio's mother had been.

"Forgive my intrusion," I said.

Curio's mask of imperturbability was back in place before I had finished speaking. "Governor Piso agreed that Thessalonica was no place for my ambition. He wrote your master who graciously gave me a place in this household. Lucius Piso formally released me of my obligations of respect and gratitude, and Marcus Crassus has done the same."

"Very generous of them both, and most unusual. I find it strange, though, that *dominus* never spoke to me about it beforehand."

"Or to me, that I would be taking direction from a slave."

That put the hammer to the egg. "I see. There are many freedman employed on this estate, or on several dozen other properties. Would you be more comfortable in some *lesser* post?"

Curio's nasality rose a muffled notch. "I should confer with your *dominus* before I did anything unilaterally."

"Be very clear about one thing, Lucius. Whether, when you stroll into town, your neck is free of obligatory ornamentation, or like me, for the past thirty years, you have devoted every waking moment to this man and his family, *everyone* in this household is a servant of our *dominus*. That includes his slaves, his freedmen, his children, his wife, me and most importantly as regards *this* conversation at *this* very moment, you. Is that understood?"

We completed our business in silence, and I almost apologized for my rant, born as it was not so much by what Lucius had said but by what he had implied: *dominus* wanted the man right where he was, and that frightened me. Later, when I asked Crassus about it, he responded by inquiring if it was now his duty to delay every decision he made until after he had laid it upon my table to receive my seal. Then he added that the day he actually *gave* me my own seal he might consider it, but neither circumstance was very likely. It was a short discussion.

CHAPTER IV

56 BCE - FALL, ROME

Year of the consulship of
Cn. Cornelius Lentulus Marcellinus and L. Marcius Philippus

I never gave the scars on my back much thought anymore; the tug and pull of the pale ridges had drifted into the background of my consciousness. One can get past just about anything, given enough time, even when one shouldn't.

Hanno was the only member of our society who regularly saw the ugly stripes. He became accustomed to the sight, but the first time it happened, unsettling for us both, he was assisting me with my bath. I had been looking forward to the moment since mid-morning; had I been paying attention I would have prepared him for such a lurid unveiling. I had folded my clothes onto a shelf and had turned from him to enter the *calidarium*. He emitted such a gasp of pain I thought he had accidentally stabbed himself with a stilus. (This was quite possible—he was constantly picking up whatever caught his eye for inspection, testing, even tasting.) Not this time. I whirled to see a look of horror on his face that slowly melted into one of pain, then sorrow. Tears welled as he came to me. He put his hands on my bare shoulders and made to turn me around. When I realized what he was doing, I stiffened and pulled away.

Hanno looked puzzled; he held up his mutilated hands to my face. "But Alexander," he said. "Look."

"No!" I said, slapping his hands away. "We are *not* the same."

After half a month of explaining, then apologizing, he still had not forgiven me. In the end, only an unfeigned recognition that our scars did indeed make us brothers brought a smile back to his face. It also brought a number of restless nights to my bed chamber as I contemplated my admission.

Now, Hanno was warming scented oil and wiping down an iron *strigil* with a towel and the heel of his hand while I soaked in the steaming waters. It was just past the ninth hour. There were at least two hours before sundown; plenty of time to clean up after the day's work before Crassus returned from the senate, which would not sit in session after dark. Romans take advantage of the light — even for the privileged class, the day begins soon after dawn and ends at sunset. As we were in the heart of winter, each of the twelve hours of the day were markedly foreshortened compared to summer, with the result that the entire city moved at a much brisker pace, not from the cold, but from the need to cram as much as possible into the shorter workday. That morning, Crassus and I had risen in the dark, before the first hour, to review by lamplight the notes for the day's speeches. He was in the forum by the time the rest of us were having our morning cup of water.

"I'm glad to see you're not using the public baths."

At the sound of my master's voice, I leapt up and whipped round to face him, as much to save him from the embarrassment of seeing his stripy handiwork as to relieve me of the discomfiture of exhibiting it. Hanno grabbed towels, pinched together by the two remaining fingers of each hand. The weight of the larger one caused it to slip from his grasp. Reddening and repeating apologies, he handed me the smaller and dropped awkwardly to his knees. Using the fallen bath sheet, he scrubbed at the water my turning had splashed upon Crassus' senatorial shoes, the black ones with a "C" stitched in silver thread on the top of each boot. This was the traditional emblem for the original number of conscript fathers in that august deliberative body — one hundred. Six times that number were now accommodated in Sulla's *Curia Cornelia*, resplendent in their white togas. Only a few were curule magistrates, allowed to wear the *toga praetexta* of their ancient office, embellished by a broad purple border. Crassus was one of the oldest, most venerated among them.

"I have instructed everyone to remain in the compound, if possible," I said, "and if they must go down into town, not to do so without an escort."

"Good," Crassus said, wincing as the seat Hanno was guiding to him scraped along the floor. "It's not safe in the city. Stop fussing, boy!" Hanno abandoned his attempt to wrestle the back of the chair into a parallel position behind *dominus'* legs and stood with his hands at his sides, his chin trembling.

"It's all right," I said. "Fetch me one as well." That brought the smile out again. He dragged another chair to me, but I stood there dripping, my towel being of a size that made it perfect for blowing one's nose, but little else. I held it bunched in my hand, deciding not to risk a flood of tears by asking for another.

Crassus said, "Sit." I sat. "Hannibal," he added, "would you mind fetching us a bowl of olives?" Hanno was off like a lurching charioteer, leaving his grin hanging in the humid air.

"Shall we move to a more comfortable setting?" I asked, hoping to change into some dry clothes and get off this chair.

"I don't know which prospect is worse — suffering that unfortunate's drawbacks or attempting to talk my wife out of keeping him. Best leave it be. And no, we'll stay here where it's warm. It's freezing outside."

He did that on purpose. Splendid. I'll be wearing the pattern of this woven cane seat on my bottom for hours. As I spoke, I thought how best to employ my towel. "Why all the precautions, *dominus*?" *If I put it on the chair, I'll have to rise to do so, and I had just been commanded to be seated.* "Clodius' faction wouldn't harm us." *If I stuff it under my buttocks to give my cheeks some relief, Crassus will think me insane, or incontinent. If I drape it across my lap, I'll appear a prude.* "He's praised you on the *rostra* and vilified Pompeius." In the end, I mopped my brow with it and dropped it casually on the floor.

"Anything to foment confusion and disruption," Crassus said. "Anything to stir up a hornet's nest of dissatisfaction. He has no real love for me or the constitution, and I have never, nor would I ever stoop to solicit or accept his praise. Mind you, even if it was a hollow gesture to gain support for his political aims, his passage of a grain dole for the poor was admirable. How we'll be able to import enough to perpetually feed 300,000 mouths and pay for it all is quite another matter.

"He is a dangerous fool, Alexander. He's destroyed hapless Cicero; if that man wasn't such a pugnacious prig,

Pompeius and I might have forestalled his exile. I would have done, too, if I had known Clodius would incinerate and confiscate the poor blowhard's property. Now Clodius' gang of armed rabble terrorize citizens and senators alike. He claims he acts in the name of the people, but in truth, anarchy is his newfound god. If my purpose was not ineluctably fixed elsewhere, I should like very much to bring him to heel."

Crassus shook his head. "This is a dangerous time for the Republic—Caesar's ambition seems boundless; I must devote all my energies to exacting our revenge, but to do so I must mimic his audacity. It is a hard thing, Alexander. To accomplish my means, I am become part of the corruption and misgovernment I abhor."

"Are you certain there is no other course you may follow?" Hanno returned with a bowl of glistening olives. Both Crassus and I held our breath until he had placed them on a small pedestal table between the two chairs and moved to stand with his back against the far wall. He took Tulio's gift from his belt and I knew without looking that his eyes soon would be glazing over with each soothing stroke of the brush.

Crassus rolled an oily green olive between his thumb and index finger. He looked as though he might crush it rather than eat it. "I am certain of nothing but that I love Tertulla and revile the man who attacked her. I will have him ruined and exiled, or perish in the effort."

I glanced at Hanno and gauged he was too distant to hear, and if he heard, to understand, and if he understood, to care. "My insides twist at the thought of your tribulation."

"Who else knows?"

"In this house, only the three of us, but there is talk. For *domina*, it is easier to bury the fact than the memory."

"We must protect her as best we can. I am sorry to disrupt the *familia*, but from this point on, my determination must brook no distraction. There is much to do, and the first step is to win the consulship."

"In other words, your revenge hinges on doing Caesar's bidding."

"You might have phrased it less painfully, but yes."

"The senate must grant him five more years in Gaul, and you must take Syria for your proconsulship."

"And from there I will march on Parthia, the largest jewel not already set in the Roman crown."

"*Dominus*, we have treaties with Parthia. The senate will never sanction such an adventure."

"Do not belittle such an achievement with the wrong noun, Alexander. This is conquest. The senate will sanction a triumph quick enough when I bring their king home in chains, I promise you. Though I suppose you're right—it will be an adventure. Wouldn't you like to see the legacy of the Great Alexander: Antioch, Hierapolis, Seleucia?"

"A tempting offer, my lord, but traveling in the company of so many legionaries is bound to bring up too many disturbing memories. If you could manage to leave them behind?"

Crassus answered by reaching for another olive.

"One thing puzzles me, *dominus*," I said. "If you must win this coming election and thus be granted Syria to govern after your year's term, why have both you and Pompeius refused to announce your candidacies?"

"Lentulus, who now serves, is a good and honest consul, and a hardened conservative. He will not be

57

bullied by any extra-legal decisions made by us at Luca. He has refused to take our names — the deadline for declaring is long past. His co-consul, Philippus, favors Caesar and the *populares*, and therefore badgers us to run. But he is not a man who can see beyond a single move on the board. I will not risk declaring myself a candidate while the mood in the city is fractious and uncertain. The senate will follow us, but between the grain shortage and the few but vocal *optimates* crying out against us, the outcome of a vote now would be uncertain."

"You are stalling."

"I am doing what I must," he said, his voice rising. "Time shoves rudely at my back, but I must not move too soon. I have this one chance, no more. I see that look on your face. Do not lecture me on legality or ethics, Alexander; it pains me more than you can know to abandon my principles, once inviolate, now doughy with expediency." His words were spoken with shaky conviction; agitation creased his brow. He stood and paced back and forth in front of my chair. He grabbed another olive and destroyed it in his mouth.

"Dough will rise," I said, "and harden when baked."

Crassus turned to me and slammed a fist down on the arm rest of my chair as he spoke. "This is no time for your *wit*, Alexander!" He spit the olive pit onto the floor. I resisted the urge to pick it up. I glanced nervously at Hanno. He had put away his brush and now stood by the wall, his ruined hands before him, nervously linking, separating, then re-linking his four digits in two interlocking circles. He was swaying from side to side, aroused by Crassus' tone. I prayed he would not speak.

"When the people are alarmed, they look for stability," I said. "The people love you, *dominus*. I was in the forum when Clodius took the *rostra* before half the city. 'Who is murdering the people with famine?' he asked, and the people responded, 'Pompeius!' 'Who wants to go to Alexandria?' he asked, and they shouted, 'Pompeius!' And when Clodius said, 'Whom do you want to go?' with one voice came the thundering reply: 'Crassus!'"

"His armies are disbanded," he replied dismissively, "and the man needs an occupation. Grain merchant suits Pompeius' abilities. Let him negotiate with the Egyptians. As sweet a fruit as Egypt is, I must leave it for others to harvest. With Parthia's riches we will buy the grain of ten Egypts, and Rome's praise will be everlasting."

"What of the senate and the people, *dominus*? You are the rock upon which they both depend."

"You exaggerate to the point of transparency, Alexander. But, fine, for the moment, I shall be a rock. Caesar, then, is a comet that has struck our world, knocking it off-balance. What, then, can this rock do but be dislodged and roll down whatever slope his shaking sends it? It will take all my art to set things right again.

"To begin, the people will need a hero. I am not that man. Not yet. Pompeius has played that role more successfully than I, certainly to more applause. Let Pompeius find the grain and wallow in the cheers of the crowd. It is what he loves best, so we will let him have his moment."

"I am surprised to hear you say it."

"Let him sweat to regain his popularity; it serves my purpose now. His theater is almost complete; it will be a monumental diversion." I smiled at his unintended pun. "And when the grain starts to flow once more, sated citizens will make for pliant voters." He suddenly looked at me as if I had just appeared in a puff of smoke. "Why are you shivering, Alexander? Here, take this." Crassus undraped his senatorial toga, exposing his purple striped tunic, further sign of his rank. He stood and meant to drape the toga over me like a blanket. I rose as well, shocked. I held the huge garment at arm's length, standing naked before him.

"No, *dominus*. I cannot wear this. Hanno, fetch my tunic. Hanno!" The boy pushed himself off the wall and took off at a sprint, which for him could be more likened to a leaping hop.

Crassus sat back down, dropping the toga in a heap on the floor. "As you wish," he said, sounding like a child rebuffed after offering to share his dearest toy.

I retrieved my hand towel, then let it fall again. "*Dominus*," I felt compelled to say, "it is a most generous offer. But that garment is not meant…"

"What, for the likes of you? Do you think I am unaware of the honor I do you? By Athena's robes, Alexander, I do not understand you. Even when I extend my outstretched hand, you refuse to take it. Is the gap between us so great?"

I sat in wondrous silence for a moment, crafting my answer. "The fissure is broad and deep, *dominus*. Your gesture is well-meant, but can you not see that the gulf is widened by it, not bridged?"

"You will take nothing from me, will you?" he sighed. Hanno returned with my clothes and I quickly tied and wrapped my *subligaculum* about me and threw the tunic over my head. As I dressed, I shook off the muddled feeling that it was I who should have sympathy for Crassus. *Let us return to politics,* I thought, *a less dangerous and more straightforward subject.*

"I don't understand, *dominus*. Why all this subterfuge?"

"Ah, Tranio!" Crassus exclaimed. "Always a welcome intrusion."

The wine steward entered with two assistants, the first of whom handed each of us large, double-handled silver cup. "I have a nose not only for the best vintages," Tranio said, "but for where in the house they are most needed." The second assistant approached and filled a third of each cup with water, and finally Tranio himself, cradling the *amphora* as if it were a baby, completed the ceremony. He waited, a barely restrained puppy, while *dominus* drank. Crassus knew his steward well enough to feign a heart attack of joy before dismissing the man. Even when the wine was mediocre, the praise might yet be effusive, for their was nothing more glum than a pouting Tranio.

When the steward had left, humming contentedly, *dominus* asked to be reminded where we were in our conversation. "Why not throw your support to the *optimates*?" I said. "They have had their man for months. Domitius has promised to recall Caesar if elected and strip him of his army and provinces. Isn't that what we want? Why aren't we supporting him for consul?"

"I cannot break with Caesar; my preparations are not complete. Caesar could return from Gaul and easily stir up a majority of senators to retake control of the senate. Or worse, if he thinks our alliance is broken and that he cannot rely on my influence, he might come back not as a politician, but as a general at the head of his army. He wants Parthia, but Gaul has not yet been subdued. I must give him no reason to abandon the West. Let him keep his focus on the Moreni and the Menapii while I take the initiative to deprive him of the East. The only way to accomplish this is to feign amity between the three of us until Pompeius and I are consuls."

"Then what is holding the *optimates* back? If your names have not been taken, why does not Lentulus simply call the election without you? The year will soon be over and he will have to lay down the *fasces*."

"Precisely. Alexander, I don't think you're spending enough time at the baths." Crassus' grin was vexing.

"*Dominus*?"

"Lentulus plans to call for elections before the month is out. His intentions must be frustrated. Do you know the baths of Numa?"

"A small *balnea* that caters to mixed bathing. A disreputable establishment."

"The tribune Gaius Cato is a regular patron."

"So are thieves and whores."

"We will not debate the man's morality, but rather applaud how he chooses to interpret it."

Understanding dawned and I said, "The tribune of the plebs may veto any call for elections."

"It is his habit to take the waters daily at the seventh hour. Meet him there," Crassus said, extracting a scroll that protruded from the pile of senatorial wool on the floor, "and give him this. Discreetly. He'll know you by your plaque."

I took the proffered papyrus, wound about its thin spool of polished ebony and tried to imagine how many zeroes were cavorting with one another beneath its seal on the letter of credit. "Surrender it into tribune Cato's hands alone," Crassus said. "Take Betto and Malchus with you."

"Malchus!" Hanno cried.

"That's right, Malchus," I said.

"I *like* Malchus."

"I know you do."

"Not Betto. He makes me confused. He talks too fast."

"That's enough now. Let *dominus* and me finish our conversation. Afterward, we'll go to the kitchen and find some grapes."

"Green or red?"

"Hannibal!" Crassus snapped.

Hanno dropped his head, pulled the brush from his belt and drew it over and over again through the tail of his hair. Two large wet circles appeared on the tiles at his feet. "Excuse me, *dominus*," I said. I padded naked to the wall where the boy stood.

"Father Jupiter defend me!" Crassus cried.

Hanno threw his arms about me as I comforted him, assuring him that *dominus* meant no harm. I looked back to where Crassus stewed. "I'm certain lady Tertulla would be grateful if you apologized."

Dominus' eyes narrowed. "Apologies, Hannibal," he muttered. "I shouldn't have shouted."

I stepped aside, holding Hanno's claw of a hand. "That's all right, Father Jupiter," he sniffed. "I forgive you."

"Now, just a ..."

"There now, feeling better, aren't we?" I said, stifling a laugh. "You wait here, Hannibal, while Father Jupiter and I finish talking, then we'll go to the kitchen as promised. There's a good fellow."

I sat down smiling.

"You are never to call me that, do you hear?" Crassus said under his breath.

"One can see how the boy might be confused."

"Never," Crassus hissed. "And you are never to speak of it."

63

"By the Vestals, I swear," I said, still working at ironing the grin from my face. "Where were we?"

"About to bribe the tribune of the plebs to forestall the elections."

"Yes. We will continue," Crassus said, "to thwart Lentulus as often as we must till his term expires."

"And then an interrex? But who?"

Crassus nodded. "Who knows? A man who will put our case before the *comitia* with more enthusiasm than our diligent but misguided consuls."

"The interregnum can last no more than five days. How long can this persist?"

"Until we find an interrex who sees things our way, but I should think that by the end of Januarius, the people will have had enough of the upheaval this regrettable ploy is bound to ignite, and will rise up to plead for a return to normalcy. I ask you, who in this city is more a bastion of normalcy than I?"

Abruptly, Crassus' bearing relaxed into almost childish excitement. "Now, prepare yourself for the best news of all: Publius returns within a week!"

"*Dominus!*"

"Arrange for a banquet during the festival of Jupiter. A perfect occasion for a celebration."

"How did you manage to pry The Bane of Aquitania away from Caesar?"

"The legions are preparing to take up winter quarters; the great general can spare my son, surely. What?"

My incredulity was showing. "*Dominus*, Caesar would never release his most celebrated lieutenant for a family reunion, no matter how well-deserved. The tribes of Gaul are as yet unsubdued."

"As are the people of this city."

So that was it. "I see. And how many will be in Publius' party?"

"A goodly number. Caesar writes that he rides at the head of twelve *cohorts*, something more than five thousand legionaries."

"Something more than five thousand votes, if I take your meaning."

"Bright as ever, bright as ever," he said. As he rose from his chair, Crassus tousled my hair. I *hated* it when he did that. "Don't tell *domina*," he said, bending to scoop up the folds of his toga, carrying it in both arms like a pile of laundry. "She could do well with a surprise such as this."

"Help *dominus*," I told Hanno. He leapt from his post at the wall, but Crassus shook his head.

"Tend to your master," he said, winking at me. I hated it when he did that, too. "He looks wet."

Somehow, within a day, everyone in the *familia* had heard about Hanno and Father Jupiter. It is inexplicable how fast confidential news such as this manages to travel.

CHAPTER V

56 BCE - FALL, ROME

Year of the consulship of
Cn. Cornelius Lentulus Marcellinus and L. Marcius Philippus

"You used to be skinny," I said to legionary Drusus Malchus as we walked down the Clivus Victoriae off the Palatine. Malchus was stuffing the remains of a meat pie into his mouth.

His voice was pleasantly irritating, like a stroll over crushed gravel. "You used to be handsome," he said, "but you don't hear me casting insults at you, do you?" He licked each of his fingers, one at a time.

"We just did," said Flavius Betto. Far shorter than either Malchus or myself, legionary Betto took almost two strides to our one to keep his place between us. His pace was additionally hampered by his struggle to keep his short sword hidden behind his cloak.

A third guard, Minucius Valens, dressed like the rest of us in inconspicuous tunic and cloak, prodded Betto from behind. "Move smartly, Betto. The girls are waiting."

"May I assist you, Flavius?" I asked, trying to be helpful.

"I've got it," he said, yanking his baldric across his shoulder.

"That's why Betto can't get laid without reaching for a few coins," Valens said. "Under the coverlet, his girlfriends keep asking the same thing." He sang in high-pitched mimicry of an annoyed woman, "'May I assist you, Flavius.' He never could figure out where to put it! Maybe you'll have better luck with your *gladius*, but it looks like the only thing you'll penetrate with that sword is your scabbard!" Valens, a stocky man no taller than Betto, but thick of arms, chest and wit, thought his jest hilarious.

"You've missed your calling, Minucius," Betto replied calmly. "With the amount of pigeon shit coming out of your mouth, you'd have made a superb *ornatrix*, bleaching the hair of dainty ladies." Valens stopped laughing, and the rest of us did our best not to start.

"Gentlemen," I said, looking pointedly at Minucius Valens. "There will be no time for fraternization. We make the delivery to the tribune and return as quickly as possible."

I did not know Valens well; he had been among Crassus' guards for a year at least, but there were just so many servants in *dominus'* employ, it was impossible to know everyone on a personal level. Not so Drusus Quintilius Malchus and Flavius Salvius Betto. I had known these two estimable characters ever since coming to the house of Crassus.

Malchus' calm and sage counsel had seen me through many a difficult night in my first frightened and perturbed days in servitude. He poured home-grown cold reason on my overheated despair: a slave I was, but in Rome, there were slaves, and then there were the slaves of Crassus. I should make offerings, he had said, to whatever gods or goddesses who watched over me that I had washed up on this patrician's shore. From the look of me when first I was brought to the auction block, I would not have lasted a week had I been sold to one of the big farms, or the mines, or any one of a thousand crueler masters. I was one of the lucky ones, he had said, and I had better learn to be content with my lot.

It was true, Malchus had been lean and lanky in those frantic days, just like me, but after a year living the softer life of a guard at the Crassus residence, the man who had helped acclimate me to my fate had been thoroughly consumed by his consumption. I had never seen anyone so in love with food. Because of his height, he could not be called 'fat,' but the man had become *big*. To those that called him 'friend,' and there were many, he was known as Malchus the Mighty. But he was gentle and kind, and his calm was almost impossible to penetrate.

Then there was wiry, fretful Betto. He, unlike Malchus, was democratic in pothering equally over every matter, whether large or small. But he was fierce and loyal, and once, not long after my arrival as a newly-minted slave, he had saved my life. The two friends had joined up with Crassus to help Sulla defeat Marius. They were rarely out of each other's sight. This, though they were almost constantly in disagreement. Betto was river to Malchus' riverbed. They gave each other form and direction; one without the other would make the world a little less tolerable.

•••

Romans are always at war with somebody. The one that eventually brought Malchus and Betto into the welcoming arms of Marcus Crassus and my grateful company was known as The War of the Allies. Slaughter, when given a name, sounds so much more palatable, digestible. No bloodstained, breathless participant, I can assure you, ever stopped to consider what sobriquet history might bestow upon the present melee while he was in the thick of it.

This particular conflagration had been smoldering for decades, breaking out just a few years before I was taken from Greece. Most of the Italian states, who for centuries had been Roman allies, were of the opinion that Rome had begun to cheat them out of their share of the spoils of war. It had. Because of a handful of Roman laws, the Italian states surmised that their land was methodically and legally being taken from the innocent multitude and redistributed to the wealthy and avaricious. It was. And after all they had done to assist in the growth of Rome's power and influence, the Latin allies felt they were deserving, at long last, of Roman citizenship. They were.

And so, being thus thwarted and abused, after a time they went to war against the teat that had fed them and then been discourteously withdrawn. They lost. Before the fighting had ended, in an effort to dilute the rebellious Italians' grievances, the senate passed a law granting citizenship to all former allies who had not raised arms against Rome. This occurred when Malchus and Betto were in their late teens. With more exuberance than forethought, the two friends who had grown up together on the same Perusian street, celebrated by breaking into a wine shop. Consequently, they were 'encouraged' by the local garrison to join its ranks. Due to the ongoing rebellion, the hurdles of their both being underage and of Betto's need for thick-soled sandals to meet the height requirement were amiably removed.

Finding that they liked the life of a soldier well enough, they had joined *dominus'* army as it rushed to Sulla's aid to overthrow the tyrants Marius and Cinna, and had stayed on with him ever since. The only time the two soldiers shed their duty as part of the company that guarded the Crassus household was the year and half they had gone off with him to put down the slave rebellion lead by the gladiator, Spartacus.

There being no other viable option, and here I use 'viable' in the literal sense, i.e. capable of remaining alive, I took Malchus' advice, and now, almost three decades after my capture, I strolled with my companions past estates, expensive shops and other wealthy pedestrians traveling the paving stones of the privileged. Citizens nodded politely to me, shopkeepers gave me a warm greeting as I passed; a fruit seller tossed me a plum and smiled. I was welcomed here and accepted — there goes Alexander, chief slave of Marcus Licinius Crassus. What a lucky fellow! It was a brisk, sunny morning, and I smiled as I put the plum in Malchus' outstretched hand. It was good to be alive.

No, nothing sinister is about to happen; I truly was as thankful as a virgin chosen for the Vestals to be out and about, amongst friends and entrusted to dispatch a weighty charge. But then, being thankful implies the existence of a repository for this syrupy, effusive gratitude, and since my enslavement had cleansed me of any pretensions of belief in benevolent deities watching over me, I wondered to whom my respects ought to be paid. Unfortunately, the only name I could come up with was Crassus. He was as close to a god as I was likely ever to meet. Father Jupiter, indeed. To be a happy slave in a foreign land is to be as plagued with ironies as Hanno was infested with lice when we found him. One is a constant irritant that distracts your attention, fills you with frustration, nags at your enjoyment of any good thing, and if you have any self esteem at all, is a condition of constant humiliation and shame. And to be lice-ridden is a remarkably similar experience.

Oh. I must correct myself, and I do apologize. Something sinister *is* about to happen. More than one something, in point of fact.

Our route lay across the forum and then northeast. The first time I had seen its broad plazas framed by temples and civic buildings of brick and stone, my awe had been tempered by my exhaustion and malnutrition. Since then, every time my sandals trod upon its worn black stones, I harkened back to the day I had been dragged past the sight of the beating heart of Rome, thirty years earlier. At the time, my own heart was more beaten than beating, led behind the horse of a magnificent centurion to be presented as a multi-lingual gift from a grateful general, Lucius Cornelius Sulla, to his heroic *legate* Marcus Licinius Crassus. I think about that centurion from time to time and wonder, had he retired to a farm in Campagna, happy with his harvest of grapes and grandchildren, or had he fallen amongst his comrades on some distant, ruined field, defending the honor and the ever-expanding borders of the Republic? What we foreigners have failed to comprehend over the centuries is that the proud centurion would have found either fate equally satisfying. This is why Rome grows, and the rest of the world shrinks.

CHAPTER VI

56 BCE - FALL, ROME

Year of the consulship of
Cn. Cornelius Lentulus Marcellinus and L. Marcius Philippus

I f there was grumbling over my insistence that our mission remain strictly business, I could not hear it, for as we crossed the Nova Via at the southeastern border of the forum, a great tumult was occurring at the other end. The echoes of a man in a toga gesticulating on the *rostra* rolled down to us, held aloft by distant cheers from the crowd.

"What's that about?" Betto asked with his usual anxiety.

"Keep moving," I said. "It is either Clodius Pulcher or Annius Milo, riling up their respective mobs."

"Are we safe?" Betto asked.

"Clodius feigns championship of the plebs, and Pompey has brought Milo up to oppose him, so either side should be content with men of Crassus."

Betto said, "So this is a polite throng, is it? They'll stop to ask us who we support before they club us to death. That's comforting."

Malchus said, "Within the hour it won't be safe to be anywhere near the forum, no matter whose side you're on."

"Which is why we must make haste." The narrow box I gripped felt suddenly heavy.

"What's all the ruckus about, anyway?" Valens asked. "Clodius hates Milo because Milo is Pompey's man, Milo hates Clodius because he forced Cicero into exile, and just about everybody but Milo hates Cicero. Politics is easy once you know who hates who."

Betto, who had picked up the pace once he got sight of the crowd, said, "We need elections. If we had consuls by now, we'd have order. The gods hate anarchy. *I* hate anarchy — it interferes with my peace of mind."

"Everything interferes with your peace of mind," Malchus said.

Moments later, even before we had crossed over to the Sacra Via, three ravens flew overhead, one following the other. "Did you see that?!" Betto cried. "Pray the augurs were looking elsewhere. As bad omens go, that one excels, mark me."

"Just do your job," Malchus said, his face set.

We headed northeast toward the Esquiline and before long turned on to the Vicus Sandaliarius. The street was choked with commerce, the smell of leather and men who balanced piles of hides on their shoulders — deer and cattle and pig. The tanning workrooms and smithies were open to the street, but other stretches kept their secrets behind unmarked doors and blank walls littered with graffiti. Shopkeepers were cranking down their awnings; those directly across from each other almost touched above the worn paving stones, concealing those beneath in yellow shade.

We were making our way through the throng when I felt a sharp tug at my neck. I looked back just in time to see Valens deliberately trip a poor fellow heading in the opposite direction. The man scrambled to his feet with dagger in hand. *That was unmannerly,* I thought. *Perhaps it was an accident; in any case Valens should apologize.* The thin, unwashed creature crouched in a fighting stance, looking for his assailant. To my surprise, a second man joined him, also armed, the hole where his left eye had been drawing as much of my attention as his knife. Street traffic recoiled in an arc around them, but Valens stepped into the open space. All at once, it became eerily quiet. *Good, Valens will say his obligatories and we can be on our way.* The one-eyed man spoke first. "Go about your business, now, there's a good fellow."

"I am about my business," Valens said. "That's a fine purse you've got strung about your neck."

"Move off," the first man threatened, "or we'll stripe you good and all."

Valens ignored him and pointed to the second man. "What's that there? Why it looks like a bulge in your tunic. A purse-shaped bulge, or I'll kiss *Laverna's* chalk-white ass. Seems like one'd be enough for any honest man."

"We're done talkin'," said the one-eyed man. The two of them moved toward Valens, who casually reached inside his cloak and withdrew his *gladius*. Three eyes widened. Before One-eye and his friend could even contemplate a change in tactics, Valens was bracketed by Betto and Malchus, each with swords drawn.

"Now," Valens said, pointing with the bright tip of his weapon, "put your toothpicks away and hand it over." One-eye glowered at his partner, muttering "idiot" to his partner as he reached inside his tunic and tossed over my purse. Before I could stop myself, I foolishly put my hand to my neck to feel for the pouch I already knew was no longer there. *I truly am a lackwit.*

"Wait a minute," Malchus said. "This one's no good; the strap is cut."

Betto said, "So it is! Lucky for us that one looks serviceable enough. Hang it here." Betto waggled his blade just below One-eye's chin. The pilferer removed his own bag and with infinite reluctance draped it over the sword. This time the look he gave the other cutpurse was genuinely lethal. "There's a good lad," Betto said. "But we're not thieves, you know. We'll just take what's owed us." With that he sheathed his sword, opened the thief's purse and dumped its contents on the street. We melted back into the crowd; people began moving again, but continued to give the two men kneeling in the street a wide berth.

"*Atriensis,*" Malchus said as we moved off, "with respect, never walk down a street like this without first tucking your valuables down the front of your tunic."

"If I were him," Valens said, "I wouldn't walk down these streets at all, not without a few good men to guard him."

Betto shook his head and rolled his eyes. "You mean like us?"

"Leave him be, Flavius," Malchus said. "You were behind Alexander, too, and I didn't see *you* stop them."

"Thank you *all*, gentlemen," I said, ending the conversation. I took both pouches, one full, one empty, and did as the big legionary advised, first tucking one inside the other. There were no other incidents on the street, and not long thereafter we came upon a door above which hung an oversized, iron *strigil*. We filed inside, but

75

just before the door closed behind me, I thought I heard distant shouts rising above the general noise of the city.

This was no typical bathing establishment. In every *balnea* I had ever frequented, women's and men's facilities had always been separate. I am convinced this was more a function of prejudice than prudery: Roman men did not want their conversation or relaxation vexed by the intrusive and inconsequential interruptions of females. In this egalitarian establishment, however, it appeared that female presumptuousness was of a kind more easily welcomed by the ruling sex.

We stood in a small anteroom that led through another open doorway to the larger changing area. From somewhere beyond came music from a lyre and pipes. Also, sounds of laughter and play, from both sexes, could be heard not far off. "If Cato the Elder were not already in his grave these hundred years," Betto said, "this would put him in it."

"Why's that?" Valens asked.

"Because he was such an insufferable prig he wouldn't even allow his son into his own presence when he bathed."

"It's a miracle he ever had a son," Valens said.

"Well spoken," Betto allowed.

A bald old man, whose weathered face and arms perfectly matched the namesake of the street in which he worked, sat behind a small table. Behind him, a bored looking guard leaned against the red-painted wall. The baths manager looked up and scanned the four of us, his gaze finally coming to rest disconcertingly on me. He narrowed his eyes and rubbed his chin, considering. Could this look of disapproval be directed at me? I looked behind me, but there was no one else there. "Hmphh," he said at last. "Four of you. That'll be four *sesterces*."

"What?" Betto objected, too loudly, as usual. "I've never paid more than a quarter of an *as*." The guard pushed himself off the wall, no longer bored.

"That will be fine," I said, placing the equivalent, a single silver *denarius* on the table.

"The baths of Numa are worth every *as*," said the ancient *balneator*, who I believe meant to wink at us but was struck by a fit of coughing. When he recovered, he tapped the coin with an age-lined nail and said, "You'd better have brought more than this, though, unless all you want to do is bathe."

"Actually," I said, leaning over the table and lowering my voice, "I'm trying to locate a particular individual."

Looking as if all his suspicions had just been confirmed, the *balneator* scooped the coin off the table and put it in his box. He scratched the stubble underneath his chin and said, "There's no one here."

"Really? No one?" said Betto. I held up my hand to keep his lips from raining further alienation down upon us.

The old man said, "No one with four big men looking for him." He squinted at Betto. "Three, anyways."

I reached into my purse and tossed an *aureus* on the table; we all listened to the lovely, dull clunk of its contact with the wood. It lay there silently, but each of us understood its secret language: "Look at me," it sighed, "isn't gold the most enchanting and wondrous of all colors?"

"First one of them I've seen all week," said the *balneator*, leaving the coin where it had come to rest, but eyeing it greedily. "He'll get lonely, he will." I placed a

77

second precisely on top of the first. Apparently, a bargain had been struck. The old man looked up with the gentle, querying interest of a librarian, and at the same time, without taking his eyes off mine, deftly swept the gold from the table and into his tunic, neatly circumventing the receipts box.

"Tribune Gaius Cato?" I said.

"Try the *calidarium*. He'll be the one with the most food at hand. Nipples the size of my fist. Go through the changing area, past the *tepidarium* and the massage rooms, then across the *palaestra*. Mind the large *frigidarium*; it's empty for cleaning. The small one's still available...though I don't suppose that's of any interest to you gentlemen. The *calidarium* is at the back, next to the toilets."

We went through into the crowded changing room where I did my best to ignore a man and woman who appeared to be changing vigorously and simultaneously at close quarters. Slaves guarded the cubbyholes where patrons had stored their belongings; in fact, there appeared to be more attendants than bathers. We were just about to pass into the spacious *tepidarium* when I heard a laugh and stopped short. I told the others to go find the tribune and walked out through the colonnade onto the *palaestra*. The large courtyard was open to the sky, at one moment lit brilliantly by the early afternoon sun, thrown into shadow the next by passing clouds. To my right was the empty swimming pool; its painted concrete bottom was quite deep. To my left, half a dozen men were lifting dumbbells and several more were wrestling on the packed earth. At the far end of the courtyard, nearest the street entrance, two games of *trigon* were in progress, but it was the one being played by three bare-breasted women that drew my attention. I might not have noticed had it not been for a shaft of sunlight that momentarily illuminated one of the players. There was only one woman I knew with hair that shade of red.

"Livia?" I asked incredulously, walking briskly toward them.

"Ow!" she cried, distracted by me and hit hard by the ball thrown by the young lady to her left. She rubbed her right shoulder, realized who had called her name and exclaimed, "Alexander! What are you doing here?" Her arms crossed almost involuntarily, pressing against her breasts.

"Oh, Livvy, I am so sorry. Shall I count those three points? No, of course not. Why are you covering your...oh." The girl who trotted up to see if "Livvy" was all right was no slave. A Roman woman could exude just as much of the aura of power and privilege as a Roman man, even one who looked to be no more than seventeen. This one's dark brown hair was threaded with gold links to hold it aloft. Her nails and toes were painted and obviously pampered; around her throat she wore a fine necklace with a gold and lapis Egyptian ankh. The two attendants from the game ran up and wrapped both women in thin linen towels, which somehow made their practically naked state even more immodest.

The third player trotted by, heading for the anointing room. "I've got to go anyway," she called. "Thanks for the game!"

"Hey! I want a rematch next week," Livia's new acquaintance called back, waving. Then she turned to me and in that same silken voice of authority said, "I am Caecilia Metella, but my friends call me Cornelia."

"I recognize you, mistress. My master is well-acquainted with your father and holds him in high regard. However—"

"However?"

I was furious, but could not speak my mind before the daughter of senator Quintus Caecilius Metellus Pius Scipio Nasica. A hundred reprimands came spilling to the very tip of my braced and trembling tongue. I do not know what goddess held it still, but to her I give silent thanks. It would have to be a goddess, would it not? Circumspection is rare in men. I could not drag Livia from this indecent establishment, so I opted for a less physical alternative and introduced myself to her friend.

"I know who you are," Cornelia Metella said, "and I apologize for stealing your Livia away." *My Livia? Had Livia confided some intimate thing to this young lady, or was my imagination spiraling out of control yet again?* "Tertulla is housebound by order of her husband, but I never miss my weekly game of *trigon*. I met Livia with my parents at one of Tully's[1]* dinner parties a few months ago. Marcus Licinius and lady Tertulla brought the new Crassus *medicus* to drum up business for her practice, which was very liberal of them, but after the introductions, everyone pretty much ignored her because, you know, she's a slave."

"Everyone except you," Livia said.

"It's not your fault," lady Cornelia said indignantly. "I find it ridiculous that people refuse to associate with

---

* (editor's note: Tully was a nickname for Marcus Tullius Cicero)

someone simply because of an accident of birth. I have friends my own age who aren't half as smart or nearly as talented. I've been having Tertulla set Livia free as often as possible this past month."

"I do recall now *domina* mentioning something about forgiving your absences. At last, I meet the young lady in the flesh," I said. The two women laughed, first one way, and then another after I said, "What, have I misspoken?"

"Alexander, you are hopeless," Livia said.

"I persuaded your *domina* to allow Livia to fill in today. She is an exemplary companion and quite the experienced athlete."

"And thanks to Alexander," Livia said, "I shall now have a bruise to prove it."

"It was stupid of me to interrupt, but seeing you in this place…"

"What do you mean," lady Cornelia asked, "'*this place?*'"

"Don't mind him," Livia said. "Alexander is a bit of a prude."

"That's so sweet." *Sweet. Just the sort of compliment every man lays awake nights hoping to hear.*

"You needn't worry," lady Cornelia said with an impish smile. "It's not like we were considering stealing any trade from the working girls. But occasionally, it is fun to watch, and to be watched. And don't think I didn't see, Livia."

"See what?"

"That muscular beauty with the hairy chest in the game next to ours—he's been eyeing you since we came onto the *palaestra*."

"You are sadly mistaken, my lady."

"You *know* it's true. And I told you not to call me that." I don't know which was worse, Livia's blush or my inability to keep my head from whipping around to spy out this rival. Why can't I realize my mistakes before I make them? As I returned my gaze to the young *domina*, the heat began to rise in my own cheeks. Lady Cornelia was beaming up at me with a look that said, 'I know all your secrets.' "Besides," she said aloud, "the Numa is perfectly safe."

"That's just it, lady Cornelia. Today, the streets are *not* safe. I am on an urgent errand for my master, accompanied by several men-at-arms. I will see you both safely home."

"Nonsense. My man waits in the changing room. Livia's never had a massage, and I mean to treat her. After which, I shall keep her company while she does some shopping."

"Go, Alexander. I've discovered an herbalist only a few streets away who carries waneb root. I promise, I will let you know the moment I am home safe and sound."

I hated leaving her, but what could I do? If I had found her alone, I could have ordered her to come with us. But now, in the presence of the patrician's daughter, I was powerless. I bid them farewell and walked toward the rear of the *balnea*, skirting the empty pool. I found my own escorts standing in the hallway just outside the *calidarium*. Betto saw me approach and said, "There you are. Say, was that—"

"No. It was not. Why aren't you in the *calidarium*?"

"Two reasons," Valens said as he and Malchus joined us. "One, it's hot, and two, he's not in there."

Malchus asked, "Weren't you just talking to—"

"No, he wasn't," Betto said imperiously.

Malchus shrugged. "The tribune is through the *calidarium* in the sweat room. But we didn't go in."

"It's a small room. You can't miss him."

I ignored Valens attempt at a joke which I did not comprehend and said, "All right. I'll be out in a minute. Flavius, you come with me."

"Can't we wait till he's finished," Betto whined.

"I don't know what you're talking about, but no, there's no time. Drusus, can you see if there's a back way out of here? And Valens, you wait for us right here. By right here, I mean nowhere near the massage rooms. Is that clear?"

"Can he talk to us like that?" Valens asked.

The Mighty Malchus said, "He can if I say he can. Do what he says. If there's trouble, then I'm senior legionary in command. Is *that* clear?"

Betto said, "Better you than me."

We separated, and Betto and I crossed the *calidarium*. It was both hot and humid in this domed room, about twenty-five feet in diameter, its circular walls painted deep blue below the midpoint, rusty red above. To the left, steam rose from a sunken soaking tub in which two women lounged and perspired, eyes closed, backs against the edge, arms stretched along the rim in watery crucifixion. A cold water fountain bubbled in the center of the room to refresh those who required respite from the fires warming both floor and walls. From the heat radiating up through my thin sandals, my feet knew we must be very near the furnace room. To the right, a semi-circle of wooden benches hugged the wall, offering the only non-heated surface. Taking refuge there were two older men deep in conversation and one young woman, curled up like a cat, naked and asleep at the far end. I averted my eyes from another young man who was disentangling himself from his bearded lover, only to be assaulted by the sight that lay directly ahead.

The view beyond the archway into the torch-lit, semi-circular apse that was the smaller *laconicum*, or sweat room, rooted my sandals to the floor and caused me to lay hold of the edge of the fountain with counterfeit insouciance. The tribune Gaius Cato sat, or rather sprawled in the dim, flickering light, his hairless, gelatinous form enveloping half the only bench in the room. He was the center of a living frieze, a lounging symmetry of debauchery. A young woman and a younger boy tended to the man's sloping breasts (the *balneator* had not exaggerated), one on either side of his shining corpulence. Rivulets of perspiration, brave explorers, circumnavigated the hemisphere of his gut. A third woman, kneeling with her back to us, her head bobbing between his thighs, held his midsection at bay with a straining forearm. Food was heaped everywhere, but nowhere more than in the tribune's own hands. They swung slowly, methodically between tables behind the bench to deposit their loads beyond the pink fish lips and into the waiting abyss beyond. Driblets and crumbs of excess fell from his mouth and down his body, a sleet of food and wine.

"I told you we should have waited," Betto muttered.

"What's that?" the tribune called in a nasal whine, bits of nut tart falling from his mouth to land in the hair of the oblivious woman laboring between his splayed thighs. "If you have business, don't just stand there, approach!"

"I'd rather not," Betto whispered.

Forcing myself to release my grip on the fountain, I walked to the border between the *calidarium* and the *laconicum.* Truly I could not have moved any closer without grave risk of becoming an inadvertent participant in the tribune's afternoon indulgence. "Sir, forgive the intrusion. I come representing my master, Marcus Crassus." Sweat was beginning to bead on my forehead and twin drops tickled as they ran a slow race down my flanks.

"I've been expecting you. Give it here." Sausage fingers waggled, summoning me forward. I reached into my tunic, removed the box and leaned between the two women to pass it into the tribune's outstretched hand. For the moment, everyone stopped their ministrations to watch the tribune struggle to unwrap the entwined clasp.

"Ach! My fingers are too fat and greasy. Crispina, petal, would you mind?"

"Of course not, husband." Long years of experience in maintaining decorum prevented me from abrupt reaction when the woman to my left detached herself and stood, her naked hip brushing against my tunic. Waves of body odor and perfume—cedar oil and vanilla—rose with her; almost overwhelming as they roiled in the room's heated air. I stood my ground and managed to keep eye contact with her husband as she applied deft fingers to the unwinding of the thin ribbon that wrapped back and forth across the two brass pins that held the hinged box sealed. When done, the lady Crispina returned the opened box to her spouse and waited with the rest of us while the tribune removed the scroll.

Having read its contents, he looked up at me expectantly. "Anything else?"

"Any message, sir, for my master?"

"Why, give him my heartfelt thanks, naturally, and inform him that, as always, I am his faithful servant." The tribune craned his head. "That small man just behind you, he's rather attractive, in a diminutive sort of way, isn't he? You there," he said, wiggling his outstretched fingers, "would you care for some lunch?"

Betto appeared to fold in upon himself, then, realizing he was still visible, stammered something that sounded like a decline. Unsure that he was communicating, he looked to me with pleading eyes for assistance. "What my companion means to say, my lord, is that he'd be delighted" — Flavius whimpered — "but he is on assignment just now."

The tribune shrugged. "Right then, everybody switch places!"

Our business concluded, I turned to go, the thought of watching the repositioning of the next phase of the tribune's entertainment distressingly non-imperative, and more disturbing than coming upon them already engaged. At the archway between the two rooms, Betto was already turning away; his fretful mumbling almost inaudible. I grabbed his elbow and walked him briskly back through the *calidarium*, across the hallway and into the *palaestra*. There we found Malchus and Valens standing at the edge of the empty pool. Malchus reported that he had found an exit to an alley behind the toilets, but I told him we wouldn't need it. "You three go on ahead. I will either catch up to you or meet you back home."

Malchus squinted at me suspiciously. "*Dominus* would have our hides if anything happened to you."

"I have business down the street which does not concern you." It was evident my old friend was not to be convinced. "Drusus, I beg of you."

"Let us check the street, at the least," he said. I walked with them to the entrance, after which my companions fanned out, returning shortly to report nothing untoward. I waved them on and they walked back the way we had come. I turned left, but after a few paces retraced my steps and reentered the *balnea*.

CHAPTER VII

56 BCE - FALL, ROME

Year of the consulship of
Cn. Cornelius Lentulus Marcellinus and L. Marcius Philippus

"*Salve*," said the *balneator*, as I reentered the baths. "One *sestercius*." He held out his upturned palm.

"I haven't left," I said affably. "I was just bidding a few friends farewell."

"There's a well-worn tale."

"No, I am in earnest. I paid for myself and three others. Ah! I see. Forgive me; I am slow to recognize humor. You are in jest." I smiled down at him. He smiled up at me, but did not withdraw his hand. Now I was confused. "Myself, plus three others in tunics and red cloaks? It comes to you, yes?"

"You just described half the men who patronize this fine establishment."

"Oh, come now," I said with frustration. "You must recollect."

"Exactly. I must re-collect one *sestercius*." The guard looked on impassively.

This is the kind of discussion from which I know I should flee but to which I am inexorably drawn, a moth to a candle. An inconsequential debate, not worth the time it takes to engage in it, but I am a fish mesmerized by the wriggling worm of another's non-comprehension. Or a fisherman, determined to prevail over the thick-witted trout with a rod and line of impeccable, inescapable logic.

"Sir, surely you recognize me from our previous conversation."

"I've got a terrible head for faces. One *sestercius*." I was tempted to tell him the reverse was also true, but knew at once that stooping to vulgarisms would not have been helpful to my cause. Instead, I said, "Allow me to refresh your memory. I gave you two *denarii* for the whereabouts of tribune Cato not a quarter of an hour ago."

"Sorry, we don't give out the names of our clients."

"I'm not asking for it *now*," I said, my voice rising a modicum higher than I would have preferred. Exhaling, I calmed myself and planned my next move in this Game of Wit*less*. "Here's a proposition for you: I'll guess where the tribune is; if I'm right, you let me in for free. If I'm wrong, I'll pay you two *sesterces*."

The old man looked offended. "Gambling is illegal," he said, crossing his arms. I waited, staring him down. Finally, he said, "Go ahead then."

"The *laconicum*," I said triumphantly.

"Sorry, he's in the *calidarium*. That will be *two sesterces*."

"You *said* he was in the *calidarium*, but he wasn't. He was in the *laconicum*."

His almost bald brows raised ever so slightly. "I said I *thought* he was in the *calidarium*."

"Aha! So you *do* remember me. My point is proved. Please let me pass."

"Where is it written that you may leave the *balnea* Numa and return whenever you please without payment?" said the *balneator*. The guard yawned.

"Does the day drag so slowly for you, sir, that this is your only form of diversion?"

"I am easily entertained, sir. I might have been able to accommodate you earlier," he said, interlacing his fingers while planting his elbows on his table, "but now, you understand, we are at capacity."

"Not a soul has entered since we began this conversation!"

"True, but neither has anyone departed."

"Take pity on a poor slave," I said, reduced to begging. "I serve Marcus...well, a most vicious master, who takes no greater pleasure at the end of the day than to scrutinize every *as* of the accounts for which I am responsible." Exasperation and mendacity—the contest was lost, if not to a better man, than at least to one with more persistence.

"You seem like a nice fellow; I'll tell you what I'll do for you: pay the two *sesterces*, which by your own rules you owe me fair and true. Then come back at a time of your choosing and I'll let you pass, no charge whatsoever! What could be fairer than that?"

I reached into my purse and let two coins slide to the table from my open hand. "What could be fairer indeed. I salute you, sir, and would stay to discuss the finer points of your victory, but I am in rather a hurry. I'll return for a written pass before I leave."

"No need," the old man called as I passed through the dressing rooms. "I never forget a patron."

Once inside, I headed straight for the massage rooms. Livia's safety is paramount, I told myself. That argument rang false, though with noble tones. Lady Cornelia had only one slave to guard them both. That reasoning was as ludicrous as it was unwise: what could I add to their party that would ameliorate their protection. Sympathy? I should have kept Malchus with me; he was both large *and* discreet.

I was not clear on what it was that I intended, only that I needed to see her once more before leaving this place. In the next few moments, instinct would serve me better than brains, not once, but twice. I was lucky: Livia was in the first enclosure. One could hardly call them rooms; they were roughly ten-foot square spaces formed by draperies which could be drawn open or left closed. The curtain between Livia's and lady Cornelia's rooms had been pulled back and tied tight against the far wall so that they might converse without obstruction. The *medicus* and the patrician's daughter lay face down on raised, padded tables, naked except for towels covering their modesty. An exhilarated cacophony emanating from the enclosure just beyond gave ample and continuous evidence that massage was only one of many offerings on the *balnea's* menu. Thank Aphrodite, the curtains, at least, were closed.

From where I stood, I was at least temporarily invisible: the men faced their clients, and both women had their heads turned in the direction of the athletic couple beyond. "Livia, darling," lady Cornelia said, "for five *sesterces* more your masseur can make you moan like that. Shall I call for Buccio to fetch my purse?"

The muscled, bare-chested masseur with moonless midnight skin was pouring scented olive oil onto his hands. His shiny, curled hair lay so fine and tight upon his scalp it scarcely looked real. He could easily have been a warrior or a prince in his own land. He was young and smooth and exotic, and I didn't much care for him at all. He must have had only a rudimentary understanding of Latin, for he showed no reaction to lady Cornelia's suggestion. Unlike myself, whose breath found a high perch and refused to budge.

"You are kind, Cornelia, and unlike any highborn I have met. Oh, but that is heaven," she said, interrupting herself as the African applied his skills to her feet. "But given the choice, and there were times when in my youth when I had none, I prefer more intimate surroundings. If you'll allow me, it would be a privilege to say 'no.'" Livia's tone had slid from conversational to that voice with which all slaves are familiar, the flat, disassociated tone needed to withstand some memory better forgotten, but impossible to repress.

Exhale.

Lady Cornelia turned to her older friend, "No one is going to force you to do anything against your will here. I promise." Young as she was, she was not naïve. She had heard the change in tone, and understood that, hard as she might try, she would never bridge the span that yawned between them with a massage or a game of *trigon*.

Livia pushed herself up on her elbows and said a most sincere, "Thank you." They both recognized that even those two words, softly spoken, had the power to push them apart, each into their separate worlds.

Lady Cornelia thought for a moment, then said, "Shall I have father buy you, and set you free, then?"

"Don't joke about such things."

"I'm serious. More oil," she instructed her own masseur. "My heels are like leather."

Livia lay back down on her stomach, her right cheek on her hands. "Free." The sound blew through her mouth with less weight than it deserved. "My mother fought for my freedom all her life."

"Where is she now?"

"Dead, if the gods are kind. She was sent to the mines. I haven't seen her or had word from her in twenty years." Livia laughed, a short, mirthless sound. "Do you know what she told me: she said you could never be happy, you could never fully experience love unless you were free. Freedom was the only thing that mattered."

"Then let me help you honor her memory by granting her most fervent wish."

"I believed her, when I was a child. But now, I don't know. Even if it were possible, Cornelia, to gain this prize, what would I sacrifice? You've seen what life is like outside the walls of your estate. Freedmen are judged almost as harshly as we are. The stigma never fades. I'm thirty-seven and no virgin. What kind of man would have me? How would I live? Without the protection and patronage of *dominus*, what citizen would pay to be treated by a female doctor?"

"But you'd be *free*. You are beautiful. You could do what you choose."

"Forgive me, Cornelia, I do not make light of your most generous offer, but I think my time for a free life has past. Even my mother might offer different advice today. If I had money, or even family…. But I will think about it, seriously, I promise." Livia laughed; now the sound was bright but dismissive. "Why are we even talking about this? *Dominus* would never let me go. He's invested too much in my training. You might as well ask him to sell

Alexander to your father. No, I am welcome in the house of Crassus, and my place is there."

"You *want* to remain a slave?"

"I have a home there, my work is respected, and there is...there are people there who care about me."

"Hm. The house of Crassus is renowned for training and keeping only the highest quality staff. If you say the life there is better than on the outside, I must believe you. Something has changed, though. My parents remarked on it – both Crassus and lady Tertulla seem different, somehow, since their return from Luca. Do you know anything about it?"

"I am only back from Memphis these few months; I really couldn't say."

"Well," lady Cornelia said, dismissing even the hint of an unpleasant subject, "I pray they are well. When my friends and I talk of the marriages our fathers will arrange for us, theirs is the one we all hope to emulate. Whatever the matter, we'll find a shrine and say a prayer for them on the way home."

"You are sweet to do so."

"Not so sweet that I wouldn't steal your man there away from you," lady Cornelia said.

"This fellow?" Livia said, gesturing back toward the African. "Take him. I have no preference."

"Thank you, Livvy. I like the thought of his big hands upon me."

"You're not going to let him...," Livia said, alarmed.

The young lady laughed. "Of course not! My father would kill me. No, I mean he would *seriously* consider it. All he talks about is making a prudent political match for me. I tease him, but I mean to make him proud of me, in every way, including the stain I leave on my wedding sheets."

Lady Cornelia said something to her masseur, who spoke a single word to Livia's, and the two made to switch places. This was my moment. Livia was turned away from me. The *aureus* in my palm was warm and basted with sweat, but held at the ready. I moved into view at the foot of Livia's table just as lady Cornelia rolled over onto her back. She saw me straight away; all was lost! I smiled at her helplessly, beseechingly. To my astonished relief, she smiled back conspiratorially. I held the coin up to the man about to squeeze past me and motioned him to make good his departure in quiet haste. He grasped the hot gold piece, his entire face smiling, and went off to contemplate how he would spend this newfound windfall. There was no time to pour more oil. The African looked only mildly surprised when I took his dripping, gleaming hands in my own and rubbed them vigorously. I winked at him and made a gesture for his continued silence. He winked back at me, but the motion was mimicry without understanding. He started to say something, which I quelled, taking his hands and guiding them to lady Cornelia's feet. Her expression said she found this pantomime at least as entertaining as her interrupted massage. I did not care; my improvisation was going well so far, providing my heart did not explode in my chest.

Before me waited the unsuspecting Livia. She lay with her ankles just off the table, toes pointed toward the floor, curtains of her unclasped hair thankfully blocking her vision.

"Oh! I think you've made a bad bargain, Cornelia." Livia sighed as I attended to each individual toe of her left foot, pressing and separating, oiling the valleys between each, intent on making each touch a caress.

"And I think we are now perfectly matched," she replied.

I had no idea what I was doing; fortunately my hands were guided by a higher authority: desire. Technique's teacher was nothing more than imagining the ecstasies I would feel if our places were reversed. I gave what I wanted to receive. I was reluctant to leave any part of her, but I could not work on her feet forever. Moving up the length of each calf, I drew my fingers firmly back down her lean muscles till I reached her ankle. When Livia released a sigh of pleasure, my chest tightened; breathing became a voluntary thing.

I watched my African counterpart; when he stopped to replenish the oil on his hands, I did likewise. When he moved up onto the exposed, slightly spread tops of lady Cornelia's thighs, I moved higher as well. Rubbing my hands to warm them, I positioned my thumbs on the back of Livia's right thigh, as close as I dared to the towel which, were it to rise by the slightest fraction, would reveal all it was tasked to conceal. Pressing gently, I moved in alternating, short strokes down to the back of her knee, then up again, cradling and stroking the front of her leg with eight other beguiled fingers as I went.

Moments passed and somehow I found myself tending to the oiled and toned contours of Livia's back. I had fallen into a reverie of tactility, no longer certain if Livia's flesh or my own hands were the recipients of such mindless, focused attention. Every stroke and manipulation moved with but one intent: to elicit a sigh of contentment or a moan of pleasure. And there were many. A stifled cry from the adjoining table broke my mediation.

Lady Cornelia's masseur had found his way to her breast, and despite her earlier protestations, her nipple rose with eager curiosity to the rhythmic rolling of his thumb and forefinger.

"I think we had better stop," she gasped, pushing his hand away.

"Oh, just a while longer, Cornelia. I am transported." Livia stretched her arms and legs, an arrow of limbs and torso. "Alexander, you have Apollo's own touch."

There's a coincidence: the masseur they originally hired for lady Cornelia has the same name as my own. Wait a moment!

Livia reached beneath her, grabbed a second towel from a railing under her table and deftly rolled onto her back as she covered herself. "Did you think," she continued, "even after all these years that I could forget the touch of your hands?" With one arm across her chest, she raked her unbound hair away from her face and smiled up at me.

I did not know what else to do, and it was out of the question that I continue to stand there, stunned and silent. So I kissed her. Livia yielded, twisting on her side, curling up into my embrace. Her hand held the back of my neck, her knees bent, prodding me closer. Once she had been mine, and I had broken her heart. I was not deserving of this moment, but I would not give it up. Wetness pushed against the eyelashes of my closed eyes. The musk of the perfumed oil swirled lazily around us, moving as slowly as our mouths. But like all infinite moments, this one, too, proved itself false.

There came the sound of a scuffle at the entrance to the *balnea*, then shouting. I heard someone bellow something that sounded like 'the enemies of Clodius!' I broke from our embrace. "Lady Cornelia, call your man."

The look in my eyes won any argument she might have raised. She shouted for him, but there was no response, at least none that we could hear about the growing tumult. Patrons were running for the entrance, but the way must have been blocked. I watched as lady Cornelia's masseur bolted for the back of the building. "There must be a back exit. Wrap those towels about you as best as you can. Quickly."

I unhooked my cloak and threw it about Livia's shoulders, forgetting my duty to serve the highborn lady Cornelia. We followed the path of the African, who had crossed the *palaestra* just in front of the empty *frigidarium*, disappearing into the hallway leading to the *calidarium*.

"What's happening?" Livia asked.

"Anarchy," I replied.

CHAPTER VIII

56 BCE - FALL, ROME

Year of the consulship of
Cn. Cornelius Lentulus Marcellinus and L. Marcius Philippus

From behind us, a voice called, "Mistress!"
"Buccio! What has happened?!" lady Cornelia cried. I have noted how often questions escape our mouths when the answers are known to us even before we begin to speak. It is my contention that we do this in order to let our minds catch up with our brains. Or perhaps it is the other way round. In any event, we stopped to give the old slave time to catch up to us. He held one hand to his head and a bundle of his lady's things under his other arm.

"Your pardon, lady," the little man said. "I did my best." Lady Cornelia grabbed her clothes from him.

"There's no time to change, lady —" I started.

"Shut up," she said, pressing a fine, yellow tunic to her man's bleeding head. I deserved that, I did.

In a voice full of apology, Buccio said, "They beat me when I tried to conceal your jewels."

We had not yet skirted the pool when a familiar voice boomed out, "Hold!" Familiar, as in recognizable, but not in any way sociable. It was the man I had heard calling the

99

name of Clodius. We turned with sinking hearts to see a knot of unsavory fellows armed with clubs striding across the *palaestra*. Their leader, a man with bushy eyebrows and a full beard was the least appetizing of all. Behind these ruffians, several more had herded a dozen or so of the *balnea's* patrons together into a frightened huddle.

"What is the meaning of this, sir? How dare you detain representatives of senator Crassus?" I heard myself say. Someone must have pushed me to stand in front of the women, for there I suddenly stood. Behind them, there was only a foot or two of dirt to the edge of the pit that was the empty swimming pool.

"That's a fair question," the heavyset fellow said, thoughtfully tapping the end of his thick club into the palm of his hand, as if to consider it. "And it deserves a fair answer, but let me ask you one first. Who the fuck put *you* in charge?" he said, jabbing the club into my stomach. My knees discovered the ground of their own accord, but my breath was undiscoverable. Livia dropped and put her arms around me to help steady me.

Through my wheezing, I heard another man lisp, "Crassus? He's frenss with that *ophtimate* bastard Gnaeus Phompheius! Clodius said..."

I tried to speak again, but a wave of nausea overtook me. The leader interrupted his accomplice, giving me time to collect myself. "Calm yourself, Palaemon. Does this look like the *curia* to you? We're not here for politics; we're here for fun."

"I wouldn't exactly call them friends," I managed to whisper.

"Hey, I know that man," a voice called from the back.

"Yes, yes, I know him, too. He's Crassus' man, Alexander." He reached down to pat my head, the swine.

"But these two," he said, swinging his club between Livia and lady Cornelia, "I don't believe I've had the pleasure. Get it," he said, turning to his men. "It's a pun." Silence. "Haven't you people seen Syrus? You must—he's very funny."

"You're no Syrus," I said, reaching out as fast as I could to grab the man's right heel with both hands and pulling with all my strength. My intent was to unbalance him, send him sprawling to the ground where he belonged, wrest the club from his grasp and start valiantly swinging while the others made their escape. In retrospect, it was probably to the benefit of all our party that the foot did not budge.

"Listen, my brave mantis," he said, pulling me to my feet by my ear. As he looked up at me, he jabbed the club in my chest, lightly this time. "I've got no quarrel with you. Clodius is being nice to your master because he knows how it rankles Pompeius. Any man who stands with Crassus is a friend to Clodius. Today, leastwise."

"An excellent man, a man of reason," I lied.

"'Velus,' he told me, 'go out, hire a dozen or so men of flexible character and administer a thud or two to any conservatives you may find.' Even gave me a list, which would be grand, except I can't read for shit. I mean I know how to read, but the gods have plagued me with the blurry eye. So I'm looking, instead, for them that's got that look; you know the one I mean, the look like they own the world and you don't."

"An astute criterion, for which you can see we do not qualify," I said, meeting his eyes, whose pupils looked as if they had been replaced by moonstones. I had seen this ailment before, but never up close. The effect was disturbing, as if the ruffian were looking through me, not at me. "And we are all four members of the Crassus household," I added, careful not to look directly at Lady Cornelia.

"But Crassus *does* own the world," the one called Palaemon said slowly, and with effort. His mouth was pulled down on one side by a scar, mangling his words as if he had a mouth full of knucklebones. The rest of his cratered face had been ruined by the pox.

"But he doesn't have the look," said Velus.

"No, of course he doesn't," I said, beginning to feel almost chummy with this ne'er-do-well. "He's a man of the people."

"Well, you see, here's the thing of it," he said, tilting his head and rubbing the club against the underside of his hirsute chin. "Clodius said 'any *man* who stands with Crassus.' He didn't say spit about women."

"What? You wouldn't dare club a woman," I cried, spreading my arms protectively. Or at least instinctively.

"No, 'course not. Not with *this* club," he said, waving the piece of wood. "It's a pun. Get it?" This time, the amateur comedian got his laugh. "Now stand aside, cousin. Don't you worry, we'll have your lady friends back to you…" he looked up at the clouds overhead as if that would assist him in his calculations, "… oh, shouldn't be more than half an hour. You lot," he called to his men in the back, "Make sure you've fleeced them proper, then let 'em all go. Keep the women you fancy."

The man called Velus stepped forward and reached for lady Cornelia, who screamed. Two others shoved me aside and went for Livia. "No!" I cried. "No, please." Livia knew better than I to struggle or protest: she went limp, having learned since she was barely more than a child that resignation would see her through her coming ordeal with the least brutality. She cast her eyes downward, her lips pressed tightly together. For one brief moment, she glanced up at me as if to say, 'it doesn't matter.' But oh gods, how it did. Strong hands held my arms, but my imagination flew free to slay every last one of these caitiffs.

From out of the shadows on the other side of the pool, the tribune Cato appeared, now dressed, the front of his tunic stretched tight across his belly, his family bunched behind him. In one greasy hand he held the roasted leg of some animal, in the other the box with my master's bribe. With his high-pitched voice he called out, "You men, unhand those women. I shall have your names, sirs."

"Gaius Cato," Velus said. "I recognize you."

"As well you should. Return these good people to their belongings and set them free. I'll have no unlawfulness in my presence."

"Ah'll tend to this," said Palaemon, starting to make his way around the pool.

"The person of a tribune of the plebs is sacrosanct," Gaius Cato said haughtily, with no hint that he and his arrogance might be in danger. "Have you prayed at the temple of Ceres? No? Lay a hand on me and you may visit all your possessions there before they are sold at auction. But you shan't be troubled by your loss for long, for presently your head will be forfeit to Jupiter."

"You first," said Palaemon, jauntily swinging a rusting scrap of curved iron.

"Wait," Velus said in a tired voice. He thought for a moment. "The problem for a tribune in a situation like this," he said, "the problem with your sacrosanctity, if I may call it that, is that you don't have any *lictors* for protection. I mean, why would you need any, if just bumping up against you in a crowd could get you thrown off the Tarpeian Rock? But the only crowd that matters here is us.

"You've seen us," he said, working it out, "so that's no good for us, and not very good for you. I could kill you, but much as I like these fellows, I don't trust 'em worth spit, and I can't very well kill them all to keep them quiet, so here's what I'm thinking. You take you and yours and go about your business, and we'll go about ours, without the killing you part. Everybody's happy. Oh, and we'll take that fancy box before you go. Go get it, Palaemon."

"This box is on my person, therefore part of my person."

"But we're not taking it from you, tribune. You're giving it to us as a, hmm, parting gift, if I may call it that, to thank us for letting you go. Isn't that right?"

Palaemon reached Gaius Cato and held out a scarlet and crooked hand. "Outrageous," the tribune sputtered, reluctantly surrendering the box. "There's nothing in here of any value to you," he said in a voice that declared quite clearly that there was indeed something of value within, if not in the thing itself, than in the knowledge of its existence. Not that bribery wasn't as common as cleaning your teeth with crushed oyster shells, bones and olive oil, it was just that it was one of the few transactions Romans preferred to conduct in the shadows.

Palaemon trotted back to Velus and gave him the box. Then he sauntered over to the two men holding Livia. "Ah'm the only one doing any work here. Ah'll take the redhead." Velus nodded, and his reprobate accomplice took hold of Livia's wrist. The crooked smile that contorted his lips made me want to wretch. I strained in vain against the hands that held me.

"I shall commit your faces to memory," said Gaius Cato.

"Fine by me," Velus said to the tribune. "I'm going to treat myself to a shave after today's labors. Best of luck remembering *this* face."

"Thass not right," Palaemon said, "Ah haff no beard."

"Then grow one," Malchus said.

Malchus!

"Or develop a limp," added Betto.

A hobnailed military boot came thrusting out from behind Velus and crashed into the back of Palaemon's leg. He fell screaming, releasing his hold on both Livia and his iron rod. It landed at her bare feet; she bent to scoop it up. Even scoundrels possess the reflex to help a downed comrade; in the instant when their grip loosened I wrenched free of the two that held me and rushed to Livia's side.

"No one move!" Velus called out in alarm. Something very sharp was prodding painfully into his lower back. Lady Cornelia pulled away from him and ran to join Buccio and the two of us. Livia held the iron rod against Palaemon's neck, not particularly careful of the pressure she applied.

From behind him, Malchus said in an amiable tone, "Velus Herclides, how long has it been?"

"Malchus? Drusus Malchus?"

"If you are speaking of the same Drusus Malchus who yanked your inattentive innards away from more than one mortal thrust, then yes, that's me. What brings a fine legionary like you to this gutter work?"

"I thought I left two men to guard the front entrance."

"You did."

Velus shrugged and sighed. "Pompeius Magnus disbanded our unit three years ago. You know me: I'm shit at anything but soldiering. Anywise, the pay's decent."

"Not decent enough," Malchus said.

"There are other benefits," the villain countered, smiling at the women. Can you imagine the acidic stew of furor and impotence in my breast? My mind, a treacherous thing, forced me to paint in lurid detail what it was he was seeing when his eyes roved over Livia. I wanted to rip his lungs out with my teeth. I looked at Malchus, looming behind Herclides, sword drawn, completely at ease in the role of savior. My friend, my hero. The phrase "what would I do without him" was for me a real and frightening question. *With good reason, slave, the fruit of love hangs so high; Unless both slave and warrior thou be, then come not nigh.* I determined that at the earliest possible moment, I would have a word with the towering Malchus, so confident in his skill at arms, and become once again, as I had been so long ago in Athens, a student.

"Not today, there aren't," Malchus answered Velus, his voice as sure as the tip of his *gladius* was sharp.

"Not at the moment, no," Herclides answered. "But the funny thing about moments, Drusus, is that there are always more of them."

"Until you're dead."

"Until you're dead," he agreed. They made it sound like they were drinking to each other's health. "You realize, this still leaves you outnumbered, what, eight to two?"

"More like six to three," Minucius Valens called from where he stood facing the two men in the middle of the *palaestra*, his sword and dagger drawn. "I wouldn't count these two."

"Velus, there are no odds here," Malchus said reasonably. "There's you, there's me and there's Camilla."

"Camilla, is that your tongue tickling my back? Hello, sweetheart! Drusus, you're such a romantic. Who else do you know who does that? Who names their sword?" Herclides started to turn around, but Malchus put a hand on his shoulder and a little more pressure on his *gladius*.

"If you tell your people to fight, Velus, Camilla will leave you ever curious—you will never know how the battle ends. Quickly now—everything that isn't clothing and isn't attached to you, on the ground."

"Now that's unkind. Leave a man a little dignity, Drusus. I've yielded. You've seen the streets; at least let us withdraw with our weapons."

Malchus twisted Camilla, at the same time adding a feather's weight more insistence from his sword arm.

Herclides cursed. "Throw down your weapons," he called. "We are done here." Palaemon's face was so contorted it was not clear, from his supine and restricted pose, if he was filled with anger, regret or relief. Except for the chill the scarred man sent rippling across my skin from the look he gave Livia as he scrambled away from her, I had never felt so unencumbered.

The ordeal over, Livia put a trembling hand on my shoulder for support. With an uncharacteristic tremor in her voice she said, "I think I'll leave the herbalist for another day."

"A wise plan."

•••

"Why did you come back?" I asked.

"To settle a bet," Betto said mildly. "I *knew* that was the healer you were talking to." I cocked my head and curled my mouth up on one side, a mannerism which, over the years, the *familia* of the house of Crassus had come to learn as shorthand for 'you're not telling me everything; out with it.' After a moment, he said, "Fine. After we left, we passed this bunch" — he motioned toward the brigands — "and saw them going in. They didn't look as if they were going to the baths for a dip and a scrape."

"Into the pool with them," Minucius Valens said. "We'll hold them here and send the slaves to the *comitium* for help."

"No," Malchus said. "Herclides, take your wounded and leave this place."

Betto said, "What? What kind of a rescue do you call that?"

"This here is a twenty-year man," Malchus said, never taking his sword from the spot where it might easily find the strapping ex-soldier's right kidney. "He's come on hard times, but no real harm has been done here. We've seen to that. So what if we rescue a few more than we intended? Eh, tribune Cato? That agreeable with you?"

"No, it isn't. Not really. The man has interfered with the tiny part of my day where I attempt to recover some sense of *otium*." He blew a blubbery breath through those shining lips. "Well, I suppose a good supper will restore my equanimity." With the roasted leg he still clutched, he waved his permission at us and skirted the empty *frigidarium* with the rest of his party.

As he passed, I said, "Tribune Cato, aren't you forgetting something?"

"Ah, good man." He approached Malchus and his captive, chins lowered, gleaming hand extended. Herclides relinquished the box.

While we waited for the women to dress, I looked in on the *balneator*. The guard was just regaining consciousness and the manager of the establishment was nursing a purpling bruise on his tanned bald pate. A pile of coins, restored by the villains under the watchful eyes of Betto and Valens, lay on the table in a heap. As soon as the old man saw me, he put a protective arm around the money.

"The deal's off," he said. "You can take your custom elsewhere." He tossed two *sesterces* to my side of the table.

"None of this was my doing," I protested. Not that I had any intention of returning.

"Look behind you," he said, patting a damp cloth to his temple. "You see that?" There was nothing there, but I could not resist the urge to turn my head. "That's trouble. It follows *you* like a three-legged dog. You get to be my age, son, you get to trust an itchy chin. Didn't at first. Ignored it when my first wife said she was going off to visit her folks in Herculaneum. Dido, you know, she made a bit of a racket of an evening, if you get my drift. The night she left, I heard an awfully familiar song. Turns out she was only three doors down and one story up." He leaned forward, put his forearms on the table and laced his fingers. "Let me tell you, when you came through that door, the sudden urge to scratch was a powerful thing. But your gold made me stupid."

"For your trouble," I said, placing five silver *denarii* down next to his two coins. Do not say it. I know what you are thinking: the crafty *balneator* coaxed those coins from a gullible dupe. Perhaps. The thing is, time and again I had seen Crassus wave his *lictors* aside to empty his purse into the dirty, straining hands that reached for him every time he climbed the senate steps. Could I do any less? The irony is not lost on me. Observing my master year after year, one of the more lasting lessons I have learned is that generosity costs nothing in the end. Then again, Crassus may simply have been trolling for votes.

CHAPTER IX

56 BCE - FALL, ROME

Year of the consulship of
Cn. Cornelius Lentulus Marcellinus and L. Marcius Philippus

I found Crassus in the main kitchen, pestering the cooks and dipping a long bronze spoon into this and that for a taste. It was almost the twelfth hour and the sun was setting. Lamps were being lit throughout the house; shafts of flecked gold slanted in through every western window, hitting their marks of floor and furniture with unerring accuracy. It was growing cool; *dominus* wore two tunics, the plain one hidden by his favorite when at home, a fine wool affair with sleeves past the elbows, dyed in broad light and dark blue stripes. In recent years, to alleviate the discomfort of the irritating appearance of bunions, he had taken to walking around the house barefoot. He wore no belt, setting free the few pounds that old age and a less rigorous lifestyle had earned him. From the *familia*, he kept few such secrets; from Rome, his vanity would never countenance such informality. A statesman must always look, and more importantly, play the part. On the other hand, most statesmen wore a gown so ponderously shapeless that it obscured all but head and feet from scrutiny.

Congratulations to the inventor of the toga, who realized that a Roman's life was often not as abstemious as his Roman statues would have us believe.

From the pantry at the opposite end of the sweltering workroom, Curio entered, scroll and pen in hand. "Alexander, I've been looking for you. The boar you ordered is tainted. I've sacked your merchant and have a list here of replacements."

I ignored Lucius, strode in and stood opposite *dominus* across the main work table. "A word, *dominus*?" I blurted with enough emotion to cause Eirene to stop stirring the pea soup. Heads turned, then froze like a crowd before the priest's knife descends upon the sacrifice.

"Oh my," Crassus said, taking the topmost deviled egg from an otherwise perfectly arranged tray. He took a bite, hummed his appreciation, and with his mouth not quite empty said, "Your *atriensis* is cross with me. Ladies and gentlemen, I must leave your good company, for I cannot bear to suffer my chastisement publicly. Come, Alexander, let us walk in the peristyle, so I may at least enjoy the purpling clouds while I discover what it is that has upset you so."

Before we could make good our departure, Hanno came lurching around the corner and skidded straight into me. "Master!" he cried, his forehead buried in my chest. I hugged him briefly and squatted to his height.

"I've told you before, Hannibal, I am not your master. Now go with Lucius to pick a new butcher."

"No! That's boring."

"Well, then, is there anyone who could use a little help in the kitchen?" A dozen hands rose, some with genuine enthusiasm. Dinner was delayed by only a quarter of an hour as a result of Hanno's "assistance."

Crassus handed the spoon to the cook standing closest to him and out we went into the cooling evening air. "That is your fault," I told him. "It was you who told him to call me master."

"I don't mind," Crassus said, licking a thumb. "Why do you?" I chose not to answer.

One of the peacocks had somehow strayed into the garden and lay beside the gravel path, the sweep of its tail an arrogant, opulent display, even in repose. It lifted its azurite head as we strolled passed, but otherwise ignored us. It had a right to feel safe. Lady Tertulla had issued orders forbidding the birds to be butchered and served alongside their artfully arranged feathers as was typical in other great homes. If they are sacred to Juno, she argued, they will be treated with no less honor in this house.

Crassus was right about the clouds: it was a singular sunset, and although our view of it was restricted by the peristyle to a rectangle of stately palaces in hues of orange, red and cream floating above our heads, the fading light fell upon us with a warm glow. How lovely it would be to stroll here with Livia, to hold her hand, to turn and pull her close. For a moment, I lost my grip on why it was we were here.

"You know," said Crassus, "it isn't that I don't enjoy a quiet walk in the garden with you, Alexander, but typically I reserve those for my wife."

Color rushed to my cheeks. "Forgive me, *dominus*. It is so beautiful this evening that I quite forgot myself."

"Understandable. I am not the perfect partner for you either, I suspect. Ah, the luxury to be able to forget oneself," he said his voice wistful, "how do you do it?" The question was rhetorical. We walked a pace or two, then Crassus regained his usual, affable condescension.

"Our strolls, however, are more seemly when liberally enlivened with the spice of discourse. Now what is it you wanted to see me about so desperately that you needed to use that tone before the help?"

"Humble apologies, *dominus*. May I speak freely?"

"You may never speak freely, Alexander, but you may speak."

"Very droll, *dominus*. I am serious."

"As was I. What troubles you?"

I took a breath. "You, *dominus*. When I first came to you, you commanded me to challenge you, to teach you all I knew and all that I might learn, and never to cower before you."

"I remember, and only occasionally regret the conversation."

"Well then, I know speak under that aegis. You are hurting the city you love, and its people. Perhaps you are blind to the upheaval you are causing, perhaps you are not. I suspect the latter. Either way, you need to know that Rome suffers at your hands."

"At my hands," Crassus said pensively, rolling the sound of my accusation around in his mouth as if he were still back in the kitchen sampling tidbits. We walked a few more paces in the dimming light. When he spoke again, he held his left hand in his right while rolling the plain iron band around his third finger. "I have never removed this ring, not in thirty years. I have heard it said that a nerve connects this one finger directly to the heart, and that the band is worn here to symbolize the bond between husband and wife. Do you know of this, Alexander?"

"I have heard it, yes, but I am aware of no autopsy proving it either true or false."

"I never gave it much thought," he sighed, "one way or the other. But now I believe the theory has merit. Why is this? Because I can no longer feel the connection that held your mistress and I so close. Caesar cut it in Luca. I felt the fiber snap and recoil that night, felt the loose ends bunch and tighten. Since then, that severed cord has spread a foul numbness from here to here," he said, pointing from his hand to his chest.

"Do not let him do this to you, *dominus*."

"It is a thing accomplished and cannot be undone." Crassus stopped walking and put a hand to his temples.

"*Dominus*, the city is in chaos. Publius Clodius sends out his gangs to replace considered government with reckless fear, and there is no one to stand against him. Pompeius replies with Milo and his men, violence to oppose violence. All this because you and Caesar, a man you hate, scheme to steal the consulship so you may share it with Pompeius, another you despise. It makes no sense."

"I have no choice."

"The people look to you for leadership. Take back your bribe to tribune Gaius Cato. Hold the election. You will win."

"I must be certain. Without a second term as consul, I lose Syria."

"The only certainty is that Romans are molested and beaten in the streets."

"I will protect our people."

"You cannot. Livia and Cornelia Metella came within moments of being raped today."

Crassus' face contorted with pain. I thought his eyes were about to water, but instead, the cry sprang from his lips. "Alexander, with what philosophy can you heal me?

Teach me some other way to repair this damaged heart, and I will be your attentive student."

"Love your wife. Repair your marriage. If Aristotle could look upon you and lady Tertulla, he would declare your lives bound in a 'relationship of shared virtue,' the rarest and most noble of loves. Do not abandon her to seek revenge. Caesar's crime was vicious and unimaginable. He believes that you are weak, that you will see no path but vengeance. If he is right, he has you. But you can be the stronger man; you *do* have a choice. Do not respond in kind. What he has done may not be forgivable, but, *dominus*, you must learn to make it forgettable."

Crassus laughed, a dark, feral sound. "No human could do this thing. It is a task for a man with a heart carved from obsidian."

"No, *dominus*." I did something then I had never done in all my years bound to this man. I put my hand on his chest. He did not strike me. He did not step back. He waited, and I spoke. "It is a task worthy of *this* heart, of *this* man." Crassus shook his head. I withdrew my hand, but did not surrender. "My lord, I beg of you, turn back from this course; only blood and sorrow lie at its end. No marriage should ever confront the test Caesar has forced upon yours. But the challenge lies before you; it cannot be avoided. Choose unwisely and everything you cherish will be destroyed. For the love of your wife, your people and your city, forget and forsake Caesar."

The light of the day had almost gone, and Crassus stood before me, an aggregate of hardened shadows. He did not strike me down or call for guards to haul me away. He looked upon my face, but his eyes were focused on a point far distant and unreachable. In his gaze, I could see what he saw: humiliation, shame, and an anger that burned and sparkled on shimmering coals of memory; they would never be consumed. "I cannot forget," he said. "I cannot forgive, and I *will* be avenged. You find *my* determination as unyielding and rigid as my sword? Know that it would crack and shatter before my lady's. We are of one heart and one mind."

"Then kill him."

"Alexander, you surprise me."

"In an hour Boaz could furnish me with the names of a hundred assassins."

"The slave master could give you a thousand, but none would serve my purpose. I will not grant Caesar the most noble of deaths, a soldier's death. I pray to Mars each day to keep him safe and unharmed until my return from Parthia. What is death by the blade but a moment's agony. What justice lies at the point of a *gladius*? Would you have him poisoned? That is a woman's way, and though it cause him to contort and foam till his bones splinter and his lungs ignite, it is yet an end too condensed, too generous for the man who raped my wife. Caesar has writ an indelible mark upon our marriage. He has besmirched our home with a permanent stain."

"*Dominus…*"

"No, Alexander. I will not be satisfied till I have penned an equal scrawl across the remainder of his soulless existence.

"I will not be satisfied until I have stolen from him and destroyed the destiny he seeks — to return Rome to the days of kings, to ascend to his newly gilded throne to begin his dynasty.

"Until the day I walk the streets of our city and hear men both great and small respond with apathy and indifference to the name of Gaius Julius Caesar, I *will not be satisfied*."

A stone bench lay just off the path where we stood; Crassus bent and reached for it. He sat, exhausted. The clouds above us, leached of color, now marched resolutely onwards, their greyed and ghostly bulks floating on the glow from a million lamps. "If you could only go to war alone," I said.

"What? I am too tired for riddles, Alexander."

"When *I* speak, *dominus*, the house of Crassus listens. When *you* speak, all Rome pays heed. Where Crassus goes, tens of thousands must follow. How many must journey to the edge of our world to mete out Caesar's castigation?" I knelt before him. "You are the better man, *dominus*. Will you travel thirteen hundred miles for honor's sake when your wife waits for you not fifty feet from this very spot? Is there an altar large enough to hold the years and the lives that must be sacrificed to balance your scales of retribution?"

Crassus spoke not in anger, but with a voice tired beyond his years. "Did you know, Alexander, that when you first came to me, there yet lingered serious debate over whether or not slaves had souls? If my judgment had fallen on the ignorant side of that silly notion as we converse here in this serene garden, it would make the task much less irksome to fetch my *pugio* and end your animal life. I am an enlightened man, Alexander, and I delight in the small barbs and vexations you hurl at me. Your soul notwithstanding, my old friend, you have gone too far. Tell me, do you hold your life so cheaply, even now that your Livia is returned?"

Livia and I were shackled to him with the same invisible chains, yet I bridled to hear him speak of her.

"She is not *my* Livia, and no, *dominus*, I hold nothing. You have graciously assumed the burden of holding my life in your hands for me since the day we met, thirty years ago."

Crassus took one of my hands in both of his; they were warm and soft, the manicured nails buffed and unbroken. He smiled as a proud father smiles at his son; as a man so secure in his vision of the future that he will see no other. "You should be grateful, Alexander. Evidently I hold it more dearly than you yourself. You must not speak of this again. Do you understand?"

I understood that in that fading light, we had wrestled on the fulcrum between two futures: one bright, one bloody. I understood that I had failed him. I had failed us all. "*I* am not your enemy, *dominus*."

"No," he sighed. "You are not." He pushed himself up off the bench. "It is dark. Let us go in."

CHAPTER X

56 BCE - FALL, ROME

Year of the consulship of
Cn. Cornelius Lentulus Marcellinus and L. Marcius Philippus

"Where's my sword?" I asked.

Malchus and Betto both laughed. Hanno stood by as my second, ready to offer a towel or a footstool which he had strapped to his back. "Here you go," Betto said, handing me a six-foot wooden pole with a leather-bound crosspiece that made the contrivance look distressingly like a miniature of a crucifixion cross. Then, without thinking, he tossed a shovel to Hanno, who had the good sense to step out of the way.

"Why are you trying to hurt me? Why is he trying to hurt me?" Under my tutelage, Hanno's Latin was improving slowly. (Lady Tertulla had implored me to assist, rightfully arguing that correct speech is the first step on the road toward civilized comportment.) The boy had already honed to a fine edge the cadence of indignation, though I cannot say from whom he had learned the art.

"Hannibal, I was not trying to —"

"You threw the shovel," Hanno persisted. "I *saw* you throw the shovel."

"Yes, I *did* throw it, but I —"

"Betto knows I catch bad. He knows."

"Betto would never hurt you. He is your friend, Hannibal."

"Friends don't throw things."

Betto muttered, "Sometimes they *feel* like throwing things." He walked with disinclination to retrieve the shovel. As he passed Hanno he said, "Sorry." Hanno looked at him as if he were a dog he wanted to pet but was afraid it might bite.

"What are you doing?" I asked. Betto had begun to dig through the dew-topped grass into the moist earth beneath.

"You'll see." We were standing just inside the track of the Circus Flaminius up on the Campus Martius. The sunrise was just brushing the tops of the hills to the north. At this hour there were few who shared the arena with us: a half-dozen chariot trainers, their riders and mounts blowing hot clouds as if they burned from within; ten pairs of men practicing with wooden swords and wicker shields in the grassy center of the field, their bare chests slick with sweat despite the dawn's chill. The shops beyond the colonnade that encircled the stadium were still shuttered. Across the street, the sharp applause of hammers and chisels could already be heard coming from the construction site of Pompeius' colossal theater. The temple dedicated to Venus Victrix, rising opposite the stage behind the great semi-circle of seating was so tall that, above and beyond the roof circling the Flaminius, I could see the gilt statues of Pompeius and the goddess burning in the morning sun.

I regarded the wooden contraption with disdain. "I thought you were going to show me how to defend myself. What am I supposed to do with this?"

"Walk," Malchus said.

"Walk? Walk where? I thought we'd be doing what they're doing," I said, pointing to the sparring men. "I know how to walk; I want to learn how to defend myself."

"You see, that's where you're wrong, Alexander." said Malchus. "You only think you know how to walk. But you're the boss." And off he sprinted toward the soldiers. "Come on, then," he waved.

I did not care for the smile on Betto's face as he paused from his excavating to watch. "Stay with Betto," I told Hanno.

"*Ave*, brothers!" Malchus called as we approached. A few grunts of reply were tossed at us, but that was all their concentration would allow. To me, Malchus said, "We agree that while we train, I am *your* superior and you promise you won't hold anything that happens during these exercises against me or Betto? Right?"

"You're not going to cause me bodily harm, are you?"

Malchus grinned.

"I am insulted," I said warily, "that you felt the need to ask. And also a little distressed. You have my word."

"Mind if we have a look at a *scutum*?" Malchus called to the nearest combatants.

One of the soldiers gave the sign to hold and his partner ceased his assault. "Mine is third from the right," he said, breathing hard. "Just put it back the way you found it."

Malchus saluted. "Go on," he said to me. "Take it out of its sack and drape it over the post. Don't throw it on the ground." I went to the line of enshrouded rectangle shapes leaning up against a long railing and unlaced the ties on the soldier's shield. I wondered why the men practicing nearby were using practice shields instead of these. I supposed the real thing was too valuable to damage.

Doing as Malchus bid, I carefully removed the oiled goatskin and lifted the semi-cylindrical rectangle by its sides. Gods, it must have weighed twenty pounds! The edges were protected by a thin frame of iron nailed into the outer leather covering, painted bright red with golden wings and lightning bolts leaping from the central, oblong, iron boss. Painted in the upper right corner in brightest white was the Roman numeral 'VI.' The inside was lined with canvas, except where a circular hole at the center was bisected by a horizontal iron grip directly behind the boss. At the top hung two iron rings which I surmised erroneously were to enable the sturdy artifact to be hung as a decoration of honor once the need for it had passed.

"Hold it proper," Malchus said, coming up. "Here, like this." He took my left hand and had me grip the handle palm down. "Now hold it up in front of you so just your head is exposed." I did. "Good. Now stay like that for a count of fifty." I made it to eighteen. Before I dropped it to the wet grass, Malchus caught it, then returned it to its covering and its place against the railing.

"You want to know why those men are using wicker shields instead of these? It's not just because they don't want to damage the pretty paint. The wicker surrounds an iron center—they weigh half again as much as the one you just held." I heaved a great sigh of defeat. "You want to tackle the likes of Herclides? You want to fight like a soldier? Then you've got to be fit like a soldier."

As we walked back to Betto and Hanno, my brow creased. "Maybe we ought to go home and release the men I hired to take your places while we're gone."

"This ought to do for starters," Betto said, shoveling the last of the dirt into a large canvas bag that Hanno was holding open for him. Malchus held the pole upright for his friend, who reached up and attached the bag to the crosspiece. "I'd say it's close to 25 pounds. Maybe 30."

"What do you mean, 'for starters?'"

"A legionary carries twice that on the march, not counting weapons and armor."

"And don't forget the shield," Betto smiled. "It hangs from the crosspiece on those rings."

"Now, Alexander," Malchus said, "shoulder that pack and we'll start you off easy: five times around the track. Off you go. Well, Flavius," he said, throwing his cloak on the dewy ground and sitting cross-legged upon it, "I hope you packed enough breakfast for everyone."

"Two portions for you, one for me. As always. Hannibal, have a seat. What did you bring to eat for yourself?"

"I'm not hungry. Can I have that apple?"

"Only if you're going to eat it," Betto said, about to toss the piece of fruit to the boy. He checked himself in time. Malchus chuckled and spit an olive pit into the hole.

The Circus Flaminius was 800 feet long and 300 feet wide. Over the next several weeks I would memorize each brick, shop and pennant along its wide dirt oval. Every day, three hours before dawn, I trudged up the Capitoline and marched with my pole and its fertile baggage, a lost, lonely ghost in the black upon black shadows of the great stadium. My right leg, pierced by one of Sulla's archers the day I met my master, grew quickly strong and its hindrance was imperceptible.

Recruits in full gear were required to complete 18 miles in five hours, then 22 miles in the same time. My responsibilities at home foreshortened my regimen, but within a month, I had become Heracles in his prime, or Milo of Croton, Olympic champion. I purchased a small, polished bronze mirror and secreted it beneath my bed, admiring my progress at the end of each day.

That was before Malchus and Betto took me off the blessedly level track and into the cursed hills. On the first incline, the stamina and strength of which I had become so proud fled like terrified children. The blisters and sores which had hardened to callus on the track were chafed and shredded anew. Muscles in my thighs and calves, corded and toned, found infant cousins I had never met, but who now cried out each night to make my acquaintance. There was no question of surrender. Come morning, the memory of Livia in Palaemon's grasp or the wild moons of Velus Herclides' eyes pitched me from my bed into the sweat-stained embrace of my cross. To spur me up the steeper hills, I dreamed it was not weighted wood I carried but Livia, heroically spiriting her away from mortal danger, some imagined, some all too real. I was so exhausted by bedtime I forgot to look in the mirror.

I was strong, bursting with stamina, and begged now to learn the offensive skills I would need to be of any use in a fight. My teachers scoffed and told me fighting was the least fraction of a legionary's skills. I told them I did not wish to become a soldier; what I wanted to avoid was the feeling of total uselessness should anyone I cared about ever be threatened again. Almost simultaneously my two friends said, "Then you've got to learn to be a soldier."

They taught me marching formations, basic camp construction and layout, how to pitch the eight-man *contubernium* tent, how to strike it and efficiently pack the mule assigned to each unit. I failed to see how this would protect Livia in a scuffle. Nor was I amused when Betto suggested I show the ones I cared about how to hide behind the mule.

One morning in early October they led me to the stables adjacent to the Circus Flaminius. On their urging, I had let Hanno sleep in. The stable master showed us to three available mounts. Betto came into my stall and was about to remove the tack from where it hung on the wall when he was brought up short by my upturned palm. "Tend to your own beast, good Betto, and let me see if I can calculate through logic what goes where."

"That would be an interesting experiment to watch, were we not of a mind to be home before nightfall."

"Let him be," Malchus said, leaning up against a post to watch.

Betto's eyes, which even in repose risked bursting free of their sockets, bulged even further. "I can't look," he said, walking off across the straw-strewn floor to prepare his own mare. "He's buying us supper if we're late."

After I said good morning to the bay gelding assigned to me, letting him get my scent and speaking polite words of introduction, I covered his back with a felt pad, secured the four-horned saddle by tying off the girth as well as the breast and breech straps. To protect his flanks, I attached pendant cloths to the saddle. The bay took the bit and bridle easily enough so, gently holding the single rein I stepped up onto the mounting block and swung my right leg over the saddle. Once settled, I nodded at Malchus. Smiling like a proud father, he unhooked the stall ropes, patted the gelding's neck and we backed out of the stall. Betto was still fussing with his mount's girth.

"On my parents' farm in Elateia. I usually rode bareback, but this arrangement should pose no problem. Race you to the Porta Flaminia and back? Whenever you're ready, that is."

Malchus said to Betto, "By the look of it, Flavius, we'll be back in time for *you* to treat us to a fine and sizable lunch."

•••

At long last, the day arrived when I stood with both wooden *gladius* and wicker shield in perspiring but determined hands. I was going to learn to how to fight. Not how to wrestle, a sport I had enjoyed with my father as a child, but to learn the way of the Romans, the killing way, with sword and shield, javelin and dagger. We stood before a thick, six-foot tall, vertical training post, identical to the ones used by gladiators preparing for the arena. I would be taught many of their own techniques: the parry and feint, the over-the-shield stab, the knee-drop and groin-thrust.

Malchus took me through each maneuver, step by step.

By mid-morning it was clear to all assembled, most especially to my embarrassed, humiliated self, that I was useless.

Betto said it best when he observed, "Malchus, he's useless!"

As much strength and stamina as I had gained, the coordination of sword and shield was simply beyond me. Within minutes I would tire of holding my *scutum* aloft, even the lighter, standard version. Practicing with a stationary post was bad enough; sparring with my friends provided proof beyond question that if my goal was to tread the fields of Elysium before my time, wielding a *gladius* against an enemy with the least particle of prowess was the surest way to transport me there. After all that work! I was uncharacteristically irate; words of solace from Betto and Malchus made my failure all the more frustrating. I hurled my shield and sword to the ground, thoughtless of the damage I might be doing to the equipment. Like a child, I stomped to the edge of the training field where I could hopefully continue my silent tantrum in peace. Betto, not one to let any hornets' nest be without shaking it to be sure that no one was left at home, followed me, chattering words of useless encouragement at my heels. Hanno made to run after me, but Malchus grabbed the sleeve of his tunic and shook his head. They stood holding hands a few feet from the training post.

Flavius, you have brought this upon yourself. I spun round; if I could not carve him to tatters with a sword, my tongue, always honed and at the ready, would serve to prick and wound. But then I had a better idea. "Betto!" I growled in a tone even I did not recognize. The look on his poor face stuffed my curses down my throat, but not my frustration. "Give me that!" I snapped, pointing to his dagger.

"Alexander," he said, suddenly timid, "I don't think that's—"

"Now!" He removed the *pugio* from his belt and reluctantly surrendered it to me, handle first, looking as if I were about to stab him with his own knife. I held it by the tip of its seven inch blade, thrust him aside and with an atavistic shriek hurled it at the training post, over thirty feet away. By the time Betto finished shouting 'LOOK OUT!' the blade was vibrating chest-high in the center of the wood. Malchus, who had instinctively shoved Hanno to the ground along with himself on top of the poor boy, rose on one elbow and let out a whoop that stopped all activity on the field.

"Very good, master," laughed Hanno, half obscured by Malchus' stomach.

Malchus slapped the flattened boy on the shoulder and shouted, "That was one throw in a hundred!"

But it wasn't.

From that moment on, my early morning exercise regimen ended with a good half-hour of knife practice. Not hand-to-hand — I was still a dead man up close, but I had found my combative niche. This gift had its limits, to be sure — for one thing, more than half the time it was the butt of the knife that hit the target, but hit the target I could! It was better than standing by helpless when help was sorely needed. There was nothing I could not do with a dagger. I threw side-arm, over-arm, blade-first, haft-first, over distances that actually drew crowds when I practiced. I could unsheathe and deliver with accuracy from either side; the normal throw when unsheathed from the right, or across the body in a single motion when flung from the left. Anything with an edge and a handle would do: kitchen knives, carving knives, butcher knives, even *gladii*. It was as if my right arm and wrist had become imbued with a godlike harmony of balance and motion any time a blade was placed in my hand.

I was, to the surprise of all, a natural.

There was no question but that Betto would be my instructor and guide. One day long past, Nestor and Pío, two jealous members of the Crassus household had conspired to relieve me of my household chores, all of them and forever. If not for Betto's skill with a dagger, not to mention the accuracy of his aim with the remnants of a half-eaten apple, the assassins those two sent to kill me would most assuredly have earned their fee. As for Pío and Nestor, one was dead, the other branded and sent to the mines — as good as dead.

News of my prowess traveled quickly; it was not long before *domina* and *dominus* requested a command performance. They brought the entire household with them. I was quite terrified, but my throwing arm knew nothing of nervous jitters or fear of failure. When it was required of me, I became an engine of accuracy. Even the presence of Livia, her white healer's tunic singular but superfluous in setting her apart from all others, did not cause my aim to falter. Our eyes met once, she smiled briefly, and that wisp of encouragement gave me more strength than Atlas. At the climax of the demonstration, Betto pegged an apple to the training post and from forty feet away I cleaved it in two. With the blade end of my dagger sunk into the wood, as well.

Crassus and Tertulla came up to congratulate me, then my lord pulled me aside. "What a surprise, Alexander. I am fairly well astounded. And it sets me thinking. You, more than any man, even my lictors, are by my side night and day. Upon your return home, prepare a posting which I shall sign and you shall lock away appointing you as one of my personal guards. But tell no one. Keep one of your daggers concealed upon you at all times. I know, I know — the law. Better keep it well-concealed or we'll both be in trouble.

"Now, you may continue your early morning exercises, that is a noble pursuit, but I require that your aim be refocused on more pragmatic targets. There is much planning and preparation to attend to, and I want you by my side in council."

As she passed, lady Tertulla let her jeweled hand rest lightly on my own, the fine blue sea silk of her shawl, held about her wrist with a golden lion's head clasp, draped over my arm like fog settling on rough ground. With the lightest of touches, she drew me down to whisper in my ear, the black curls of her perfumed hair brushing against my cheek and neck. "You are faithful and wise, good Alexandros." *(My birth name!)* "Stay close to him. Speak your truths as no other dare. Know that both our minds and hearts are fixed on Parthia; do this for your love of me and the will of your lord. He has need of you now; his need will be greater once Brundisium has faded behind the wake of his ships." The lips which, by those words, funneled the separate fates of thousands into a single destiny now moved lightly to kiss me on the cheek. In the next moment, she had reached for her lord's outstretched hand, and was gone.

I looked for Livia before she left, but my lady's appeal and the ebullient arrival of Betto and Malchus blocked both sight and chance of seeing her. In the end, it was just us three and Hanno left to clean up after the display and put the field back into pristine preparedness. Two hours later, as we were walking back down the hill Malchus said, "What other talents have you been hiding in that skinny frame of yours?"

Betto scratched his head. "Can't think what more there is to teach you. Never seen anything like it. Did you see the look on the faces of those veterans? Alexander, you're an artist with a blade." He slapped me on the back with such force I missed a step. The harder the smack, the greater the affection.

Hanno rushed to my rescue. "Stop it!" he shouted. "Don't hurt my master's back. He doesn't like—"

"…for you to call me master," I finished for him.

Malchus stopped and squatted on his haunches before Hanno. "He has scars, Hannibal. We all know that. But you mustn't be ashamed for him; you must be proud. Our friend Alexander is a brave man. Did you know he fought a Roman general to earn those stripes?"

"He did?"

"That's right, boy," Betto said. "And anyway, I was just trying to hand him a compliment. You know what a compliment is, don't you."

"I know. A compliment is a nice thing to say about a person."

"That's right!" Betto said, impressed.

"Malchus gets them all the time. You don't."

"Kid, have you ever heard the expression, 'respect your elders?'"

"No. But once I heard Father Jupiter say to master, 'respect your betters.'"

Malchus sputtered. "Give it up, Flavius. You're outmatched. "

•••

Later, as we acknowledged the guards and passed through the tall gates into the estate and home, the sight of the wealth and privilege that had swallowed me whole was depressing. I thought of *domina*; did revenge make her blind to the toll their plan would take on her husband? On herself? The rest of us were so far beneath their scheming and their plots, though I stood on the Palatine, a Roman Olympus, to them we served but one purpose, to be the expendable instruments of their designs. The memory of her extravagant scent returned, an insistent rippling of juniper and cypress lapping against my senses, no less seductive than Circe's perfume was to Odysseus. Unlike the hero, I would never possess any holy herb of moly to defend myself against my lady's wishes. She might ask, but there was no choice implicit in her perfumed entreaty.

I thought I had carved out a miniscule refuge of freedom within this life, but after years of hiding I could feel the crumbling slide into a deeper darkness, dragging me toward yet another fate I would never have chosen for myself. I looked at Betto and Malchus and poor Hanno, terrified that they, too, would slip and stumble into the abyss, all of us falling helplessly into the darkness. Something about my practice these past weeks, at once troubling but unformed, chose that moment to coalesce into evanescent thought, and recognizing it, I snatched it from the air. "It is not enough," I said before we parted company at the atrium, each to our assigned tasks. "You say I am an artist, Flavius? If we stop here, then all my works must remain incomplete, for I possess but half my paints and brushes."

"Has it occurred to you," said Betto, "that while you were out looking for the next great lecture series, most of the rest of us were happy just to get laid without our pricks falling off."

"I beg your pardon?"

"What in Cerberus's two tongues are you talking about?"

"I need more skills."

Betto looked dumbfounded. "Why couldn't you just say that?" He turned to Malchus. "Why couldn't he just say that?"

And so it was that Betto and I began our training all over again.

CHAPTER XI

56 - 55 BCE - WINTER, ROME

Year of the consulship of
Cn. Cornelius Lentulus Marcellinus and L. Marcius Philippus

I t was several weeks after our mission to the *balnea* Numa before lady Cornelia and Livia could both be released from their social and medical obligations to travel together into town. The streets were still unsafe, and would remain so until after the elections, which Crassus would continue to have postponed until Januarius. I forbid Livia from this outing; she laughed. Why is it I will not be taken seriously? Neither her personal safety nor the threat of rain would make her see sense, and I could not bring myself to have the guards confine her. She argued her position with a whispered kiss against my ear. "You'll thank me next time you suffer from one of your migraines." The headache would arrive either way, for the thought of her out and vulnerable in the city was making my temples throb and the cords in my neck turn to iron.

After a promise that our itinerary would have a single destination and no impulsive excursions, Malchus, Valens, the lady's man, Buccio and I escorted the women to the herbalist's, a tiny shop down a crooked street little more than an alleyway. Betto had wanted to come as well, but *domina* was out preparing for the parties that would festoon Sulla's Victory games like banners. Crassus had sent so many men to guard her, including Betto, that you could barely see her litter, let alone get near it. We opted to abandon the use of such a carriage, as it would attract more unwanted attention than our paltry guard could comfortably accommodate. As for Hanno, he had discovered the stables, and the horses had discovered him. Love grew unbridled, if you will forgive the pun, by horse and boy alike.

The games were of particular importance to the Crassus household, since they were held to honor Sulla's victory against Marius and Cinna in the Civil War a generation earlier. There was not a Roman alive older than forty who did not remember that the battle at the Colline Gate would have been lost had it not been for Marcus Crassus and his 2,500 Spaniards. Sulla's forces were about to be overwhelmed when my master, right beneath the very walls of the city, broke through Marius' Samnite defenders, allowing Rome to be taken into the loving but brutal arms of its conqueror. Some of the older *optimates* could still be heard to murmur that had Crassus been just a little older (he was thirty-three at the time) the city and the dictatorship might have gone to him. Rome loves nothing so much as a hero.

I have reminded you on several occasions that I am no Roman. While Crassus would be the man of the hour for the last week of October, this celebration, of all the dozens of festivals held throughout the Roman calendar, was most reviled by this chronicler. Before Sulla had himself declared dictator of Rome, he and his armies had been preoccupied with the sacking of Athens, abducting everything of value, from our books, to our art, to our greatest minds. To whit, me. To be fair, at nineteen, my mind still had some small way to go before it would come fully into its season. That point aside, this festival had special significance for me: not long after the butchery had abated I was captured, brutalized and chained; given as a gift of gratitude from the victorious general to his young lieutenant. While Rome drinks, eats and whores itself into a stupor to mark the occasion, for me this holiday must in perpetuity commemorate the end of my freedom and the beginning of my life as a slave.

If this were not reason enough to abhor these games, I have another. For over 700 years the festival that honored mighty Zeus was held in Olympia near the town of Elis, a celebration of man's feeble but worthy attempt to mimic the gods in prowess and speed. It is no coincidence that these two festivals, one infant, the other ancient and venerable, are held at the same time of year. As I have previously perhaps overstated, when Sulla's armies trampled our fair city, the dictator transported everything he could lay his hands on to Rome, including the Olympic Games themselves. Fortunately, he died two years later and no one objected when the official competition quietly stole back to Greece, where it belonged. As Greece honored Zeus, so Rome continues to venerate Sulla with its imitation of the Olympiad. And Rome, being the repository for all the world's stolen wealth that it is, keeps offering greater and greater prizes for the winners in each event. The celebration of Sulla's conquest is an irresistible cynosure for every athlete within a thousand miles. They stream to Rome to compete, leaving our original celebration destitute of quality competitors. I spit on Sulla's Victory games. In private, naturally.

•••

I paid little attention to whatever ointments and herbs Livia was purchasing. My eyes, and those of Valens and Malchus, were trained on the crowded street, scanning for trouble. Buccio kept a rear guard at the back entrance to the shop. All of us had short clubs looped into our belts, save for our two real legionaries, Malchus and Valens, who kept their hands on the pommels of their ill-concealed swords. And of course, there were my knives.

We came to grief at the intersection of the wide Nova Via and the Porta Mugonia at the base of the Palatine. To our left loomed the vined and hoary columns of the temple of Jupiter Stator. The wind rose, the bare branches of the trees above us on the hill argued with each other in coarse, scratchy voices, and it began to rain. We were just about to start our climb to home and safety when Livia called my name with low urgency. We turned to see twenty of Clodius Pulcher's brutes walking quickly down the cream brick steps of the temple. Most were unknown to us but their leaders had sickeningly familiar faces. To a man they wore the look of smug imprudence that comes from being on the side with overwhelming odds in its favor. Two of them wore the trappings of gladiators: a *retiarius* with his net and trident, and a *hoplomachus*, with padded leggings, a small round shield on his left forearm, a dagger in his left hand and a stained lance in his right. Neither of them wore helmets, but their expressions were as hard as armor. Those two stood on either side of Velus Herclides. There were only four or five long strides between us.

"*Furina's* feces!" Malchus muttered under his breath. "This is not good, Alexander."

"Drusus Quintilius Malchus," Herclides called, smiling like a cat with a sparrow beneath its paw, "How do you like me without the beard?"

"This crossroads is a sacred place," Malchus called back as Herclides' men moved in, forming a semi-circle in the broad plaza of the gate. Behind us rose the Palatine.

"I was hoping you and I might have another *moment*."

"And you've just brought weapons into a temple."

"But as you can see, we've brought them back out again." His men chuckled.

"Bad luck to spit in the face of the gods," Valens said. His gladius slid into view, whispering a soft farewell to its scabbard. Behind Herclides, the scarred Palaemon leered.

Malchus held Valens back with an outstretched arm, then stepped in front of him. "Your complaint lies with me, Velus. Let us walk apart and settle our differences privately."

"You?" Herclides said with surprise. "You're a fellow legionary. How could you think a bone with any meat on it lay between us?" His face was smiling, but his eyes, flitting left then right to check the positioning of his men, made my legs weak. "It's the women we want, same as before."

I called out, "What would Clodius Pulcher say if he knew what you were up to?"

"Well, if it isn't the Mantis. Best guess? He'd probably say, 'save some for me.'"

When the laughter died down I said, "You know who we serve." Somehow, I kept my voice from flying off into the upper registers. "Let me remind you: Marcus Licinius Crassus."

"Mantis, hadn't you better start praying?" This evoked a drool-laced cackle from Palaemon.

"Back then," I continued, fear spilling words from my mouth like bees fleeing the nest, "you must have been, what? Fifteen? Twenty? Old enough to remember. The Via Appia? Spartacus? You are no more than twenty assembled here. Marcus Crassus was in a hurry back then, what with wanting to nail up six thousand as quickly as he could. With you lot, he'd most probably, and this is just a guess, of course, but I shouldn't be at all surprised if he took his time with you and your men. You'd be begging for crucifixion by then, that is, if you still had tongues. Is that how you picture the end of your days, Velus Herclides."

"That's good, Mantis. Truly." Herclides' voice wavered just a fraction. "But if you keep needling me, who's going to be around to tell him? Besides, I can always grow another beard."

"You know I can't allow this, Velus," Malchus said in a low and steady voice, his weapons drawn. His hands had been empty, but now, as if by sorcery, *pugio* and *gladius* circled slowly in each hand.

"Why Camilla," Herclides said to Malchus' gladius, "aren't you looking bright and shiny today." He rubbed his roughly shaved chin with a hand fairly covered with coarse, black hairs. Tufts of the same sprouted from the back of his rough-spun tunic and climbed the front of his chest to the base of his neck. "I might spare you," he said. "But you'll have to wait. You shouldn't have interfered, Drusus. As many as we are now, it'll take hours to get these lovelies back to you. Think of the time you would've saved if you'd have let the Mantis hand them over back at the baths."

Valens turned to Malchus and said quietly, "The road up the hill is narrow. Easier to defend." Then he walked up to Herclides, his sword point two feet from his chest. "You sure your blurry eye is up for this?" he asked.

Herclides shrugged. "For what? Nodding my *fucking* head?"

Which he did.

"Valens!" Malchus yelled. The *retiarius* threw his net from Valens' left. Minucius leapt right to dodge its iron entanglement, and stepped into the braced and waiting point of the *hoplomachus'* lance, a trap the two gladiators must have planned from the outset. Valens made no sound that we could hear above the hiss of the rain. Minucius dropped his sword and grabbed the wooden shaft with both hands to try with all his might, his strength sapped by agony, to stop what he knew would happen next. The gladiator pushed and twisted, then yanked the weapon out from his body with a sickening tearing sound. Minucius Valens fell dead in the street.

Many things happened either in quick succession or simultaneously, I cannot remember clearly. Malchus bellowed, switched dagger and sword hands and threw his *pugio* into the neck of the *hoplomachus*. The gladiator had enough strength to pull the blade from his throat, gripping it as Minucius had held the lance that had killed him. Then he fell to his knees, pitched forward onto our fallen friend, his own blood spreading across the back of the man he had killed.

There were only two daggers in my belt. Now one of them lodged just below the neck of the villain nearest Malchus, the thrust of his sword aborted by my blade. It is a terrible thing to witness death by violence, a thousand times worse to hold a man's life in your own hands and to willingly, consciously take it from him. Acknowledged or not, something noble has been scoured from your insides, never to be replaced. You saved a friend's life, and there lies ample justification. But never peace, never balance, never the same. At least that is how it seems to me.

Brutal death is a thing unnatural, a foul insult to whatever order holds sway in the universe. Or a bloody argument that we are lost in the midst of Chaos. Valens was the first victim laid upon the altar of Crassus' revenge. A man I never knew was the second. So many would follow, I weep to think of it.

Drusus screamed for us to run. We turned our backs on our assailants and fled up the hill, knowing there was no hope of escape. Livia and I did our best to shepherd our small flock away from the wolves who loped confidently behind us. Fifty feet ahead the road narrowed. If we could make it that far, we could turn and defend ourselves. It would be the most logical place for us to fight and die. Only an instant before I had wondered what kind of man gives his life for those he barely knows? I wanted to hate Valens because I was unable to find another way to end this. Because I knew such pointless bravery was beyond my understanding, beyond my emulation. Valens had once joked that a hero is a fool too afraid to have the good sense to turn and run away, but his last act among the living gave that jest the lie.

They say in moments of great fear or desperation, a man will always make a choice—either to flee or face his enemy, but choice requires thought, and in the moment when you know for certain that death is stalking you with strides you cannot outrun, there is no time for thought. You do not choose. Like Betto, or Malchus, or Valens, you act, doing either one thing or the other. Now I understood the lesson Minucius had taught us. I glanced at Livia, her knuckles wrapped white around a small club I had not seen her conceal, her features constricted with determined antagonism. I was furious and wretched to think of all the things we were all about to lose.

Then we stopped. Everyone stopped. There came a noise so startling, so magnificent, that all who heard it were compelled to seek it out, their eyes drained of will, filled with terror. If there was a herald to announce the eruption of a volcano, if the gods trumpeted a warning before the earth split apart and solid ground became as jelly, this was that noise. It was the sound that birthed all despair. It was doom proclaimed in a register so low with so many discordant voices the rain itself lost hope and abated. Malchus was first to regain himself and shout for us all to resume our flight.

The best gladiators are inured to distraction. This sound was curious, but no immediate threat to the *retiarius*. He turned to look behind him, saw nothing and returned to the task at hand, the task assigned to him and paid for by Velus Herclides. He hefted his trident, shifting it ever so slightly in his upturned palm to settle in that well-worn place of perfect balance. In that moment, flesh and black ash and iron were all as one. Malchus, protecting our rear and retreating backwards up the hill, made a large and unavoidable target. Thirty feet separated the gladiator from Drusus. Another sixty lay between my friend and me. I pushed Livia up the hill and ran the other way.

The *retiarius* was about to release his spear. He was too far away for me to risk a throw on the run, but by the time I could get close enough it would be too late. I shouted, "DOWN!" and hoped that Malchus could hear me above the din. Though he must have heard my feet slamming on the path above him, though his back was to me, Malchus did not waste time turning round to question his orders. He kicked his feet back and threw his hands out in front of him. The trident was moving through the air, but I had called my warning too soon: the gladiator had adjusted the angle of his throw. Its three barbed points would pierce Drusus through his left side. My knife was out; for this to work, the spear's living target would be but a blink away from my own. I aimed my blade, leading my mark at a point just to the left of where Malchus' knees were when he was standing a heartbeat before. The knife spun at an oblique angle into the tines of the spear, disrupting its flight just before I crashed into Malchus myself. His main weapon spent, the tactical situation on the ground changing in an instant, the gladiator bolted. Malchus and I scrambled to our feet; I found myself warding off our assailants with the gladiator's trident alongside an extremely put out Camilla.

•••

The noise was unbearable. To our left, from the direction of the forum, the Nova Via emptied into the plaza about one hundred yards from our vantage point. Now, bursting from the wide avenue came a running throng. They did not stop to admire the temples or basilicas that lined its borders, but ran as if safety lay *without* the city walls. Many of them were shouting; some were screaming. They were pushed, almost physically, by stentorian blasts echoing and rebounding off every surface. Herclides tried to rally his men, but except for Palaemon, they had voted with the majority and were heading in a diagonal stream across the plaza to blend into the mob and escape whatever horror approached.

I saw what at first I took to be a Roman general sitting tall and imperious on a black, high-stepping stallion, both

144

horse and rider adorned in polished silver furnishings. But no, this was no Roman, but a daemon in human guise. It was bald, yet from the top of its head sprouted two curved horns, each almost a foot in length. Its ears hung thick and low to its neck, framing a gaping, scowling mouth below flattened nose and slitted eyes. It turned to look in our direction and I flinched, fighting the urge to run. Then it pointed at us and I did shut my eyes, but only for an instant. I don't think anyone noticed.

The origin of the terrible noise now became visible, but seeing the source did nothing to quiet the argument between the frantic voice of reason urging me to flee, and the wonder-struck curiosity cooing foolishly to tarry and behold this spectacle. The impostor general's minions appeared, row after row of bare-chested creatures in motley leggings and boots of rough-cut hides. Their skin was a brilliant blue painted with swirls and slashes of crimson; the hair that sprouted from below their nostrils hung almost as low as their braids. Each of them held aloft a vertical, six-foot tall length of brass that ended in a bristling head, some with the likeness of boars, some dragons, some horses. As they entered the plaza, the notes they blew from these instruments leapt from deep, droning tones to shrill barks and earsplitting yips. It was enough to make one beg for a return to the first noise that had set our skin to crawling, sonorous by comparison; or at the very least for a good pair of waxed ear plugs. The instrument, I later learned, was called a *carnyx*, and there would come only one other time in my life when I heard a cacophony of sound that constricted my heart with more dread.

As soon as the last barbarian herald cleared the narrow neck of the street, chariots spilled out and around the marchers, their horses eager to find their legs. The occupants of these careening vehicles appeared to be shouting at the top of their lungs, but we could hear nothing above the braying of the brass and the rumble of the iron wheels. The drivers crouched low in front, their vision in danger of being obscured by the flying tails of the two stout horses that seemed to be barely under their control. Around these horses' necks were strung a decoration of large bells, but again, they made no sound that we could hear. Behind the men with the reins stood warriors taller than any Roman with oval shields and raised javelins, their bronze helmets fearsome with spikes, fat horns, even full-sized statuettes of ravens in flight. As they flew ever closer, we could see that the woven sides of their chariots were adorned with the grisly evidence of their prowess: the shriveled heads of their enemies, tied in place by their own knotted hair. These trophies bounced and knocked about with each turn of the wheels. The racing steeds wore no necklaces of silent bells — they too were draped with grisly gourds now empty of the essence that in life had made them men.

The chariots split into two streams — one made to cut off the escape of Herclides' gang, the other curved with wild precision toward where we stood. Behind these barbarians marched what appeared to be a *century* of regular, Roman legionaries, but by this point, armed soldiers inside the *pomerium* made little impression. They, too, headed our way.

Herclides' men, never having been able to reach the main throng of rioters, had been rounded up and herded back to the base of the Palatine, including a defeated but stoic *retiarius*.

Livia was by my side and we were holding hands. I do not recall who had reached for whom or when. Our helplessness before this fractious army was complete, and that knowledge wedged itself tightly between myself and the pleasure in which I otherwise would have rejoiced. I backed her up the hill as far as we could, watching the heathen general rein in at the base of the road upon which, only moments before, we had expected to die. Turning to Herclides and his men, he warned in perfect Latin that any man whose hand still held a weapon by the time he finished speaking could later reclaim their severed property by withdrawing the nail that would in short order be driving said appendage into the temple door. There was an immediate clatter of arms.

The rider looked up at us; we looked down at him. His stallion snorted and shook its sleek black head. Startled into action, I let go Livia's hand in order to step in front of her, grasping the trident once again with both hands. Alexandros, the brave, skinny shield!

To Malchus, the apparition said, "Sheathe your sword, Drusus," his voice muffled by the silver face mask. I knew then, to my shame, that my terror had transformed metal into living flesh. Fear is an excellent mathematician— dividing allies with mistrust, multiplying misgivings into dread. "You are relieved, legionary," the splendid terror continued, "though I see we have arrived too late to make this a perfect rescue." The stranger's horned head turned toward the bodies on either side of his mount. His horse had not shied—it was either well-trained or well-accustomed to the sight and smell of human blood. Malchus cocked his head and lowered his weapon. "As for you!" the masked rider said, turning that hideous visage up to me (*to me!?*), "Is it really your intent to skewer your favorite student with that thing?"

My poor befuddled brain, while recognizing that danger had just o'erflew us like the dappled shadows from a murder of crows, was as yet bereft of the power of speech. I stood there, able only to cock my head like a dog that has just heard a strange noise. Which, you may be sure, we had.

"Master?" the rider asked. "Are you unwell?"

A gentle punch in the back from Livia jarred my ears and tongue at last.

"Publius? Publius!"

Pulling the Celtic helmet from his head, Marcus Crassus' youngest son laughed. "Apologies, master, I could not help myself! You looked about as frightened as my brother and I were the day you burned your sandals onto your feet saving Father." He slid off his horse and stepped smartly to stand before me. Relief turned to joy as I held out my hand to the little lord I had entertained and tutored for over a dozen years.

"I didn't save him—" I started.

"Oh, no," Publius said, slapping my arm aside, "we'll have none of that." He threw his arms around me, pressed his head into my shoulder, squeezed the breath from my lungs, then hoisted me into the air as if I were a sack of lentils. A very light sack of lentils. "Gods, but it's good to be home!"

"Your homecoming *must* have been timed by the gods," I said, struggling to regain my composure after he set me back down. "Tragedy was imminent."

"I know. I saw. These two weren't citizens, I trust?" He referred to the dead gladiator and the man I had dispatched. Gladiators rarely were, though none of us could say, and Herclides was silent. "Father wrote to tell me how badly we were needed. Apologies, though, for this one," he said, pointing to Valens.

Malchus said, "He was your father's man. Valens. Minucius Valens. He fell to buy us a little time...from these," he added, pointing.

"Then he died a soldier's death, a hero's death, and earned a soldier's sendoff. We'll cremate him with all honors, if his own people will permit it."

"Sir," Malchus started, "his family will be honor..."

"Livia!" Publius declared, his attention too magnanimous to linger in any one place, "I'd recognize that hair from a thousand paces."

"*Dominus.*"

"Tell me true, now, did I see that hand of yours in my tutor's?" Four cheeks reddened, but there was no time for reply. Publius suddenly and rather startlingly sank to one knee before Cornelia Metella. "Aphrodite come to earth!" he said, holding out his arms. The lady Cornelia smiled in spite of herself. "I beg you, tell me by what name you wish to be called while you grace us with your immortal presence. I shall replace every one of our house gods the moment I have crossed our threshold with dozens, hundreds of your likeness." Publius rose without waiting for an answer, unclasped his red cloak and gallantly swirled it over the women's heads and wrapped it about both their shoulders.

"Do that," lady Cornelia said, tilting her head ever so slightly, "and you will bring the wrath of all the gods that protect the house of Crassus down upon us. I don't think I'd care for that. It might interfere with your plans to court me."

"And bold as well," Publius said, snapping his fingers without taking his eyes off lady Cornelia. The closest legionary removed his cloak and ran to his commanding officer. Instead of draping it over any one or two of the rest of us shivering lot, he clasped it about his own shoulders.

"*Dominus*," I said, "may I borrow one of your men to announce your arrival?" Publius called forth a rider; I instructed him to speak only to Crassus, letting him know that his youngest son would be home within the half-hour. Speak only to him, I told the man, and be sure lady Tertulla hears nothing of it. He saluted, then turned to ride up the Clivus Victoriae at the double.

A heavily accented voice asked, "General, these?" We turned to see a blue-faced man with beard and pigtails of the most extraordinary yellow tilt his head toward the penned-in prisoners. His battered helmet matched his hair: a gold-painted overturned cup crowned by two large, golden balls suspended by a cross-shaped spike. One could not help but interpret their design anatomically. After he spoke, he clicked his tongue and eased his reins to the left. His dappled horse side-stepped into Herclides, congregating the captives into an even closer assembly.

"I'm not a general, you know," Publius said conspiratorially. "But don't tell them."

Malchus scanned the plaza, which continued to fill with hundreds of men now focused on one man. "I don't think rank has much to do with it, sir."

"I'll tell you, Malchus, there's only one thing that separates a Celtic warrior from a Roman legionary. Discipline. Without Roman discipline, my head would be hanging from that pommel right there. Isn't that the meat of it, Culhwch? Discipline?"

"True enough, by Macha. But now we, too, have discipline. Lucky for you we like your food better. And your gold."

Publius laughed. "Culhwch is my *Praefectus Alae*, commander of my cavalry. Alexander, you'd better make certain that something extraordinary is prepared for our guests' dinner."

"I shall see to it personally, *dominus*."

"Ahem!" lady Cornelia interjected. And was ignored.

"My son, Brenus," said Culhwch with no small hint of apology, meaning the youth on the small grey who had ridden up beside the unlikely *praefectus*. Brenus was no more than twenty, his sparse beard making a stouthearted but doomed effort to cover his freckled cheeks. He had red hair, darker than Livia's and almost as long. He wore no body paint, which in his case made him all the more frightening. His nose, a hilly palette of outlandish colors, was swollen and crusted with dried blood, bent unnaturally to one side. He was intent on ignoring the pain he must be enduring, yet his eyes watered. I glanced at Livia.

"His beard is thin; I blame his mother," Culhwch said mysteriously.

Brenus spoke, his nasal voice deeper than I would have guessed. "My heartwall, Taog." The individual of whom the young Celt spoke was just behind him — a warrior so tall his horse appeared to be six-legged. The sight of him was the living seven-foot definition of his unfamiliar title, and none of us needed to ask for an explanation. He did not speak, but his pale eyes, shadowed by the brow and nose guard of his helmet, were alert and vigilant.

"Nobody asked you for introductions, boy," Culhwch said. "Waste of a warrior," he muttered, eyeing Taog. "If a man needs looking after, he's not a man, is he?"

"Take that up with Mother, if you ever pass her way again," said Brenus.

"And you were not spoken to, either!" Culhwch said.

Well, this was rapidly getting out of hand. It was time for diplomacy. I opened my palm to catch the agitated father's eye. "Your Latin is impeccable, sir."

Culhwch turned to me and grinned, showing a mouth full, mostly, of yellow teeth. I did not like that look, not one bit, suddenly feeling as if the Celtic leader's frustration had found a less contentious target. "Someone must have stretched *you* between two trees when you were a babe, eh?" *Height isn't everything,* I thought. *I may be taller than average, but height is a relative manly virtue: Brenus' heartwall could wrap one of his hands around my neck and his fingers would touch. But attend, the Celt speaks again.* "Impeccable, you say? Do you mock me with your big words? I've noticed that Romans who talk big are small in battle. Are you truly weak, or do your words have mystical weight? Are you a wizard?"

"He's no wizard," Herclides said, speaking up for the first time since he and his gang were overwhelmed. "He's just a slave." Culhwch's left leg shot out and his boot caught Herclides in the chest, knocking him into several other men in the makeshift corral of Celtic riders.

"A spell spoken by a slave works just the same as one said by a free man," Culhwch said. "If they know the art, and the words, and speak them *impeccably.*"

Lady Cornelia stepped forward, pulling Livia with her beneath the borrowed cloak. "Do you think you men could continue this riveting conversation after we've had a chance to change into some dry clothes?" I looked up; it did appear as if it might rain again.

Culhwch did less than ignore the young mistress; he went on speaking to me as if she was not even present. "I'll teach you some of our tongue while we're here. You'll probably choke to death on the first sentence."

"If the stench of your journey does not kill me first." I know. How impolitic of me. How spontaneous. How convenient that Crassus' warrior son stood so close. Livia gave a short laugh, underscoring the magnitude of my impertinence; the sound was mirthful and mischievous. Diplomacy aside, I could not let the Celt's callousness and disrespect stand. It rankled. Even in Rome, *especially* in Rome, a few of the rules of civilization must be upheld, or if not, what is left to uphold civilization?

In any case, you cannot let these barbarians get the verbal upper hand. It encourages unmerited arrogance.

Culhwch was far from insulted. He let out a great belch of a laugh and made to slap his son on the back, checked himself and instead kicked one of Herclides' men. "He's a sharp-tongue," he cried, making the balls on his helmet swing as he nodded. He took to the game like a hunting dog to the fallen prey. "Men like you are revered story tellers in my tribe," he said, continuing to nod, "as long as they are entertaining." He leaned forward on his horse and his eyes grew wide. "If we become bored by their wit, we cut them up and feed the pieces to the dogs. That always gets a laugh from the little ones." *Well. I'll concede the first round, then.*

"That's enough," Publius commanded. "You heard lady Cornelia." Culhwch looked disappointed.

"Do we kill these ones?" he asked.

"Who among you are citizens?" Publius asked, reining his mount to face the captives. Only Herclides and Palaemon raised their hands. "Put those two under separate guard, and I'll sell the rest." A centurion, without being told, took sixteen men and herded the future slaves toward the forum markets. Strange that not a single protest was throated among them. Why waste your breath debating the inevitable?

"These two deserve execution," Malchus said, pointing his *gladius* toward Herclides and Palaemon.

"What, and lose two votes in the coming election? In case there was any doubt," the general said to the men who had caused us no end of grief, "you'll be supporting my father and Pompeius when the time comes. And between now and then, you'll be campaigning for our noble senators. Clear?"

"Yes, general," Herclides said, his head bowed so you could not see his eyes. Palaemon nodded.

"Good. Tribune!" Another officer, the trailing main of the blond horsehair on his helmet as combed and cared for as his beard, rode up beside Publius. "See that these two find a place in camp where we can keep an eye on them."

"We'll squeeze them in, sir, nice and tight."

"What about him?" said Livia, pointing to the *retiarius*. "He tried to kill Drusus."

"I wondered what you were doing holding a trident," Publius said to me. "Hand it over. It makes you look silly. You—out here." The gladiator moved from the middle of the captives to stand before Crassus' youngest son. "Are you a citizen?" Publius asked, inspecting the six-foot trident as if he had never seen one up close before. The bigger man, his left arm-shield his only protection was hanging at his side. He shook his head; his jaw was set, his eyes fixed on the young commander. As Publius said, "Too *bad*," he thrust the weapon into the gladiator's bare chest, yanked it out and dropped the trident on the ground. Legionaries on either side of the fighter had caught the man before he fell and were dragging him off while he expired. The son of Crassus, it seemed, was a child no longer.

"I killed that man," Livia whispered.

"You saved him," I countered, "from having to think about the time and place of his execution." A weak argument, but what else could I say?

"Post men about the city as we've discussed," Publius was saying. "We are here to keep the peace until elections are held. I intend this campaign to be a success like any other. Culhwch, don't have your men wash off the woad. The word's already about that I've crossed the *pomerium* with armed soldiers. Let's make sure all factions know we are both armed *and* frightening."

"Petrocorii need no woad to frighten tiny Romans. It is a wonder to my men that such a little people have built such temples. We have decided you have somehow enslaved a race of giants. Or wizards." He looked pointedly at me. "The blue stain stays as my general commands. Who wants to wash it off? By Lugos, water is not for washing; it's for making ale. Hah!"

"It's a drink worthy of the gods," Publius conceded.

"You Romans wash too much to be true men. Washing is for women, to clean our breeches and our vests. And even they barely let their toes touch the stream! Hah!"

CHAPTER XII

56 - 55 BCE - WINTER, ROME

Year of the consulship of
Cn. Cornelius Lentulus Marcellinus and L. Marcius Philippus

As our little troupe, minus the valiant Minucius Valens, made our way up the hill toward home, I watched Publius leading his horse, walking beside lady Cornelia, flirting without shame. What had happened to the irrepressible six year-old scamp playing in the dirt, digging for worms? The line of the boy's future had been drawn along a Roman road paved with golden stones. Here was the man, but it was the child I remembered, squirming like one of his captive night crawlers while I tried my best to tutor him in his studies. All he wanted to hear were tales of gods and the heroic deeds of men. Now, here he was, uniformed, magnificent, lethal, his helmet tucked under his weather-bronzed arm, the embodiment of his childhood fantasies, leading his black stallion to walk beside the lady Cornelia. Publius was newly twenty-six, but this was a different man entirely from the one I had last seen leaving for Gaul almost four years ago.

Physically he was much the same: blue eyes, short, black hair, rectangular, ill-shaved, stony face. Still cocksure, still confident he could get into a brawl and come out smiling, though bleeding and bruised. But now, every last vestige of 'boy' had evaporated. This was not only a warrior, but a commander of men, men he had beaten in battle and yet, with his own personal magic had been able to forge into auxiliaries as loyal to him as any wolf to its pack leader. Perhaps a greater achievement — he had the admiration and respect of Roman officers twice his age.

In addition to the twelve *cohorts* now making camp on the Campus Martius, which Caesar had relinquished to insure my master sat for the second time in the curule chair of consul, Publius had arrived in Rome with one thousand Celtic horse; one thousand, can you imagine? A calculation I tried unsuccessfully to avoid making in my head was the total number of trophies, bereft of body, now dangling from their saddle horns.

•••

Tertulla was blindfolded and laughing, a hand to her mouth. Crassus stood behind her, his arms about her waist as they stood waiting before the tall cedar and iron double doors. From the interior of the atrium, I thought I saw Hanno peek briefly out from the shadows, but then whoever it was, was gone. We stopped at the circular fountain of Neptune, pounded by the crash of foaming marble surf, his painted green torso kept glistening by an invisible pipe hidden in the top of his head. The watery regurgitations from the mouths of twenty marble fish surrounding the god splashed into the basin below, masking the sounds of our approach. Publius held out the reins of his horse without taking his eyes off his parents, assuming with confidence that some lesser person would immediately obey the implicit command to take them. I did.

Livia stepped up beside me, abandoning Publius' cloak to the sole possession of lady Cornelia. As much as I loved the animals, I had a frantic urge to rid myself of my sweating, equine charge. I caught the eye of a stable boy and passed the reins to him. He led the beast away to be dried off, brushed, blanketed and fed. Here we stood, alive. When I was first forced into slavery, I had wished for death, but that was a far distant memory now. I had never been so glad to find myself taking one breath and then the next. I felt newborn and rash. I reached for Livia's hand once more, and she did not resist the gentle intrusion.

Members of the *familia* were emerging as quietly as they could from both sides of the house, some with tears in their eyes. Lucius stepped from the front entrance, beguiled by this scene of reunion. I caught his eye and our heads nodded; we smiled at each other in appreciation and understanding.

The look in my lord's eyes was childlike with excitement. He practically vibrated with giddy pride as he held Tertulla, as if he could barely keep himself from ruining the surprise of Publius' return by shouting out or even dancing. It was as close as I had ever seen him come to losing his dignity altogether. Publius tip-toed closer, but his boots on the white gravel were intent on betraying him with each step.

"I'm not a fool, you know," my lady announced when he was within a dozen feet of the couple.

"Whatever do you mean, *columba*?"

"I mean," she said, ripping off the blindfold, "I want to see my son!" Tertulla broke free from her husband and ran into Publius' arms. He swept her up into the air and spun her round to shouts of joy and welcome so earnest you would think we were all cousins, nephews and nieces. The moment he set her down, *domina* grabbed Publius' face in both hands and kissed his cheeks over and over. "You are safe! You are home!" she repeated until her energy was spent. Then, taking his hand in hers, she raised it on high and turned in a slow circle, the roses in her cheeks watered by happy tears. This was the remembered Tertulla of the twinkling eye and wise, carefree smile. It was the first time she had returned to herself, without effort or guile, since Luca.

Dozens of the *familia* now present moved as close as they dared to their lords and masters, which was not so close that my lady did not now have to raise her voice. "Is not my son the most beautiful creature ever to descend from Mt. Olympus?" A heartfelt cheer. "Come, let us give *Virtus* deserved rest from his labors and summon Bacchus to quench the thirst of battle, victory, and the long road home!" A more raucous noise was stamped to silence by a single word.

"HOLD!"

Crassus stepped down onto the gravel, and though he was dressed in nothing more authoritative than his house tunic, his voice brought the stunned quiet that follows the thunderclap. The *familia* froze, including Tertulla and Publius. Then, more gently, he spoke above the clamor of the disobedient fountain. "May not a father greet his son?"

Publius pressed his forehead against that of his mother, kissed her cheek and walked to stand before the *paterfamilias*. He was several inches taller than his father, but in force of presence they were equals.

"Father."

"You look well."

Publius smiled. "I am fit."

"You are unwounded?"

"No harm that won't heal." Tertulla approached to stand two paces behind Publius, but no closer. She would not enter that sacred space between a Roman father and his warrior son. The men stood facing each other, almost at attention. Not even a cough escaped the rest of the *familia*.

"Did our letters reach you?"

"Forgive me for not writing. Gaul is a reluctant mistress, and Caesar is an unrelenting conqueror."

An awkward silence, to none but *dominus*, *domina* and myself.

Crassus looked down, recovered himself and again met his son's eyes. "You have acquitted yourself well in Aquitania."

"I had hoped I would arrive before the general's letters. I wanted to be the first to relate my adventures to you."

"I shall pry every detail from you at dinner."

"We will bore Mother."

Crassus' hands twitched at his sides. "That is extremely doubtful." For several moments, their eyes did what formality forbade: they embraced each other in silence, the old, crafty grey holding the young, impetuous blue. Tightly, tenderly.

"You look well," Crassus said at last, then smiled at the redundancy. Publius grinned, and the spell of formality was broken.

"My son," *dominus* said hoarsely, reaching for Publius and gripping him with a strength that belied his sixty years. They held each other close, unmoving, Crassus substituting the pressure of his grasp for what he could not voice: *'I was sick with worry for your safety'* – *'I prayed for you twice each day'* – *'When letters came from Gaul, your mother and I would only open them at the temple of Bellona after making sacrifice; one time I vomited at the foot of the altar and had to give the appalled priest a thousand sesterces for his trouble.'*

We watched in silence, many of us crying openly now. Publius cradled his father's greying head against his shoulder. *Dominus* squeezed his eyes shut, but could not stop what nature and love demanded. They stood as statues, and we, barely breathing, completed the courtyard tableau.

CHAPTER XIII

56 - 55 BCE - WINTER, ROME

Year of the consulship of
Cn. Cornelius Lentulus Marcellinus and L. Marcius Philippus

t was past the *sixth hour* of the night. The family had retired over an hour ago. Publius' homecoming meal had been simple enough: bacon-wrapped chicken, steamed mullet and flat bread. By comparison, the feast to mark the celebration of his return to Rome was a Herculean task: 200 guests including senior senators, both *optimates* and *populares*, entertainments and a menu which must be provisioned and prepared in only five days, on the third day before the Ides of Ianuarius, between the festivals of the Agonalia and the Carmentalia. None of the preparation could be started until now, not even the invitations, for fear of spoiling the surprise of Publius' return.

I sat on a stool at one of the two long work tables in the kitchen, oil lamps casting slats of shadow and light through the pile of wax tablets on my left, one for each runner. Our six house scribes had their own work—in the morning I would have Curio send men throughout the city to wait while the invitations were printed by copyists-for-hire so that the scrolls could be delivered by midafternoon. Before me blurred a list Nicoteles had handed to me when I sent the bleary-eyed cook to bed. Nicoteles was talented, but I missed our old cook, Atticus, who had died at the venerable age of 59.

I perused Nicoteles' inventory of items not already in store which would be required for the celebration's menu, and it was not funny in the least:

500 dormice

6 boars

10 lambs

300 wheels of bread

10 gallons of *garum* (in addition to the three gallons of the fish sauce we always kept on hand)

5 large *amphorae* of honey

5 more of olive oil

3 baskets of almonds and 8 of fresh figs

All that and a veritable field of salad greens and vegetables.

Enough! I could look upon the interminable list no longer. Taking the weights from the scroll I watched it curl upon itself like the capital of an Ionic column turned on its head. The short lines of the missing items, in itself a poem of excess, gulled my reluctant attention back to the rash and idiotic blunder I had committed only hours before in a moment of irretrievable optimism.

After the servants had been fed, I had summoned Hanno to my *tablinum*. There I had instructed him, before he retired to the servants' quarters, to deliver two scraps of parchment to the medical clinic at the front of the estate where Livia made her bed. The same bed where her mother, Sabina, had slept before her. He scooped them off my table with his customary technique of interlocking the remaining fingers of both hands to hold them securely.

163

Then off he loped, may Hermes pluck the feather from his one good heel! I had changed my mind the moment he disappeared, but the hour would not allow me to call for him in a voice much louder than a whisper. He was gone, and with him, the middle ground above despair and below elation which I had so carefully constructed, then inhabited ever since Livia's return to Rome.

They were little poems, gods defend me! Insignificant scraps of nothing that would destroy the modicum of harmony I had gingerly pieced together after years of misgiving, awkwardness and distance. Yes, I had kissed her on the massage table, but two months had passed since that impulsive moment, and curse my ignorance and innocence, I was more flustered and unsure now than ever I was before. I did not know how to approach her without feeling ridiculous, and having a hundred household duties as excuses, I had employed virtually every single one to avoid her.

Her rejection of me was imminent, of this I was certain. She would come to me with sad, green eyes, take my hand (this time in sympathy, not in fear), and tell me how much my friendship meant to her. Playing the scene in my head made me want to regurgitate.

Who is the greatest poetess of love, beguiling hearts down through the centuries? Sappho, as any schoolboy knows. Any schoolboy, it would seem, could teach me more of this art of the interplay between the sexes than I have gleaned from my paltry experience. (Not that I would take the advice of a pimpled coagulation of base impulses.) All that I know of love came from Livia herself, but that was twenty years ago; we were barely more than children when Eros kindled the fire in our eyes. Here, I might as well share with you how I tightened the noose around my own unworthy neck. I sent her this:

> The sweet apple blushes on the end of the bough,
> At the very end of the bough which gatherers missed.
> Nay, missed not, but could not reach.

If only I had tempered my ardor and left it at that, Livia might have taken the sentiment as a genteel compliment and nothing more. At that moment, alone with my wine and my misery, I was convinced that life was a string of "if only's" leading from one self-inflicted bungle to the next, until at some point, that phrase became one's final utterance, and one expired with regret on one's lips.

If the first lines did not mark me for a fool, then what followed surely would. There was a young poet who had been causing a stir around town with his frank and irreverent verse. His name was Valerius Catullus. My master was particularly fond of him because occasionally his caustic wit would nip at the heels of his nemesis:

> Caesar, I have no great desire
> To stand in your good graces,
> Nor can I bother to inquire
> How fair or dark your face is

It was from one of Catullus' other short poems that I stole the following fragment...

> Once, bright days shone for you,
> when you came often drawn to the girl
> loved as no other will be loved by you.
> Then there were many pleasures with her,
> that you wished, and the girl not unwilling,

truly the bright days shone for you.

… and sent it off to Livia.

If one cup of honeyed wine steadies the hand that drinks it, then a second will surely calm them both. Pouring one, then another and downing them quickly, I filled a third and stared at it, wondering if I might not be straining the boundaries of this dispirited philosophy. What was I thinking? Earlier that day, when we believed the line drawn for the length of our lives had been abruptly shortened with alarmingly little notice, Livia took my hand. What of it? In such a moment of fear and stress, I might have clung to Malchus had he stood but a little closer. What foolery to misconstrue the reflexive grasp of a friend's hand as a token of love.

The unexpected fragrance of sweet rush and myrrh joined the cool breath of air that flowed from the peristyle, across the colonnade and into the kitchen. I looked up. Livia drew aside the heavy portiere and padded barefoot through the opening. "I'm cold," she said, walking to the opposite side of the table where I sat. Without invitation, she picked up the untouched third cup of wine and drank its contents without pause for breath. "Better." She threw off the thick, woolen shawl draping her shoulders, tossed a scrap of parchment toward me and leaned over the table, hands askew, elbows locked.

Misery! She had thrown the poem back in my face. I could not bear to look at it. Instead, I stared wide-eyed at her transformation. She wore a skin-tight, ankle-length dress in the Egyptian style, of a fabric so sheer imagination became as superfluous as thought. The wide, beaded collar around her neck stopped just above the swell of her barely covered breasts. Her eyelids and lashes were darkened by galena, matched by wings of malachite that

166

swept up from below her eyes to reach almost to her temples. Her hair was tied at the base of her neck but she had draped it over her right shoulder and bound its mass with a coiled, silver snake. There was heat in her eyes that outshone the glow of the lamps.

"You have avoided me ever since that day in the *balnea*."

"You have been drinking," I said.

"And it's working, too. I have almost forgotten the day's events."

"Where are you going dressed like that?"

Livia laughed. "Back to bed, if you're not quick. I'll have more wine."

I poured and as she drank, admitted, "I *have* been avoiding you."

"You're afraid of me."

"I'm afraid of being spurned by you. Again." I hope you'll agree that I deserve some modicum of credit for confessing that one as intelligent and quick-witted as I might at the same time be as callow as a Vestal.

"I'm here, aren't I? Maybe you should read that," she said, gesturing at the scrap of parchment before me.

I took a breath, picked it up and found a different fragment by Sappho:

The sinking moon has left the sky,
The Pleiades have also gone.
Midnight comes — and goes, the hours fly
And solitary still, I lie.

"Have I not made my feelings clear," Livia said, "or was my kiss that day not up to your standards."

Andrew Levkoff

I shook my head and lowered my eyes to the table. "What standards? One needs to have a base of comparison..."

"Stand up."

"Why? What are you going to do?" I rose, not as steadily as I had planned.

"Be impetuous." She leaned further across the table. "Now put your mouth on mine."

Her lips were glossy with the taste of honey and cassia. I disappeared into that kiss, and if thinking were a talent I still possessed, I would have wished that the soft mingling of breath and lips would never end. Breaking that embrace was a fall from timeless skies to a mundane present, and neither of us had a desire to remain earthbound.

"Where can we go?" she asked.

"Don't move," I said. I pushed the lamps and wax tablets aside and to the astonishment of us both climbed up and over the long worktable and into her arms. It was simply too far to go around. We held each other's faces in our hands and for a moment let our eyes speak the language our mouths had just relearned.

"Take me to your room," she said.

"We can't. It's just down the hall from *dominus* and *domina*. The clinic?"

"Too far. I will wait no longer. What about there?" She pointed behind me to the locked door of the pantry. I fumbled in my tunic to pull out the chain holding the key. A second necklace, entangled in the first, glinted dully.

"My scallop," Livia said. "You've kept it all this time." Her eyes had become brighter in the lamplight.

"If that bracelet of shells had not come undone that day under the statue of Apollo..."

168

"But it did, and we are here now. You were so clumsy trying to retie the string about my wrist you woke me from my nap. This is fine silverwork," she said, untangling the two chains.

"Not my doing. *Dominus* insisted his *atriensis* wear a chain worthy of the station. He meant it as a gift, but I prefer the string."

"Perhaps these links were made with metal mined from Laurion." My smile crumpled. "How ironic if a gift from Crassus to you had something of my mother forged within it."

"Livia."

"Forgive me, that was a stupid thing to say. I cannot help but miss her, but you are not to blame. It is you that I want, Alexandros. Very much. It is my curse: my mouth will be speaking long before I even think to advise silence. You know," she said, her eyes atwinkle, "perhaps I acquired this evil trait from you."

I laughed, and surprised myself by saying, "I shouldn't wonder. But you have taught me how two mouths may hold each other speechless."

"Then let us be silent, but not still." We walked to the pantry door holding the lamps and each other.

With the key in the door, I turned to Livia and said, "Are you certain?"

"My sweet man," she said, caressing my cheek, "*this* is the time for you to be silent."

Once inside, we kissed again. The press of our bodies soon made plain the state of my arousal. I pulled away. "Livia, I…"

"Shhh." She put her fingers to my lips. "You are safe with me," she said.

"I am unschooled," I said, my face reddening.

"Then, for once, I shall be your teacher."

CHAPTER XIV

56 - 55 BCE - WINTER, ROME

Year of the consulship of
Cn. Cornelius Lentulus Marcellinus and L. Marcius Philippus

N ow that the first of the year had passed, an interrex had been "found" friendly to my master's cause; the names of Crassus and Pompeius had finally been put up for consul. In the morning, Betto and I met the line of shivering clients waiting to greet their patron in the daily *salutatio*. We told them *dominus* was sleeping late, took their lists of requests and promised to pass along their good wishes. Betto then gave each client a purse of 2,000 sesterces with instructions to spread the word among the people that stability and the end of violence could only come with the election of these two venerated conscript fathers, Crassus and Pompeius. They trudged back down the hill, blue-lipped but content. My own people would be following close behind with campaign encouragement in the guise of jingling leather purses.

That evening, the weather was cooperating only in that it was not snowing: it was bitterly cold and getting colder, it being near the twelfth hour of the day.

Fortunately, the company need not rely solely on their own conviviality to keep warm: the furnaces were stoked and hot air was blowing beneath their slippered feet, heating not only the floors but the walls themselves. There were so many people filling every public room of the Crassus home that the *triclinia*, of which there were three, accommodating 27 diners, had been abandoned in favor of an endless buffet and an army of servants offering drinks and treats. The front entrance looked like a bootmaker's workshop, piled high with all manner of footwear.

Dominus and *domina*, the elegant heart of Publius' homecoming celebration, were followed wherever they strolled; just now they stood in the main atrium, pressed upon by dozens of well-wishers, eavesdroppers and a few junior senators who I am certain had received no invitation. One who was conspicuously absent: Gnaeus Pompeius had declined, claiming his young wife, Julia, Caesar's daughter and Pompeius' fourth wife, was unwell. She was often ill; the excuse was not entirely implausible.

In time, Pompeius would marry yet again, as one tragedy heaped itself upon the one beneath it. The gay and carefree nymph he would later claim as his fifth bride was in attendance this night. But that day was yet to come. Tonight, her eyes and heart were fixed with unshakeable attention upon another. Children — their untroubled, idyllic vision of the future is almost always shattered. Sooner or later they learn what all youth must — that life is the cruel fate that awaits them while they make plans for a tomorrow that will never be.

•••

I looked for Livia in vain. She had told me she would not attend; when I balked, she gave me two highly rational proofs. "First, you will be in your element, fussing over every detail."

"I do not fuss," I sniffed.

"Second," she said after an exaggerated inspection of the ceiling, "I love the way you look at me, and so will everyone else should they see us together. We have not yet presented our affiliation to *domina* and *dominus*, and you are incapable of keeping that boy-who-has-found-a-little-fox look from your face."

"It is a most wondrous and beguiling *vulpecula*," I said, my face relaxing unconsciously into the very expression to which Livia alluded.

"This is Publius' day. Let him have it." There was no logical response to that, but Livia did invite me to bring her a plate of pastries when the last guest had departed.

•••

"Father, guess where Caesar intends to march his armies next? Go on, guess!" Publius popped a *globulus* into his mouth, a fried ball of cheese curd and semolina rolled in honey and toasted sesame. He licked his fingers, held his hand aloft and a dining room slave stepped forward to wipe each finger clean with a damp cloth.

"Forgive me, son, but I am too old to play guessing games."

"You won't believe it. Parthia, of all the wind-swept, graceless places on earth. But that isn't even—"

"What!" Crassus almost choked on a hard-boiled egg dipped in honeyed *garum*.

Tertulla gave him water to sip and whispered urgently, "Husband?!"

"I know!" Publius said. "If it hadn't been Marcus who told me, I would never have—"

"Wait. Marcus, your brother?"

"Who else, Father?" Publius said, impatience snapping into his voice like the whipping of a wet branch. The boy at play in the dirt had grown into a soldier unaccustomed to interruptions, even by his own father, the holder of *patria potestas*. "He stopped me just before I rode for Rome."

"What did he say?" Tertulla asked.

Publius could only laugh. "Mother, Father, I am *trying* to tell you."

"Perhaps we should wait and speak of this later," Crassus said. "This is your homecoming, not a campaign."

"Do you," Publius said slowly, his voice spiked with exasperation, "or do you not want to hear the bizarre words of Caesar?"

"Yes," said *domina*. "No," said *dominus* in the same instant. Though the law favors the *paterfamilias*, sometimes a look may overrule the highest court. "Go ahead, then," Crassus said. "But try not to shout."

"My brother, Marcus," Publius said, explaining for lady Cornelia's benefit, "hardly ever leaves the general's side when he's in camp."

"Possibly he believes it better to have a Crassus beside you than behind you," said my lady.

"That was unkind, sweetheart. Caesar is our friend," *dominus* said.

"What do you mean, lady Tertulla?" lady Cornelia asked.

"She jests," Crassus said flatly. "Publius, continue." *Dominus* looked at his son as if to say, *later*.

Publius and everyone else within earshot wondered at my lady's remark, and when Crassus' son spoke again, it was as if each word were a stone poorly balanced in a crocodile-infested stream. "Marcus is the general's *quaestor* and paymaster: it is fitting they should converse frequently. Here is the heart of it: Caesar told Marcus he had consulted the Sibylline Oracles and had discovered an entry stating that 'the kingdom to the east will never be conquered save by a man who wears a crown.'"

"Extraordinary," Crassus managed to say.

"So," lady Tertulla spat, her face pinched with self-control, "he fancies himself a king now, does he?"

"There is more. Caesar then turned to Marcus and said, 'your father will try, but he will fail.'"

"Outrageous," lady Tertulla muttered.

There were murmurings all around, and Crassus tried to drown them out with a laugh, saying, "Either you misheard, Publius, or else Julius referred to another enterprise, perhaps political, like my campaign to offer assistance to our provincial tax collectors." Too late. The dormice had scampered from the kitchen.

"How dare he make such a villainous prophecy?" Cornelia Metella said, after an extended sip of wine. Her goblet was refilled almost without her notice. She had staked out her place beside the young commander and was not about to yield it to any rival. Publius seemed well-pleased by her attention, a fact which later would be happily noted by his father and mother, who also cleaved to their son like flowers following the course of the sun.

Publius said, "My lady Cornelia, forgive me for exposing possibly the only two things you, with your superior education and intellect do not know: first, you cannot know what you are talking about, because you do not know what *I* am talking about. And second, you cannot know what I am talking about, because I myself am baffled."

"Ignorance is an underrated virtue, my lord. I could give a fig for your reasons," she said, choosing a cheese-stuffed fig from a passing tray. "If something has been said against the house of Crassus, a home where my entire family has found hospitality and friendship in equal measure, then I am that man's enemy. Even if it be your commanding officer, the noble Caesar."

"Imagine how you'll feel," Publius said, "when you've known us more than a week. Lady, may I take your wine?"

"If you're thirsty, find your own," lady Cornelia said, twisting away from his proffered hand. "I know my limits."

Tertulla suddenly spoke up with such bitterness, a dozen heads whirled to attend her. "*Noble* Caesar is but a man. Men make mistakes. Caesar has made yet another: he underestimates my husband."

Publius appeared ready to speak, but discretion held his tongue. I know what he must have been thinking: *'so it's true, then?'*

"*Columba*," Crassus said, lightly squeezing his wife's hand, "one of our children has come home to us. Let us make our guests feel as welcome as our son."

"What's this is I hear of crafty Crassus failing?" asked a new voice. "The gods, if one could find them at home, would stumble and fall from Olympus, should this be so."

"Tully!" Publius cried, shaken from his puzzlement. "How I have missed Rome's greatest voice! With apologies, Father," he added quickly. The young man embraced his old friend and mentor while Crassus looked on with ill-concealed frustration. The famous orator was old enough to be Publius' father, yet almost a decade younger than *dominus*. He was balding and more than adequately filled his toga; you might also care to know that when seen in profile, his nose was as prominent as his ego. Like Publius' father, I viewed his friendship with *dominus'* son and *my* student with the same mild distaste. I know the man's reputation, and grant his capabilities, but I simply cannot be drawn to a person who carries himself with both the arrogant and aggrieved bearing of one who believes he has no equal, yet cannot comprehend why others have not leapt to the same self-evident conclusion.

"Cicero!" Crassus exclaimed, putting his arm about his critic's shoulders. "Welcome! How we have missed you."

The statesman looked almost as bewildered as those other guests who were also aware of the stormy history between the two senators. Which was everyone. "I would rather have stayed here in Rome than be missed by those who remained at home."

"Oh, that nonsense is long past," Crassus said.

The orator had referred to his forced exile by Clodius Pulcher. Their enmity was legendary. Cicero had appealed to *dominus*, Caesar and Pompeius for help, but they had turned their backs on him, it is rumored as payment-in-kind for the time he spurned their offer to participate in their coalition at Luca.

"I see reconstruction of your house is continuing apace," Crassus said, glancing at me to summon more food servers. I, in turn, gave the nod to Lucius Curio. I would not miss a single syllable of this! Curio turned with a huff from his own place in waiting, and even among the crowded assembly, I could hear the sound of knuckles cracking as he departed.

"No thanks to Clodius," Cicero answered. "We will never be rid of the stench left by his arson, or the acrid reminder of what Roman politics has allowed itself to become."

"Now, now," Crassus said, "let's leave politics at the door this night. This is a happy occasion."

"Of course, you are right, dear friend. Politics and happiness can no longer co-exist in the city, let alone in the same house. I am done with politics, and shall concentrate on the rediscovery of happiness. I shall withdraw from active pursuits to concentrate on my writing. But you, Marcus, your political star rises to heights even Icarus never knew. Of course we all know what happened to him." *(Oh, the man never rests!)* "No, after Luca, I have willingly surrendered to the will of the people, or at the very least to the will of Crassus, Pompeius and Caesar. Thank the gods that you three know what is best for the rest of us. Will you drink with me to the Republic, Marcus?"

"With all my heart." Crassus raised his goblet. "To the Republic!" he cried, and the toast was repeated as it surged throughout the house.

When the noise had died down, Cicero resumed. "Is it not a blessing that the interregnum has passed? Black, you may be unaware, is my least favorite color." He paused for a long moment, but Crassus refused to fall into his trap. "What, you took no notice of those senators who refused to attend the games, who shunned the Latin festival on the Alban mount, and who declined to feast in the Capitol on Jove's sacred day? You must have seen them, donning black togas as if in mourning? How stifling, to suffer so throughout the summer, the poor dears."

"I *did* notice one thing," my lord said offhandedly. "*Your* toga remained as bright and pure as the snows on

Vesuvius." *Well spoken, dominus. Yet I fear there is much truth in Cicero's accusation. The world is out of balance.*

"I stood in sympathy with them, Marcus Licinius, yes, in sympathy. I was as unhappy as any with your manipulation of the elections, but I have a skin condition, you see…"

"Where are your wife and daughter?" Crassus asked, casting about not only for Terentia and Tullia, but for a change of subject.

"They have little taste for parties these days. Their home is in ruins, after all. I only stopped by to congratulate you, Marcus, on your election. Consul for a second term. Well done."

"I am honored by your confidence, Marcus Tullius, but you know as well as I that the vote will not be taken until next week."

Cicero laughed, a short, nasal snuffle. "Oh, I take your meaning now, Marcus," he said, as if comprehension had just dawned. "You would have me harken back to a time when the outcome of a contest was not known until *after* the voting. How nostalgic."

"Honored Father and illustrious friend," Publius interrupted, "do you know the sign of an unsuccessful party? I thought not. Permit me to tell you. It is when the conversation begins to bore the ladies."

"As so often happens," Cicero said, waving off a platter of roasted chicken legs practically thrust beneath his nose by a server pushed at arms length by Curio, "it is the children who must lead the old ones out of the woods. Enliven us, and recount Caesar's prediction of your father's failure. I am intrigued."

Publius glanced at his father. "I fear I have misspoken. It was nothing."

"It was *some* thing, else you would not have voiced the sentiment with such scorn."

"Why, little Roman," said a new voice, "do you insult this warrior by pressing for an answer different from the one he has just given you?"

"Merciful—" Cicero started off with his hallmark scorn, but censored himself mid-huff as he turned into the barreled expanse of Culhwch's chest. The Celt had cleaned himself up for the party: his breeches were almost stain-free and he wore a shirt. This did nothing to improve his scent. I was having him followed wherever he went by two slaves swinging thuribles practically on fire with as much incense as could be stuffed into them. Every now and then Culhwch would swat at the boys halfheartedly, but they were nimble and appeared unhurt.

"There are only two reasons to piss on a man's name before his family and friends—either you are a witless swine, or you wish to challenge him in battle." The Celt looked down on the senator, braids swinging. "We know it's not the second one, don't we, bacon-that-speaks," Culhwch said, smiling.

"How extraordinary," said Cicero.

"Culhwch," Publius said, "remember where you are. This isn't Corterate."

"Praise Macha. Do you know," the Celt continued, pointing a ruddy, lined finger at Publius, "in one battle alone, this same man slew 30,000 of the 50,000 who faced him. Hope that he is as merciful with you."

I must give Marcus Tullius credit. He craned his neck, stood toga to tunic with the huge fighting man and said in a low, heartless register, "I would have killed them all."

That took Culhwch by surprise. "Would you now?" He turned to his general. "Would he?"

Publius said, "You never can tell. We Romans are unpredictable."

"My head on a pike! Maybe you're not such a pig's ass after all. That's the same advice I gave the young general. He didn't take it, Macha's balls. What was it you said, general?"

"What I always say: leave the vanquished living reminders of their defeat." Publius looked very pleased with himself. "After we've gone, who better to speak for us of the futility of opposing our domination than those who have witnessed it firsthand?"

"Well spoken, my son," said Crassus.

After Publius had introduced Culhwch all around, and the ladies had finished either scrambling from the room or touching the Celt so they could recount their bravery to their friends on the morrow, Cicero waited the minimum number of polite beats before asking how it was that a man like him would leave home and hearth to follow a conquering foreigner. The big Celt looked to Publius, whose only response was an amused look that said, 'you're on your own.' My young master took this opportunity to invite lady Cornelia to inspect the remarkable Armenian tapestries hanging in the hallway leading to the baths. They were remarkable indeed, for they did not exist. Although, there were some unused *cubicula* in that very place.

"Why does anyone do anything?" Culhwch began philosophically. "For gold or a woman. For me it was both." Culhwch grabbed a handful off a platter of sliced roast boar carried by Lucius himself. I'd have to remember to commend him on his initiative. The enunciation of Culhwch's next words fought for ascendancy over his chewing. "I prefer gold — it is *always* beautiful to behold;

when you possess it, you will *always* cherish it—when it is gone, you will *never* rejoice."

"Are they all as polite as you in Gaul?" Cicero asked.

"I don't know; it's a big place. Does polite mean honest? Then I'm more polite than most."

Crassus said, "We could use a man like this on the floor of the senate. Think how he'd lessen the hours of squabbling."

"Think," Cicero answered, "how he'd lessen the number of senators."

"Your senate is a place for speeches, not for Culhwch. Your son and I have struck a good bargain: you keep your robes and talk and tell us who to kill and we will take our spears and our horses and ride out with your soldiers and kill your enemies by your side. We will take a few heads, you will give us a little gold, then everyone is smiling."

"An excellent bargain," *dominus* said. "Tell us then, my lord, how you came to ally yourself with my son."

"I am a prince of the Petrocorii. We work the iron mines; nobody in the land you call Gaul makes better weapons. My father was chief of Corterate; still is unless someone's jabbed a spear through his black heart. Corterate is smaller than Vesunna, just to the east along the river. In Vesunna, the people are richer, the women are prettier and the beds are softer. Especially the bed of the daughter of the headman, a dung heap of a bastard who, it must be known, is a very good friend of my father. Hah! Everyone had it in for me, but I did them a favor. There's no comparing my seed to the jellyfish she calls 'husband;' now they'll have a strong son who'll make them proud. Unless they tossed him to the dogs when he was born." Culhwch took a swig of wine. He added thoughtfully, "That's what I'd have done."

"You took another man's wife," Cicero said, "in his own house, an ally of your father, and got her with child?"

"Are you deaf, or have you not been listening?" Culhwch asked. He wagged a nail bitten forefinger in Cicero's face. "That would not be *polite*." Cicero flushed, searching for those in the crowd of listeners guilty of laughing, but Culhwch had already moved on. "Your son, lord," he said, addressing Crassus, "had just vanquished the peoples of Armorica and had fixed his eye on Aquitania. I made parlay with this young Roman commander who had blood in his eyes. When he told me he would first make war on the Sotiates, copper-mining scum if you've never met one, and after that pursue the gold miners of the Tarbelli, that was all I needed to hear. I swore fealty and offered those few cavalry and charioteers of my father's who were loyal to me and looking for a little excitement. Couldn't go home after all that, so here I am."

"A thousand such warriors is no small offering," Crassus said.

"Why make war on your own people?" One could see that Cicero was reluctant to pose another question, but could not help himself.

"First, they are not my people. My people came down from the great island to the north you call Britannia. The southerners of Aquitania, well, who cares where they came from? Second, iron is good, gold is better."

"I am deeply humbled and gratified by your loyalty to my son."

"He is a good fighter and a better leader of men." A scream, too familiar to my ears, came from somewhere near the front entrance, but Culhwch continued as if this was a prosaic celebratory noise. I fought the urge to leave my post, but Crassus gave me no signal. "Impetuous, but he is young," the Celt said as others moved off toward the disturbance. "You have raised him well. Would that I had a son like him."

"You are most gracious," said Crassus. "Let us see what this fuss is about, shall we?"

We came upon a semicircle of guests framing a scene of frozen confusion. Let me see if I can describe it accurately for you. Hanno (it was his ear-piercing squeal we had all heard) was standing against the far wall to the left of the inventory of guests' footwear. I had assigned him the simple task of keeping the outdoor shoes organized and fetching those required by departing guests. Remarkably, he could place every pair with its owner's feet without a single instruction from the reveler. When guests were ready to depart, Hanno unerringly and instantaneously found the correct pairs of shoes amid the wall he had built upon everyone's arrival.

Now he was crying. Kneeling before him was Brenus, Culhwch's son, his arms devoutly wrapped about the poor boy's knees, his head lowered in apparent prayer. Almost blotting this pitifully unique sight from view was Taog, his back to his master, brandishing with one hand a seven-foot wrought iron floor lamp, its spilled oil leaving a sputtering arc of dying flames on the tiles. Cradled under Taog's other arm was the top of a struggling Roman head. But before we get to Betto (whose head it was), I should note that arrayed against the Celtic giant were Malchus, his lethal mistress, Camilla, naked and gleaming in the lamp light, plus several armed guards and guests. Swords and daggers made small, ominous circles in the air, vipers ready to strike. In moments, blood and oil would mingle on the floor.

"Lay down your weapons, gentlemen." Crassus strode between the antagonists and lowered his arms. Every exposed blade followed the gesture as if attached to his hands by invisible strings. The voice of Marcus Crassus turned adversaries into contrite children. Even Taog righted the lamp, humbled by the courage of the master of the house, unarmed and vulnerable, walking to a place easily within his grasp. Thankfully, at that moment, Brenus finished his prayer and released his hold on Hanno's legs.

"Master!" the boy cried, running into my arms. "Sorry. That man frightened me. I'm really sorry. His face is ugly." Brenus had allowed Livia to treat his broken nose, but she could do little more than clean him up and offer him a draught of poppy-laced wine, which he refused. He would heal over time, but until then, the unnatural colors and shapes of his face would startle anyone not prepared for the sight, especially a boy like Hanno. "And he touched me. I didn't want him to, but he did. So I screamed. Sorry. Sorry. Sorry."

While I comforted the boy, Brenus quickly rose to his feet. "He is a child of Lugos. He made the sign and I was bound to pay homage."

"Sir," Crassus said, looking up at Taog. "I must ask you to release that man."

Before he could comply, Culhwch came up behind *dominus* and shouted, "You pustule on a whore's teat! You've shamed us all!"

"Hold, Culhwch," Crassus said. "You are not shamed. I sense nothing but a misunderstanding here."

The Celtic warrior shouldered past *dominus* and raised his hand to strike his son. Taog made a low noise deep in his throat and took a step toward Culhwch, relaxing his grip on Betto's head.

"I will not have this," Crassus said. "You are a guest in my home."

Culhwch grinned and a blade appeared, far too close to Crassus' person for the comfort of any Roman present. Or me. As our lord held up his hand to stop the Romans trembling to intercede, I stepped between the Celt and my master. Culhwch flipped the knife to his left hand and grabbed me by the neck, pressing his spoon of a thumb against my throat. After that, I don't think he paid me any attention at all. "How will you fare, Brenus," he said, "when your heartwall has crumbled and you've nothing to hide behind?" Taog gave the knife no heed, but he clenched his fists, his knuckles making sounds like walnuts cracking. I could not help but think of Lucius Curio. There he was at the edge of my vision, peeking out from behind a statue of Mercury.

Where was Publius?

"Whew! I was about to suffocate in there," Flavius Betto said theatrically, drawing everyone's attention. Having wriggled free of Taog's head lock, he had dusted himself off and was sauntering up to our little group as if we were all friends at the local tavern. "And the smell!" He came straight up beside Culhwch and clapped him on the back.

The Celt leader let out a little laugh. "He does stink, doesn't he."

"Let's be fair," Betto said, "compared to us, you and yours smell like you all rode up from Hades on your chariots. Nothing else like it above ground, I'll wager. Then again, I hear you fight like daemons from the underworld, so I'd say it's more than a fair trade."

"I like this little Roman," Culhwch said, sheathing his knife.

"Call me Betto. You know, sir, you're choking my friend here."

"Hah! I was just holding him out of the way. I would not let any harm come to my lord Crassus' man, or any Roman, unless ordered." He let me go and shook my shoulder with affection. I think. Then he turned to *dominus*. "If you say there is no shame, I must believe you. Still, my people and I have disrupted your celebration. We will go." The tension was leeching rapidly from the area.

"There's no need for that," Crassus said, but he was using his oratorical voice.

Betto, sensing his work was not quite yet done, turned to Taog and poked him several times in the stomach. "You understand, *dominus*," he said, "I refrained from committing violence upon this fellow, it being a party and all. You behave yourself from now on, you hear? This is the house of Crassus; you remember that next time." The grey-eyed giant looked down at Betto. He knew exactly what the little soldier had done, and laughed with closed lips, a sound like a boulder thrown down a flight of stairs.

Crassus smiled. "I thank you for your forbearance, Flavius. Come to my office tomorrow morning, when you're not on duty."

"Yes, *dominus*." When Betto left our lord's *tablinum* the following day, he would find himself a thousand *sesterces* richer.

"Hah! A country of comedians," Culhwch said, shaking his head. "How we ever let you beat us." His smile disappeared when he looked at Brenus, still standing near the wall that displayed the glowing family death masks. Culhwch pointed a finger at his son and

187

said, "I've had enough of you for one night." He paid his respects to Crassus, ignored Tertulla and made for the door. Hanno pushed away from me and hobbled to the wall of shoes. In no time Culhwch was putting on his boots, which frankly would not have been that difficult to find, even with eyes shut.

"Make the sign, boy." Hanno formed two interlocking circles with his four remaining fingers.

"Hmph. So it's true." The Celt left without another word.

"He cannot bear the thought," Brenus explained, "that my heart lies with the priesthood, not with soldiering." The crowd was leaking away like air from a bladder, drawn to other entertainments, of which Crassus had provided many, though none as thrilling as the prospect of unscheduled violence.

"Are you a Druid then?" I asked, so intrigued that I had spoken without permission.

"An initiate, yes," he said, delicately dabbing with a fringed *orarium* at the yellow and purple lump that was his nose. "I saw the child standing with his four fingers thus, making interlinking circles; this is the sign of Lugos. I knew that we had been guided to this place; that our destiny did truly lie with your son, our friend and commander. I meant no harm to the boy."

Lady Tertulla walked briskly up to us, her blue eyes flashing—never a good sign. *Dominus* followed close behind. "Then why," she said tersely, "did you not release Hannibal the moment he screamed?"

"I could not, lady. Not until my prayer was said. Your Hannibal is a Godsend, a human talisman of protection and strength."

"What kind of god," *domina* said with disgust, "allows his priests to frighten a harmless child?"

Curio insinuated himself into our group. "Forgive me, *domini*. Titus Lucretius is about to begin his recital in the main atrium."

"In a moment," lady Tertulla said. "We will arrive shortly. Have him wait."

"I didn't do anything wrong?" Hanno whispered, back in the dubious safety of my protection.

"You are a Godsend," Brenus said, moving closer until *domina* held up a wary hand. "We revere you and will serve you if you let us."

Hearing this, Hanno smiled his smile and the entrance hall grew bright.

The small crowd of guards and armed guests, still mistrustful while two Celts remained, stayed within earshot. Betto turned to Malchus, his friend visibly relieved as he sheathed Camilla. "Nice work," Malchus said.

Betto muttered, "I had to inhale the breath of Cerberus so we could discover Hannibal's a good luck charm?"

"Be thankful," Malchus said, eyeing Taog warily, "that the giant left you with a nose, and your head."

"I have heard of these Celtic gods and their Druid priests," Crassus was saying. "They build wicker prisons in the shape of giant men, twenty feet tall. When they are victorious in battle, they crowd their captives within and set the entire structure alight."

"Lugos must receive our gratitude, or we will fall from his favor. We serve our god. When you parade your tortured, captured kings, slaughter your enemies and take them for slaves, what god do you glorify?"

"You disgust me," Tertulla said. "Marcus, I do no want these people in our home."

"I swear, no harm shall come to the boy from us," Brenus said. "If you allow it, I will share my heartwall to insure his protection."

"We shall see," Crassus said. "For now, I think it best that you retire."

One of the young men who stood beside Malchus ready to defend the city's patriarch was a brooding, beardless, light-haired man of thirty. In the days to come, I would see his knit brows often, furrowed as frequently in concentration as in consternation, and would learn to respect his counsel. His name was Gaius Cassius Longinus. Julius Caesar would come to know him as well.

CHAPTER XV

55 BCE - SPRING, ROME

Year of the consulship of
Gnaeus Pompeius Magnus and Marcus Licinius Crassus

I was not present for my lord's investiture as consul, nor could I have been. Should any person not a senator, least of all a slave, enter the *curia* while in session, civic deliberations must by law cease immediately. The moment he took his office and sat in one of the senate's two curule chairs (Pompeius was yet abroad, returning from his mission to secure new and more reliable grain contracts), *dominus* proceeded openly with his plans to leave both his newly won post and the city as soon as preparations could be completed. He was beset by friends and adversaries, *optimates* and *populares*, calling for him to reconsider this precipitous, not to mention illegal plan. He ignored them all.

Publius was brought into his counsel, but was never told the true reason for his father's obsession. Crassus was rightly afraid that if he knew, he could not be restrained from assassinating Caesar himself. But that was not *dominus'* plan. All Publius knew was that his father was intent on making war for the glory of Rome. The young legate's eyes glittered at the prospect as he said, "Gaul is cold and wet, and I have no desire to suffer more of the same in Briton. Father, enough of stories. Let me demonstrate in Parthia with lance and sword the qualities of which your son is made."

In his office, Crassus paused before speaking, emotion clogging his throat. "No father could be more proud than I. But is such a thing possible? Caesar will never release you."

"Release? I am practically my own man in Gaul. Caesar is but half its conqueror, his letters to the senate notwithstanding. I tell you truly, and I make no boast, I have done more with one legion than he has with six. Did he guide my hand while I conquered all Armorica? Where was he during my conquest of Aquitania? The war against Ariovistus, King of Germania, would have gone quite differently for our legions had not my cavalry charge broke the enemy lines and dispersed them in disarray. 120,000 heathens learned their final lesson that day. What a fine sight to see what was left of their ranks fleeing back across the Rhine, their tails tucked beneath their hairy behinds. Now don't misunderstand me, Father," Publius said, "Caesar is a decent general. For an old man."

"Do not discount the wisdom of age and experience, my young hero."

"Father, for age, I shall rely on *you*, but for experience, you must admit no commander twice my age has more."

"I certainly can think of none with more self-confidence. Well then, we shall make a fine pair of generals, old and young. But how will you get away? I must sail before the end of the year. Gabinius, the man I am replacing in Syria, would like nothing better than to lay claim to Parthia; we must make haste."

"Why worry?" Publius said. "If he is but a governor and no king, let him try. According to Caesar, Parthia will still be ours for the taking when your Gabinius fails."

"I'd rather not give him the opportunity, despite Caesar's confidence in the Sibyl. You and I are true kings—rulers of our own destinies. We cannot help but succeed. But you have not answered my question."

"If you let your dog run without a leash, you cannot blame the dog if it runs away."

Crassus swept a grey lock from his forehead. "I don't follow."

I said, "You strike me, young master, as more wolf than cur."

The old Publius would have winked at me. The new Publius glanced at me sideways, a rebuke for interrupting. He continued to his father, "I am practically autonomous in Gaul. My men follow me, not Caesar. I will return to Gaul and make my peace with him; honor demands it. But as I pass through the north, I will tarry. There are thousands of Pompeius' men breaking their backs in rocky fields, as suited to farming as a whore is to marriage. One whisper in their ears of a march to glory and you will hear the sound of scythes dropping and sword belts tightening from Vercellae to Ravenna. By summer's end you'll have enough men marshaled on the Campus Martius to conquer a dozen Parthias."

"One is all that I require."

"Master! Father Jupiter! Look at me!" Hanno shouted, galloping past the entrance to Crassus' *tablinum* on the shoulders of the Celtic giant, Taog.

"Hannibal! Taog!" I snapped. "What are you doing here?"

"It's all right," Crassus said. "Your mistress is visiting lady Cornelia today."

"Play outside, then. Where's Brenus?"

"In the workshop," Taog said, making a final turn around the *impluvium* before ducking carefully through the atrium doorway.

"Father Jupiter?" Publius said, his eyebrows reaching for the black curls of his hairline.

"It's nothing," Crassus said, reddening. "The boy is tainted."

"I can't get him to stop calling me master, either," I added. To Publius, the explanation was insufficient. "I have told Hannibal over and over again that *dominus* is master, not I. With his muddled logic, he reasons that if I am, well, who I am, then *dominus* must be a god."

"And neither of you did anything to discourage this?"

"A little," Crassus said, avoiding his son's eyes. "Let the lad have his delusions. I don't mind, really."

"No, I'm sure you don't," Publius said, then burst out laughing.

"Once Hannibal gets an idea in his head…" I said, my voice trailing off to wherever feeble excuses go to die.

"Oh this is rich," Publius said. "Why didn't you bring the thing out at the party? Have you taught him to sing or do a little lopsided dance?"

"Shall we get back to the matter at hand?" Crassus said.

Publius composed himself, barely. "Yes, of course. Forgive me." He cleared his throat. "Do you remember Cassius Longinus?"

"He attended your party, ready to use his dagger for more than spearing fruit, as I recall."

"That's the man." Publius pressed his lips together as if trying to prevent something from escaping. "Wait a moment!" he blurted. "If you are Jove, and Mother is Juno, then I must be Mars Invictus!"

"Yes, that's quite droll, Publius. Just let us know when you've finished reciting the panoply."

"All right, all right," he said, holding up his hand. "Yes, Cassius." He took a deep breath, calming himself. "He's a good man. With your permission, I will approach him and ask him to join us. He is ambitious; he told me he feels held back, as well he might under Caesar's command."

"How do you know him?"

"He came down with me from Gaul. I met him years ago at Cicero's. I know, I know — Tully is not your favorite exemplar of Roman resolve, but he has always been kind to me." Crassus gave his son a stern but less than withering look. "To the point," Publius continued, "Cassius had just returned from Rhodes and was invited to one of Cicero's study sessions comparing the Academy Skeptics to the Stoics. You talk about your drunken confederacy of dissolute whoremongers, well…" *Dominus* and I stared blankly at Publius; after a moment he shook his head and continued, as much disappointed with his audience as we were with his japes. "That's where we met. Cassius enlisted with the 7th and I've known him ever since. He's trustworthy, a good soldier and strategist. If he accepts the commission, I'll have him levy the troops, get them mustered in the south, and I'll join you as soon as I am able."

•••

Thus it was decided. But before he returned to Caesar, *dominus* helped pave the way for his son to climb the ancient, revered, but ofttimes ignored political ladder whose ascent was assured by his victories in Gaul. He was too young to become *quaestor*, the first official post in the *cursus honorum* (the position had a minimum age requirement of 30), but his father had him stand for two other respectable posts to start him on his way. He was elected almost unanimously to both.

Only one golden link remained to be forged: though young for his military prowess, Publius was beyond the age when wealthy Romans traditionally found an advantageous pairing for their male children. His sojourn in Gaul had postponed any thoughts of women beyond fleeting, forgettable couplings with camp followers and local whores. Returned to Rome, the boy who never once stared with trembling lower lip into the abyss of want continued his uncanny good fortune as a man. Publius was one of those rare individuals upon whom the gods never frowned, despite his arrogance and presumption. It was not that he expected through the privilege of his birth that good things must always come his way, for that would require contemplation of desire denied. Publius Crassus lived from one perfect moment to the next, heedless of the wonder of his charmed life. Once he crossed the *pomerium*, Eros was armed and ready for him the moment he leapt from his horse.

Priests were engaged to inspect with meticulous scrutiny the steaming entrails of an unwilling pig, whereupon they made their pronouncement. The entire month of Maius was rejected as unacceptable, that being the time reserved for making offerings to the dead. Which was a happy coincidence, because most senators fled to their country estates for the six-week recess beginning in mid-Aprilis. Not Crassus. Not this year. The priests chose a bright, auspicious day in early Junius, just before Publius was scheduled to depart Rome for the north. His marriage to a most willing Cornelia Metella would be the event of the season. And of course, she was the perfect match.

•••

The day after Hanno and Taog had interrupted our meeting with Publius, the boy and I were sorting the mail into piles: legal, political, supplications and personal. As it did every day, legal had the largest mound, followed by political argument, then requests for everything from money to land. There was one interesting application from one Gaius Octavius, a legate who had fought with Lucullus against Mithridates, king of Pontus. He was the first of several experienced military officers anxious to join this most public of Crassus' secrets, the expedition to Parthia.

I left my office and with Hanno in tow walked to the next one down the hall, the large but spare *tablinum* of my master, who was at the *curia* in session with the senate. Before I could lay the letter on *dominus'* table, we were intercepted by Brenus, who was smiling like a father. Hanno ran to him and said, "Is it done? Is it?"

"It is indeed, young master."

"I am not master. Master is master." Hanno laughed, coaxing smiles from us as easily as one would pluck a daisy.

"Here," Brenus said, handing the boy an oilcloth chunky with its contents. "Try them on." The Celt's broken nose had shrunk to something recognizable as such, and the colors were fading beneath his freckles.

Hanno fumbled with the string and finally extracted two strange-looking gloves. Brenus helped him get them on his hands with difficulty, Hanno was so jumpy with anticipation.

"Surprise! Surprise, master!" he said, waving what appeared to be a set of brown leather, two-fingered gloves. The pinky fingers were absent, but the thumb looked normal enough. It was the middle finger arrangement that drew the eye, as if the three fingers adjacent to thumb had been fused into one broad digit. Hanno put both hands so close to my face I had to back up to focus on them. He was flexing the middle "fingers," which bent in an almost natural motion. "See? See, master, see? Hannibal has all his hands now." He turned and flung himself into Brenus' arms and hugged him in that fierce way he had.

"It's all right lad," Culhwch's son said, patting Hanno on the head. "You go an practice with 'em and don't worry, I've made an extra pair just in case."

Watching the boy dance away, waving his new prosthetic, I said, "That's a fine piece of work, Brenus. How did you do it?"

"He slips his third finger into a ring; when he pulls down on it, it carries with it articulating blocks of wood inside the leather attached here, and here. He will not have the same grip as real fingers, of course, but with practice, it should help him grasp objects with more ease."

"You've just made a friend for life."

"The boy is holy," Brenus said. "Lugos commands we watch over him."

"Surely not you personally?"

"He makes the sign."

"Yes, I have seen it. If Hanno could choose between the sign and six more fingers, you would find nothing in him to revere."

Brenus spoke as if I were a child. "Use your eyes, Alexander. The choice has already been made. The boy belongs to Lugos."

"What you see is coincidence, not religion. Look around you, Brenus. Hanno is quite well-looked after right where he is."

"You are not Druid."

"No, we are not. If the sign is so important to you, why then did you give him those gloves to cover it up?"

"A man may wear shoes and still know he has feet."

I sighed. "Understand, everyone recognizes that you and Taog have been very kind to Hanno. You have befriended him and made him very happy. He is fond of both of you. He talks of little else. But be reasonable, Brenus, you cannot seriously be suggesting he'd be better off with you?"

"We would protect him."

"No. Where you are going, there will be war. Not even your gods are powerful enough to guarantee his safety. On the battlefield, only one god decides who lives and who dies. His name is Chaos, and he is heartless and inconstant. But here, in Rome, another god holds sway: he is Crassus, and in his house, he alone can keep Hanno safe."

•••

One morning the following week, Tertulla came to me almost frantic. She could not find Hanno. Leaving her with promises that calmed her like sleet on snow, I gathered help and searched the house. When he was not found, I asked Betto if the Celts were drilling. "They're up on the

Campus, shattering decent Romans' nerves with the din from their chariots. I've been telling myself that the roaring in my ears is from the bath water that lodged itself there yesterday, but it just might be the sound of their wheels crashing around in my head. They're wasting their time, if you ask me. Are you asking me? I'll tell you anyway. Has anyone told them where we're going? I can't wait to see what happens when those chariots drive through a foot of sand."

"A simple 'yes' would have sufficed."

"I don't think it would have, no."

"So, you're coming with us to Syria, and beyond?"

"Do I have a choice?"

"Well, I shall enjoy your company."

"What a relief, Alexander. I wouldn't be tagging along if I knew you weren't coming. We'll plan a picnic every day. I expect I'll have nothing to do anyway but lay about and take the Mesopotamian sun."

"Good. You could use some color. By the way, lord Publius informed me the Celts will be horsed, not in chariots, so there is one less thing for you to worry about." I turned toward the front entrance.

"I'll find something to replace it, don't *you* worry. If you're going up there, bring some wax for your ears. Though I doubt cruel Ulysses himself could keep that unholy racket from driving his ship up onto the rocks." I decided to ignore the flaw in Betto's metaphor: Odysseus would be unlikely to encounter a Celtic chariot on the waves, and if he did, it would only be for a moment.

I found my quarry sitting on the edge of the track of the Circus Flaminius, snug, happy and lost in Taog's enormous lap. At last I could look down on the giant Celt. Barely. Hanno was playing a game he had invented himself. He would rummage through my garbage—repository of the best pieces of discarded parchment—find a draft or an invoice and mash it up into a ball. Then he'd toss the missile between one hand and the other and pull the blocks in his glove at just the right moment to create a makeshift pocket in which to snag the projectile. He was becoming quite good at it.

Betto was right about the noise. Imagine that this entire conversation was shouted.

"Master! We're resting." Hanno threw a crumpled old requisition high over his head and plucked it deftly from the air before it hit the ground. Taog and I applauded. As did Hanno.

"So I see. Are you having fun?"

"Oh my, yes! Brenus took me for a ride in a chariot! I was scared but then I wasn't, but then we had to stop because Brenus' father's face got red. Do you know what Taog told me? He said his people get buried in the ground when they die and all their stuff goes into the hole with them so they can use it in the afternoon."

"Afterlife," Taog said, tussling the boy's head. If anyone was carrying on a conversation in the halls of Olympus, Taog's voice was how I imagined they would sound. Minus the accent, of course.

"And if they're good, they get to come back and live again."

"That's right," said Taog. He began tightening the laces on Hanno's gloves.

"That is a fascinating concept," I said as enthusiastically as I could.

"That's what I want to do. Can I, master? I want to die and come back as someone else."

"Who would like to come back as, little warrior," the big Celt asked.

"It doesn't matter. Anyone else is fine."

"I think you should stay with us for awhile longer," I said. "You're far too much fun to have around."

"I know. How much longer can I stay?"

"As long as you like. I know for a fact that Lady Tertulla has been looking for you. Why don't we walk down together? I think she may have a treat for you."

"Bye, Taog," Hanno said, climbing out of the Celt's lap. "There's Brenus! Look at him go! Taog is too big to drive the chariot. I can't make the sign with my gloves on. But we can pretend." He pressed his hands together and bowed his head. "Watch over others," he began.

"As Lugos watches over you," Taog finished. He also bowed and linked his fingers. I don't know what came over me, but I too made the sign, spoke the opening words and bowed my head toward Taog. He finished the prayer, but before his expression of wonder could fully form, I had already turned with Hanno in hand to walk back down the hill.

•••

On the last morning of Februarius, Hanno ran to tell me between gasps that the clinic had been closed for the day. As soon as Crassus finished with me, I walked quickly down the path to the front of the estate. There, the thick walls that kept the *familia* separate and ignorant of the travails of the human swarm below also housed our school and clinic. The sun was just about to break over the hills.

"I knew you would be here the moment you heard," Livia said. She lay on the *lectus* in her small room, pale and lovely. "Take that look from your face and come sit by me." I did as I was told. There was a sour smell in the room and a cloth-covered pail by her bedside. Livia took a sprig of mint from a vase by her nightstand and held my hand while she chewed it thoroughly. Then she lifted the cloth and spit the remainder into the pail.

"I'm not ill. Here, feel. Gently." She guided my hands to her breasts and I felt their swollen weight. "Now," she said, pulling me to her, "come kiss the mother of your child."

Is it manly to cry at such joy? Why should grief be the only beneficiary of our tears? After all we had endured, there were salted drops enough that fell for sadness. I bathed my *vulpecula's* cheeks with my happiness and did my best to balance the scales. We laughed between caresses and whispered breathless words of affection to mouth, eyelash and ear, but soon there was only one way remaining to express the distillation of a thousand lyric poems. I pulled away from her and asked with insistent eyes. She nodded once and raised her tunic. We were soon lost in a place we hoped never to be found. The sounds we made we did not hear. We were so close, yet still apart, maddened by the atoms that kept us separate. At last, even ecstasy flew apart and we disappeared entirely, blown into a space without thought or boundary or time. At the end, when I found myself in myself again, Livia was there to meet me, breathless and smiling. We lay quietly, holding each other, listening as the sounds of the world slowly became real again. Having gone to that emptiness together, it felt almost sad to return.

•••

Slaves are forbidden to marry. They may form a *contubernium* if the master permits, they may cohabitate, have children, live the simulacrum of a life. When I came

203

to him in his office with the request and the news of Livia's pregnancy, Crassus rose from his chair and came around his desk. I thought he was going to shake my hand, but he held me by the shoulders, told me I deserved every happiness, then embraced me like a brother. I blinked with surprise and suppressed pride. When he finally released me, his lips were pressed together in a tight smile and his eyes were shining. He rummaged through the clutter that surrounded his work space, but finally beaten, told me to take 25,000 sesterces for myself from the treasury. It wasn't as if I did not know where the money was stored. I complained of his generosity, to which he responded it was worth every *as* to see an end to the pining he had had to endure for years.

With his wealth and the number of slaves already in his employ, another mouth to feed meant nothing to Crassus. His happiness for both Livia and myself was unsullied by greed. Not so with almost every other Roman slave owner, by which I mean practically every Roman citizen or freeborn. Even soldiers taking up the non-military life see that their "wives" have at least one, two if they can afford it. The more slaves, the more status. Coupling and procreation by their property is not only permitted but encouraged, for who would not be pleased to get something for nothing. Every child of a slave is born into that same condition, with no rights or property save those given them by the generosity of their masters. Anyone fortunate enough to own a mating pair of slaves is further gratified by the fact that, considering the foreign captives trudging to Rome each year by the thousands, they will be increasing their household with one whose native tongue will be Latin.

Malchus and Betto had conspired to have crafted a gift they were wise enough to present to me when Livia was absent. It was a set of six throwing knives and a supple leather belt to sheathe them. To Livia, they gave a pair of gold earrings with drops of carnelian swinging from gold strands. She thanked them from her heart, but chided that this was not a gift for both of us. While Malchus was saying that I had only to see her wearing them to know they were as much a gift for me as for Livia, at the same time Betto said that this was as much as they could afford. It is surprising that, considering the number of times Malchus has slapped his friend on the back of the head, Betto has not developed a bald spot.

With her husband's permission, Tertulla gave us the most stunning gift: a week at their summer villa in Baiae, with no responsibilities or duties other than those small and gracious labors of affection we chose to give to each other every waking moment of each day. Of the nights, suffice to say that Livia was a patient teacher, and I an willing and adventurous student. In our absence, Eirene had eagerly volunteered to watch over Hanno and he, in turn, was not unhappy to share her little *cubiculum* with her until our return. Her fondness for him was genuine, to which the boy readily responded.

While we were gone, I never gave Lucius Curio a single thought. Not even once.

Upon our return, Livia moved her things into my quarters. Most of her trinkets were Egyptian. I was especially fond of her beaded collars and anklets. By 'fond,' I mean they stirred something base and primal within me, and I am at a loss to explain it. One of the myriad lessons Livia taught me was that some things lend themselves better to experience than understanding.

Knowing my taste in this, she would sometimes greet me in bed wearing nothing but a necklace of nephrite lozenges, strung tight about her neck, and a gold anklet above her painted toes. This was the playful Livia, not the workaday version. Her preference was to wear no adornment, but the Egyptians were renowned in the arts of arousal, and during her years there, Livia had learned them all, and learned them well. It was not my place to ask how, or with whom. Or to think about it over much.

I could not wait till Livia and I could share a cup of wine, hold hands and speak of how the day had gone. It became ritual for me to watch her unbind her hair and comb its lengths made gold-red by the lamplight. I sat mesmerized on our bed. She would call me a romantic fool, and I would ask her, who of us, then, was the greater fool, the besotted lover, or the woman who loves him? Waking in the luxuriant stretch of her arms was a miracle that to my amazement, repeated itself each morning. Romans may not have called our pairing a marriage, but it was that in every way but name. We knew that Crassus would never dream of it, but he could, if he was of a mind, sell either one of us at any time. Even though the threat was virtually non-existent, its lesson was clear: life is tenuous, joy is fleeting. Who knew this better than we? Some nights when we made love, we found that we could weave 'forever' from one timeless moment to the next. It was enough. It had to be.

The spring of our *contubernium* was a time I shall always think upon as a gift beyond all measure; I had never been as happy or content. Yes, I was aware that had I not been enslaved Livia and I would never have met, never fallen in love, never created a child together. The irony of my circumstance would prod me from time to time, but I was quick to let it go. What did it matter? Had I any choice in the matter, would I sacrifice my freedom to spend even five such bliss-filled days with this woman. I would. I swear that I would.

There were no clouds to mar this bright bliss, save for the growing shadow caused by my lord's preparations to make his vengeful war. Many were the times that Crassus would be forced to rap his knuckles on the table to rouse me from a daydream, but he was rarely cross and most always playful. I think he saw in us something of the way he and Tertulla used to be before Luca. He could confide in no one, for even Piso was more ally than friend, and the political risks, to say nothing of the personal shame, were too great. I yearned to offer him a place to unburden himself, to be the ear he could find nowhere else. But each of us had our roles. And we would play them until the end.

CHAPTER XVI

55 BCE - SPRING, ROME

Year of the consulship of
Gnaeus Pompeius Magnus and Marcus Licinius Crassus

T wo events occurred in early Aprilis which I feel compelled to relate. Each goes some way toward comprehending, if not excusing, the unfortunate events that follow. Were this chronicle to be remembered...Forgive me. I leap—a performance restricted to pen and ink for this ancient of 86 years—I leap ahead to the present day, to our island refuge to pause for just a moment. Here I sit, scrawling for no one's amusement but my own, hilly knuckles clutching a fresh reed pen, soon to join his countless, splintered brothers in the trash. The previous conceit has caused me to laugh out loud, but that happy noise has quickly resolved itself into a fit of coughing that has turned my grizzled face crimson. My mind wanders; it is this heat. As I was saying, if I *were* to be remembered, it would be as a master of understatement: 'unfortunate events' indeed. You see? It only takes the lapse of three and a half decades and a decaying mind to make plains of the memories that once were mountains.

Pan's hoof. I seem to have worn myself out. Perhaps a short nap, then I shall begin again.

•••

There is a bowl of figs by my hand. I do not know how it got there.

•••

Since my arrival in Rome, I have had many opportunities to wonder if compassion's opposite is cruelty, or to reflect whether or not indifference would serve as a better black to its white. Do you recall how Curio had vanished from my mind while Livia and I dallied in Baiae? Why must there always be a price to pay for every indulgence, and why must it so often be withdrawn from the bankrupt accounts of the innocent?

We returned late to the city. The house was quiet. Livia fell to our couch without unpacking and was instantly asleep. Her mind and body were at rest, one untroubled, the other exhausted. My mind and body, as so often was the case, were at odds, and sleep would not come. I walked through the darkened house, scratching lists onto a wax tablet. Finding myself in the servants' wing, I saw a light. I knocked lightly on the wall beside the portiere and a voice said 'enter.' I pulled the curtain aside to see Hanno on his knees fellating Lucius Curio.

"Hanno," I said, the word half-choked on the revulsion that filled my head and pushed itself hot and wet out my eyes. "Come here."

"Oh, really," Curio tsked. "Must you?"

"Master!" Hanno flew to me. I caressed his hair, adjusted his head band and told him to return to Eirene's quarters. I would see him first thing in the morning. Taking two long strides to stand directly before my assistant, I slapped him hard. His head snapped sideways.

"How dare you?!" Curio cried, incensed.

With the back of my hand, I slapped his other cheek. He recovered, keeping his hands at his sides, but his cheeks flamed from far more than the sting of my hand. "I see," he said. "I did not realize your claim was exclusive."

I hit him again, struggling to keep from making a fist.

"You cannot blame me, now that you have somewhere else to spill your seed…"

The backhand was harder this time. Much harder. Curio almost lost his balance. When he righted himself, he held the back of his own hand against the corner of his bleeding lip. He said, his voice low, "You will pay for this, slave."

A guard appeared in the doorway, surrounded by other sleepers roused by the noise.

"Leave us. Pull the drapes," I commanded.

They withdrew, but I knew they would be listening intently just down the hallway. I reached behind me, and as I pulled the blade from the hidden sheathe in my tunic, I whispered, "The fault is mine, Lucius Curio."

"Are you mad?" he said indignantly. "You cannot carry a weapon!"

"*Familia* will never be to you what it means to us."

I put my left hand on his chest and pushed him back upon his sleeping couch, then fell upon him, my thighs straddling his chest. His head was bent up against the wall. I put the blade against his neck and my mouth close by his ear.

"Touch the boy again," I whispered, "and you will watch the last of your life's blood wash these tiles."

"You have no idea what is happening here, do you? Get off me. Do you think your years of service have earned you a dram of *anything* more than you had the day you came to this house? You are a fool, no better than that deformity I use to pleasure myself. Now leave me. I have a busy day tomorrow."

In the morning, we were both summoned. Crassus would hear no complaint from either of us. He advised Curio that while it may have been different with Piso, though he doubted it, under his roof, it was the practice to engage in sex solely with consenting partners. Children under twelve and individuals unaware they were engaging in sexual activity were not to be approached. He enjoined me from disturbing the sleep of the *familia*. And that was all.

•••

The average Roman, I have found, has a strong stomach and a hard heart. By day they are robbed and bullied, hounded by hunger; they take advantage lest they be taken advantage of. By night they cower, shut in their tiny rooms at sunset, prisoners deafened by the wagon wheels of commerce until the dawn makes the treacherous streets safe again. They wilt in summer's heat and shiver in winter's rain. They watch unending yet unequal streams of misguided country cousins and newly-minted slaves trickle into the city each day, one lot to seek their fortune, the other to see its end. They live in overcrowded apartments, beset by poverty, crime and disease. But this is their Rome, the greatest achievement in the history of mankind! How is it that their senses can deceive them so?

Rome is a hollow place, and the people are cruel. I have seen it all firsthand, from their conquering armies to their stolen culture, from their marvelous engineering to their addiction to superstition and fear. But I had never yet seen anything like this. Why do I post this footnote to my tale? For it is nothing more than that. One Roman may be kind, a dozen forgiving, perhaps, but put them together by the thousands and they become the slavering Beast, their better selves subsumed by the riotous appetite of the mob. In all my time in Rome, never before had I seen compassion from the masses, and I believe that because we would soon be on our way to war, where mercy is unwise and kindness has no place, it is incumbent upon me to admit that once before I left this city, never to return, I was witness to its existence, however fleeting.

It was the festival of the Veneralia, honoring Venus Verticordia, the changer of hearts. Apparently, by purifying themselves in the men's baths while wearing nothing but a myrtle wreath while drinking a concoction of crushed poppy flowers, milk and honey, a woman's prayers would be heard by Virile Fortune. Satisfied by their offerings and ministrations, this forgiving god would then agree to conceal any physical blemish or abnormality from sight. I think it more likely that the potion itself obliterated any perceived unsightliness, or at least the minding of it. You may imagine that on this annual day of devotion, congregations of naked, drugged, bathing females were followed about by throngs of young men and boys eager to make new friends.

Not so this year, not on this day. For this was the five-day dedication of the Theater of Pompeius. The general, having finally returned to the city to accept his consulship, was resplendent in the gold wreath and embroidered toga that this gift to the people entitled him to wear. To celebrate, he had conceived of entertainments that designed to put his name on the lips of every Roman for months to come, for eternity if Pompeius' prayers were answered. You, who find these scrolls, will know if Magnus got his wish.

The first four days of games were conducted in the Circus Maximus, a more appropriate setting than the theater for the hunting and slaughter of five hundred Gaetulian lions, all male, some as long as ten feet from nose to tail and weighing five hundred pounds. At least Livia was allowed to remain at the clinic, claiming her stomach was in a delicate enough condition without such entertainment, even though she expected to see no customers. Low barriers of shrubbery meandered throughout the track, simulating the wilds of the north African plain. Having been starved in their cages, the black-maned cats were released in the Circus, angry and bewildered, at the rate of about twenty an hour. There they were speared, beleaguered by darts and shot through with arrows until the day's light faded with the roaring of the crowd. For variety, when it appeared the people might grow bored, four hundred and ten panthers, seen by many spectators for the first time in their lives, were put on display, then butchered.

How it was that tens of thousands of everyday citizens — tradesmen, husbands and wives, families out for a picnic, munching on snacks and sipping drinks — how was it that these Romans could watch the staged executions, hour after hour, their eyes never tiring of the bloodletting? I could not find a way to comprehend this. That is, until *dominus* explained it to me. Here, he told me, a spectacle is made of the art of the symbolic. Each ferocious beast represents the wild and untamed world threatening the peace and prosperity thriving within our borders. The hunter, armored and armed, is Rome. At the end of the day, as the bloody corpses of our "enemies" were dragged from the field, every citizen, regardless of station, could feel vicariously the exhilaration of victory, could walk hand-in-hand with his children back home to a meager supper, proud that Rome had once again metaphorically triumphed over an uncivilized world.

Remarkable.

We came to the fifth and final day of the festivities. The highlight of the inauguration was to be presented within the theater itself. Faintly nauseous, my heart thumping in my stomach from having had to endure these allegorical massacres, I followed *dominus* and *domina* up to the Campus Martius. I prayed silently to no god in particular that the smaller venue might actually afford the kind of theater an enlightened Greek was accustomed to attend. Thirty years in Rome, and I had yet to learn my lesson.

Until now, there had been no permanent theater in the great city; such a thing would be considered vulgar. The people loved a good show, but censors and senators, arthritic in both limb and righteousness, found them unhealthy and indecent for the general welfare. They were outlawed within the city walls. This from an aristocracy who bred gladiators to shed their bright blood and fed criminals to wild beasts for the amusement of the cheering crowd.

Romans, and actors in particular, being nothing if not resourceful, were not to be denied. Thespians and the backers seeking to supply what was already in great demand resorted to building temporary stages for their performances of Greek favorites, mime and ribald comedies rich with sexual innuendo. These wooden structures were only meant to last a matter of weeks before being dismantled, if they did not collapse before then. Soon they would spread again like weeds in some other part of the city.

Pompeius had constructed something else entirely. Its massive square blocks of tuff and travertine, supported by giant concrete vaults, its gardens, temples and amphitheater, these had never been seen before, nor is their equal ever likely to rise above any city's outline.

Some say it was to impress Julia, Caesar's daughter, whose marriage of the past four years had helped bind one general to the other. But she, being of refined sensibilities, would rarely attend. Others, like my lord, contend it was to regain his popularity, frittered away in the years since his military victories, replaced by nothing more spectacular than marrying a girl less than half his age. Whatever the reason, Pompeius' pride was bruised by the inattention. As a Roman, he should have known that the people's memory is as short as the hairs on his shaven chin. Pompeius was like a man who, before he leaves on a long journey, lights the lamps in all his rooms and is surprised to return to a darkened house. Romans, like oil lamps, need constant attention and frequent replenishment.

We already know where it stands, adjacent to the Circus Flaminius up on the Campus Martius where I exercised and learned the art of the dagger. Building the first permanent theatrical edifice of stone outside the *pomerium*, Pompeius circumvented the censors' squinting probity. I will be brief, but you must see this monument to one man's insecurity in your mind's eye to better visualize the acts of inhumane cruelty which I shall shortly relate.

The word 'theater' barely does the vast complex justice. First, imagine a rectangle 650 feet by 450 feet.

Attached to the western wall of the theater itself, this was the Portico of Pompeius, a colonnaded garden lined with plane trees, statues and fountains. Visitors could stroll among its shaded lanes during intermissions, make offerings in any of several adjoining temples, purchase food in shops or seek shelter in the columned arcade should it rain. In the center of the Portico's western wall, opposite the great theater, Pompeius built a *curia* where the senate might gravitate to debate, another incentive for moral lenience. The conscript fathers succumbed to the beauty and comfort of the meeting house on many occasions, but only one proved memorable. Within its marbled walls, just shy of eleven years from the celebration of the theater's opening, Julius Caesar would be assassinated at the foot of a larger-than-life statue of Pompeius himself. Neither Crassus nor I were present for the turmoil that followed, for we had escaped the Rome of his dominion and my confinement, each in our separate ways.

Let us continue east into the theater itself. Walking through the rows of red and gold columns that formed the back of the proscenium, we will find ourselves on the 300-foot wide stage. To reach its edge, nearest the audience, we must travel another 60 feet. There we could look up at the great semi-circle of the amphitheater, where Pompeius once again side-stepped censure. Above the highest tiers of seating rose a lavish temple to Venus Victrix, Pompeius' personal deity. This was not a theater, he insisted, but a monument to the goddess. The semi-circle of rows rising to the heavens were not seats; they were steps leading to her home. No one complained in a voice loud enough to overcome the sound of construction, or the cheering of the people once it had opened.

At its highest point, the golden statues on the tiled roof of the temple looked down upon the performances from a height of 150 feet. But our attention must tumble to the floor of this architectural masterpiece, to the smaller arc of the orchestra just below the raised stage and directly in front of our seats. Pompeius had spent a fortune on the theater's design and construction. His favor with the people could only soar by such a gift to the public. It should have been so, but Pompeius would find that even the bloodthirsty citizens of Rome have their limits.

(Editor's note: illustrations of the theater may be seen in the glossary under "Theater of Pompeius.")

There was no charge for admission, but seating was limited. Every plebeian was required to present a clay ticket stamped on one side with a likeness of the great general so kind in execution he was barely recognizable, on the reverse with an image of his pretty, young wife. (When speaking of Pompeius' spouse, these two adjectives almost always preceded the noun.) Two weeks before the opening, within a manic 24 hours, the ticket windows were shut and locked, their stock of clay tablets depleted. 25,000 elated citizens would be privy to the final inaugural performances of the greatest theater ever built. Those unfortunates who were denied entrance crowded the street outside the curving walls for the chance of hearing, if not seeing, the spectacle.

On this morning, the plebeian crowd of ticket holders cheered, waiting as senators, patricians and knights filed past them to take their seats. The late morning sun was warm, but not oppressively so. At least not to the lower classes. Crassus and Pompeius paid the price that every senator and person of status must at public events: dressed in their formal togas, their faces were flushed,

217

their bodies damp with perspiration. The heavy wool draping was not meant for spring or summer. But the custom was rigid. The two consuls were almost invisible, surrounded as they were by a small army of *lictors,* twelve guardians assigned to each, jostling to stay near their charges. These two men, who had never seen eye to eye on almost anything, waved amiably to the people, smiling at everyone, even each other. Pompeius had assigned six servants to throw coins over the heads of the *lictors* into the sea of waiting hands waving like kelp fronds. I had chosen a dozen for the task, but Crassus bid me instruct half their number to keep their bags tied. I saw his point.

Crassus cared as much for such entertainments as he did for Pompeius. The man might make a decent merchant, but his ability to govern inside the *pomerium* was universally recognized by those who mattered as staggeringly fairish. When they first shared the consulship fifteen years earlier, they could agree on almost nothing. Pompeius did not understand the workings of the senate, he had flouted the time-honored *cursus honorum* and many senators, including *dominus,* thought him unworthy of his wealth and status. But had Crassus not attended today, the people would have cried out in protest. There must be amity between the city fathers who protected and fed them. Especially these two; now that they had finally taken office, the turmoil must certainly end, mustn't it?

Crassus held his wife's hand, slowly making his way along the arc of the aisle to sit in the first row beside his co-consul, Gnaeus Pompeius Magnus. Above the amphitheater, the vault of the sky was the unbroken blue of a wood thrush's egg. The box of honor was festooned with white and gold banners, golden statuettes and four splendid and imposing guards, one at each corner. The colors of their uniforms matched the cushioned chairs to which *dominus* and *domina* were led, a goblet of spiced wine pressed into their hands almost before they were comfortably seated.

Senators and knights stopped to offer their congratulations before they found their own places. A purple rope designated 300 seats reserved for the conscript fathers. After them, non-senatorial patricians arrived, followed by those of the equestrian class, the knights. These nobles were only slightly less venerable than patricians and therefore markedly more arrogant. They were assigned the fourteen curving rows behind the seating reserved for the senate. As the plebs poured in, the shadow cast by the temple looming high above and directly behind us crept up the travertine rows of benches like a reticent supplicant to the goddess.

"A stunning achievement, Gnaeus," Crassus practically shouted.

"Gratitude, Marcus. With luck, my gift to the people will divert discord and channel harmony back into our streets." *And drown you in a renewed flood of popularity.* "Ciro!" he called to a servant sitting beside me in the row behind the box. "Food for our guests!" He looked over, nodded and said, "Alexander."

"Congratulations, my lord," I said, "on your election to consul for a second term."

"So gratifying to see your solemn Greek face again." He turned back to his guests. "Marcus, you honor your man, bringing him here, but I warn you, there is talk: it is said that if one wants Crassus, one need only seek out Alexander."

"I find his counsel useful."

"Indeed? A shame his station must bar him from our consular deliberations."

"Indeed." In communication, tone is everything. With the way *dominus* delivered that response, one could almost see the insult sailing high above the head of Magnus. If one wanted an unobstructed view, one need only have looked for the smile that played briefly upon *domina's* lips.

"Have you discovered," Pompeius continued, "some invisible thread from the East with which you bind him to your ankle? I hope for your wife's sake you untie him at bedtime." He turned to laugh with whoever had overheard his jest, but was disappointed to find there was no one of consequence within earshot.

"He goes where he is bid," said my lady.

"Truly? Alexander, you are the quintessential servant. Have some wine."

Ciro handed me a cup. I bowed my head in thanks, then toasted both Pompeius and his creation. As I drank, I looked about me. This was one of those moments, more and more infrequent over the years, where I stepped outside myself to see what had become of me. On this day, nowhere in Rome was there a more important place to be, and if that were true, then I was indeed sitting at the very center of the world.

I had lost everything, and what was taken could never be retrieved, yet fate or luck or Melyaket's goddess had brought me to this place, basking just outside the light illuminating these demigods of Rome. I smiled, not because of what even I must admit was my good fortune. Now I had a reason to suffer my servitude. She waited for my return at the place we called home. And what passed between us was ours. We shared it. We owned it. It could not be taken from us.

I turned my attention back to the most powerful *nobiles* in the city. Save for his height, Marcus Crassus had the look of the ideal Roman patrician—his grey hair cropped tight, his eyes clear, his cheeks hollow, his mouth fighting against the gravity of both age and the knowledge of what life has in store for all of us. Even if you're a demigod.

Gnaeus Pompeius Magnus, though younger than my master by nine years, was not faring near as well. He had gained more than a few pounds since I had last seen him on the *rostra*. Touring his several country estates with his wife...I beg your pardon – pretty, young wife...must have agreed with him. Unfortunately, this extra weight, packed into his round face and stubby nose had only served to further pinch his nasal speech. And it did nothing at all to diminish the inevitable, indelicate whispers of porcine disrespect.

"I'm sorry Julia is not here today," Tertulla said. "Is she unwell?"

Pompeius leaned across Crassus. "On the contrary. She *is* feeling poorly, but only because..."

"Oh!" Tertulla said, taking the consul's hand across her husband's lap. "Joyful news!"

"Isn't it wonderful?" Pompeius said. "Julia told me this morning. I am destroyed that she cannot be here to share this moment. This is going to be the best day of all."

The arranged marriage of Caesar's daughter to Pompeius, his fourth and second-to-last, had been born of political need, but despite their difference in age, there was true affection between them which only grew over time. His love for Julia would make Pompeius a laughingstock, but the old general cared not a fig for their jokes and jealousies. Destiny, however, would be unkind, and their union would end tragically. In only three months, violence would erupt at the elections for the *aedile* magistrates. Several people would be killed. Pompeius would intervene unsuccessfully, and in his attempt to separate the parties, would be spattered by blood. His servants would bring him a fresh toga, returning the stained garment to his home. There, Julia would chance to see it. She would become so upset at the sight of it, thinking her husband had been wounded or worse, that she would faint. Landing badly on the hard floor, a few days later she would lose the child. Livia's and Julia's pregnancies must have begun only weeks apart, and we would weep to hear of her sorrow. The following year, she would recover well enough to try again, but she was such a frail creature. She would die in childbirth, and her daughter, seeking the arms of her mother, would follow her to the underworld only a few days later.

I tell you this, not in order to inundate you with yet more tragedy, with which these scrolls already drip, but to make you understand that as this marriage began with politics, so it ended. Julia was one of only two tenuous threads holding the alliance between Pompeius, Caesar and *dominus* together. With Crassus on his way to Syria, the once-tight ball of power that bound these three would be well on its way to unraveling.

•••

Pompeius was a child with a new toy. Unlike most children, myself included, he at least was willing to share. A dozen horn blowers took the stage and sounded a fanfare, while behind them, workers folded the segmented purple curtain and pulled it aside. "You must excuse me," Pompeius said, getting to his feet, his smile plumping his cheeks to the size of ruddy apricots. "The people want to hear from me."

Tertulla leaned over to her husband and as the crowd quieted I caught her saying, "Doesn't he have that the wrong way around?"

I will not bore you with Pompeius' opening speech. It was just another litany of his accomplishments, which the crowd acknowledged politely but with only modest enthusiasm. I have always held that lists of one's triumphs sound considerably more grand and are more likely to be cheered when they are spewed from someone else's mouth. Even if true, when self-touted, achievements are by some arcane mystery less likely to be believed. Humility is the best braggart.

Other than the grain contracts, Pompeius' victories had grown stale with age. This encouraged my master, who became even more convinced the time was right to bring a new province home to the Roman masses, thereby undercutting Caesar's lesser contributions in Gaul. If the rumors of Parthian riches were true, Gaul would seem a paltry conquest by comparison.

The morning was filled with music and gymnastic competitions. When the great tragedian Clodius Aesopus took the stage, the raucous applause multiplied with such amplitude in the acoustically perfect bowl of the amphitheater that I was obliged to hold my hands to my ears. After several soliloquies, the aged actor spied his old friend, Cicero, and called upon him to ascend the stage. While this galled both consuls, there was little to be done about it without appearing ungenerous — they were forced to endure an unscheduled performance by the orator. Cicero, like Aesopus, never missed an opportunity to perform, but he was gracious and blessedly brief,

223

congratulating both Pompeius and Crassus (which visibly annoyed the former) before taking his seat once again.

A small group of players took the stage and spent a moment tuning their instruments. The crowd grew quiet. Then, from the opposite end of the stage, a woman of roughly forty years emerged from between the giant columns so quietly and unobtrusively that the audience, their attention drawn to the greater activity and noise of the musicians, did not notice her entrance. When at last a knot of those in the lower tiers saw her and recognized her, their enthusiasm swept up the curved rows until the entire amphitheater was on its feet. Galeria Copiola, the most famous of all the interlude dancers of the Roman theater had been coaxed out of her six-year retirement by Pompeius. She had given up her art at the height of her abilities, having found that wealth, of which she had accumulated much, was preferable to fame, of which she had had enough. "Better to leave," she is reputed to have said, "to the cry of tears than the outrage of offended jeers." A lesson learned by far too few of the politicians who witnessed her final performance that day.

The interlude dancer provided entertainment while actors and stage hands prepared for the next act in the play, which was always a comedy, since dance and pantomime, especially of Copiola's sprightly energy, did not lend themselves to tragedy. This performer and her talent were so beloved that when she was on the bill, she packed the old wooden theaters regardless of the play being performed. While her performance this day was as memorable as the leaps and twirls of her teens, forgive me while I allow the lady Galeria to lapse back into her early retirement so that I may rush ahead to describe the day's finale.

224

Within moments after her final number, an army of stage hands began to appear between the tall columns at the back of the stage. Each pair of men carried a segment of iron fence, six feet wide by ten feet tall. Three vertical bars were topped by gold-painted spikes and weighted at the base with heavy iron plates. The workers quickly created a barrier about the entire circumference of the orchestra and stage, each segment linked to its neighbor by heavy bolts through each crosspiece. When it was done, Pompeius walked through an open section directly before us, crossed the semi-circle of the orchestra and climbed the stage. He stood inside the enclosure, dwarfed by a fifteen-foot tall statue of Venus draped in fine, green wool, the color of the goddess. The marble likeness smiled down upon him, peering over the bars that separated them.

Someone high up amongst the *plebeians* shouted, "Magnus, the great hunter, has captured himself!"

From the opposite side of the theater, someone else called, "At least the goddess knows on which side of the iron to stand!"

Pompeius, normally one for whom the dimmest star was more discernible than his own inchoate sense of humor, smiled and soldiered on. "On this the final day of dedication of my theater, what goddess better exemplifies the Roman spirit than Venus Victrix, embodiment of both beauty and victory. Today, I place upon the largest altar ever built in her honor a sacrifice of such proportions it will dwarf any offering that has come before.

"The creature *loxodonta africanus pharaoensis* is no stranger to Romans. Our ancestors knew them, fought them, captured them, defeated them. King Pyrrhus brought them to our shores to wage war against us. Your forbears have seen them but two or three times, always on

225

display, docile, chained, paraded about like pets on their leashes." The crowd began to stir, and I, too, had the sinking premonition that there are times when the best seats in the house are those furthest from the stage.

"Today," Pompeius continued, "A story for your grandchildren. You will pass on to them the lesson learned first by Epirus, then by Carthage, both to their undoing: no army, no creature on earth is a match for Rome's indomitable legions! Never before have the monstrous beasts you are about to see fought so close to the city walls. Not until today! I give you…the African War Elephant!" A fanfare sounded while Pompeius crossed back to his seat. As his section of fence was bolted shut behind him, from the shadows of the proscenium, a small, dark and barefoot man, wearing nothing besides a loincloth and a willow switch backed onto the stage. He spoke foreign, halting words and gently tapped his branch on something lingering in the shadows.

"Quick, Ciro, fill my cup." Pompeius turned to *dominus,* noting how his wife clung to him. "Tertulla, there is absolutely nothing to fear. We rehearsed with bears yesterday, and no one received so much as a scratch."

Crassus said, eyeing the few feet between the iron bars and where they sat, "Bears? You might as well have practiced with puppies."

My lady did not look reassured, but even she, like the hushed crowd, was struck by the wonder of the animals being led into the light. The elephants were over ten feet tall at the shoulder, fifteen feet in length, with long, curving white tusks that flanked their drooping trunks. Their ears, thin and veined, were larger than the feathered fans that waved us cool in summer. It should have been the most terrifying site any of us had ever seen, yet their eyes looked out at us with benign intelligence and unutterable sadness. I thought I must be ascribing human feelings to the moist, black orbs which gazed at us, but when the creatures' trainer, having lined nine of the elephants up on the left side of the stage returned to lead the second group out, there was no mistaking the tears that stained *his* dusty cheeks. When all were assembled, he walked up and down the line of eighteen males, reaching up to pat their cheeks, soothing them with lies. As he passed, several of the animals blew gusts of air or raised their trunks to sniff at him.

"Do they not look ridiculous?" Pompeius asked. "They are as brainless as they are massive. I know, for I hunted them in Africa back when Sulla was dictator."

"They look vulnerable," Tertulla said, "but I see no sign of stupidity, nor any indication of aggression. They just stand there."

I could not restrain myself. I leaned forward to our host and said, "Aristotle has studied these creatures. He has called them 'the animal which surpasses all others in wit and mind.'"

"And fierceness," Pompeius said. "And fierceness."

As if having heard us, one of the animals let out a low grumble and swung his trunk to curl it about his neighbor's. Another down the line raised his snout and trumpeted, answered by an exclamation of astonishment that rose as one voice throughout the amphitheater. Many patricians seated in the front rows stood and clambered up the aisles to the laughter of those already seated high up. We held our ground. Pompeius rose to calm the people's fear. "To represent our brave legionaries in today's exhibition, behold the hunters of Gaetulia!"

Behind him, from each side of the stage, eight tall, olive-skinned men costumed in Roman military tunics, sandals and helmets entered the fabricated arena and lined up, their backs to the audience. Their shields were not Roman, but small and round, painted with designs of white and brown. If anyone looked ridiculous, it was they. There was one, nearest Pompeius on the other side of the bars whose bronze helmet bore the black and white plume of an ostrich feather. He, like all the others, balanced a long, smooth lance in his right hand, much different than the Roman shield-piercing *pilum*. The legionary spears were tipped with soft iron, meant to be thrown once to disrupt an enemy's line, bending upon impact lest they be hurled back at our own troops. These African weapons, with their flat, leaf-shaped spearheads were designed for deep penetration.

The gates through which the Gaetulians entered clanged shut, startling the animals. They brayed and bumped into each other, clearly becoming more agitated at the sight of what they recognized as their assailants. Their trainer had retreated to the far right corner where Pompeius had stood before the statue of Venus. The little man leaned with his back against the bars, eyes closed, hands pressed together. I doubted his prayers would be heard.

Several of the animals took a step or two forward on the stage. Others made strange and unsettling sounds. "The people must see we are their masters," Pompeius said, pointing. "Kill them; start with that big one near the end." He turned to Crassus, pointing straight down through the iron fence. "I've had a store of weapons laid in against the wall. Fear not, the hunters will never run out of javelins."

The soldier with the ostrich plume said something to his men and stepped forward. He hefted his spear, calling out to his victim, motioning with his free hand. Stepping forward with his left foot, he threw the javelin with such speed and grace the spear cut the air as if it had been loosed from a bow. The point entered just below the animal's left eye, deftly skirting the armament of muscle and bone to rend the soft center of its life, killing it instantly. Its legs, lifeless pillars, buckled; the corpse crashed to the stage, snapping the spear with a stomach-twisting crack as the creature hit the ground. On both sides of the fallen giant, the animals screamed and side-stepped away in terror. The elephant furthest to the right smashed into the fence with force enough to break several of the iron crosspieces, shoving the marble Venus into the column behind it. The head of the goddess broke and fell, then the body toppled in a crash that sent the animals in a wild-eyed search for safety. The crushed trainer lay in a crumpled, lifeless heap, spared the sight of the carnage to come. Perhaps his prayer had been answered after all.

The audience's cheers were ecstatic.

Rather than charge and retaliate, the elephants appeared desperate to escape. Javelins were now being flung at them by all the hunters. Believing the place where they had entered the arena was the way to their salvation, they bunched about at the rear of the stage, crying out as they pressed against the bars, being wounded all the time in their flanks and legs. Their grunts and cries, pitiful wailing notes were pressed indelibly into every ear. Tertulla turned away. Our eyes met and I could see the water welling brightly in hers. The crowd grew silent, their jubilation extinguished.

Suddenly the elephants turned and rushed away from the rear of the stage, stampeding toward their executioners, stumbling over the bodies of those already dead or dying. At first we could not discern the reason why they reversed direction, but then we saw that men with torches had appeared at the rear of the theater, jabbing with their flames, denying the stars of this last day of celebration their freedom.

"Madness!" Crassus shouted, grabbing his wife. "Stay here, Alexander. Be my witness." They were already up and moving. Truth to tell, had I wanted to flee, my legs would have betrayed me.

The Gaetulians circled round to the right. The elephants, only ten remaining now, ran wildly toward the curving fence, straight at us. Iron had never looked so flimsy. Pompeius crouched horrified, his hands clutching the wreath on his head. His guards and *lictors* huddled about him.

The animals' flanks were exposed, and the hunters loosed a barrage of javelins that thumped and tore into their thick hides. Instinctively fleeing from the source of these new wounds, the victims collided with their brothers, the entire herd smashing headlong into the barrier just beyond us. The fence folded outward over the first rows of seats like a jaw dropping. I saw two men knocked flat and bloody by the iron bars; there may have been more. These were not senators, who had already fled to higher ground, but fools looking for a better view.

Voices rose behind us, a new noise of protest. People were on their feet, demanding that Pompeius stop the killing. When their cries went unanswered, their shouts turned to curses. A cup of wine careened off my shoulder, splashing Magnus's back with scarlet.

One beast separated from his fellows and turned toward the hunters. Blood stained his hide black. His ears flared in defiance; he trumpeted with rage and stumbled forward, cutting off his attackers' retreat. He was driven to his knees, but reaching out with his trunk, snatched a shield from a screaming African and flung it into the stands. It arced high overhead, as if the animal had been trained to perform a trick. His head sank to the ground and the hunter drove his spear into the neck at the base of the elephant's skull. 25,000 groaned as one.

Only five of the original eighteen animals were left alive, all with mortal wounds. They gathered at the front of the orchestra, facing a stunned and horrified crowd, seeming to plead directly with them with raised trunks and cries of the most pitiful nature. The audience jeered the hunters and hurled curses down upon Pompeius. Many stormed from the theater, their tears mingling with vows never to return again. As the remaining elephants' strength gave out, they sank to their knees, their breathing rattled and labored, yet powerful enough to blow dust up to sparkle in the afternoon sun. The hunters approached, spears held high. Incomprehensible shouts of "cowards" and "barbarians" pelted the foreigners from above; the garbage flung down upon them was in a language more easily understood. The chief Gaetulian shook his spear at the Romans, returned their epithets in his throaty tongue and ran to stab the nearest elephant for spite. As he raised his javelin, the animal rose up on his front legs, using the last of his strength in a final attempt to get away. The hunter with the ostrich plume moved in close enough to touch the beast and grabbed his spear with both hands for a killing thrust to the heart. But he was too late. The elephant moaned, one of the saddest sounds I have ever heard, and died. The hunter jerked back to avoid the rolling corpse, but one bare foot was caught by the dead animal as it rolled on its side. Off balance, the headman squealed and jabbered as he fell backwards, kicking with his free leg at the grey wall descending upon him. I could not hear the bones of his legs break, but I could see his eyes bulge like eggs as the lower part of him was squeezed up into the upper half. His countrymen rushed to his aid, pulling his arms to free him from an embrace from which there would be no release. He screeched at them until the wave of his jellied insides pushed their way out his mouth. Then he was silent. It was the first time I had heard the crowd cheer since that same man had killed the first elephant.

While this was happening, Pompeius left the theater, crouching under the shields of his guard, without comment or apology. Eighteen elephants were slaughtered that day, along with any hope that Pompeius' millions had bought the renewed love of the people he had so wished to purchase.

•••

A gladiator crying for succor, running from his opponent would be jeered and reviled; but let that same behavior be exhibited by a herd of lumbering, implausible creatures and the empathy of the crowd is aroused. There is no logic to it, except perhaps this: the elephants could easily have overpowered the hunters and crushed them. That they appeared to spare them, offering their own lives instead, was seen as noble.

Was it this that touched the heart of the ordinary citizen? Was it not the Gaetulians who represented the best of the heroic Roman spirit, but the elephants lying slaughtered on the bloody stage of Pompeius' amphitheater? Would any Roman voice such an admission out loud? I doubt it.

CHAPTER XVII

55 BCE - SUMMER, ROME

Year of the consulship of
Gnaeus Pompeius Magnus and Marcus Licinius Crassus

O ne may develop a taste for jellied eel, and though I personally have never found it appealing, I admit the possibility that, however unlikely, my taste may someday change. I cannot say the same for a steaming plate piled high with confrontation. This dish, I can assure you, I shall never relish. To Livia, it is practically the staff of life.

"Why in the name of Isis," Livia said, "would *dominus* take you to Syria over a trained and experienced healer?"

It was the end of the day. We were in my wife's clinic across from the old schoolroom where I used to teach Latin and Greek. Though Livia was not legally my spouse, we used the words 'husband' and 'wife' whenever we could, in thought and in speech, though not too loudly. Livia was in her six month. I had never seen her look more beautiful. But her demeanor had swung measurably toward what honesty demands I catalog as 'cantankerous.'

Figurative eggshells lay shattered across the floor wherever we tread.

"*Dominus* has a hundred healers. He is a family man. He would not tear a mother from her newborn child."

"Maybe he'll insist we both make the journey."

"Nonsense. Even were you not with child, there is one compelling reason for him to take me and leave you behind."

"I cannot imagine what that might be. No offense, Andros, but I have seen you try to lift a legionary's shield."

"Droll, but off point. I am *dominus*' closest advisor. My effectiveness would be paralyzed were I constantly distracted by worry over your safety."

Livia's eyes narrowed. "I hate how you overturn an argument by saying something sweet. But you see," she said, heading for the larder, "that argument works both ways. Which is why he'll leave you behind and make me his personal *medicus*."

The last patient of the day had left, another satisfied referral from *domina*. The elderly lady with the uncooperative bowels had departed with a paste of macerated melilot and dates. In the sealed jar's place, she had left a sizeable gratuity. While this *peculium* did not legally belong to Livia, Crassus had promised her the same arrangement he had bestowed upon her mother: any money left over from the expenses of running the clinic was hers to keep, to do with as she pleased. Sabina, regrettably, had forfeited all—her money, her freedom and her family when she had been proved guilty of murder. By me. An image of her in the choking dark of Laurion's silver mines would always hang between Livia and me, a noxious cloud. She had forgiven me, but I would never be at peace. Had I made the right choice? Someone much wiser than I would need to be my judge. Until then, I would rely on Livia's absolution. In those days, the only solace I could give myself was to wish her mother the release of an early death.

Livia was cleaning her instruments in a large bowl of water. "What are you doing?" I asked. "What is that you have there?" My curiosity was too fervent to be genuine, but Livia decided to play along.

"Brenus gave it to me." She held up a foamy, grey ball.

"Brenus?" Hanno asked expectantly. He was at the door, sweeping dirt into the street. His gloves were a tremendous help. He almost never dropped the broom. "Where's Brenus?"

"He's gone, dumpling," Livia answered.

"He left with Publius last month. Do you remember?"

"Taog, too?"

"I'm afraid so, Hanno."

"They'll be back," I said. "Don't you worry; you'll see them again."

"When?"

"I don't know. Soon."

"How long till soon?"

"I don't know, Hanno, perhaps in a couple of months?"

"Will I see him tomorrow?"

"No, dumpling, not tomorrow. We'll let you know as soon as we find out. Now let Livia talk to Andros. You're doing a wonderful job with your broom."

"I *am* doing a wonderful job! Thank you!" The smile came back.

"You were saying…"

"I was saying how you are staying and I am going. Now, do you really have any interest at all in this?" She waved the grey ball at me. "It's quite remarkable."

"I'm listening."

She lowered her voice for the first few words. "Our Celtic friend showed me how to make it. It's mostly goat fat and beechwood ash, if you can find it, but any fine ash will do. You mix it with water and it cleans everything, even clothes. He calls it *soap*."

"Remarkable."

"He also claims it makes your hair shiny," she said.

"You've used it on your hair, haven't you? I can tell. You look stunning."

"Don't try to flatter me out of going and thank you."

"Livia is beautiful!" Hanno said.

"Why thank you, dear. You're beautiful, too."

"Yeah!" Hanno dropped the broom and clapped by bumping the heels of his hands together in rapid succession.

"Where are your first gloves, Hanno?" I asked. "Those look newer. They are the second pair, aren't they?"

Hanno nodded. "I don't know." He thought about it hard, and realizing he had no idea where he had left them, his lower lip began to tremble.

"They're probably in our room," Livia said. "Don't worry about it, dumpling. We'll find them." She dried her hands on a towel and turned to me. "One of us is going to have to stay behind to look after the baby." She patted the ball of her stomach.

"It cannot be me. And the thought of you here, safe with our child, will give me strength on my journey."

"Crassus is going to *war*, Andros! Whose skills do you think are more valuable, a healer's or a scribe's?"

"Scribe indeed. Your sense of humor blossoms when your humors are out of balance. Think on it, love — when has *dominus* ever gone anywhere without me?"

"I'm going," Hanno said.

"That's good, dumpling. It's almost time for supper. Please put the broom in its place and be sure to wash that dust off before you come to table."

"No, Livia. I'm going to war with Father Jupiter. Want to see me march?" He began to limp about the room.

"Hanno, *you* are not going anywhere." Seeing his face begin to crumple, I quickly rephrased. "Because we have a very important job for you. We need you to stay here and help look after little Marcus when he comes."

"Or little Sabina."

"Are they coming with Brenus and Taog?"

"You know, they may just. One or the other. You and Andros will have such fun playing with the baby while I'm away."

"I refuse to have this discussion with a pregnant woman. Besides, it is entirely academic. We need only put our cases before *dominus*."

"Let's go to the kitchen, then. I have an insatiable craving for a plate of jellied eel."

•••

The truth was, neither of us was anxious to go before Crassus to plead our case. Whatever his ruling, if he was determined to forego the sight, scent and touch of his beloved wife for two, maybe three years to achieve his goal, he would not think twice to demand the same of one of us. For a generation I had belonged to the growing, fortunate *familia* of the Crassus household. But now, just at the moment when Livia and I were about to make our own true family together, Crassus would snatch it away from us. Throughout my life, experience has been there to be my willing teacher, yet what a poor student I have made. Why can't I remember that not once have I ever seen a coin, whether grimy copper or bright gold, that had but one side.

PART II

A HARDNESS OF STONE

CHAPTER XVIII

55 BCE - FALL, ROME

Year of the consulship of
Gnaeus Pompeius Magnus and Marcus Licinius Crassus

A s you came to the end of the last scroll, you who read this, did you laugh at our folly? I could not blame you if you had clucked or tsked, but can we be faulted for imagining that Crassus would take *some* interest in his newborn property and show *some* regard for its parents? He did neither. It was *both* of us he wanted and both of us he took. Livia was as skilled a doctor as *dominus* had ever seen, the equal of her mother and more, for Sabina had lacked the knowledge of the ancient Egyptian healing arts. Of course Crassus would take her, though I begged on my knees for him to leave her behind. When that failed, I had nothing more to say, for I would never ask for him to take her and leave me, even to be a father to our son.

Yes, a son, Felix, born to us on the 3rd of October, seven pounds of soundless, red-faced fury that melted into entranced repose the instant he found his mother's nipple. Our master's plan was to set sail from Brundisium in November. Five weeks. That is all the time he gave us. So we held him, fed him and inhaled the indescribable scent that belongs only to new life. We stayed up nights to comfort his cries, then lay exhausted with him curled between us, lulled at last by the tiny rasp of his breath.

You may wonder at our choice of a name that means happy, blessed and lucky. Wonder no more. The choice was not ours, but lady Tertulla's. Do not forget we were but pets, and never has there been a bitch that names its own litter. Yes, I was bitter. Far easier was it to absorb the consequences of a life without choice when I was the only one suffering those consequences. Now one had become three, and it was as if I had been enslaved anew. Curio's harsh words rose like bile; I drank to drown them out, but I cannot hold my wine. Livia held my forehead as I kneeled over the basin. She ground mint and waneb root (the herb she had insisted on buying that day at the baths) and suffused them into a tea. Within minutes I was still bitter, but at least my stomach and head were much improved. We decided Felix was a name hard to dislike; perhaps, for once, this would not be another instance for life to laugh at us poor mortals with its sadistic sense of irony.

Hanno was entranced. The moment his stable chores were through, he dashed to our quarters to thrust his head into Felix's basket to see what 'little brother' was up to. That is, after he'd passed inspection.

"Don't you dare touch that baby till you've washed your hands, young man." Livia guided Hanno to the basin.

"Sorry, sorry, sorry." Hanno scrubbed away as Livia had shown him, rubbing the tops of his hands and the bumps where his fingers used to be.

"Soap," she reminded him.

"It's very slippery! I can't hold it."

"Do you want me or Andros to help you?"

"No, I can do it by myself! I like the bubbles. They have shiny colors." The boy chased the ball around the basin, splashing water on the floor. "It's very slippery," he repeated.

"Would you like some help now?" Livia asked gently.

"Yes, please."

Hanno was very gentle with the baby; to watch them together only multiplied our sense of loss.

•••

We gave Felix all the love we could for as long as we could. Then we handed him to lady Tertulla and followed our master to war. The separation from Hanno was unspeakable. He had to be physically restrained and no amount of affection or reassurance would stop the flow of his tears.

Those partings chipped another piece from the foundation of what I had convinced myself to think of as my friendship with Marcus Crassus. It fell to the ground, and though it might be repaired with care and time, I would not, could not ever be the one to bend my scarred back to pick it up.

•••

Dominus was not totally heartless; in fact he was generous beyond measure, though his kindheartedness bore the cruelest of ironies. Not only had lady Tertulla promised to personally see to the care of little Felix, our lord made this pledge: if the fates were merciless and neither Livia nor I returned to claim our son within three years, Crassus, or Tertulla in his absence, would go before a magistrate with *dominus'* written instructions to perform

245

the ceremony of manumission. He showed us the scroll — a guarantee of our boy's freedom, including a stipend of 5,000 sesterces a year, until his 25th birthday, at which time a place would be found for him to continue working on the estate as a freedman, if he so chose. All that was required to satisfy this generous arrangement was that both his parents be casualties of Crassus' war.

But what if we lived? What if *dominus* was right and the Parthians were easily overcome? To survive would condemn the child to a life of servitude. Coming home would be tantamount to making our own son a slave. The obvious and literal escape clause was easily blocked: should either of us run away or attempt to flee, the offer would be rescinded. The only way to free Felix was to die.

To understand how Crassus could imagine that we would be comforted by such an offer, you must see it from his point of view. To him, choosing freedom, a life outside the aegis of his beneficence, was a poor decision indeed. The security, housing, sustenance, sense of *familia* — the life he gave his slaves was better by far than anything that could be imagined beyond his influence. He was undoubtedly right; Crassus was an exception to the Roman norm. But he also understood, because I had explained it to him on numerous occasions, that servitude to an enlightened master was a viper with seductive and unshakeable fangs: the more a slave was injected with the venom of comfort and security, the more numb he became to his own condition.

So Crassus, knowing what it would mean to Livia and me, would give our son the choice, should we not return, of making his own way in the world. Felix Alexandros would be able to choose his own destiny. From that moment on, there was not a day that passed without the contemplation of our cruel dilemma. We were determined to give our newborn son the chance to become a free man.

•••

The day before Crassus was to hear the decision from the senate regarding his invasion plans, I made yet another attempt to dissuade my master from his costly revenge. We sat together in his office.

"Don't misunderstand me," he had said. "I *believe* my wife was raped. I am going to war because I believe her."

"She would never betray you," I said quietly.

"Let me tell you a story," Crassus said. "I named Publius after my brother. Before he was murdered, one time when we were children, I came upon him playing with a toy catapult that belonged to me. Publius had broken one of the strings that secured the basket and was trying to repair it. I pushed him aside, looked at the damage and saw how easy it would be to fix. I left it in the dirt, and never played with it again."

I did not know what to say. "You need time."

"I do not think I am not alone in my misgivings about that night," Crassus said, "Your lady is finding it more and more difficult to accept what happened that night in Luca. True, it was she who had warned me away with her eyes. But it was I who froze, as hard and as unmoving as quarry marble. And when at last my indecision thawed, what action did I take? I faded into the darkness. I cannot tell you with certainty whether it was her silent plea or cowardice that finally moved me." He paused to rub brusquely at his eyes, as if by doing so, he could blind himself to that one memory. "We do not speak of it."

"With respect, *dominus*, could it be you, not *domina*, who is finding your…predicament more difficult to accept? My lady adores you. She wants things as they were. I can see it in her every movement, in the way she looks at you when she knows you cannot see. She wants to reach you, *dominus*, but grows afraid she no longer knows how."

"I would have been no match for him. I know that. But better to have died in that accursed room than live with what I have become. I am no coward, Alexander. I can *not* be a coward."

"You have both suffered; there are no cowards in this house."

"It does not matter," he said, sounding beaten and exhausted. "The logic of it, the political expediency, the weighing of pros and cons — it is all beside the point. He was there, she succumbed, I did nothing. These facts are irrefutable. Though we love each other still, the wound is open and foul. I know of only one balm that will heal it."

"There is another, *dominus*."

"If the plant from which it grows lies not in Parthia, it is a false cure."

I took a breath. "Forgive *domina*. Forgive yourself. Forget Caesar."

He turned on me suddenly. "I told you once before not to speak of this again. You have no idea what you ask. Your words of comfort offer none. They are noises you make with the vain hope that I will find the sounds pleasing and logical. You know *nothing* of this!" I flinched, thinking he was going to strike me. "Sounds without meaning, Alexander. Your philosophy is useless here." He walked behind his table and sat, resting his arms on the gilt lion paw armrests of his chair. His fingers caressed the grooves of each claw.

He spoke again, his voice soft and terrifying. "You will never understand, Alexander. No. You can never know. But I can show you; there is a way. Do you wish to know? Do you want to feel it in your heart till it cracks from the knowing?" His words flowed black and thick, a spume noisome and vaporous. "Then do this," he said. "Put Livia in that room. See Caesar's hands on her breasts, Alexander. Hear the rustle of fabric as he pushes up her tunic and thrusts his cock up inside her." Crassus exhaled with a sound like a bull before the priest's blade falls. "Then, when you can see him grunting behind the only love you have ever known, when you have done that, then you put yourself in that doorway. And you stand there, and you watch. Watch and do nothing. Look at him. Look at the tears on her cheeks. Now, tell me again. Tell me to forget Caesar. Go ahead, Alexander. Tell me to forgive myself. Tell me. TELL ME!"

I stood quite still, trying to shut out the image that once envisioned, would never depart. Crassus, now disgusted, waived his hand at me as if he were swatting a fly. "Get out. And if you ever ask that of me again, or attempt to move me from my course, I will have you flogged, or worse."

•••

I waited for Crassus on the steps of the *curia*. Clouds with flat bottoms moved across the sky as if they glided on the surface of a calm sea. In my mind's eye I saw the forum, the people, the entire city under water; the real world was up there, and we were the dark reflection beneath. Behind me, the double doors of the senate's meeting house finally creaked open and a dozen blinking *lictors* stepped into the light. They formed a double line into the center of which my lord strode. Following close behind were his legates and senior officers, junior senators themselves. Crassus adjusted his toga with a yank and

249

nodded for our company to proceed down the steps. He was not happy.

"Bad news," I said, elbowing my way without opposition into the channel of refuge made by his guards. "I see the others did not adjourn."

"I consign the others to Pluto's ass," Crassus said, holding out the scroll with his invasion proposal. I took it.

"You expected this," I said as we walked through the forum. People stopped to stare or wave. Many applauded as Marcus Licinius Crassus passed by. Our pace remained steady. "Therefore you cannot be exceedingly disappointed."

"I am the dog who sits patiently by the dining couch night after night, swallowing his drool at the prospect of scraps that never come. Foolish dog. Octavius!" A man in his mid-thirties with short, unruly hair and flushed cheeks who still managed to look boyish rushed up, the hem of his toga bunched up in his hands so he wouldn't trip while running. His was the first letter we had received asking for a commission.

"General?" Octavius asked.

"Where is Cassius?"

"On the Campus Martius, taking inventory, laying in the last of our stores."

"Good. The senate, as you heard, has dismissed us."

"Why stay where we are not welcome?" the legate said. I liked his sense of humor. It had a certain ring to it.

"Precisely. Alexander, you will leave for Brundisium the moment you are able to prepare for the army's arrival and accommodation. We will follow in haste."

We walked the rest of the way in silence. Crassus never rode to the forum; he always walked. Walking, he claimed, was the best exercise. If true, the months ahead would make many tens of thousands fit indeed. My disposition leaning naturally toward the morbid, I thought of those poor, fit souls who, when our labors were through, would never make the return trip, and prayed their number would be few.

Crassus bid his *lictors* and lieutenants enter the *domus* with us, rather than make them wait in the street. After they greeted the lady of the house, to their delight and our surprise, her handmaidens ushered them into the great hall where *domina* had prepared a feast of rare foods and wines in honor of our imminent departure. We left them toasting each others' success and returned to the first atrium, where I took up my primary post as a silent ghost. The room, lit by a mote-flecked bar of sunlight from the rectangular opening above the *impluvium*, was done in Carthaginian marble of the deepest reds and yellows. Quite rare, quite expensive. It was, however, purchased at a substantial discount — Crassus owned the quarry.

Tertulla's image was reflected in the atrium pool, hands demurely clasped and folded in front of her. She wore a plain, white *peplos* held by two gold brooches at the shoulders, and once again had abandoned her *stola* in favor of a second tunic. It was dark green, artfully hung off one shoulder before falling to her ankles. The matrons of society had clucked behind her back at her refusal to dress respectably, but she dressed only for *dominus*. One thing they could never reprove was her loveliness. A belt of golden threads cinched her waist and gave form to her figure. She wore her hair in the style Crassus favored most: black curls arranged to frame her pale forehead and cheeks. Longer wisps spiraled in front of her ears, which were adorned by the slender gold pendant earrings her husband had just given her for her forty-sixth birthday.

"I've heard complaints," Crassus said, taking her hands in his. She cocked her head, completely unalarmed. "Indeed. I have heard it whispered that your eyes are too blue, too large for such a perfect oval of a face."

"I'm ashamed to admit it is true." She scrunched up her expression and squinted. "There, is that better?"

"Don't bother, it only helps a little. There is more: your grooming is too carefree, your hairstyle disheveled. But to me," he said, "everything about you is as perfect as Plato's forms."

They stepped into each other's arms, gripped by an awkward hesitation before their lips met in an unsure kiss. I had never seen them so tentative before. Thankfully, their embrace was interrupted by servants led by Curio entering with refreshments which they set before Crassus.

"Wonderful. Thank you, Lucius," *domina* said. He nodded, taking his place against the wall opposite mine.

"Ah, plums," my lord said, biting into one whose tartness was instantly apparent. "My favorite," he said, wincing.

"Everything is your favorite," *domina* said.

"Alas, I am a politician."

"I wish I could convince you to remain a politician. Remain, husband."

"What's this? *Now* comes a change of heart?"

"Every day steals hours from this moment until the instant of your departure and pushes them between us and Caesar's offense, making it more distant. Revenge is close upon us. It is real and terrible, and Luca fades. I am afraid, Marcus."

"Now, now, we cannot falter, *columba*. We must be strong."

"Is there no other way?"

"It is the way upon which we have agreed. It is the way for which we have planned since Luca."

"The senate has denied you." Her voice was a stew of regret and hope.

"It is of no consequence. As proconsul and governor of Syria, my commission is invested with *imperium* and absolute authority over both civil and military decisions. We leave for Brundisium."

"Allow me, then, to travel at least that far with you."

"No, love. Let us say our goodbyes here, in our home, surrounded by things familiar and cherished. I would rather my memory paint your face in this setting, than bid farewell to you among strangers."

"In that case," she sighed, "I have a surprise for you." Her voice was bright, but brittle. She held out her slender fingers and for the most imperceptible of moments, Crassus hesitated to take it. He did, of course, but by then it was almost audible — the sound of another stone being set in the wall that had been rising between them, keeping them from being at ease with each other. Ever since that night.

Caesar, the silent mason.

We followed them out through the *tablinum* into the smaller of the two peristyles, the one framed on all sides by the portico supported by eighteen granite columns. The tangled vines of wisteria that clung to the gutters were bare, a gnarled and forlorn beard framing an open rectangular mouth. How different they would seem in summer: clusters of fragrant, pale purple hiding the ugly bones from which they always sprang with such elegant enthusiasm. I would not see their blooms next year, or ever, but I did not know that then. Like these vines, we cling to the rhythms of what we know. Change is never without its perils. I could do with less of it.

When we walked past the *lararium*, I could see that Tertulla had made an offering of honey cakes and wine in the little alcove, arranging them at the foot of the image of the *paterfamilias*. *Dominus* smiled at her and she graced him with a look I hadn't seen in months. I followed them out into the open courtyard, past the near fountain and the painted marble statues spaced between the symmetrical rows of rosemary, silverbush and planters of passiflora.

Tertulla's personal servants had carried the master's couch from the dining room and set it among the six lotus trees that mark the center of the *peristyle*. Their leaves rustled, tugging at the smooth, grey branches. Every now and then a glossy, golden spear would heed the whispering wind, forsaking its anchor to sail in its first and final spiral to the ground. I watched the leaves take the only journey they would ever know and wondered, is there freedom in death or, as the leaves learned each autumn, death in freedom?

Once again, Curio and I made ourselves inconspicuous beside opposing pillars, both to our masters, and each other. Where was Hanno? He would usually come running for a hug and a head scratch the moment he heard I was in the *domus*. He was probably with the stable master; still, I felt an acute need for one of his hugs. I worried about Hanno being left on his own. I worried more about leaving little Felix behind, and most about Livia not being able to stay safe with him at home. We would be gone so long our own son would not know us upon our return. So many choices over which to fret. My mind was clogged with worry. And the culprit once again: change. Did perturbation increase in direct proportion to the amount of change? I think it must be so.

Before the *lectus* was a low table holding an *amphora* of Falernian wine, a wheel of warm bread, a variety of cheeses from Trebula and date plums which had ripened on the bows above our heads. A large wooden chest sat nearby on the gravel. Tertulla bade *dominus* sit, and he reclined on the couch reserved for the head of the house, while she arranged herself on the pillows at its far end, lying on her right side so she could face him. She nodded at a *ministratore* who broke the clay seal on the wine and poured it through a strainer into a mixing vessel. My lord and lady looked grateful for the formality and familiarity of the serving rituals to put them at their ease. The slave added half as much water to the wine and poured the diluted mixture into two silver drinking bowls. Another servant tipped a ewer of perfumed water over their hands, then dried them with a soft towel.

"Mars awaken!" Tertulla said, holding her bowl aloft. "May Jupiter Invictus grant victory to Crassus and Rome."

Dominus told her that he went for her, not for Rome.

"Then do not go," she said lowering her bowl and her voice. "Let us find another way."

"I am resolute," he said. "And I will be victorious."

Domina complained of the time they would be apart. "Who will be my hero," she said, "and catch the mice for me now? We shall be overrun by the time you return."

Crassus took her hands in his and kissed her cheek. "That was a long time ago," he said, not unkindly. "Is that the surprise?" He pointed to the chest.

Tertulla sighed with resignation. "You're going to like this," she said as cheerfully as she could. She got up, went to the chest and pulled the lid up to reveal its contents.

Dominus rose respectfully to join her. The trunk was filled with clothes and armor. There were extra tunics and two pairs of hobnail *caligae.* Beneath these were a fine silver balteus from which would hang a new *gladius* with a golden hilt and a smaller *pugio* dagger. Crassus dug further into the chest, admiring first an embossed leather cuirass, then a padded *subarmilis* to keep his armor from chafing. It was complete with leather *pteruges*; he ran his hand appreciatively down the finely worked fringed strips. There were several sizes of cloaks, boxes of toiletries, and other packages containing little gifts, sweetmeats and remembrances. Wrapped in muslin was a small bronze statuette of one of our household *lares.*

"It is a duplicate," Tertulla said. "I will implore mine to perform its task well—to protect and preserve our family, *all* our family" (*she looked at me, I glanced at Curio*) "and to bring my loved ones home to me, safe and unscathed."

Crassus closed the trunk lid and turned to his wife. The words escaped his lips before thought, drawn out by some malicious sprite. "By rights Caesar ought to pay for at least half of all this."

Lady Tertulla stood and turned her back to *dominus*, blinking away tears. He begged her forgiveness, but the damage was done, the scab picked at yet again.

She said, "We will never put it behind us, will we?" It was barely a question. Crassus went to her and stopped, his hands frozen just above her shoulders, the distance separating them measured by fractions and continents. He glanced at me and I could see he was afraid to touch her lest she pull away. There are senators who call him one of Rome's greatest orators, but now he stood mute. At last he lowered one hand to her bare shoulder, not daring to embrace her. After a moment, she reached up and covered his hand with her own.

My lord laid his head on her shoulder and they stood like that among the lotus trees, listening to rustle of the leaves. Finally, he told her that he would rather fall on his own sword than intentionally cause her harm. "But a green harpy lives inside me and will out no matter how I reason with it."

My lady said, "Then do not reason with it, mighty Crassus. Bury your sword in its craw and be done with it. You have no cause for jealousy."

Gently, *dominus* turned her around and wiped the tears from her eyes. "In my mind I know this to be true. It is my heart that yet writhes with the memory. I would tear it from my body, but then how would I love you?"

My lady smiled weakly. "There are enough senators to call you 'heartless.' I shall never add my voice to theirs."

"I apologize for speaking to you as I did. Your gift is magnificent, as are you."

"It is my fervent prayer," she replied, "that you will have the entire trunk thrown into the Tiber. If you still love me, stay and put aside this war. We were rash, and we are wrong to seek revenge at such a cost." Tertulla took his hands in hers and stared at him with such intensity that by this look alone she might have deflected him from his intended path. "You need not go further away, husband, to bring us closer together. You do not have to go. The people would have you stay. *I* would have you stay."

He took both her hands in his. "I cannot turn back, nor would I. Caesar has taken enough from me. No more. When I return, I will retrieve the *bulla aurea* of my childhood and wear it in the triumphal procession. This I

257

swear to you and to any god who will listen. I did not act that night in Luca, to my everlasting disgrace. I must act now."

"Then," said my lady, "I will pray for you daily. Twice daily." She reached up to *dominus*, and drawing him down to her, pressed her body full against his own and they kissed as I had not seen them do in many months.

"I have loved none but you, I love you still, and I shall love you always."

She said this to him then, and he shook with emotion when he heard it. "I summon Venus and Mars to join in both love and in war. Come, Venus Victrix, come quickly now. Forsake Vulcan and with You, Father of Warfare, take pity on us, turn evil aside from us, and preserve my husband's and my sons' life. Gird them with the strength of Hercules and the cunning of Mercury. Vanquish any and all who oppose them. Let not the scales of victory hover above the blocks, but fall decidedly in favor of, and with the full weight and power of Crassus."

•••

Many months later, as he kneeled in the bloodied dust of a strange and desolate land, Crassus would marvel at the clarity of his recall of their last moment together—the warmth of her skin through the fabric of her tunic, the smell of almond and bergamot in her hair, the soft pressure of her arms about his neck. He wore the memory of her embrace like armor, and though he knew it would not save his life, it would be all that was left to him to ease his passage into whatever lay beyond.

CHAPTER XIX

55 BCE - FALL, ROME

Year of the consulship of
Gnaeus Pompeius Magnus and Marcus Licinius Crassus

"We could be home within a year," I whispered. Felix was asleep in his crib. From his own cot, Hanno kept shushing our every sentence with a noise louder than our speech. I lit another lamp to aid in my packing.

Hanno said, "Bright."

"I am sorry, son. It will only be for a little while. Try to sleep."

"If I try, it never works." I smiled at his exhibition of logic and he smiled back, knowing he had pleased me.

"I can't leave him, Andros," Livia said, moving from our bed to stand over the crib. Under one arm she held a bundle of my folded tunics; with her free hand she tucked Felix's blanket up under his dimpled chin and bent to kiss his forehead. "I can't do it."

"We have no choice."

"That is what angers me the most." I took the tunics from her and laid them neatly in the open trunk that lay in the center of our bedroom, a *cubiculum* so well-appointed and lavish it would put many senators' own lodgings to shame.

"Why are you still here?" Crassus stood in our doorway, the portiere drawn aside. His hands were not empty.

Livia and I turned and spoke simultaneously, "*Dominus!*"

Hanno sat up in his cot. "Father Jupiter! Hug?" At least the boy had learned to ask.

"Not now, Hanno. Father Jupiter is displeased."

"That's all right," Hanno said, completely oblivious of our master's tone. "I'll wait right here."

"I thought," I said, "to spend one more day with my family before departing for Brundisium."

"I told you I needed you there by the end of the week. You were supposed to have left today. It was not a suggestion, Alexandros." Crassus only called me by my birth name when he was truly angry.

"*Dominus…*," Livia started.

"The answer is 'no,' *medicus*. I did not send you to Egypt to learn to be a wet nurse. You and your skills will follow the army." Livia looked at the floor. Thankfully, her unbound hair hid her expression.

"If I leave the day after tomorrow, all will be in readiness for your arrival."

"You will leave at first light. I will not have you depart the day the cover is removed from the *mundus*. It will be seen as an ill omen; bad enough we'll be leaving the city before the Plebeian Games have ended."

"Yes, *dominus*."

"I am sorry to put you through this," he said, a shade less put out. He peered into the crib like a proud grandfather. I noticed that he was barefoot, and wondered how the coming months would treat his ailing feet. "Your *domina* will tend to your son as if he were her own, you have my word and hers. He couldn't be in better care."

More and more, it seemed my lord was letting words fall from his mouth without permitting them to first pass through his brain. I could feel Livia vibrating by my side.

Crassus opened his hand to reveal a golden amulet on a gold link chain. He held the chain and let the *bulla* swing free. "Your mistress will keep it for him to wear, when he is older."

"That is very generous of you, *dominus*. But a slave cannot—"

"He can, if I will it so." He dropped the heavy ornament into my hand. I felt the heft of it, then handed it back to him.

"May we all return safely to see it adorn his neck. Livia, these are for you." He held out two tunics trimmed with wide red stripes, the sign of a senior *medicus*. For a heartbeat, I thought she would refuse them, but sanity got the better of her and she mumbled gratitude.

To me he said, "I was going to have your mate surprise you with this honor when she met up with you in Brundisium, but I see I shall have to rob her of that pleasure." He handed me a 4-inch gold disk hung from a broad purple sash. The thick medal was reminiscent of the *phalerae*, awards centurions displayed proudly on their chests for deeds of valor. This one was inscribed with writing that encircled the entire circumference: "Alexandros, beloved of Crassus. Harm him, harm me. Disobey him, disobey me." Within the circle, facing each

261

other were two engraved likenesses, his, and my own. Between them was an image of one of the lotus trees from the *peristyle* at the estate in Rome. On the back, these words were etched:

> A face once effective
> May one day be erased
> For one need having perished
> May find it's been replaced

"What does this mean?" I risked asking.

"Should you ever require the knowledge, Alexander, your intelligence will guide you. Now finish here," he said curtly. "You have an early start."

On his way out of our room, Crassus detoured to allow Hanno to throw his arms around his true master. The boy never looked so happy as when he had just been given the gift of human touch. After we had given him our own hugs of good night, Hanno settled down and was in blissful sleep within moments.

"I hate him," Livia whispered after Crassus' steps had receded down the hallway.

"I know that you don't. *Dominus* does what he must."

"You didn't even argue with him."

Livia wanted a fight, and I was close, posing no threat. "Argue? With him? Come, let us pour a cup of honeyed wine before bed. The packing is almost done."

"Finish it then."

"Livia, would you take Felix with us to Syria and beyond?"

"I would have the right to choose to take him wherever you and I decide."

"As would I. But such talk is nonsense. Besides, what finer care could there be than that of our lady?"

"The care of his mother." She stood rigid, her hands at her sides.

"How I wish I could comfort you." I placed my hand close to hers, without touching.

She was crying softly. "What a fool was that happy, whistling child." Her fingers slid into mine. "Life is not what she imagined it would be. I was treated less cruelly in the house of Boaz, the slave merchant."

"Never say that," I said, kissing her forehead. "Never think it." We curled into each other's arms, and Livia let me hold her until her sobs subsided.

"I hate for you to see me cry," she said, pushing me far enough away from her to hold me by my elbows.

"Why? You will always be beautiful to me, no matter how red and puffy your face."

"It's not that, dolt."

"To say nothing of the glistening of your runny nose."

"Enough." She kissed me hard on the mouth. "I don't care about any of that. I don't want you to think I am weak."

I laughed, kissing her eyes and nose, then, between each sentence, with increasing fervor, her mouth. "Concrete is weak. Marble is weak. Even Margianian steel is weak, compared to you. Now come, *domina*," I said, tugging lightly at her hand. "Who knows when we will be able to share a bed again?"

A short while later, Crassus reappeared, poking his head through the otherwise closed portiere. Barefoot to ease his bunions, we did not hear his approach, though had he stomped through the hallway in his *caligae* the surprise would likely have been no less. "I neglected to tell you, Alexander," he said, stifling a yawn. "In your absence, Lucius Curio will perform your duties as *atriensis*.

263

CHAPTER XX

55 BCE - FALL, BRUNDISIUM

Year of the consulship of
Gnaeus Pompeius Magnus and Marcus Licinius Crassus

O n the fields to the east of Brundisium, before the troops prepared to board the ships, Crassus assembled the army. There he offered up many cleansed and garlanded sacrifices: seven lambs, seven bulls and seven pigs. Seven sets of three throats to be slit to ensure the safety of each legion. A city augur, proud of girth and unashamed of excess, possessed of such capacious jowls they'd have made a roomy pair of mittens, this practical priest had allowed his mouth to be stuffed with bribes too prodigious for a lesser man to swallow. A positive result having thus been secured, the relief of the gathered thousands was no less genuine when, after the sacred birds had been released, the blessed father interpreted their flight as an auspice that our enterprise was looked upon favorably by the gods.

Crassus had had crafted seven of the most exquisite and opulent standards, taller and richer than any soldier had ever seen, crested with eagles of hammered silver and gold. The priest had blessed and anointed each with sacred oil. They were mounted in a row at the back of a raised reviewing stand, seven sanctified emblems that were the soul and strength of each legion. Beneath them, rustling gently in the slight breeze were many mounted, tasseled, purple *vexilla*, banners numbered with gold thread and images of wild animals, woven from the finest Tarentum lamb's wool. Before these flags and standards stood the senior officers of the army, their helms and breastplates shining as brightly as the standards above their plumed heads.

It is said the Hebrews would march to war carrying a small cabinet containing stones marked by the hand of their god. With this gilded ark leading them into battle, their armies would be blessed and protected; their god would not let them suffer defeat. Now Judea and its boxed god, their people rebellious and troublesome, squirm under the heel of Rome. Every army finds some pretty mystery on which to pin their hopes of victory: success proves faith justified, but defeat will not strip it away, for faith is impervious to calamity and disaster. Yet here they were: seven blessed standards, and every soldier who saw them, even the skeptics, believed with all or some part of his heart that with them marching before us, we could not fail.

I dimly remember possessing this glazed look of wonder as a child. When I grew to manhood, I discovered that one of three things was true: either the gods had abandoned me, I was beneath their notice, or they did not exist. Soon the elegant proof of a boot in the back had me rethinking the lessons of childhood. The logic of starvation, when the most appetizing offering on the menu was a maggoty hunk of something that used to be bread, this evidence argued relentlessly for the reevaluation of the idea that someone above was keeping a lookout for me. The irrefutable theorem illustrated by men unafraid to meet your eyes as they beat you — these daily insults were better proof of the way of things than anything I had been taught as a child. They filed away at the chains of my reliance on the gods till they broke, and with almost no effort at all I was able to turn my back on them. Finding myself spiritually on my own was a revelation. I was alone, and better for it.

Unless everything has been taken from you and your soul scraped clean of the last stains of foolish dependence on help from above, you cannot imagine how freeing it is to depend on nothing but your wits and the occasional bit of good luck. No, I put no stock in those seven eagles staring down upon us with cold metal eyes. I took far more comfort from Malchus' sword arm, multiplied and compounded by thirty-eight thousand men with hard eyes and rigid discipline.

•••

I had arrived in the port city weeks ahead of the army, to meet with the priest, inspect the ships, inventory the cargo and smooth the way for our departure. I took quarters in the finest inn Brundisium had to offer, The Whistling Pilum. The name made me think of Livia, who was on the Via Appia at that moment, in all likelihood annoying one of the other healers with her tuneless tunes. I wished she was here to annoy me. When the engineers began arriving, they went right to work building a city of their own on the fields outside Brundisium's walls. Hundreds of citizens poured from the port to watch, but were rebuffed when they offered to help. They were told they'd only be in the way, which was true, but feeling slighted, many returned to their tasks behind the walls.

•••

At a trumpeted signal from two dozen *cornicines* standing on a separate platform, men secreted among the 420 *centuries* raised thirteen foot tall standards stacked with bronze disks, silver wreaths and purple tassels that ended in a honed and oiled spear point, itself over eight inches long. (As I have said, the warlike Hebrews marched into battle with but a single divine emblem of their invincibility; Roman history was rife with evidence that where one sacred symbol was good, hundreds were better.)

As each decorated pole was offered humbly to every *century's* standard bearer, the shout that went up from the troops created such a noise that within the city walls those that were not already watching the spectacle were joined by everyone else, bringing commerce, shipping and the entire city of Brundisium to a standstill.

As he mounted the wooden steps to the main dais, Crassus handed his plumed helmet to me and smiled. I marveled at the weight of it, but he seemed to wear his armor lightly. His eyes were alight as they had not been since before Luca, the grievous events at that meeting having both darkened and narrowed his vision. He stepped crisply up to the raised wooden platform, his armor glowing dully under the overcast sky. The roar of the army escalated to madness as soon as his grey head could be seen climbing the steps. He took his time, greeting and complimenting his lieutenants, warmly grasping their forearms, each in his turn: Cassius Longinus, his *quaestor*, brave Octavius, loyal Petronius, ursine Vargunteius, Antoninus, Ignatius, and the one

267

remaining officer whose memory I dishonor by my shameful inability to remember his name.

Giddy with the enormity of this spectacle, I imagined what it would feel like to don the general's helmet, to wear, just for a moment, the trappings of a god. Until that moment, I suppose I had never truly understood the power of the man to whose fate my own had been lashed. (Though ever since the night of our return from Baiae, the assistant who had become my replacement had succeeded in unnerving me on just that subject—decades of service and not even a private chat to break gently the calamitous news.)

As the general spoke, his slow, careful words, having been memorized by the banner-bearers, were repeated loudly from where they stood so that all in the great multitude could hear. The timing was imperfect, creating eerie waves of words, cresting and falling in dissipating ripples.

"Have you ever seen a legionary weep?" Crassus shouted. "I don't mean the man who has lost at knucklebones ten times running; that poor wretch has cause to cry." The general waited for the light breeze of laughter to pass. "I speak of a soldier, battle-dressed, armed with *gladius* and *pilum*, brilliant in polished helm and painted *scutum*. No, not this man, trained, strong, deadly: this is not a man who weeps. Yet today, your general stands before you, water welling in his eyes. Shall I tell you why? Because in my forty years of service to our people, I have seen and fought with many armies, but none such as this. The *cohorts* that blanket this field are the finest group of veterans that Rome has ever assembled! We are a Roman army—there is none finer in all the world! So, should my tears fall," he shouted above the roar, "should my tears fall it is because I stand here, now, with you and for you, at the proudest moment of my life! And because you men of valor have chosen to stand here with me...," Crassus continued to speak, but his final words went unheard, buried in an avalanche of cheers.

When the uproar had died down, aided by the outstretched arms of the general, my master said, "Many of you veterans, if you are like me, have either misplaced or worn out much of your equipment. When you fought with Pompeius or Lucullus or Caesar, the army supplied your weapons, your shield and your helmet. Everything else, from your cook pot to your armor came from your pocket or your pay. Is it right that the man fighting next to you is better protected just because his purse is heavier than yours? No, it is not right, and in my army, *every* legionary will be as safe as I can make him.

"Centurions! See the posting outside the *quaestorium* for your appointment time. Cassius Longinus and his people will supply each legionary with freshly forged *lorica hamata*, chain mail for *every* soldier!"

This time *dominus* had to wait even longer for the cheers to subside. "You all know we march to Syria. Do you think proconsul Gabinius is such a poor governor we must come to his rescue with such a force? Last I heard, Antioch still stood." Now Crassus' voice rose in volume and authority with every sentence. "Does this look like a relief force?" The "NO!" that answered each question was a thunderclap. "Are you nursemaids for infants?" "NO!" "Will you be content to gaze at palm trees from the safety of a sleepy garrison?" "NO!" "Are you armed and girded for peace?" "NO!" "I know men on their way to WAR when I see them!" The cry of affirmation was deafening. I had to put my hands to my ears, almost dropping the general's helmet.

Crassus waited and let his eyes sweep across his legions. "You must also know that the senate has withheld its blessing." Boos and whistles swarmed like locusts. "The day *that* decision was made the senator's *wives* must have gone to the *curia* while the men rummaged through their houses searching for their testicles!"

While he waited for the laughter to subside, Crassus looked down and scanned among the closest ranks, men of the first *century* of the first *cohort*. Then he looked up again and called out, "Would you like to know the secret of our invincibility?" He was departing from the script and the banner bearers were forced to keep up as best they could.

A legionary shouted, "We march for the First Man of Rome!"

"Gratitude," Crassus said, pressing the cheers to silence with outstretched arms. "But our strength does not come from me, nor from any you see upon this platform. For the answer, I shall demonstrate. "You," he said, pointing. "Leave your shield and ascend the rostrum."

Behind me, a stunned Drusus Malchus hissed under his breath, "*Furina's* feces!" He broke rank and the safety of anonymity to join his general. Behind Crassus, the legates were smiling. The stair planks creaked as Malchus climbed, gripping the rough-hewn hand rail for the equilibrium that had suddenly forsaken him. A large splinter speared his left hand and before his mind could stop his mouth he shouted, "*Fucking* son of a whore." His brain reminded him where he was before he finished speaking so that the last word was more miserable whimper than curse. Face flushed with crimson, he let the long sliver remain rather than risk any more unmilitary outbursts. He could be whipped for such an offense. If that was his fate, he'd have plenty of company: those within earshot, and there were many, laughed out loud with as much lack of intention. It was hard to say who was more embarrassed.

To break the solemnity of such a moment was surely an ill omen. Next to me, Flavius Salvius Betto clucked his disapproval. Crassus saved the moment by laughing along with his men. Betto clucked even louder, but with such lofty permission, the wave of fellowship spread until Malchus had made the top of the stage. He came to parade rest several feet from the general, as if the aura surrounding Crassus were an invisible shield he could not penetrate. Even with cradled helmet, Malchus was still a full head taller than anyone on the dais and half again as broad. Yet pulled from his place in the ranks, the poor man looked like a gasping fish tossed up onto a hot beach; the sea of his brothers-in-arms beckoned just beyond reach.

"Do you need a medic, son?" More guffaws. Drusus shook his head spasmodically. "Let's have a look then," Crassus said, motioning him closer. There was a stirring of awe as their godlike leader took the legionary's hand in his own. Crassus gave a crisp, hard yank and pulled the two-inch sliver from Malchus' palm. There was a tumultuous cry as he held it aloft.

"Let this," he shouted over the cheers, "let this be the first and last casualty of our campaign!" Crassus grabbed Malchus' hand and as he finished his next sentence flung it aloft as if the legionary were the winner of an Olympic wrestling contest. "Let Mars Invictus cause Parthian spears to fall as harmless splinters against our Roman shields!"

By my side, Betto whispered, "They'll have to be very tiny Parthians."

Crassus waited for the noise to die back down, allowing the men a good deal more license than he would once we were on the march. "Tell us your name," he demanded. Then, under his breath, "You're a good sport, Malchus. This will all be over in a moment and you can take cover."

Malchus nodded gratefully. "Drusus Quintilius Malchus, sir."

"Any women in your life, soldier?"

"Several, sir." The requisite answer, which still got a laugh from those few who heard him.

"Well then, Malchus, your sweethearts will want to hear about this day, but they're not likely to take your word that you stood with your general and his legates before the entire army. Get some witnesses: let them hear you back in the sixth *cohort* of the seventh legion. Again!"

"DRUSUS QUINTILIUS MALCHUS! SIR!"

"That's more like it," Crassus said, taking a step backward, his left arm extended to present the soldier to the army. "I give you Drusus Malchus, legionary: first *century*, first *cohort*, first legion." Thousands cheered and whistled, none louder than his *contubernium* mate and best friend, Betto. His especially raucous praise was a mixture of pride and relief that the general's pointing finger had come so close yet passed him by.

"Well, Malchus, I shall have to commend the cooks. You have obviously found no fault with the food." My friend reddened and grinned, but kept silent, his inventory of replies having been exhausted by remembering and saying his name.

Now Crassus paced slowly across the stage as he spoke, tens of thousands of eyes following his every move. "Legionary Malchus achieved his status of rank through constant training and practice, expert sword and shield work, applied in the only furnace hot enough to temper his skills to the hardness of steel—the field of battle. I know this without asking because the same is true of every man in his *century*, I'll wager in his legion. They could not have earned their posting otherwise. With whom did you serve, son?" he asked with a wink.

"With you, sir. Against the rebel slave Spartacus."

"Of course you did," Crassus said. "Like Malchus, most of you served under Pompeius, or Caesar or Lucullus or me. To face and engage the enemy, there is no substitute for this metal—forged with strength and rigorous training it is a most deadly alloy. And those of you whose sword points are as yet unblooded—know that every *century* is crammed with men of experience ready to guide you."

Crassus walked to the edge of the platform. "Training, strength and experience—a most deadly triumvirate." He pointed back toward giant Malchus, who flinched at the gesture. "Legionary Malchus has them all. Is this what makes us invincible?"

"Yes!" cried the multitude.

Crassus raised his arms as if to enfold the entire field. "You are my children, and as a father loves his sons, I swear by Jupiter, I love each and every one of you. And so, to keep you safe, I must answer 'no.' These things makes us deadly, but they are not what makes us unconquerable. Know that each day we march I will sacrifice to Mars

Invictus so that when this war is over, we may *all* return to our beloved families and homes. Every one of your lives is precious to me; that is why you must heed me now and learn this lesson above all others. Those who have been tested know this truth, but all must share in the sacred secret of our indomitable strength."

The silence that followed was stunning and strange amongst that throng, especially after the good-natured jesting and camaraderie. The general paused to let the stillness grip every man, then called out, "Legionary Drusus Malchus did not come to this field alone. Nor should he stand here, alone upon this stage. Bring his tent-mates forward."

Betto and six other serious faces marched up the stairs, their joyous relief at not being singled out short-lived. "Come, come," Crassus said, gesturing with his hand, "stand beside your worthy companion here." He spoke directly to the soldiers on the stage, but his voice was loud and carried far. "I will trouble you with no more questions, but speak plainly. When we bring the battle to the enemy, when *pila* are thrown and swords are bloodied, when ranks are closed and the press of bodies weigh upon your shields, remember for whom you fight.

"You do not fight for Rome.

"You do not fight for glory, or for riches.

"You do not fight for your centurions or your legates.

"And you do not fight for me."

There were no looks of puzzlement from the legionaries on the stage, but two of the officers standing behind the general, Ignatius and Antoninus, frowned and shifted uncomfortably.

"Look at the men around you," he continued. "Meet their eyes and take their measure. From this day forward, for as long as we march together, your tent-mates are your brothers. Your mother is Rome; she spat you from her womb to stand side-by-side with your brothers-in-arms. Fight for *them*. Protect *them*. When they stumble, *you* help them stand. When they tire, *you* give them encouragement. And when the enemy is but a gladius length away, you *kill* for *them*. Do this, and they will do the same for you.

"You think you fight for fame or spoils? Do not let the play of your anticipation distract you from the work of your sword. You think you fight for your sweetheart or a child left behind? Your wives are far away, but your brothers are right beside you. Fight for them, and live! Fight for each other, and we will return to Rome with such treasure it will take a thousand mules to bear the weight of it!

"I make this promise, witnessed by these officers: when we return victorious, laden with Parthian gold, a bonus of 5,000 *denarii* awaits every fighting man!"

It started somewhere in the middle of the army but rapidly built to a crescendo, a single voice amplified thirty-thousand times: "Crassus! Crassus! CRASSUS! CRASSUS!"

CHAPTER XXI

55 BCE - FALL, BRUNDISIUM

Year of the consulship of
Gnaeus Pompeius Magnus and Marcus Licinius Crassus

C louds black and purple as bruises swelled over the busiest port of Calabria, the grand peninsula that jutted into the sea to form the northern arm of the Gulf of Tarentum. With lumpy, distorted faces these airy witnesses looked down with dismay on a harbor choked with over four hundred vessels: *triremes*, troop carriers, cavalry transports and cargo ships. Their masts swayed in the wind like the spiny back of the monster Cetus. No lightning could be seen, but thunder rolled, deep and ominous, over the 4,500 light infantry auxiliaries, 3,500 cavalry, 30,000 legionaries and an equal number of support and supply personnel all waiting for the order to sail. To a man they were wishing they were on dry land. Myself included. Thunder without lightning? And in November? The whispers spread throughout the fleet: could this be the curse of the tribune at work?

Thirteen hundred miles due west, the empty Mesopotamian desert waited quietly, parched and alien beneath a vacant sky. This was the unimaginable home of Melyaket who, with an unrefined and ignorant vitality which more than likely rivaled that of his horse, had wasted his youth in any number of barbaric and unsavory pursuits. Now, after the expenditure of thousands of hours of preparation and millions of *sesterces*, my master was about to make good on his vow to close that prodigious gap in order to annex the country where the youth had gamboled: Parthia, the Eastern Empire, quiescent but grand, Rome's rival for no other reason than it existed.

As I worked to maintain my balance on that massive, lurching deck, I wondered if the rolling thunder were a harbinger announcing the end of my relative good fortune. The climb up years of servitude to stand at the side of one of the rulers of Rome seemed pointless now. What had I hoped to achieve? Now, my thoughts were only for those I could not see. How was little Felix faring without his mother? Was Hanno safe? Would Curio stay away from him? I needed to focus and somehow survive this perilous adventure. Then Livia and I must find some way to return to our family.

I clung to the swaying main mast, a thick tower of wood slowly scribbling invisible messages on the heavy air, watching closely as Crassus struggled with the silver *fibula* that secured his cloak over his right shoulder. I would not offer help if none were needed. Transformed by his resplendent military attire, it was as if I were seeing him for the first time. Does what we wear express or hide our true character? Was Crassus more authentic in uniform or draped in his toga?

The whipping wind put the simple task of fastening his cloak beyond him. Lips pressed into a line of concentration, he struggled against the heaving foredeck of his flagship, *Scourge of Ctesiphon*. The *quinquereme* was tied up at the very end of the breakwater so that it could lead the fleet; the sea here was growing alarmingly choppy. A covetous blast almost whipped his Tyrian purple *lacerna* out into the Adriatic, but the general retrieved his cloak when it became entangled in the rigging of the foremast. Now my assistance would not be perceived as insulting. I rushed from my post, and without a word between us, gently pushed the old man's hands aside. I attached the *fibula* while the general held on to the unruly garment. Crassus, while offering no word of thanks, favored me with a fleeting and preoccupied smile.

Something chewed at this incarnation of Roman perfection. The pieces were all present: grey hair cropped close, nose thin and jutting, jaw strong enough to lend dignity to any coin of the Republic. Curious that in his lifetime he minted but a few. The armor made him look older than his sixty years. Clothed for war with breastplate and helm, though custom-made to precisely gird his aging body, it seemed ill-fitted, more costume than the resplendent trappings of a consular general. I closed my eyes and imagined my lord in his toga, and instantly beheld a master of Rome. That cloth spoke so much more eloquently of his wealth, influence and authority than the plume and bronze and leather. Yet another more recent image elbowed its way into view. Could it be that it was neither the garb of war nor of politics that suited him best, but rather the comfort of his favorite house tunic, barefoot at home in his kitchen, wooden spoon poised to dip into whatever bubbling pot drew his fancy?

Where was Livia?

•••

Turning his grey eyes downward, Crassus stared at the backs of his tanned, still strong hands as they gripped the railing. He blew air sharply through his nose — a self-mocking snort of laughter that sent his self-confidence tumbling away on that same breath. The clouds overhead bunched closer, darker, lower. "Crassus, you old fool," he whispered so that I could barely hear him, "what are you doing here, when you could be soaking in a hot bath at Baiae, sipping honey wine? I am a play actor dressed for the wrong part." *Had I been speaking aloud? Had he read my thoughts?* He adjusted his leather breastplate and ran his fingers over the gilded and embossed "muscles."

"I will employ her presents, Alexander, to bring the world to her feet. Look on't," he said, smiling. "We have not yet departed the Italian shore, and already her gift of armor has saved my life."

"I do not follow, *dominus*."

"If I'd been forced to wear my old uniforms, squeezing into them would have asphyxiated me long before we reached Syria. Sixteen years since I rode out against Spartacus, and at least as many pounds. I'm not the soldier I used to be, and truth be told, I was not born to it like Pompeius or Caesar."

"Some wars," I tried, "are won on foreign soil, some on the floor of the senate. No general is more accomplished on that bloody field than you."

"That is as may be. But a long time has passed since I last traded a toga for the *lorica* of battle. I must be mad. Or senile. Can I do this? I must, if this contest is to become my salvation, and Caesar's ruin." Thunder mocked with brief applause over our heads.

279

The conscript fathers, their senatorial robes shaking with outrage, had chafed and brandished their fists in vain. Crassus had abandoned his consular duties and marched from the city at the head of one of the greatest war machines ever assembled by a single man. Unsanctioned by the senate, here was a rogue army to match any sponsored by the state. If the people's coffers had not been opened to pay for this enterprise, how, you may ask, was it possible for Crassus to amass such a force? Before Publius left Rome for Gaul, he estimated that based on existing intelligence reports, three legions would have no difficulty subduing the backward desert dwellers of the Euphrates. "If three will do," his father responded, "then let us add five to the two already billeted in Syria and thus make seven. Seven will do more, do it faster and do it more safely. And seven," he said finally, "will impress upon the tribes of Mesopotamia that Rome has come to stay." Crassus received not a single additional *as* from the senate or any other source. The entire enterprise was equipped, salaried and provisioned by the Croesus of Rome, Marcus Licinius Crassus.

Since that day, *dominus'* enthusiasm had faltered. The general looked out over the rail and sighed as he surveyed his army. "I am not happy to be here, Alexander."

"Why is that, *dominus*?"

"I had hoped never to pass this way again."

"I understand, general. This place holds less than Elysian memories for me, as well."

Crassus ignored me, but he knew it was through this place that Sulla's army had dragged me from ruined Athens when I was little more than a boy. "When last I saw the plains of Apulia," he continued, "all those many years ago, they were piled deep with the corpses of those I slew. And for what? For a cause so hopeless it curdles the blood to dwell even a moment upon the monumental waste. Every man of them a fool. Brave, to be sure, but fools nonetheless. Did they think we would allow them to unravel our way of life like a cat with a ball of yarn? Rome could not let it stand. I could not let it stand."

"Your logic is unassailable."

"And your impertinence is tiring." Crassus gave me a sidelong glance. "The Thracian brought his fate upon himself. He could have fled across the Alps, but instead he turned south and what, thought to challenge the might of the Republic? Madness."

"By then he was cut off. Lucullus had landed here in Brundisium. Pompeius was approaching from the west, you had split his army in two and your own legions were moving in from the north. There was nowhere to run. He had no choice but to stand and fight."

"And I had no choice but to destroy him. How many did I slaughter that day? Forty thousand? Seventy thousand? For certain, it had seemed as if Pluto had risen from the underworld to reign upon the earth. I left the field thinking so much blood must surely stain the land forever. Jupiter's gentle rain would never wash it clean. But it is not so. The seasons have returned, the grass has grown green again and to the north fields yield crops sweet and untainted by the gore that watered that soil. So too in time the name of Spartacus will fade to nothing along with the memory of his rebellion."

Crassus swept his eyes out over the bay so full of men and ships we could scarcely see the water. "His fate will not be mine."

•••

"Forgive me, sir." The legate of Legion II had come up behind us.

"Yes, Petronius? Are we ready to sail?"

"Sir, I am come from the council of the ships' *trierarchs*. They have asked me to petition you to delay our departure until this freakish weather clears. Not one of the captains advises leaving the harbor now."

"I understand their concerns, commander, but I must insist that my own need supersedes their fears. I cannot allow that maniac Ateius another opportunity to delay us. Once away, his histrionics will shred and fly apart on this pernicious breeze." Crassus thought for a moment. "Prepare four oxen for sacrifice. We will satisfy both Jupiter and Mars. Place the altar on the highest of the harbor islands so that all may see. Advise the legates to meet me there. I will conduct the service myself. After the gods have had their portion, distribute the best of the meat to the *trierarchs*. The men *must* take heart, Petronius — Parthia awaits; all we need do is reach out with a mighty grasp and take it — for the glory of Rome."

"For the glory of Rome." Petronius saluted and left.

"Doubly ingenious," I said. "Satisfy the gods and forestall the captains by filling their bellies."

"Yes, I thought it would appeal to your sense of parsimony. It's a wonder you let me have any pocket money at all."

"A rich man will not remain so otherwise."

Together, we slowly paced the deck. Although we were actually the same height, it did not appear so, thanks to the lifts Crassus had had built into his *caligae*. I wondered how his feet were faring, though I thought it best not to ask. Though he was ten years my senior, he at least had a full head of hair. Only a prematurely greying wreath crowned my otherwise bald pate. My eyebrows seemed to be the only place on my head where hair would grow. Crassus would chide that with my thin nose, close-set eyes and round head, when I raised my bushy brows in skepticism or thoughtfulness, as I often did, I looked remarkably like an owl. If one must be compared to our avian cousins, what better choice for me than brother owl: noble, wise, silent and ferocious in the hunt.

Upon reflection, I must be honest and content myself with but two of the four analogies.

Still, when Livia's arms were wrapped about me, and her teeth held the lobe of my ear a willing captive, I far preferred to be called her sweet *pelargós* than his *bubo*, no matter how noble or wise. But I must not think of such things.

"Come now," Crassus said, "you lead a leisurely existence, compared to most."

"Not if by 'most' you mean your twenty thousand other slaves. You put me through twice as many paces as any three of them."

"Twenty thousand? That is the count? Truly?" Crassus could not keep the pride from his voice.

"Truly."

"Well, they are lucky, the lot of them, to have such a generous master."

"Indeed. Not a one of us would fare better on our own. As Aristotle has said, *'from the hour of their birth, some are marked out for subjection, others for rule.'* I would not trade places with you, my lord, for all the world. Which I dare say is practically within your power to bestow."

"It is a sign of the times, Alexander. A Roman who would serve his city needs money, not to hoard but to spend. Money breeds popularity, and popularity wins votes. Nonetheless, I have little doubt that your Aristotle would be quick to lump me together with those who '*turn every quality or art into a means of getting wealth; this they conceive to be the end, and to the promotion of the end they think all things must contribute.*'"

"Aristotle might, but I would not. No, in spite of your riches, I know you to be no shallow man. But, how then, shall I address you, if not consul? Praetor, censor, tribune, champion of the Servile War, and now proconsul and governor...you've garnered them all."

"You have me confused with someone else, Alexander," Crassus said sarcastically. "Pompeius himself wrote to Rome that *he* had ended the war with Spartacus, and as Magnus speaks, so Rome hears. I am afraid that unlike me, both Pompeius Magnus and Julius Caesar wear glory like an apple wears its skin. I am but a servant of Rome; they are its masters."

Yet again, I thought to myself. I had heard this tale a dozen times. "What is told and what is true are more often distant relations than identical twins. History will recognize you, even if the senate does not." A slave from the temporary galley came tottering up with a tray of bread and cheese. Crassus tore them in hunks, handing some of each to me. I had the tented kitchen constructed for Crassus' convenience; it would be dismantled before we sailed.

"Thank you, Simeon." He nodded to the servant, who departed, then turned back to me. "This is in the distant past," he continued. "Pompeius has always loved the adoration of the crowd. Let him sing for it. Though I admit, it pleases me to remember his most recent miscalculation in his courtship for the people's love."

"The elephants."

"Remind me, upon our return, to purchase a pair. I should like to keep them as pets, and as a reminder of that day."

"May that day arrive swiftly."

"Come, come, Alexander. Show a little spine. Does not your philosophy require observation? War is part of life. You must see it to understand it. Think of this adventure as my gift to you for the advancement of your studies."

"I would rather hear about it from the forum crier."

"At this moment, he is probably detailing the chaos of my departure."

"Yes, I am sorry to have missed it. I hear it caused quite a stir."

"You do not know the half of it. But I was pleased to find all in readiness for my comfort at the port, thanks to you. I regret the need to separate you from your son, but you are the only member of my household I would trust for such a task. You're a good *atriensis*, old friend. Half my friends would pay seven figures to steal you away for their own houses. I've had offers, believe me. Curio won't do near as well, but it can't be helped. I need you with me."

"He's quite competent. I'm sure he'll make an excellent replacement."

"Now don't pout. It's only temporary. You are foremost among my slaves, Alexander, and always shall be. You know what that means, don't you? To do what you have done, you could just as well have governed a good-sized town."

"When you grant us our freedom, general, I shall find a village and run for mayor."

"When I give you your freedom, Alexander, I shall be a poorer man by half."

It was a game we often played, but in thirty years, I had never won a round. My abilities were my curse. Crassus would never release me. But then, maybe Curio would prove to be so efficient, *dominus* would have no more need of me, and he'd release both me and my family. A faint and ironic hope. "You were about to tell me what happened at the forum," I said, trying to ignore the intermittent spatter of the agitated waters against the hull.

"As you know, my old friend Marcus Cato had already tried to convince the senate that my candidacy for the consulate was a sham, meant to accumulate more wealth and armies. The man is as blind as Homer. I have no more need of wealth than he has of purple-hemmed togas or parchment for his speeches. As for armies, I already own one; two would be gluttony. Nevertheless, he convinced the senate to withhold its sanction for a war against Parthia. And our noble collection of accountants and lawyers agreed. Why pick a fight, they asked, with a country who has harmed us but little? They missed the point entirely."

"If the political reasons were relevant, they would be many," I countered, knowing the darker motives which moved my master. "Orodes seems content to stay within the palace walls at Ctesiphon. And although he is king, his dominion is not much more than a patchwork of loosely confederated states. They do not seem capable of posing much of a threat, even if they should wish to expand their borders. They tried for Armenia, but she is now under Rome's patronage, and as a client state bent to Rome's will, Armenia is an effective buffer should the East awaken."

"Thank you, Alexander. You have made my argument for me. It is for these very reasons that Parthia is ripe for the plucking, and why the senate should have rushed to drape the *paludamentum* of command about my shoulders. Orodes is newly crowned; wet behind the ears. Our spies say he is completely preoccupied with simply keeping his throne, let alone ruling from it. He cannot possibly mount an adequate defense. We will sweep along the Euphrates like a honed scythe through dry wheat. Rome has many mouths to feed, Alexander. What flows from the breast of war but the milk of tribute, spoils and slaves? Rome is an ever-hungry infant that needs constant suckling. I will see to it, through this conquest, that its growth and health continue undiminished."

There was no point raising the objection that Rome had existing treaties with Parthia, and that breaking them would weaken the Republic's integrity throughout its sphere of influence. The light in my master's eye would brook no argument; it would only be extinguished by his success or, gods forfend, his failure. Politics aside, I had no desire to be whipped, as *dominus* had threatened. Once a lifetime is sufficient for any man.

"Where was I?"

"Cato."

"Yes. You would not believe it, but he convinced his co-conniver, that lunatic Ateius to reverse my proconsulship of Syria. Thankfully, his veto was overturned by another more 'reasonable' senator, who at this moment is on his way to inspect his new estate in Puteoli." The general winked. "Occasionally, excessive wealth has its uses, if only to let it flow where it is most needed."

"Do my ears deceive me? Or did I just hear you define your wealth as 'excessive'?"

"In the hearing, Alexander, you are not deceived. But in the interpretation, most beguiled. To the casual observer, my wealth may appear...extreme. To me, however, a *denarius* is but a tool, ten thousand *denarii* the means to many ends. And as any good carpenter knows, you can build anything if you have the right tools. Now stop trying to goad me to argument, or do you not wish to hear the end of the tale?"

Bowing contritely, I bade him continue.

"I left the senate, gathered my *lictors* and entourage, and was preparing to leave the city when this vaunted Tribune of the Plebs shows up again. This time Ateius, failing to incite the crowd to detain me, attempts instead to have me arrested!"

"I understand Pompeius intervened on your behalf?"

Crassus' expression darkened. "It is true, and it rankles deeply that I was forced to accept his assistance. Like it or not, he does have a following, and with his soothing words and paternal smiles, he parted the crowds in the *comitium* as a *liburna* under full sail cuts through hospitable seas.

"Why would he aid you? With respect, your enmity is mutual."

"Why else? To hasten us out of the city and so out of his thinning hair. Our alliance is broken. Both Pompeius and Caesar would like nothing better than to see me fail, or if the gods might grant their secret, special prayers, to find themselves on the speaker's *rostra* draped in black and reciting the *laudatio funebris* in my recently departed honor.

"Are you certain, my lord? Did not Caesar write from Gaul to encourage you?"

"Of course he encourages me! Think on it, Alexander. He believes my failure is fated, because I do not meet the requirement of the Sibylline oracles. I will fail because I am not a king. And when I do, the senate will grant him as many legions as it takes to avenge me; they will withhold nothing from him, including a crown."

"And so he allows Publius to slip away, to become another martyred hero?"

"I believe that is his thinking, yes." Crassus tilted his head toward the roiling sky. "Once I counted him an ally and I had thought, a friend. I believed I could take the measure of any man with but a glance, but it shames me to think how blind I was to his true nature. If I could be so wrong about Caesar, who is to say the image I hold of myself is not equally warped and contorted?"

"For that answer, you need only look into the eyes of your wife and sons."

"My wife, yes." Crassus' eyes drifted away, then refocused. "You were present the night Caesar became my enemy. Publius must never know. As for Marcus, my eldest, he is an accountant, not a warrior. Let Caesar keep him as *quaestor* to guard his swelling treasury. The general has little to fear from him, and I frankly, have little use for him in Parthia. He will stay in Gaul to be our ears in Caesar's camp.

"Do not look so dismayed, my old friend. I mean to turn their scheming to advantage. As much as Caesar and Pompeius think they will benefit from my departure, how much more then, will their stars fall when I return triumphant? I am no virgin legionary on his first sortie. Orodes cannot throw against us but a fraction of the army

Spartacus managed to put into the field. And what became of him and his rabble?"

The memory made me grimace. "I have seen the fate of six thousand of them—survivors caught and executed after the final battle. For more than a year after the war, unless you had a fast horse, a stomach made of Margianian steel or a wagonload of *ampullae* filled with Egyptian perfume, you could not travel the Via Appia between Capua and Rome without retching. A brace of nailed corpses every hundred feet for *sixty miles*, the sky black with crows for months—*dominus*, the horror and cruelty of it was too much."

"Because I love you, Alexander, and because I know that in matters of education and philosophy, you are at least my equal, I will not have you beaten for what I would consider impudence in any other man. Leave politics to the politicians. The crucifixions were a harsh but necessary deterrent. If I had it to do all over again, I would change nothing. And that is the point, is it not? By executing the survivors in the most ignominious, dishonorable way possible, I have insured that 'doing it all over again' will never be necessary. And mark me, Alexander, I will deal just as severely with Orodes, should he have the temerity to face me."

I stopped and turned a resolute face to my master. "I have served you, Marcus Licinius, for more years than I probably have left to live. I believe that, save for your wife, I know your heart and mind better than any man. I have seen your cunning, your intelligence, your business acumen and your political savvy. I know you to be a man of extreme generosity, good humor and loyalty. I cannot imagine what it must have been like as a young man to see your father and brother slain before your eyes. I know this is why you are so passionately protective of Tertulla, Marcus and brave Publius. You have suffered greatly, yet you have persevered and gained the world. In your heart, there is goodness, and in your mind, the desire to do the right thing. I do not believe that you are a ruthless or barbaric man, for I understand that the subtleties and intricacies of great sculpture must first endure the insults of chisel and hammer.

"All I am asking, *dominus*, is that you allow me the freedom to be absent should you ever speak again of the necessity that forced you to adorn the Via Appia with such stern politics." My voice was like the slow, persistent squeeze on the neck that extracts every drop of venom from the cobra's fangs.

Crassus was silent. The game piece had been moved. We never spoke of it, but each knew the rules. I would push the limits of my master's patience, or his tolerance, see how far and how often I could bait him until finally he snapped and reverted to the basic, fundamental nature of our relationship. Even if I lost, I won, for I would see the victory of pain in his eyes as he witnessed whatever punishment he imposed upon me. But it was a dangerous game, for men like me were cheaply bought by men like Crassus, and the silver mines were always hungry for more human fodder to chew and choke. Yet I was compelled. I had nothing that was not given me, nothing that could not on a whim be taken away. Except this. My prize was a shred of dignity that covered nothing but my naked shame. His prize, if he kept it, was a shred of humanity which he shared with no one.

Finally, Crassus spoke slowly and softly, a knife slipping gently between the ribs. "*This* freedom, Alexander, I shall grant you." Before I could offer my thanks, he said, "Now go fetch me an apple." As I turned to walk toward the shuddering galley tent, conceding the round to my master, he added without emphasis or emotion, "And bring one for yourself."

Ah. A draw then.

•••

The apples were crisp and tart. Resuming our discourse beneath the pregnant sky, I said, "You have not yet told me of the curse, of which I have heard little else since your arrival, from everyone but you."

"Alexander, I tell you, that man practically caused a riot. I approached the *pomerium* just at the sixth hour with my *lictors* and only the first *century* of the first *cohort* as escort. The sun was high and made blinding mirrors of their armor. Their weapons waited for them outside the city walls. There, like a recurring nightmare, at the *Capena Gate* stood Ateius, who had raced ahead to block the exit with his retinue. Before him a lit brazier was already aflame, the incense and oils he was pouring into it causing a stench as foul as low tide and burning blood. A large crowd had gathered by the time I stood before him. Billows of noxious yellow smoke rose even to the ramparts above the arch where spectators were climbing, scrambling for a view and cleaner air.

"Ateius screamed at me once more to abandon my plan to ignore the will of the senate. I calmly replied that I would not. He stared at me wild-eyed for a moment, his jowls turning red like a fat, mating lizard. Truly, he looked as if he was about to burst. At last he shouted, "So be it!" Then he threw off his toga to reveal yellow robes streaked as if stained with blood."

"A *magus*," I whispered.

"Yes. There was an audible gasp from the crowd as he raised his arms over his head. He began to wail in an unnatural, shrill falsetto that sent shivers through everyone, including me. This was not your typical malediction for the return of a stolen bath towel, scratched into a lead tablet and thrown down a well. No, this was a searing, hate-filled execration aimed not only at my total destruction, but everyone associated with the undertaking. He read from a parchment to increase the potency of his excoriation, and he'd obviously put much effort into its composition. He cursed me, my family and all my descendants to the seventh generation. He cursed the legionaries who marched with me, the auxiliaries, the cavalry; he even cursed the horses!

"Then, as if that wasn't enough, he began chanting incoherently; I didn't get all the words, some were Latin, some sounded Etruscan. He called upon Hades, Vulcan and Jupiter, along with demons and monsters of whom I'd never heard.

"Women threw their hands to their ears or covered those of their children. Others tried to get away; some were trampled. Merchants and soldiers shouted for him to stop. My guards would have strangled him on the spot had I not enjoined them. I would not have his blood on my hands as I departed. Now that *would* have been a foul omen."

"The people were not confident in his ability as a *magus*?"

"Certainly not. I myself knew him to be a student of the law; no one had any idea he had also delved into the mystical texts. And of course everyone, from plebeian to tribune knew that if Ateius made one little slip in word or gesture, his curse might very possibly rebound and return to fall not only upon himself, which I'm certain no one would have minded at all, but onto the city as well."

"I have heard tell of such things." Though I did not believe them.

"Attend, there is more to come. He concluded his imprecation by saying the most peculiar thing. I was so struck by it I had Sabinus write it down." Crassus opened a pouch tied to his belt and unfolded a piece of papyrus. "He said, 'If you do not turn aside from this adventure against a people that has done Rome no injury, and with whom we are at amity, you will surely be undone. Your purpose will be wrecked utterly. You and all that follow you shall perish in ignominy, your bleached bones left to inhabit the desert. Before all this has come to pass, even then Melek Ta'us may take pity on you and grant you understanding, so that upon your death you may repent, and thereby cause some future good to yet spring from your own wrongdoing.'"

"Remarkable," I said.

"I was thunderstruck, and I had no idea what this rant might signify. I said to him, 'Tribune Gaius Ateius, whatever happened to Jupiter Capitolinus? Or Mars Invictus? If I am to be sent to the underworld in shame, at least I should like to know a little more about the deity who is sending me there.' The crowd about us fell silent. I asked him if he did not think it unusual to end a curse with lenience. Ateius looked almost as bewildered as I and replied that he had been instructed to say these things by the goddess. 'This Melek Ta'us,' I presume. 'The very same,' he replied. 'And who is Melek Ta'us?' I inquired. He said he did not know. 'This is becoming tiresome,' I said. 'How is it, then, you come to invoke his name?' 'Her name,' he said."

At that moment, Petronius came back on deck. "Your leave, general." He saluted by hitting his closed right fist upon his breast. Crassus nodded. "Preparations for the sacrifice will be ready within the hour. Rain approaches from the west," he added, hoping Crassus would reconsider his decision to embark.

"Then we'd better get those oxen slaughtered," came the disappointing reply. "Where was I?" he asked as Petronius clambered back down to the jetty.

"This goddess…"

"Ah yes. Ateius told me she had come to him in a dream, in the form of a peacock. This Melek Ta'us assured Ateius that my purpose was made of stone and that I would not be deterred, but that, short of violence, he should try to dissuade me nonetheless. I said in a louder voice for all to hear, 'It augurs well that the gods know my purpose and determination, even if they be gods unknown to and unsanctioned by Rome. Now, you've done your duty and your conscience should be clear. You have also disrupted the tranquility of this city and put needless fear in the hearts of your countrymen. For this, you shall most likely have to answer to them when I have gone, but that is not my concern. Now stand aside and let us pass.' And that was essentially the end of it."

"I would have to say," I said, glancing at clouds so heavy and leaden they appeared to be straining with the effort not to burst, "that this is as inauspicious a beginning to an expedition as ever one might dread. These are powerful signs, lord. Dare we ignore them?"

"You don't fool me for an instant, Alexander. You put no stock in omens and incense. You see them for what they are: pacifiers for children. Your fear of this undertaking does not become you. There is no Roman death more honorable than one earned on the field of battle."

"Alas, I am no Roman." I imagined the Via Appia as Crassus had left it after his defeat of Spartacus. How was the fate of those six thousand eyeless sentinels, their limbs given an occasional twitching, false life by the maggots that consumed them, any different?

To a corpse, honor meant nothing. Death on the battlefield or on a cross was death all the same.

Crassus threw the core of his half-eaten apple over the side. "Don't mistake me. The gods have their place; fear of them may keep the peace as handily as a veteran legion. I, for one, though I observe the forms, am too busy shaping my own destiny to wonder whether public prayers are heard or not. Politicians make ready use of religion, but press us beyond our devout mouthings and you will find little faith."

I said nothing, but nodded toward the canopy in the stern, and shelter. In the distance to the west, a grey curtain of rain marched steadily toward the port, and lightning finally broke through the clouds. It crackled and hummed as the gods wrote a brief but illegible note on the landscape. Whether benediction or curse, who could say?

CHAPTER XXII

55 – 54 BCE - WINTER, ON THE MARCH

Year of the consulship of
Gnaeus Pompeius Magnus and Marcus Licinius Crassus

Those of you with decent memories will recall that the tribune Ateius invoked the name of the same goddess of whom Melyaket the Parthian was so enamored. It is a strange coincidence, I grant you. Yet there are many wondrous things between the instant we perceive our own mortality and the final moment when, with our last exhalation of disappointment, we resign ourselves to death's embrace, of which we have no understanding. Do I believe there exists a divine Peacock Angel (Melek Ta'us in the Parthian tongue) keeping a feathery eye on us, her mortal charges. I do not. You may do so if you choose, but with apologies to Aristotle, life among the Romans has caused me to edge closer to Epicurus on this issue: the gods have no time nor interest in the comings and goings of man, and their reality is in all likelihood so far removed from ours that they are entirely unaware of our existence. If a divine peacock has somehow slipped its celestial confinement, someone ought to herd it back to its pen.

•••

The crossing from Brundisium to Dyrrhachium would have taken a single *trireme* less than a day and a night sailing under fair skies. Our passage took three times as long. Which meant we would have been very hungry and very thirsty, had we been able to think of such things without retching. Before our voyage was over, what food we did have in our bellies was heaved up on deck, washed overboard or onto the rowers below. The storms were relentless; not for even an hour was our captain able to raise the sails and grant the oarsmen a rest. Some were broad-backed free men, mostly Greeks from Syracusae working off their twenty-six year contract to earn Roman citizenship. From what I could hear of their labors through the decking, they earned every one of the four sesterces credited daily to each man's account. Most, however, were our own legionaries, chosen from among those with the least seniority, to help man the 170 oars. There was room on deck for no more than a *century*, less if the *trireme* was carrying cargo or animals.

These cedar ships were meant to sail along the coast for a single day, then dock and take on stores for another short journey, on *calm* seas. *Triremes* and other ships of war are not built to withstand winter storms. If you were an eagle soaring high over the Middle Sea at this time of year, your keen eyes would be shocked to find the white-capped waters filled with our frail centipedes, oars beating a desperate, funereal rhythm against the iron waves.

By the time *Scourge of Ctesiphon* shipped its oars under clearing skies in Epirus Nova's finest harbor, the last of our storm-battered fleet was barely halfway through their own ordeal. Never had the Adriatic done so much to dissuade so many from the Eastern journey. We arrived drained, drenched and shivering. And behind us, on an ever darkening horizon, lightning silvered the grey sea.

The bosom of Dyrrachium's port may have been welcoming and blessedly unmoving, but its outstretched arms could only accommodate a fraction of the numbers Crassus had amassed. Weeks passed while thousands of men waited for their turn to disembark, steaming themselves dry in the cool air. Even at the rate of ten ships a day, thousands spent over a month just getting themselves off those accursed boats. The town had to ferry food and water to the queued ships while the men gambled, sharpened their blades, and baled harbor water from their chastised transports.

I say this: if man had been meant to ply the seas, the gods in their wisdom would have given him a stronger stomach. If destined to tread the earth, surely he would have been created with the legs of a lion and the feet of a pachyderm. One must be forced to the conclusion that the unerring gods blessed man with a form best suited for contemplation, study, and a life undisturbed by travel.

(Even an atheist may invoke the gods by way of expression and turn of phrase. I defy you to deny it. The supposition, I maintain, is nevertheless accurate.)

•••

Scanning back across the decades compresses time, like a length of string held taut in both hands, then slowly turned till it is looked at from one end to the other. How odd to think back on that time now. Events tumble one upon the other. A mere six years after we departed Dyrrachium for Parthia, Caesar would descend upon the port to face a resolute Pompeius. There would Magnus give Caesar such a thrashing that the war between them could have ended in Caesar's defeat, had Pompeius not halted the rout before the final blow could be struck. Of his narrow and inexplicable escape Caesar would remark to his friends, "Today victory belonged to the enemy, if the enemy had only been led by a victor." Of this and all that followed my master would be beyond caring.

Was it better for my lord that the Fates cut the thread of his life and dropped him into the black ignorance of death before learning of either of his rivals' fate? Though the Spinner had been distracted and the Measurer had lost track of Time, though the wool of *dominus'* life wound round his life's spool far more than most, I say it matters not. Like many blinded by their passions, clarity struck Crassus only when the hot breath of his mortality moved the hairs upon his neck, when the oiled, preparatory snips of the Cutter came close upon his ear. He saw, only at the last, the folly of his quest for vengeance. Too late, too late. A multitude would suffer; life would change in uncounted ways as shards from the collisions of his choices' children spun off in all directions.

Time and the world will rumble on without him, leaving brave Tertulla to grieve and go on. They will roll over each of us in our turn, as they had Pompeius and Caesar, Antonius and Cleopatra, as they will Melyaket, Livia, our son, me, you, your progeny and theirs, on into infinity until one or the other grows tired and decides to grind to a halt.

•••

Being assigned to Crassus as his non-military aide did have its benefits: we were the first to disembark to anemic welcoming noises made by magistrates, citizens and manifestly amateur musicians. Never mind. I had to restrain myself to keep from embracing each in his turn. Romans, as you are probably aware, do not have the world's finest reputation as sailors, and with apologies to the 300 oarsmen and 50 crew who got our flagship safely to port, as I stepped off onto the dock, my first thought was to ask myself how much longer it would take on the return trip to go the long way around on solid ground.

My immediate objective, after finding suitable lodgings for *dominus* while the engineers laid out our first temporary camp to the south of the city, was to locate Livia. It is good to have objectives, for they are the ropes by which we pull ourselves through this life from one milestone to the next. I advise, however, moderation in this task of setting goals, or else risk becoming tangled up in a Gordian knot of life's many disappointments.

By way of example, take my desire to find my wife. Frantic to know if she was safe, I longed to hold her and to hear every detail of how she had weathered the crossing. Then, having secured a room adjacent to and almost as fine my lord's, I intended to sup with her, bed her, and assure her that I would stand by her and protect her until we were safely returned to our home and our son. And I cannot claim to have had, by way of excuse, even a solitary cup of watered wine.

I dined alone that first night, while Crassus met with his legates. The next day, I waited on my master, and when dismissed, dove into the confusion of the docks in search of my lady. This I repeated each day of the first week, and again on every day of the second. A ship came into port carrying Musclena, the chief *medicus*, but Livia was not on board. I found Octavius, legate of Legion I, and second-in-command. He could not say for sure, but he thought the remaining two *triremes* carrying the field hospital and the rest of the medical supplies and personnel would be another week at sea. In spite of being pulled in a hundred directions, the commander took the time to put a hand on my shoulder and reassure me that now that the weather had eased, the rest of the fleet would arrive safely.

And they did, but was "the rest of the fleet" *all* of the fleet? There were rumors. Before they could be substantiated, Crassus' patience ran out, even as a dozen sails crawled over the milky horizon. I begged my lord to allow me to tarry in Dyrrachium, but his deteriorating handwriting sentenced that hope to an early death.

Even before we left Rome, Crassus had been finding it more and more difficult to hold a pen. Once we had departed the city, he wrote more than ever, composing at least one letter to my lady each day without fail. I offered to assign a scribe to him, but he would not hear of it. I was the only one he would entrust with the intimate details of his dictation. I made two copies: one would accumulate to be sent home by courier in a bundle at the end of each month; the other I would secure as insurance against the original failing to reach its destination. When I asked him how this cramping might affect his sword arm, he assured me it was only the narrow grip of the writing instruments that troubled him.

"If we fought with pens," he said, "I would be forced to fall upon mine."

That evening, I sat wearily in my master's tent, scrawling listlessly to Tertulla of the weather, the scenery and varied matters of equal import. We were to learn later that of the original 36,000 souls that left Brundisium, two thousand legionaries, five hundred auxiliaries and five hundred cavalry would be lost at sea, twelve ships sacrificed to Poseidon. Or to Crassus. Since I have never seen the water god, where else can the blame lie but at the feet of the mortal?

•••

As soon as one of the grain ships was offloaded, we broke camp with four legions; Octavius stayed behind to await the remainder of the army; Crassus himself led our troops. I left the port, turning in my saddle as we rounded the last hill that would put the sea from view. There were many more sails now sitting upon the water with stripes of red and cream, and from their number I took hope. I turned from the sight and whispered a brief appeal to no god in particular to bring her safely to port.

Strange, is it not, how even those of us who scoff at divine intervention will fall to our knees and clasp our hands the moment we realize our futures are defined by uncertainty and hazard. A thoughtful man would never leave his knees. A wise man would never drop to them. In any case, it wasn't really a prayer, but one does like to follow convention now and then.

•••

Two weeks later, still ignorant of Livia's fate, Crassus dismissed me until after the evening meal. He wanted to have a bath. If I hurried, I ought to have sufficient time. It was only an hour's ride south of camp, a place unknown to me as a child, then denied to me as a man. Yes, I had been given permission to ride rather than walk all the way to Syria! There was no prestige in it — it was the only means of keeping pace with my master and his wants. Apollo was a reliable, if sedentary dark brown bay, but to me he was Pegasus. On the march, from my equine elevation, the endless sight and oceanic sound of thousands of men marching men six abreast almost made me feel guilty. (You may be interested to know that I named my horse for the statue at whose feet Livia and I first kissed. Yes, I have a romantic nature; it is a character flaw which should be viewed with pity, not derision.)

The engineers had chosen a field between a sloping cherry orchard and a rushing stream that lay a mile to the east of Edessa. Fresh water and decent grazing—these were the two most important criteria for camp selection. In the distance came constant thunder from an unseen cascade whose waters raced past us with a jubilation I did not share. A light rain was falling. It was early afternoon and legionaries were still tramping into the unfinished camp from the morning's march. My tent lay between my master's magnificent structure—you could hardly call it a tent—and those almost as grand assigned to the army's legates. There was my humble goatskin shelter, the standard ten feet on a side, a bug caught between giant hands. But then I didn't have to share it with seven other coarse, foul-mouthed, reeking soldiers, did I? No sharing, but no sleeping either. For the first few nights, this blessed oblivion proved all but impossible to achieve, curled up in my cloak on the straw-strewn floor, save for a few nightmare-encrusted moments.

Do I sound unaccountably bitter? Perhaps, but I can account for the sentiment, I assure you. I mentioned this once. You may have forgotten, but I never shall. When I had first become a slave, dragged with Sulla's army back from Athens, a boy of nineteen, it was in a tent just such as the one which I now called home where I had catered to every need, imaginable and unimaginable, of eight men indistinguishable from the thousands surrounding me now. I recoil as I remember their callous indifference to my suffering, their almost bored creativity as each day they subjected me to some new indignation. I served at their pleasure for over a year. The decades had helped me push those memories into a corner of my mind where I shuddered to look. There it was never quite dark, but always illuminated by the same dim, yellow light that filtered down through my tent's hide to settle on my shoulders like a shroud. Now, they came again, bright and raw and new. Old friends.

I wrapped my *sagum* about me and burst through the tent flap to stand in the camp forum gulping the misty, bright air. It was clogged with the smells of wood, dirt, dust, horses, mules, and sweat. Perfume, compared to the rank, memory-laden air of my lodgings. A ride would do me good.

I looked behind my tent across the narrow aisle at the empty patch of meadow; Betto and Malchus had not yet arrived, but I had heard that they had made a safe crossing. The tent-mates originally assigned to their *contubernium* had not been as fortunate. Ridiculous as it sounds, I looked upon my friends' survival as a special favor from the heavens to me. Malchus had a way of making me see through to the best outcome of any bad situation. I needed him now. And Betto's whining was sheer entertainment, plain and simple. Some men use bravado to hide their fear; with Betto it was the opposite: strip away his complaining and superstitious caterwauling and you will never find a braver man. I mourned for the drowned men, but took great comfort from the knowledge that at least my friends, assigned by Crassus himself to the first *century* of the first *cohort* of the first legion would be nearby. But where was Livia?

There were no women in the army. You might find one or two in the arena, where survival depended on no skills other than your own, but here, in this machine of war where each part depended upon the other, no. No women.

Camp followers grew like a scruffy, wagging tail with each day's march. In this quotidian, aberrant reflection of the legion's art, a child's grotesque imitation of its parent's craft, you would find slaves of wealthy soldiers who could afford more than the one servant assigned to each *contubernium*, sellers of anything from blankets to good wine, and it was here you could also discover women in profusion. They might be merchants, selling fresh bread, their bodies, fish oil or cook pots. Or they might be "wives" of the men, who were not theoretically allowed to marry, though those were few, true and hardy to make this trip. But inside the camp itself, nary a one. Within our walls was precision, engineered and obsessive, everything in its place, each man accounted for. Give me the name of any soldier, his legion, *cohort* and *century*, and I could walk across our vast encampment of an evening and point to his tent with unerring regularity. The squalor and chaos of the army's bustling town, reborn each night outside our walls, would give me greater challenge. When Octavius met up with us, that is where I would find Livia.

•••

That is not where I went now. I walked with contrived purpose down the length of the parade ground, past the *rostrum* where Crassus could address the assembled troops, past the tent where the standards were housed, past the sacrificial altar, down to the rear gate and the picket lines where I had left Apollo. Flags placed by the engineers who had arrived hours ago still marked the boundaries of the camp and also the location of the four gates. The ground had been leveled and cleared, the sod for the ramparts collected, and work by the legionaries not guarding the rest of us was proceeding with such orderliness and efficiency it surpassed even my own captious standards.

Since there were no enemies about, Crassus had allowed the trench around the camp to be dug to a depth of only three feet. The dirt was thrown inward to build the rampart, faced with sod and finished with logs. The palisade in this friendly territory was only five feet above the ground, its floor and outer wall bound with stakes carried by each legionary. It took these men a remarkably short three and a half hours to erect the entire encampment which, when complete, would house our abbreviated army of four legions plus auxiliaries. To make our evening's home we stole from the landscape an enormous rectangle 1,300 by 1,800 feet, consuming over 50 acres. Each day. When the army was completely reassembled our encampment would grow to over 60 acres.

I found Apollo and told a stable boy to prepare him. Just as I was about to step up onto the mounting stool I overheard a voice from the palisade calling out to someone down the line. "Linus, you slug!" he shouted. "My dead grandmother would have those stakes tied off by now. Pretend there's a five-story *insula* right across the street; it's burning and any second a wall of fire is going to come crashing down on your head." That voice! Like a saw pulling through wood, so familiar, but I could not place it. Until I heard the man say the word "fire."

"Ludovicus?!"

The big man with the shaved head and eyes the color of rainwater on a stormy day turned in my direction. His skin was so darkly tanned he looked as if he'd already been to Parthia and back. He squinted, then recognition dawned and he shouted, "My favorite Greek! I heard you were here. Come on up, so I can see how bad you look. That's an order!"

"Hah!" I called back, making my way up the planed logs that served as steps. "If I remember correctly, the last time we spoke it was you who were taking orders." Then I lost my wind as Ludovicus grabbed my arm on the last plank and pulled me into what I have learned to call a "Roman crush." All along the palisade legionaries of lower rank were tamping down dirt, laying boards or tying stakes. It seemed we were the only two at rest in the entire camp.

"Yes, but not from you! I see, stork, your 'feathers' have either fallen off or turned white." I was elated to see him, but should I have been?

"What are you doing in uniform? You should have been pastured years ago."

"They tried," he said, twisting his features into a mask of rage, "but I made a face and the bull fainted."

Ludovicus had been a freedman, part of the Crassus *familia* when I first came to the house. Over the years, he had been promoted from handyman to commander of Crassus' fire brigade, and together, we had "engineered" the acquisition of many buildings on behalf of our patron. Whenever a fire broke out, we would rush to the rescue, but only begin putting out the fire with our pumps and hoses when *dominus* himself had negotiated a purchase price a fraction of the value of the ruined property.

"What happened to your career in farming?" I asked.

"Let me put it this way: the army beats shoveling shit onto a field that's already covered in shit. I quit that *latifundium* in Cremona and joined the engineers over ten years ago. Then I discovered I enjoyed swinging a sword more than a hammer. Next thing you know I'm with Pompeius fighting pirates in Cilicia. That was great fun, that was. Bit of a lull after that, but then I heard, along with everyone else in Latium, that Crassus was building an army, and here I am."

A part of me wanted to hate this mountain of muscle, but it was a small part. Even with cause, he was a very hard man to dislike. Some would say, if only in an indirect way, I had cause enough. But the truth was, Livia's mother was to blame, not Ludovicus. Sabina had loved the brigade commander with singular ardor; none of us ever imagined the depth and breadth of her jealousy until it was too late. It had never been proved that Ludovicus was cheating on Livia's mother with Tessa, the gardener, but Sabina had all the evidence she needed. Before she could be stopped, Tessa was dead, Sabina was on her way to the mines in chains, and Livia had taken back her heart and left me devastated and alone.

"You two!" a very unhappy voice yelled from below. It was Lucius Vinicius, *primus pilus* of Legion V, a position of high honor. He was smacking his vine stick into his hand so hard it whistled. The sound made me think of Livia. Which proves that almost anything could remind me of her.

Vinicius was transparently unhappy with his posting; he had hoped to be awarded *primus pilus* of Legion I, but that honor had been given to Vel Corto, an Etruscan, which rankled even more. He hadn't even been assigned as high as Legion II. To him, it was a disgrace. But he had been told that in Crassus' army, tradition was followed to the letter, unless merit proved the old way the wrong way. For the same reason, there were no military tribunes on the general's payroll. Crassus called them "ducklings." They were the darlings of the senate: their downy chins were too young to have gained any real experience, they made lots of noise and waddled around in circles without doing much of anything. Useless on the battlefield.

"Mercury's feathered testicles, centurion, what kind of example are you setting for your men? You, slave. On your way or I'll have you striped!"

"Sir!" Ludovicus saluted and gave me a look that said, *we'll continue this later. Go.*

"Centurion," I said, turning around to face him. I wasn't wearing my gold disk of immunity, for there was little need of it in camp. I hated wearing it, hated even more making use of it, for what was a slave doing with a vine stick, even if it was round and gold? Besides, it was heavy, clanked against my "identity" plaque and in any case, everyone in the army knew Crassus' first slave, Alexander. "I sincerely hope it won't come to that. I shall descend on the instant."

To his credit, when he recognized me, Vinicius did not wilt. "Sir, you have no business on the palisade. These men are on a tight schedule. You're obstructing the completion of the fortifications. However...I apologize. Sir. From behind I thought...you look just like..."

"No need to apologize," I said. "It is difficult to distinguish between one six-foot-one, balding slave in a tunic and another. The camp is overrun with us."

The centurion opened his mouth to speak again, thought better of it, turned on his heel and walked away. We could hear the slap of his vine stick against his thigh fading down the rampart. I pitied the next underling who crossed him, and knew that the only thing that stood between me and a flogging or worse was the universal knowledge that I was the general's personal, inviolable pet. I would never earn that centurion's respect, but I had been wrong not to try. Oh well.

"That was both surprising and gratifying," Ludovicus said. "Vinicius is cruel. His men hate him."

"Then Legion V is weak. Shall I tell the general?"

"Don't bother. From what I hear, these Parthians are nomads, scattered and disorganized. Even Vinicius will distinguish himself. Now, what was I going to ask you? Oh yes, I remember—let's hear it, Alexander, have you joined the brotherhood of men since I saw you last? Or are you still paying visits to the left-handed whore in your tent?"

I was too old to blush. I think. "It is comforting to find that some things never change, Ludovicus. Like your manners." I suppose my cheeks did color. A year or so after I had first been given to Crassus, Ludovicus had volunteered to pay for my entry fee into the world's most non-exclusive clubs at one of his favorite brothels. The outing had the unintended consequence of underscoring both my ignorance in all matters amorous and the certainty that I would die a virgin.

"Livia and I have formed a *contubernium*," I said. "We have a son."

"You and Livia?" Ludovicus' look was one of suspicious incredulity. "But you...her mother..."

"That was twenty-five years ago. We fell in love, once in youth, then again as man and woman. I am the most fortunate of men. So, to answer your uncouth question, in my entire life, there has been only Livia, and Livia only has filled my life entire."

Ludovicus laughed and shook my hand. "If you could tame that firebrand, perhaps it is you who should have been teaching me about women. I am well-pleased, Alexander." Thinking more on it, he added, "Isn't she about half your age?"

"Yes, if I were twenty-four and she were twelve. She's here, you know. Or will be soon." The centurion's grey eyes widened. "She's a *medicus*," I said, "like her mother. Crassus insisted she work in the camp hospital."

Ludovicus frowned. "In that case, I'd better pray to Mars I don't get wounded and wind up under her knife."

•••

An hour south of our encampment, in the shade of Mount Vermion, with directions from a villager in the town of Mieza, I found the Nymphaion. Approaching the glade with reverence, I slipped from Apollo, and while he grazed, walked slowly along the path to the base of the escarpment. It seemed impossible that the place had been abandoned, yet the columns of the portico were overgrown with vines of orchid, the stone benches crowded round by beds of mossy campion, as if their pink stars, now extinguished by the season, had huddled close, straining to hear the echoes of words spoken here three hundred years ago. Spikes of mullein, their yellow blooms now brown and sere, stood like withered sentinels; Nature would still pay homage to this place, even if man did not.

My feet walked where he had walked. My lungs inhaled the same air that he, with each exhale had imparted the wisdom of physics, politics and ethics to his young charges. A father had sent his thirteen-year-old son to this untroubled spot, away from the bustle of the capital, to study for three years with the great philosopher. It is said that this Alexandros, one greater than I or any other who ever shared that name, would in later years never go to his rest without two comforts beneath his pillow: the unsheathed dagger of the vanquished Darius, and a copy of *The Iliad*, edited and annotated by his teacher, Aristotle.

I could not tarry, for the sun had already descended to the stony brow of the mountaintop. I bowed my head to let this place of reason and science infuse me with its neglected peace and hope that somewhere along the road ahead the same would lie in store for me and those I loved. Apollo came when I called, and we made our way back up toward the Via Egnatia. The path was narrow and the trees grew thick; I did not see them till they were upon me. Scouts, Roman, their lances lowered, surrounded me almost before I could give the password chosen when the army split. If it was a full *turma* there would be thirty-two of them, led by a *decurion*. By the look of them, these men were as high-strung as their mounts.

I reached for my disk of immunity; Pan's hoof! Now, when I needed it, I had rushed off without it. That was a mistake I fervently wished to be given the opportunity to make again.

"Sand!" I cried.

Their captain looked surprised and responded, unable to keep the disappointment from his voice, "'And Blood.' All right, you're one of us. But whose slave are you? He must be rich to give you a name plaque of silver. Hand it here." The lances remained pointed at an unfriendly angle.

"It is not silver. It is *urukku* steel." I saw no harm in acquiescing, considerably more by refusing.

313

"There is nothing written here. It's blank. Is this a joke?"

"I'm afraid it is. My owner has me wear it as a symbol of his trust in me." The captain stared uncomprehendingly. "That I will not run away," I added.

"Look at the swirls of color. I once saw a sword of Margianian steel, but Margiania is east of the Mare Caspium. Almost as far as Bactria. How did you come by this?"

"Our trading partners' reach extends far to the East. That is all I am permitted to say." I held out my hand and the *decurion* returned the small, chained breast plate. I hung it about my neck.

"I don't think I like your attitude, slave."

"Few do. Alas, captain, it is my only possession: an abundance of attitude."

"For the last time, who owns you?" My tunic sank under the pressure from the tip of his spear. But I decided I was more afraid that Apollo would step forward than I was of this soldier. Something in his eyes told me he wasn't in a killing mood. And that made me impertinent.

"My master, *decurion*, is your master." A few of the riders laughed. The look in the captain's eyes went cold. Had I misjudged him? My father always told me my mouth would be the death of me. Although I doubted the man would actually go that far. However, *any* length, I thought, glancing down at his spear, would be too far.

From the back, a deep voice called, "By Lugos, I know that man."

Someone else said, "Move aside," and to my amazement, they did, although when I saw who it was who had spoken, amazement faded, replaced by astonishment.

"Taog. Brenus! Praise the gods!" The giant Taog cleared the way until he and Brenus were part of the circle that surrounded me. "Wait a minute. What are you two doing here?"

"I'll ask the questions!" the *decurion* said to Brenus.

Culhwch's son hesitated, then said, "My father requested it. I'm not your master's son—Crassus could not ride with Publius; Culhwch *would* not ride with me." He spoke as if each word were a spider in his mouth.

"You're out of line, Brenus," said the captain, "Speak to me when I address you. You vouch for this slave?"

"I do. He is...*attensis* to Marcus Crassus."

"*Atriensis*," the captain corrected. He held the Celt's eyes, looking for truth, then motioned with his free hand and the lances rose till their tips no longer pointed at my vitals. "If you were mine," he said to me, "I'd beat some of the arrogance out of you."

"You would not be the first to wish it, sir, and I expect you'll not be the last to discover that, on occasion, it has been done."

"Good to hear. Training and discipline, man. Training and discipline."

"It is our life's lot. Both yours and mine."

He scanned my face for insubordination, but mildness was all I let him see. "What were you doing out here, *atriensis*? We might easily have skewered you," he said wistfully.

"I was looking for you," I said breezily. "My lord is anxious for the army to be joined."

"Off the main road? Without an escort? General Crassus must be less happy with you than you think."

"That is always a possibility," I said. "What news of the fleet, captain? How was your voyage?"

315

The *decurion* wiped the sweat from his brow and adjusted his helmet. When he was finished, he was a different man. "It was a Herculaneum holiday. What do you think?" He turned his horse and rode off.

The scouts escorted me back to camp. No one would talk to me about the crossing. They were bringing some good news, though: if tomorrow Crassus would halt his column after fourteen miles instead of eighteen, Octavius would march twenty-two; by evening we could be whole again. On the way back, I tried to engage the Celts, but Taog was silent and Brenus' answers were curt and guarded. I asked if they had seen Livia, but they said they knew of no one by that name. Of course! She had not attended the celebration for Publius; they would not even know what she looked like. Then why did the two of them fairly ripple with discomfiture?

CHAPTER XXIII

Year of the consulship of
Gnaeus Pompeius Magnus and Marcus Licinius Crassus

The following afternoon, on the open Macedonian plain, Crassus declared a day of rest to honor the army's reunion. Sacrifices were made in the new, larger camp forum; lamb, beef cattle and wine were purchased by Cassius from a cowering village nearby, and the centurions were hard-pressed to maintain any kind of order till curfew the following sundown.

The tumult of over thirty-five thousand soldiers settling in for an evening of revelry stole through the walls of the general's tent as quietly as a triumph. But I was not yet done writing the day's letter to Tertulla. Somewhere out there, I prayed, Livia waited for me. My lord had just said, "how I miss the sound of your laugh, the touch of your soft cheek, *columba*…," but instead of writing "dove" I had begun to spell "Livia." Horrified, I crumpled up the parchment and begged *dominus'* forgiveness. Crassus stopped his pacing and walked over to the table. He

317

snatched up the ruined lump, picked its edges open and read. Then he put both hands on the writing table, leaned toward me and said, "Go. And don't let me see your face till morning." I leapt from my seat spewing thanks, but before I could escape, he added, "Don't throw that out. We'll finish it tomorrow. You're not the only one who misses his wife." There were so many layers of irony in that statement I almost choked. Before my mouth could betray me, I fled into the light.

I ran down the Via Praetoria, the center street of the camp, until some unsympathetic *optio* put a hand on my chest and insisted I walk. Skirting the *quaestorium* at the opposite end of the camp from dominus' tent, I overheard Cassius chastising a subaltern for a daily inventory coming up short one wheel of cheese. Well done, Cassius; a man after my own heart. I left the fort through the *Porta Decumana*, the western, rear gate. Wading through the six *centuries* assigned to guard duty, I must have been asked at least that many times if I was sure I knew the daily password without which I would be denied re-entry. At last, I made my way into the muddy puzzle of tottering sheds and unskinned tents selling everything from jewelry to cookware, shoddy armor to burned bread. Aisles of food kiosks were fully manned by sweating men and women frying, baking and yelling, the smoke of their battles to win the war of commerce rising grey against the pink sky. Shouting merchants clamored in tongues only their wares could translate, all trying with laughable success to emulate the order and precision of the Roman camp to which they clung. I had entered the city of camp followers.

Thank Apollo for my love's idiosyncrasies, and for my ardent love of almost all of them. (It must be noted,

Elysium be praised, Livia chose to crane her neck to look past far more of my own peculiarities.) I approached a large, well-staked goatskin tent. Just outside, two black-skinned women, wrapped head to toe in a discord of colors so bright they blinked the eye, sat cross-legged on reed mats mending other more mundane pieces of clothing, a tunic and a *subligaculum*. From within, I heard the sound of humming. Even had I not recognized that non-melody of happy preoccupation, the two legionaries stationed at either end of the tent stakes assured me I was in the right place. Saying another little prayer to Crassus for finding her and arranging for her safety, I doubled back, found a wine merchant and haggled very briefly for a corked skin of *mulsum*, boiled wine and honey, for only three times its cost in the city. Then I returned and stood outside her tent flaps and called, "Healer! I have a hangnail that requires attention."

The humming stopped immediately. The legionary on the left winked broadly, then his face returned to stone.

"Sorry, soldier, I'm off duty," she called. "Try the clinic—it's on the Via Principalis halfway between the Praetorium and the left gate." The sound of the laughter in her voice was honey poured on sweet pine nut custard— almost too much to bear.

"Ow," I cried. "It really hurts. I can't walk."

"You're such a baby," Livia said, throwing the tent flap aside as she ducked and stood upright. "Nebta, Khety, this is my heroic Alexandros."

The two women looked up from their sewing and giggled.

"Oh," I said stupidly, because I was looking at Livia, and saw that she had changed. There was a newness about her, a veneer of transcendence that lay about her like a

319

shield. Her red hair was pinned up, and like me, she wore a plain, mid-thigh tunic, belt and sandals. A red cloak was thrown casually over her right arm. Otherwise, we were dressed the same, save for my throwing knives and badge of office (I remembered it this time), the red trim on the tunic Crassus had given her declaring her a healer, and a smudge on her left cheek. We stood three feet apart, toes curling to fling ourselves into each other's arms, savoring the agony of postponement. A smiling legionary I did not know passed behind me and patted me on the shoulder.

"Nebta and Khety are your friends," I said, more statement than question.

"And now they are your friends." There was a story there, which I immediately accepted.

"They are indeed."

"Pleasure to make your acquaintance, master," the woman on the left said. Her voice was thick and sweet with an accent that rose and fell like song. "I am Nebta." Nebta wore a small gold hoop through her left nostril.

"Nebta." I nodded. "Call me Alexandros. I am no one's master."

I do not know why, but this set the African women giggling again. They spoke to each other in a new language, one I had never heard before, full of sounds as exotic as their dress. Their voices were huskier than their laughter.

"Where did you learn to speak Greek?" I asked.

The one called Khety answered, the large gold hoops in her ears bouncing off her graceful neck as she spoke. "The whole world learned to speak Greek after the other Alexandros came."

"They're from Oxyrhynchou Polis," Livia said. "South of Memphis. I met them...just outside Dyrrachium. They were looking for work."

Something caught my eye. I went to lift the cloak from Livia's arm but she pulled away from me. "What are you hiding?"

"It's nothing."

"I am relieved to hear it. Then show me this nothing." Livia reluctantly draped the long cloak over her other arm, revealing bright bruises on her legs and what appeared to be a long, deep red rope burn on her forearm. I shuddered. "How did this happen? Are you all right?" This last question is one of the most useless one can ask once an emergency has past, yet it is also one of the most ubiquitous. One simply cannot help oneself from asking it.

"I'm fine. I'll tell you later. When we're alone." She made it sound like an amorous thing, which it clearly was not. Nebta and Khety found it funny enough, but I was beginning to suspect a fine mesh in the netting of things they did *not* find humorous.

"Well, it has been extremely nice to meet both of you, Nebta and Khety, but I have not seen my lady in a very long a time and I am hoping she will join me for a stroll. There is a copse..."

"I am very fond of copses," Livia said, shifting the cloak back again to cover her injuries.

Soft hands flew to mouths, repressing mirth. I am generally opposed to romantic displays in front of an audience, mine or anyone else's, but these two simple innocents, so pure of heart, made me want to drop to my knees and embrace them. This I resisted, but they did pry a smile from the old stork. They were irrepressibly, infectiously happy.

"Gentlemen," I said to the legionaries. "What are your orders?"

"To guard the *medicus*," said the non-winking soldier.

"Do either of you have any problem taking amended orders from me?"

"We know who you are," said the winker.

"Good. You will also protect *all* the occupants of this tent, whether inside or out, to the best of your ability. You will follow the *medicus'* orders as if they were my own. You will also remain with Nebta and Khety while the *medicus* is under my protection. You will pass these instructions on to your relief. Understood? Thank you."

"You are a kind man, Alexandros of Elateia," said Khety, handing the mended tunic up to the legionary on my right. He touched his hand to his helmet and handed her a coin. She reached behind her into the tent and pulled out two beautiful woven cloaks of black, yellow and green. "Take these. It will be cold on the plain."

Nebta handed the patched piece of underwear up to the winker. "With respect, sir," he said, snatching the *subligaculum* from her and stuffing it away while gesturing at my knives (which, since we were outside the *pomerium*, I wore belted and visible), "are you really expecting those teeth cleaners to get you out of trouble better than this here." He patted his *gladius*. The underwear peeking out from his belt stole more than a little of his masculine swagger.

"No, legionary, I am expecting these teeth cleaners to have the good manners, when the time comes, to look the other way." Finally, a grunt of laughter from the silent soldier. "Now then, doctor," I continued, "shall we walk? It's not too far. Still, we might raise a thirst." I hoisted the wine skin like a trophy, then felt relief pour through me as

Livia slipped her hand in mine. Could there be a man more proud in all of Macedonia?

"Why the extra cloak?" I asked as we turned to go. "Your friend was kind enough to loan us these. You don't need to conceal anything now."

"It rained yesterday," Livia answered. "The ground may be damp." Nebta and Khety's African/Greek chorus of titters continued till we were beyond hearing.

•••

The army's camp was surrounded by farmland; it was not easy to find seclusion. When we arrived at a wooded depression split by a small stream, we were not surprised to discover we would not have the place to ourselves. I wanted to leave, but Livia spread her cloak beside a legionary-free cypress and pulled me down beside her. Truth to tell, no one seemed interested in us at all. And when Livia kissed me, my disinterest in anything not Livia became flawless.

There is lovemaking that is gentle, leisurely, laced with amorous whispers and the romance of long, slow kisses. But there is another kind, serving another purpose. Ours, on the day I discovered that Livia had survived the Adriatic crossing, when we held each other in a foreign land on our way to a foreign war, was to rail against our plight with our bodies, and for a few precious moments to reclaim our destiny with our passion. Our need for each other was ardent, urgent and swift.

I am ancient now far beyond my fair share of years. I need only look at the blue rivers pushing ever higher against the weather-beaten surface of my crooked hands to see the proof. But this skinny old stork is not me. Alexandros is not this old man; he is hiding *inside* this wreck of a body. Can you understand this? Let me

323

explain. There comes a time, somewhere between adulthood and the deathbed, when we become the people we are intended to be. Given time, we continue to learn, we continue to grow, but we are shaped, and that shape is fixed, for good or for bad. When does this happen? Only the gods know, for no man lives so completely in the present to be able to recognize the moment it occurs. But from that instant ever onwards, if he is lucky, while his bones grow brittle, his heart will remain supple; as his eyes grow dim, the world will still lay clearly before him. For me, I am fairly certain that the day I lay with Livia beneath the spear of a Macedonian cypress was the day that I stopped aging.

•••

Afterwards, we lay on our backs, breathless. A light breeze blew; we pulled Khety's colorful handiwork about us and let time and the world right themselves once again. After a while, when we had drifted back into our own bodies and our own separate thoughts, I said, "Tell me how you came by those marks."

"I feel wonderful, don't you?"

"Fine. Tell me, then, about your new friends."

"There's not much to tell," Livia said, kissing the tips of my fingers. "They're whores, I love them, and they saved me from getting raped. Oh yes! Let me tell you about Musclena."

"They're prostitutes?!"

"What did you think they were?"

"Seamstresses. Tailors, menders."

"Well, they do that, too, of course. They're quite resourceful."

"I can see that. I'm sorry, did you say 'rape?'"

"It was nothing. No one touched me. I'm perfectly fine." I stared at her. "I swear by our favorite statue of Apollo in the garden of our master."

"Certainly, then, by all means, do tell me about Musclena."

"You remember, of course," Livia said, sitting up to throw her tunic over her head, "he's my superior, chief *medicus* for the army." She reached behind her with both hands to withdraw her hair from the inside of her tunic and bind it as she spoke. "He's a fine surgeon, by all accounts, but the type that knows what he knows and anything outside of that is ignorance. So of course we got off on the wrong foot. Which is quite funny, when you think about it."

"Was I expected to understand that reference, or wait a bit?"

"Wait, my sweet *pelargós*. I caught up with the healers two days after we left Dyrrachium. Dario Musclena is willful and stubborn. How do I know this? He was walking beside one of the medical supply carts when he should have been riding in it. He had a pronounced limp. I hopped up into the cart, grabbed one of the walking sticks and jumped down to offer it to him. He refused it! I tossed it back up where it was no use to anyone and walked beside him, which I think pained him as much as his foot.

"Did you know, Andros, that you cannot sneer with just your lips; you've got to use your nose, too. If you want to practice, I'll introduce you to Musclena. You know his type: he looks down at you no matter how tall you are. No question, though, the man's good looking, if your taste runs to superior intellect in Olympian form — grey curls, blue eyes, thin lips, elegant nose."

"How fortunate for me your taste in intellect lies elsewhere."

"How fortunate for me," Livia said, "it lies right here beside me."

"Let me have it then, brag away, how did you heal the healer?"

"I haven't, but I shall. You know how I love to make a nuisance of myself to arrogant men, so looking at his swollen, bandaged foot, I asked him if he'd ever traveled in Africa. He said he didn't see how that was any of my concern. 'I'm a healer,' I said. 'You're not *my* healer,' he told me. 'One,' I said to myself. I asked him, lifting the red trim on the sleeve of my tunic if it would be an appropriate time to introduce myself. He said he already knew who I was, and as far as he was concerned, the slave plaque around my neck carried more weight with him than the clothes I was wearing. I could take it as a standing order to stay out of his and every other legitimate healer's way. I admit, that surprised me.

"I'll speak to *dominus*."

"You'll do no such thing. That will make matters even worse."

"You and I are here, miles away from our son; what could be worse than that?"

"Stop it, Andros. We *are* here, and there's nothing we can do about it. We'll get through it, somehow."

"Of course we will. Go on."

"That's it, really. I said to myself, 'Livia, you made a decent effort.' Before I walked off ahead of him, whistling as loud as I could, I said to him, 'By the way, there's a reason they call it dragon worm.' I laughed when he called after me, 'Nonsense.' And that was two."

"Don't you usually count to three?"

"Would you?"

"Perhaps not in this case. You're not going to help him?"

"In the end, when he starts howling from the pain, he'll remember me and we'll become the best of friends."

"What is his ailment?"

"You don't want to know. It's too disgusting."

I growled, a regrettable outburst only Livia has ever been able to wrench from me, although Melyaket has come close. "Then perhaps we might return to the first subject over which you were so quick to gloss?"

"I told you, nothing happened."

"Livia, please do not torture me this way. It is not kind."

"You're right. I apologize. First know that I am here, with you, and unhurt. That other thing was nothing. I'll tell you about the bruises. The truth is, our ship was caught in a bad storm."

"Gods! *Dominus* knew better than to set sail after the winter storms set in. He knew! He plays knucklebones with all our lives."

"The storm was an ill omen. But I am here, safe; is that not also a sign?"

"That was no ill omen, love. It was an ill mind manifest."

"Andros!"

"Tell me what happened."

"There was another ship caught in the storm, sailing south from Pistum."

"Not of our fleet."

"No, a merchant vessel, trying to reach Dyrrachium like the rest of us."

"Fools! Those ships have nothing but sails and two paddles for rudders."

"Our oars were beating, but I don't think we were going anywhere. I've never been so scared, Andros. The waves were like green mountains; they kept moving beneath us, tilting us up till the rain poured straight into our eyes, then sliding away, dropping us into a trough black as tar. Every time we hit the water there were screams from below and the crack of wood."

"What of the merchant ship?"

"There were about a dozen of us clinging to the ropes securing the medical supplies. I was one of the lucky ones who'd found a place on the deck where I could wrap my legs around a cleat that held one of the ropes. Some of the others who were standing further along and higher up along the ropes…they were swept away, Andros."

"I was wrong to ask. You don't have to do this, Livia."

"I think I do. I think I need to get it out of me. The *trierarch* was shouting commands that no one at our end of the ship could hear. A piece of an oar came flying toward us, bounced off of the rope nearest by head and struck a man in the chest. When we crested the next wave, he went sliding away down the deck. The thrum of the oar on that rope — a note plucked by a Titan. I will never forget that sound.

"It was still reverberating in my head when a lightning strike blinded me, painting an image on my eyes that would have made me laugh were I not so terrified. A giant swan came swimming toward us on the crest of a wave."

"Oh gods. Cargo ships are often fitted with such ornaments on their sterns."

"There was nothing we could do — the ship came over the swell aft-first and carved into us, shearing off our oars with cracks like lightning striking a hundred trees. Their stern crumpled into ours; the swan broke right over our guard rail as though to board us. The impact must have spun us round so that the next wave hit us full-on broadside because the next thing I knew I was in the water; I don't remember being thrown from the boat, or how I got these." She displayed her marks. "I swam with my eyes closed, but the pressure in my ears was becoming greater so I turned the other way, hoping that I was heading away from the wreck. My hand hit something hard and I grabbed it. It felt like an oar. You cannot imagine how strong the urge is to cling to something solid in such chaos. I wanted it to float me to safety, but something was wrong. An oar should be shooting to the surface, but this piece of wood was moving too slowly. It must be sinking, not rising. My eyes flew open. The stinging depths showed me nothing, yet I knew something was there, just beyond my sight, and it wanted me. I cursed whatever horrible weight was tugging that oar to the bottom, then thanked it for helping me get to the surface. I grabbed the wood with both hands, it was almost vertical, and pushed hard against it, launching myself like a spear. I kicked as hard as I could, praying that the water above me was clear.

"When I broke through to air and rain, I was still close enough to the burning wrecks I could hear men shouting and see their faces."

"Burning?"

"Lightning. Oil lamp. I don't know. Whatever it was, it saved us, because daybreak was already upon us and the smoke was seen from shore. The storm fled with the sun."

"Curse that merchantman. Their captain should have known better."

"Why, *pelargós*? Is it so strange that a captain should answer to a higher authority?" She wore the look of happy smugness that came whenever she thought she had won an argument.

"Our fleet captains follow orders. That man's higher authority was most likely the empty, open chests in his hold."

Livia stared at me for just an instant, long enough to be sure I understood that Crassus had no better motive, and risked far more. "Too true," she said. "Though they'll only be filled with salt water now. He sailed with whores to follow the legions."

"I am sorry for his loss. And theirs. And ours. But I care only for you. You might have been killed."

"If not for Nebta and Khety, I would have been."

I closed my eyes and shook my head and grimaced, preparing myself by repeating that she was here now, safe beside me. "Go on."

"Broken oars moved back and forth upon the rolling sea like a child's game of sticks. When a foaming crest broke, it would send them skidding down the wave wall like tiny spears. Every now and then a sea lion would raise its shiny head and stare at the mess we humans had made upon their waters. They were one with the rolling waves — their whiskered heads would suddenly appear, as if the sea had eyes; in the next moment they'd be gone. When they looked at me, and they did — right at me — the flames danced in their black eyes. I couldn't tell if they were curious or sad because they could not help us.

"The bigger pieces of the ships that were still afloat and not aflame were crowded with men and women. Those frantic people had lost their minds; not just those who kicked and jabbed to keep the rest away, but the ones who tried to clamber aboard and join them. When the decking went under, as it must, they clawed at each other and brought their own ends down upon themselves even faster. I turned away.

"The biggest piece of wreckage still afloat was our *trireme*, more than half the ship. But it was on fire at the prow. There were seven or eight soldiers, our captain among them, their backs to the flames, swords drawn. They were keeping everyone else off the ship. Anyone who tried to climb up onto the wreck was knocked back into the water!"

"Why?!"

"They were protecting the fire. The captain wanted the ship to burn, but those in the water wanted to cling to it. Naturally."

"What happened?"

"About a dozen men with lengths of oars climbed aboard and tried to rush them. One of the captain's men went down, but the others were all killed. The ones who wanted to put out the flames jumped back into the sea when they saw their brothers slain. The captain was furious. The storm was letting up by then. He ran out into the middle of what was left of the ship—by then there wasn't much—and yelled that he'd kill any man who so much as spit on the fire. But that was later."

"What was the name of that *trierarch*, do you remember?"

"I don't. I'm sorry."

"I hope he lived. He is surely another reason why you sit beside me today." Livia tilted her head. "The smoke from the flames, rising in the dawn. He knew it was a beacon, the only way a rescue party could find the survivors. And keeping people off the wreck might keep it afloat just long enough to save the rest."

"It seems heartless and cruel."

"It was, by one rod. By another, it saved lives. The captain had to have believed it was his only choice. But heartless and cruel, *vulpecula*, either way. What did you mean by 'later'?"

"I'd been floating for almost an hour when the fight on *Circe* took place. Before, when I first burst to the surface and filled my lungs, through my stinging eyes I saw a legionary clinging to a narrow bit of decking, no more than ten feet long and half as wide. A piece of railing opposite to where he clung made the scrap resemble nothing so much as a large child's boat. His head lay upon his crossed arms. He was balding at the back of his head and it made me think of you. A large wave rolled down upon us and suddenly he jerked upward, throwing his arms in the air. I saw the 'o' of his mouth and the stubble on his chin. His eyes blinked as the rain pelted his upturned face. The wave pushed the scrap of decking past me and I grabbed at it and managed to catch the railing. I couldn't believe that soldier would relinquish his hold on the raft. I shouted out to him. For a moment I couldn't see him as the swell passed, then an oar rolled up into the air. It was embedded in the poor man's back like a mast. He floated past me face down."

"Livia…" What a useless thing to say. But we have to try, don't we? To attempt to console, though we know that consolation lies not within our power, but in Time's alone.

We make noises of comfort, but when even we are not convinced, how then can those sounds be heard by those they are meant to soothe? My wife's stories were suddenly making me very much afraid. Not for the ordeal she had been forced to endure, but for those yet to come. This was no place for us.

"It's all right," she said. "I've seen my share of bloated corpses floating down the Nile."

I knew she hadn't, for Egyptians were scrupulously hygienic about such matters, but I let her go on. Each of us has their own way of declining comfort. "I climbed up on the wreckage," she said, "without turning it upside-down. There must have been something heavy underneath acting as a keel. I was still catching my breath from the effort, thinking how lucky I was when a grizzled old legionary came swimming toward me with a great deal of shouting and cursing and splashing. He'd shoved two oars through his belt and was swimming as fast as this awkward arrangement would let him. In the swell beyond him, between him and the wrecks, I saw first one, then another sea lion raised its sleek, black head to watch for awhile, but when I turned to look back again, they were gone.

"'Sorry, dear,' he said, grabbing the far end of the planking, 'this one's taken. Whew! I'm exhausted! Ever try to stay balanced on two of these things? No, I don't suppose you have.' His head was as square as one of *domina's* pretty amber earrings, though 'pretty' was the last thing anyone would ever think to call him, *including* his mother. He had a big dent in his forehead on one side and that eye was blind, the cornea gone completely white.

"I knew what he was about and I wasn't going to argue with him so I told him, 'Fair enough, take it, but let me have the oars.' He shook his head while wrestling to get them free of his belt. I was astonished. 'One, then.'

'"Afraid not,' he says.

'"Look,' I said, and by now I'm glancing frantically about for something I can pry loose for a weapon, 'you can't have the decking *and* the oars. It makes no sense.'

'"Makes perfect sense,' he said. 'I'm stealing your deck. I give you an oar, you'll bash my head in, take it back, and with my last breath I'd be the first to congratulate you.'

'"Soldier, I'm a doctor. I don't hurt people. We can help each other, get through this together.'

'"No, don't think so,' he says. 'These are difficult times, dear, difficult times.'

'"I'll give you the raft, I swear, just give me a chance. One oar. I'll float away with the current, and you'll never see me again.'

'"If you're asking, ask for two. How do you know I won't give you a swift crack across your back with the one left behind while you're making your escape?'

'"Escape?! Man, pull yourself together! We are trying to survive a tragedy. Look about you. Do you not see what is happening here?'

"Then he tells me this. 'Oh, I see right well enough. I've survived worse. And I'll survive this. But you're right about one thing. We need to take care of what my centurion likes to call 'variables.' I don't know what that means exactly, but it's got something to do with whittling down the number of things that can go wrong.' He checked to see which way the current was flowing, hefted one of the oars like a spear and hurled it as far in that direction as he could, which was right over my head. He did the same with the second oar while I watched in disbelief. He was mad, and I told him so.

"A big wave washed over us from behind. It hit the back of his close-cropped hair and sprayed over him like a green, hooded cloak, then hit me full in the face. I held on to the rail with one hand and with the other frantically wiped my hair and salt water from my eyes. He hadn't moved. But the sea lions had popped up again, this time closer, about thirty feet away.

"'You're the one who's fogged over,' the soldier said, 'and you've got twice the sight as me. You poor dear, can't you see I've been talking to a corpse ever since I showed up?'

"'What?! You don't need to kill me.' I scrambled to the farthest end of the decking and held on to the vertical piece of railing, and while I was doing this he reached down below the water line and came back up with a dagger. There was ten feet of flotsam between us. I tugged hard at the jagged spike and felt it give a little.

"'Here, I'll reason it out with you,' he said. 'But don't think that sliver is going to be much use to you, even if you do wrench it free.' He put the dagger between his teeth, pressed both hands flat on the deck and tried to hoist himself up. He couldn't do it. He slipped. He tried again and failed. I thought about swimming away, but I couldn't bring myself to get back in the water. Instead, I pushed and pulled with all my strength at the railing, hoping the sea and the collision had done my work for me. Thank Diana, it had, and that at least kept him on the far side of the wreckage, when he saw me crouching and wild-eyed, holding a four-foot spike of twisted iron and wood.

"He said, 'Congratulations, darling, but let me set you straight. Seeing as you're a healer, it's fair to say you deserve an explanation. I've threatened you, understand, so damage done. You're important—look at them red stripes on your tunic. You might tell, you might not. You see my point, dear. Me, I'm a twenty-year man, but that won't stop them. They'll stone me till I'm good and stove in if we get picked up. So there you are. You're a variable.'

"'Not if I swear to say nothing.'

"'Swear all you like, you're still a variable. But if you're down there,' he said, using his knife to point to the sea floor, 'then all's well and good.' The he shouts at the top of his voice, 'FUCK ME!'"

"Must you, Livia?" I asked. "He said those precise words?"

"To the letter. On either side of him, but just out of reach, the sea lions had risen again, the water sliding off their black pelts like oil. Except that they spoke. Were they Nereids, come to my aid, or sirens, risen from the deep to finish what rain and wave could not. I resisted the urge to stop up my ears, for that would mean having to let go of my weapon.

"'Everyone got trouble here,' one said, tilting her head back toward the burning wreckage. Her hair was as black as her eyes, so short it looked painted on. She rose higher in the sea, water streaming off her breasts.

"'Everyone who got goodness,' the other one said, 'this be the time to cast it about them like a net.' She was also naked, as far as I could tell. It was Nebta and Khety, in case you hadn't guessed by now. They were survivors from the merchant ship."

"I surmised. So there were no actual sea lions."

"Oh, but there were. At first. Later, when the girls were following the legionary, my eyes saw what they expected they would see. The soldier laughed and said, 'Wouldn't you know the only time *Fortuna's* ever handed me three all to myself, terra firma and anything decent to grab hold of for purchase is miles away.'

"'We been watching you,' Khety said. 'You got no net to cast.'

"The look of the happy brothel patron fell off his face like a mask and all that was left was the soldier-killer. When he spoke again, the knife moved in a flat arc back and forth between them, with me at the center. 'Don't understand a thing you're saying, dear, but don't care much for your tone, neither.'

"'How much you pay for them oars?' Nebta asked him. The soldier looked like he'd been smacked with one. He stared at her. 'A good man, he give you one.'

"Khety said, 'But you got to have two, and you make that good man pay, you make him pay good. Why you think your breath smell so much sweeter than everyone else?'

"'Tell you what, dear, swim a little closer and I'll give you a whiff of it, maybe even let you and your friend take a grip of this here decking, one on a side to help balance it, understand?'

"'Variable,' Nebta said. 'Understand?' She rose in the waters, paddling with strong hands by her hips, drawing the soldier's eye with the swell of her rising breasts, her nipples, black on black perfection, holding his attention as they had uncounted men before him. With his head turned, he didn't see Khety slip silently below the surface.

"In the next moment, he was gone. The last I saw of him were three fingertips, white with the strain of clinging to the soggy deck. They looked like little pieces of biscuit dough waiting for the oven. A final tug from below and they vanished. Nebta, too, disappeared. I was alone for several moments, but in that time, as the storm grew bored with us and the sky lightened, as below me the women drowned the soldier who would have murdered me, I wrapped my arms about that railing and knew you and I would find each other again. Somehow I knew it."

I pressed my forehead against Livia's and sighed. "Little fox, you are a storyteller of singular merit. It would do my heart good if you never recounted another such as this again."

"I won't, but don't you want to hear—"

"No."

"I must tell you about the—"

"I really wish you wouldn't."

"Hmph. I thought you'd take at least a *little* interest in my rape story."

"Oh gods, I'd forgotten. But you *weren't* raped."

"No."

"Then, please, love, I beg you, just the summary points."

"As you wish. If you remember, Nebta and Khety grew up in a city on a canal just west of the Nile." I nodded. "And you know they're whores."

"And strong swimmers. And large-breasted. Yes, these things have been established. And for them all I am truly and eternally grateful."

"So, my breasts do not please you?" Livia pushed herself together to emphasize her cleavage.

"I love your breasts for many reasons. I love their breasts for the part they played in saving your life. And given the opportunity, I would immerse my hands in scented unguents and offer up unto that entire harvest of pendulous fruit the careful, methodical, caresses of infinite gratitude. Do continue."

"And you haven't even *seen* them. Once ashore, the three of us became inseparable. I couldn't sleep with you…"

"I begged *dominus*. He could have made an exception, made you his personal physician, placed your quarters adjacent to his. He said it would destroy morale."

"And he was right, Andros. Inside the camp is no place for a woman."

"And outside is better?"

"It's not so bad. Our tent is large, the girls are popular; they've even hired on servants and a mule."

"I suppose it could be worse. At least *dominus* was thoughtful enough to post guards for your protection."

"Oh, that wasn't *dominus*. That was Octavius. He posted legionaries at all the brothel tents to maintain order. A good thing, too, or my rest would go from little to none. Which brings me, once again, to my clever friends." Livia unsealed the wine skin and drank.

Octavius? Once again, I had failed my lessons in the Academy of Crassus. What presumption to think that my thirty years of service, my *contubernium* with his own house healer, my advice and loyalty would raise the two of us above thirty-odd thousand others in his thoughts. At the sight of those guards, I had believed *he* was looking out for us, protecting my wife, displaying some concern for us beyond our use as pieces in this vindictive game he played. Why am I not inured? Why with each passing year does it become more urgent that Crassus show me some genuine sign of understanding, appreciation, friendship?

"*Pelargós*, why aren't you looking disgusted?" She poked me. "You weren't even listening, were you?"

"I am sorry, love. Am I completely mad, or did I hear something to do with frogs?"

Livia sighed and repeated another tale of the resourcefulness of Nebta and Khety, and this time I did my best to pay attention. The two prostitutes had insisted their new friend share their tent (easily purchased after a night's work in the crate-clotted alleys off the Dyrrachium docks). It was the evening of their first day's march up out of the city, before Octavius had organized guards for the camp followers. One very inebriated, very determined young legionary could not be convinced that Livia's red-hemmed tunic was anything but a costume and was willing to pay double to play "healer and patient." Khety stayed the attentions of her own client, pulled her hanging veil aside and told the man he did not want this woman, that she was sick with the river slime. Livia was on her knees, her back against the tent wall. Khety set a lamp on the hemp rug. "Look for yourself." Livia jumped as Khety lifted her tunic. The man leaned in to leer at the target of his lust, swallowed heavily and lurched backwards from the tent. "You touch this woman," she told the soldier as he staggered off, urgently looking for any safe place to deposit the contents of his stomach, "you never be able to touch another, not with anything between your legs, I promise you that."

"Am I to understand then, that Khety reached under your tunic and smeared green slime on your vagina before showing your nakedness to a stranger?"

"Green slime with little black dots. Frog's eggs. The women collect it by the riverbank, store it in jars and take it out whenever the need arises. What's your preference, husband, show it to a stranger, or let him take it?"

I grimaced. "Does it...are there...you know...?"

"Wash off? Smell? Are there little tadpoles swimming around inside me? Does that encompass all your queries?"

"Give my imagination time. Tonight I may wake in a cold sweat with more."

"At least you have a tent to yourself."

"A pity we cannot trade. We would see who gets more rest. Crassus is plagued by nightmares." *Dominus* had sworn me to secrecy, but that was before my "marriage," before Felix, and before I had almost lost my wife to the madness of our master's scheme for revenge against Caesar. She had a right to know. After I had finished telling her the story of what had transpired at Luca, I was stunned by her reaction.

"You make too much of it, Andros. These men will do what they will do. You say you don't believe in Olympus, love, but you are wrong. There are gods, but they don't live in the clouds, they walk the earth. The best we can do is stay out of their way and keep from getting trampled."

CHAPTER XXIV

55 – 54 BCE - WINTER, ON THE MARCH

Year of the consulship of
Gnaeus Pompeius Magnus and Marcus Licinius Crassus

The sun was still bright, but the chill of the afternoon was beginning to bite through our layers of blankets and clothes, and there was no mulsum left to warm us. Our talk of Luca and Caesar was ill-timed. I had poured vinegar over honey.

"I miss our son," Livia said.

"He is safe."

"No. He is not here. But he is not safe."

"Crassus will be victorious, we will return home in triumph, then *dominus* will exact his vengeance upon Caesar."

"And condemn Felix to this." Livia hooked a finger under the chain of her slave plaque, lifted it off the ground and dropped it again.

"There must be a way for us to live and also for Felix to be free. The solution will come to us."

"War will come to us." She shrugged.

I turned to face her, smoothing the hair from her face. "I have failed, Livia. Wait, let me say this to you, for I have never spoken of it to anyone." I picked a twig from her tunic and took a breath. "When I was young, before I was captured, I used to think I would achieve something extraordinary with my life. Not that I was *destined* for greatness, mind you, but that if I applied myself, I could make great things happen. I *would* be a great man. Now don't laugh, this is hard for me to admit. I used to think, there will be famous men among my generation, why shouldn't I be one of them?"

"What was so important about fame?"

"When you're young, you think anything is possible. Even fame. But I wasn't seeking notoriety. I wanted to make a difference; perhaps become a great philosopher and change the way we see the world. Or a sculptor. A playwright. I don't know, *something*. Have you never felt this way?"

"Not ever. But I love that *you* feel that way."

"Felt. When I was taken, I could hear the gods laughing."

She took my hand and kissed it. "I am here, and I am not laughing. You would have done it, Andros. You are just the sort to make such dreams come true. If they'd only let you be. I curse them for it."

"But, love, that's the thing. After Luca, I began to think I'd been given a second chance." Livia cocked an eyebrow. "Caesar's attack on our lady. A tragedy for our brave mistress, and I weep for her. But she is a woman…"

"And women are skilled in manipulation, but hold no other power."

"It is the way of the world — women must stand in the shadow of men, both great and small."

"Not this woman."

"No, most certainly not you. But Caesar casts a shadow Crassus cannot escape," I said, lifting a chin in the direction of the camp. "See what a man who *has* achieved greatness may accomplish by the sheer power of his will and his purse. *Dominus* has always held us gently in the palm of his hand, but now he has closed his fist. I fear for us all. He is consumed by Luca, and will not be content until he has avenged himself upon Caesar."

"You call this greatness?"

"No, Livia. I do not. Yet Crassus is a great man, a lord of Rome. And I stand by his side. He has stumbled, and I have tried to right him. If only I could have reasoned with him and steered him from this madness, there would be greatness enough in that. But I have failed."

"In Egypt, I lost many patients who should not have died. I am certain it is because they did not wish to be healed."

"I believe you. But you tried. You did everything you could to save them. That is your way. Now, here I am with two patients, one who does not wish to recover from his wounds, and one who I believe would heal the past if she could. How can I do less than you?"

"What are you saying? Lady Tertulla no longer wants this war?"

"I believe she loves as we love; each day the longing for her husband grows stronger. Her doubts could be tipped into the certainty that thousands need not perish to satisfy her need for revenge. And she is the only person other than myself who could help *dominus* find a different path. She could bring him home."

"You are a dreamer, Andros. You have as much power over *domina* as *domina* has over *dominus*. Less."

"It doesn't matter, Livia. I am the only one who has any chance of success. How can I stand by and let it pass?"

"I do you love you, *pelargós*, but you are a fool. Thank Athena, your foolishness can do no harm. We are here and lady Tertulla is in Rome. There is nothing you can do."

"You may be right. But I do know that I have not done enough. This could be it, Livia, my chance to make a difference. What if we could stop this war? What if you were out of danger? I would live the life of a slave ten times over to see you safe."

Livia kissed my cheek. "You should put that brain of yours to work on how we are going to see our son safe — and free."

"I don't know how, but somehow I have the feeling all of it — the war, Felix's freedom, you and me, it is all connected."

"There lies your greatness — to discover the connection."

"Did you know that when you patronize me the green in your eyes turns muddy? I happen to be very serious about this."

Livia sighed. "You are already great in my eyes; it is you who must learn to open yours."

"Then I will only see myself through your eyes, whether green or grimy. Still, I fear for us all."

"Being afraid is a good way to waste time, Andros. Who knows? Maybe you'll think of something. In the meantime, I will dress the wounded or toss three handfuls of dust upon the dead. And then we will try to find our way home. What more can we do?"

"What happened to you in Egypt? You have grown philosophical."

"Possibly, or else it is only your perception that is improving."

I rolled onto her and kissed her gently. "That must be it." I rose and straightened my tunic. "Now I must leave you briefly to find some privacy."

"You are funny," Livia said, sitting up.

"Me? I am comedy's antithesis."

"And there you prove it yet again. Andros, it was only a moment ago you were willing enough to take me beneath this tree among a community of lovers," she said, looking about at the few remaining couples still dotting the woods, "but to relieve yourself, you require a place free from prying eyes. You are funny."

"In the first instance, if you recall, I had but little choice in the matter."

"Go. Do you what your quirky self needs to do. If you did not, you would not be Alexandros, and I would love you the less for it." Livia hung the plaque about her neck and uncorked the wine skin. She wrung it from belly to neck but coaxed only a few drops onto her tongue.

I went a short distance away to find and unoccupied tree, and Livia went to the stream to squat over its mossy stones, cleaning herself to lessen the odds that our union would get her with child. This would be no time for Felix to become someone's older brother.

Later, as we pulled the cloaks about us for warmth, I said, "We could take Apollo, ride south and in five days be in Elateia."

"You're not serious?" She turned her head to scrutinize my face. "You're not."

"No. I am not. It is only that in thirty years, I have never been this close to the place of my birth."

"Do you know what has become of your family?" she said, propping herself up on an elbow.

"Gone. Dead. Does it matter? After he sacked Athens, Sulla moved north to engage the host of Mithridates. Half of Phocis was a smoking ruin. The battle ran south from Elateia, and many towns were sacked and put to the torch. I do not know what I would find there now. But I am certain my memories are sweeter."

"But your parents might still be alive."

"That is unlikely, but were it true, then their son is dead. Even if they managed to survive, even if old age has not yet claimed them, I would not haunt them with a shade they would barely recognize. Alexandros, son of Theodotos is no more. Better to keep the perfect lies of the past than to discover an unbearable truth."

"You are Alexandros to me."

I kissed her cheek. "Please, do not ever stop calling me that, for I love the sound. I cherish every moment with you, as I am now, as you are. You have suffered greatly, yet I have never met anyone with your capacity for joy, for finding happiness no matter where it is hiding."

"You will always be my Andros."

"I will. I promise. But who can I be to anyone else if not the slave Alexander, *atriensis* of house Crassus. Would those guards back at your tent take orders from Alexandros, son of Theodotos? No, do not look sad. I am the most fortunate of men: a man with two births."

"And two deaths."

"Speak rather of the man born the day the first one died. What would have happened had he not been stripped bare and dipped in the hot tallow of Roman ways, month after month, year after year, till nothing of that Greek boy remained, save the frail string that was his center? I will tell you — he would never have found you."

She took my hands in hers and put them to her lips. "Still, I weep for that poor child."

I would have spoken of her own ordeal as a child, sold by her father to pay his gambling debts to the slave dealer, Boaz; rented to any house that would pay; watching as her mother sacrificed her own freedom to buy back her daughter's liberty. But I could not speak of these things. Because of me, that woman had by now died in the silver mines of Laurion. Instead, I said, "Do not cry for me. For Alexander burns bright, a good Roman candle, and here, in your arms, he has found his home." The kiss that followed was long and tender, and would have been longer still had not a shadow fallen over us.

"Isn't this a ph...phritty sight."

We recognized that voice instantly — a man talking as if he had a walnut jammed up under one cheek. We shaded our eyes and looked to see a legionary in full uniform, his face scarred, pockmarked and leering. He was smiling, though his grin was hampered by the tough, ropy flesh that pulled at one side of his mouth, exposing two lonely teeth and the gums that held them on the left side of his mouth.

"Palaemon."

"Good memory, Mantis." He spoke to me, but his eyes were on Livia.

"What are you doing here?" I asked, though the answer was obvious.

"Come to fuh...feh...*fetch* you. The general wanss ephryone back in camph."

If one didn't know his character, one could almost feel sorry for him. Almost. We stood quickly. Other soldiers were about, rounding up stragglers. "I meant, what are you doing here, on this campaign?"

"Same as you. Come to get a share of that Pharthian gold. Only difference is, *Ah'm* getting army phay." There was nothing to do but walk back to camp with this criminal from the baths of Numa strolling right behind us. I was furious, and frightened. If the legions' ranks were drawn from the likes of him, I shuddered to think how we would fare once the enemy was engaged.

"What about Herclides," I asked. "Is he here, too?" Palaemon nodded. "Interesting. I suggest that as soon as we get back to camp, we find him and introduce him to Octavius. The legate will be most interested to meet the two of you."

"You're chust like all the rest. You think because of this," he said, pointing to his torn face, "because Ah'm ugly, I'm stuphid."

"No, Palaemon. I do not think you are stupid because you're physically scarred. I think you are stupid because science has yet to discover a tool able to measure the imperceptible level of your intelligence."

The felon's pale eyes registered anger. While he worked out how he had been insulted, he rested his hand on the hilt of his *pugio*. "Ah'm here," he sneered, "there's nothing you can do about it, and you'll be seeing more uff me, espheshelly you," he said, tilting his pockmarked chin at Livia. That was all I could bear; I prepared to pluck a knife free from its sheath, but as in most things, while I made preparations, my wife acted.

Livia turned and stood with her face so uncomfortably close to Palaemon's he took a step backward. I wondered if anyone had ever voluntarily come as close to that wreck of a face without being paid. "Why don't I just visit you in your tent?" she said sweetly. Rummaging in her shoulder bag, she added conversationally, "Did you know my mother was also a healer? I'm like her; I always carry my tools wherever I go. Alexandros will tell you; one time she sliced a man's throat with one scalpel and slit his wrist with another. She did it in less than five heartbeats, and he was three times the size of you. It runs in the family: we're just as good with either hand," and now her voice lowered, "and we don't like being threatened."

"We'ff that in common," Palaemon said, but his voice was uncertain.

Livia extracted a long, thin, bronze tool from its pouch; it had a fine hook at one end. "I've got several of these; some have blunt ends for probing. Not this one; this I use for retracting tissue." She twirled it in front of his cratered face. "Do you know what else it will do?" Palaemon shook his head, making the cheek protectors on his helmet flap on their hinges. "Once, in Alexandria, an African prince had an inflammation in his groin. As it happened, one of his testicles had gotten infected. I picked up his swollen sac and spread the skin tight." She made the motion with her thumb and forefinger just in front of his nose. "With a scalpel, I made an incision, only an inch or so." Palaemon, fascinated, tried not to look horrified. "Then I took this hook," she said, reenacting the gesture, "reached inside and felt for the cord that held the diseased ball to the rest of him. One little tug and out it plopped, right into my hand, neat as you please. A snip with a scissors and he was half the man he used to be."

"You don't scare me," Palaemon said.

"Really?" she said, leaning in and holding him with the green of her eyes. "That's surprising, because, you see, I *liked* him."

"There's a centurion up ahead. Octavius will send both you and Velus Herclides packing as soon as he hears there are criminals in the ranks. Centurion!" I shouted.

"Ffeelus said you'd say that. When you did, he told me to tell you and all your friends this: congratulations on your little son. Felickth, is it?" We froze. "You're a long way from Rome. And Ffeelus left many frenss behind. So lesss us be frenss, too, and effryone gess what they want. We get our share of the treasure, your boy stays healthy, effreybody's haffy."

"What is it?" The officer was short, squat and ugly, the opposite of his plumed helmet and five *phalerae* strapped across his chest. He must have spent hours polishing those medals which he wore with casual pride as they glowed in the afternoon sun. I imagined he was equally proud of the scars on his arms and legs. In three, maybe four heartbeats I weighed the probability that Velus was bluffing (Palaemon was nothing more than his mouthpiece), and even if he wasn't, no one could ever get close enough to Felix to harm him. I could not even confirm that Herclides was here. "Well?" the centurion pressed.

I was about to have him lay hold of Palaemon when Livia said, "I've got something for that arm. Looks like it hurts." We were walking again. The left gate was only a few hundred feet away.

"This?" he scoffed. "I did that to myself this morning. Tripped on a guy rope. Don't deserve any salve. And if my men saw it on me, they'd laugh and then I be forced to beat 'em with my vine stick." He waved the gnarled and glossy emblem of his rank in her face. "You don't want to be responsible for that, do you, miss?"

"Look—" I started.

"Of course not," Livia said. "I hear the general has something special planned for tonight."

"That he does. Got some musicians to entertain us. Brought 'em in from Cyrrhus. Dancing girls, too. Though I guess there's no pleasure in that for you."

"Oh, you'd be surprised where I take my pleasure," my wife said, staring pointedly at Palaemon. He felt her eyes on him, I am sure, but kept his gaze rooted to the dirt at his feet.

CHAPTER XXV

55 – 54 BCE - WINTER, ON THE MARCH

Year of the consulship of
Gnaeus Pompeius Magnus and Marcus Licinius Crassus

The higher up the chain of authority it traveled, the less the news of Palaemon's and Herclides' presence in the army was of interest. Malchus was furious, demonstrating his ire with personal threats and vows of bloody retribution should anything unfortunate befall *any* person *any*where, not only my family, as a result of contact with those two criminals. Once he'd caught his breath, Malchus then complained to his centurion, who spit, cursed and railed bitterly to Vel Corto, *primus pilus,* that his two sons had been turned away when they might have had a place in the ranks but for this breach in army regulations. Corto, the highest ranking centurion in the army, annoyed that he had been interrupted during a winning round of *latrunculi* with legate Petronius, had the soldiers brought before him. Both men were in the 9th *cohort* of Legion VII, not a particularly senior posting. But the lead identity tags in the pouches around their necks were in order. Malchus said he would bear witness against their treachery, so Petronius said there was nothing Vel Corto could do but refer the matter to Gaius Octavius, legate of Legion I. Velus Herclides, his beard regrown so full it almost hid the sly grin he'd been saving for this moment, handed Octavius the letters of recommendation signed by P. Crassus himself, and that was the end of that.

•••

"Read me that last one again."

We were encamped near Pella. No, that's not true. Our camp was close by the few shoddy structures crouched disrespectfully among the cracked and fallen columns that was once known as that great meeting place of nations, but this ruin did not deserve to claim the name of Pella. Here there had been art, intellect, grace and science, for this had been the capital city of Philippos of Macedon, father of the great Alexandros. But neither man nor Nature had smiled upon this once-great megalopolis. More than a hundred years ago, Pella had suffered the same fate as a thousand other city-states: everything of value had been spirited away by the Romans, and what they left was not worth keeping. The soul of the city had been torn away, and the tatters that remained were enough to mourn, but not to give hope. Any stout-hearted citizens who endured to begin rebuilding were thoroughly discouraged not long thereafter, when an earthquake that would have knocked the teeth from a Titan razed what little the Romans had left standing.

Now, Pella is a monument to the Ephemeral. Alexandros conquered the known world, and this is what has become of his palace in a mere three hundred years. How will it look in a thousand? Crassus wanted to march his army all the way to India and the Outer Sea. When I think about these things, even now they still make me chuckle.

I reached into the courier's tube and withdrew the innermost among several dozens of letters. We were in the general's tent; Crassus lay on his side, ready for bed in his night tunic, his head propped on pillows at the foot of his *lectus*. We had waited to begin reading Tertulla's packet of letters until after the young man sent by Livia had left. The apprentice healer had massaged *dominus'* feet with a salve meant to alleviate his soreness and the pain from his bunions. The jar of brown paste my wife had concocted now sat open on the general's night table by his glossy toes, creating an eye-watering zone guaranteed free from arthropod or human incursion. I sat in his big chair with two oil lamps between us. Crassus claimed his eyes grew tired toward the end of the day, but he could have waited till morning to read her letters. Did his father read to him as a child? I would have asked, but I was within slapping distance.

"This was written not long after we departed Brundisium.

> Dearest husband, I pray this letter finds you well and without care. You are barely gone, and I find that either I have shrunk, or this house has tripled in size. How larger-than-life is the man I have married! I never knew till now how Marcus Crassus could fill a room. And such a joyless void is left behind when he departs.
>
> I must take lessons from our daughter-in-law. Cornelia is a delight. She is full of optimism and gaiety and has made it her solemn duty to infect me with her cheer while we wait for the return of our victorious husbands and son. I fear her task is Herculean. My melancholy may be forgiven; not

since you left to put down the rebel Spartacus have my bed and I spent so many nights alone. We are vexed.

Curio is a master of order, and the estate has never run more smoothly, but at least Alexander was not an insufferable bore. Yesterday, I innocently asked Lucius if there were any women in his life and with a face as straight as an arrow he replied, "You are the only woman in my life, mistress." When I laughed aloud, he took offense and retired. I haven't seen him since.

One of the peacocks has died, and I mourn alone. Cornelia wanted to eat it! And Curio lobbied to pluck its quills for writing pens. I told them such customs might be practiced in other houses, but here there is only one way beauty and the passing of all things wondrous are honored — on the pyre.

Tell Livia that Eirene and I fight over Felix daily; he is the happiest, fattest baby I have ever seen. No wonder, with three girls offering their breasts every time he yawns. Send her my love and remind Alexander of his promise to me to keep you safe.

He had better, since it is now he who pours your wine, who has discourse with you on all matters great and small, and when his work is done, it is he who may walk but a few steps to hold his Livia. He has you both while mountains and seas separate me from you. It is unfair beyond bearing, and if I did not love you so, I should hate the both of you fiercely. You must ignore this jealous old hen, and kiss me in your thoughts.

Eternally, Tertulla

"She is the most magnificent forty-six year-old hen ever hatched, is she not?" Crassus asked, taking the letter and inhaling its perfume once again before I replaced it in its tin with the others.

"In this tent, she is first among all women. In another, she is second only by the width of a hummingbird's tongue."

"Love has made you a diplomat," Crassus said. "Multiply that craft by three hundred, the issues by a thousand and behold, you are ready to take your place in the senate."

No, I will not say 'I am happy where I am.' "Shall we answer this one before retiring?"

"Tomorrow. Rest well, Alexander. Rest well."

361.

•••

The way across Illyricum, Macedonia and Thrace is made almost bearable by a lovely bit of road some thoughtful Roman had built right across the entire northern peninsula. This twenty-foot wide paved and drained marvel made it clear why Roman planning is so vital to its empire: imagine an army tramping through the countryside day after day, negotiating rivers and mountain passes without them. These feats of engineering increase speed and reduce fatigue, taking soldiers, settlers and commerce swiftly to their goals—usually a conquered province. Romans' chiseled sense of purpose is as wondrous as it is terrifying.

The road is the Via Egnatia. It stretches 700 miles, from dreary Dyrrhachium all the way to where two seas press the land to the thinnest of strips, where the petals of so many peripatetic cultures had converged to form the rose of what, for six hundred years, we Greeks called Byzantion. You Romans know it as Byzantium. But we were not itinerant travelers, nor could we tarry. I whimpered as we marched past banners briskly snapping atop the city walls and crossed over into Asia Minor. That leg of our journey took over two months. And it was the easiest by far.

When I say "we marched," or "our journey," understand that these unassuming pronouns bear the weight of a multitude so vast that when I speak of it your imagination will stretch and tear to comprehend and contain it. Not since Alexandros swept through Persia and beyond had such a "we" been amassed by any conqueror. Oh, generals had and would command larger armies, but they were sanctioned, salaried and provisioned by the state. The army of Crassus was the army of Crassus. Tens of millions of his own sesterces, heaped upon the promise of untold plunder drew dismissed and disbanded veterans like bears to honey. They didn't seem to mind at all that at the midway point of their journey they would be required to fight a war. Some of these men had been given land or taken retirement; others labored as laymen; a few, like Palaemon and Herclides, who could not or would not return to peaceful society, chose to live outside it as criminals. But none would ever, as the Hebrews falsely prophesied, "beat their swords into plowshares and their spears into pruning hooks." These fighting men turned farmers, tradesmen, husbands and fathers, leapt to sharpen their sheathed swords and polish their tarnished belts. By the thousands they sloughed off the trappings of lives lived as play actors and ran to answer the siren call of adventure, camaraderie and glory.

This was the juggernaut that Crassus led to Syria. I must warn you that to describe the spectacle of a Roman army on the march to one who has not seen it for himself is an undertaking as futile as depicting the breadth and majesty of the star-pierced heavens to a blind man. In truth, unless one grows wings and takes to the skies it cannot be done: from the ground one has but a dust-veiled inkling of the ferocious whole.

Why will you veer, Alexandros, from the narrative of your tale to take time and parchment to set down the size and nature of the army of Crassus? Why must you send your readers back to school, perhaps against their will? Why risk them wandering off to some other distraction, when there is so much more to tell?

The answer is simple: to comprehend the scale of the tragedy, one must understand the magnitude of the undertaking. However, if you have no interest in the bowl, but crave only the pudding, then by all means, skip ahead, skip ahead.

•••

The column was preceded by scouts — archers, slingers and one *ala*, a wing of cavalry, about a thousand men all told. Then, still ahead of the main body came a vanguard of one legion and another *ala* of cavalry. Our army was already diminished by the tragedy of our crossing from Brundisium. Casualties of a war that had not yet begun.

Behind the vanguard came surveyors and engineers, marching alongside mules laden with their tools and instruments. Each night they built the fortified town that was the army's camp. A day's march averaged about eighteen miles, depending on the terrain and the roads, if any. The camp would be laid out and protected by the time the remaining legions began arriving some five or six hours after the start of the day's march. If it could not be found within the camp's boundaries, pasture would have to be found and secured for 25,000 horses and mules. Every night.

Crassus and his officers came after the survey teams, surrounded by an elite *cohort* of bodyguards, 450 legionaries, mounted to keep pace with the general. I had seen to the purchase of a most magnificent tent for the general: it took five mules to bear the poles, leather and trappings. His personal gear was borne by twenty-five pack animals. It was my task to oversee his forty personal servants who followed at the back of the column with cooks, doctors, including the limping chief *medicus*, Darius Musclena, and a thousand other non-combatants. After the legates and other officers there then followed the mass of the army: five legions flanked by cavalry. The baggage train, seven miles long of its own accord, was protected by the seventh legion and 1,000 auxiliary cavalry. The remainder of a total of 2,500 horsemen patrolled up and down the flanks of the column.

From the first scout to leave at dawn to the last mounted archer to arrive at the finished camp, the army of Crassus snaked through the landscape for over fourteen miles! And that was marching six abreast. When the way was narrow, the length of this ophidian behemoth grew longer still.

•••

Now both Nature and man strove to impair our progress. The mountain ridges of Bithynia had either to be scaled or circumvented, and its rivers and streams, as many as three in a day, had to be forded. Once, the earth shook so violently beneath our feet, the steep hills dislodged a rocky attack upon our flanks. Many men were unbalanced and thrown to the ground, upsetting the military precision of our progress into jumbled, cursing chaos. Sometimes broad, sometimes narrow, often in need of repair, the Via Egnatia's poorer country cousin pinched our ranks and caught at our feet. I am told that it is a Roman general's duty to apply his engineers and legionaries to the health and recovery of these cobbled arteries to ease the passage of those who would follow. Not Crassus. He pressed forward, leaving this frivolous task to armies of the future, for whipped by the terrors that afflicted him by night, he was not to be impeded by day.

That is until some fifty miles northwest of the Galatian capital of Ancyra his way was blocked at a wide crossroads by Deiotarus. He rode at the head of a hundred chariots disturbingly reminiscent of the Celtic variety that had drained the pink from my cheeks when Publius had returned to Rome. The memory was fresh enough to produce the same effect, and I instinctively turned to search for Livia in the haze of men behind me. At least no severed heads dangled from the charioteers' belts or harnesses.

Deiotarus, like Culhwch, was an ally, but unlike Brenus' father, this cunning ruler with ruddy complexion and braids of white was no prince, but a king. It was the source of his crown that rankled my master. Deiotarus, a tetrarch of Galatia, had assisted Pompeius a decade earlier in his fight against the obstreperous Mithridates, king of Pontus. As a reward, Pompeius had given him sovereignty over the other Galatian tetrarchs and lobbied the senate on his behalf to bestow upon him the honorific of King of Lesser Armenia. Reluctantly, at the urging of Cassius and Octavius, who recognized that a hundred thousand sore feet could do with a day of rest, *dominus* tarried at the king's invitation to admire the construction of the king's new fortress at Blucium.

Supper in the impressive but unfinished dining hall was as lavish and varied as the conversation was not. At least the roof over our heads offered protection from the elements. Though a huge fire hissed and popped in the grate, we were none of us warmed by the chill spread by my master's sullenness. Standing behind him at my customary wall-bracing post, my stomach churned with embarrassment at his ill manners. He made no effort to engage his host in conversation, answering his inquiries with little thought and fewer words. My lord had hardly touched his food, but his wine cup was well-caressed.

"So," the king said, swallowing a mouthful of roast lamb and wiping his fingers on a square of cloth, "on your way to pay a social call on King Orodes, are you?" They sat next to each other at the high table.

"The business of Rome is none of yours." *Dominus'* stare followed a fly's spasmodic progress across his plate. "Highness," he added reluctantly, in lieu of an apology.

"'Not what I heard." Deiotarus waited for a response, got none and said, "My sources tell me you're not *on* Rome's business. How could you be, when you left the city shy of one blessing: the auspices of the senate."

"Let me rephrase, then: my business," *dominus* said, stifling a belch, "is none of yours."

"Fair enough," said the king. "You could just be taking up your post in Syria…" Crassus tilted his cup to his lips and emptied it. "…with an invasion force, to govern a province? If I could raise an army this great—"

"If you could raise an army this great by even a third," Crassus interrupted, this time belching in earnest, "I might find the need to suffer your impertinence."

I winced. From where he sat at Crassus' right hand, Octavius whispered a caution.

"Calm yourself, legate," said the king. "We are all friends here. The proconsul knows I have no wish to offend. Cursed with a curious nature, I am. No harm meant." Some men simply refuse to appear insulted.

"Oh, of that I am certain," Crassus said. "For why, with my *invasion* army at your gates, would you risk my ire."

But then, having felt the sting from the slap on their cheek, know just where to slip the knife, their smile never fading. "Now there, proconsul, is something I am certain I do not risk. Why waste your time on a people your good friend Pompeius has already subdued?"

Crassus smacked both hands to his armrests and made to rise from his seat, but was undone by the wine in his belly. Before he had gained his feet, the Galatian vintage was arguing persuasively for a second airing. He sank back in his chair and instead of making response, drank half a cup of water. Octavius rose instead, and Athena be praised, Crassus' second in command wisely took that moment to call Brenus and Taog forward from where they waited by the great doors at the end of the hall. Crassus did not, or could not object to the interruption; I could tell by his drooping shoulders that he had grown weary. The legate had invited the Gauls, thinking the king might wish to trade tales of their common Celtic ancestors. Deiotarus had as much in common with these Petrocorii as he did with Crassus' forebears, but decided that he, too, would welcome a change in the direction of the conversation.

Places were made for the Celts at the king's table and they spoke amiably for several minutes, more about Taog's size than about the migrations which had brought them so far from their ancestral island origins. As the plates were being cleared for a course of sweets before a display of Galatian entertainments, a side door burst open. Thrust inside by a rush of wind and a spray of rain came Hanno, careening at speed, arms flailing to keep his balance. He was followed moments later by an out-of-breath and terrified Livia, her red hair turned to dripping ropes of rust, a modern-day Cassandra.

Simultaneously, my wife, Brenus, Taog and yes, I am afraid even I lost all sense of decorum and shouted "Hanno!" all in varying degrees of shock, horror and alarm. Guards and guests leapt to their feet, Hanno slid to an arm-paddling halt before the high table, and Octavius rose with his hand on his knife pommel. The horror was displayed primarily by myself, for four things were instantaneously obvious: not only had someone secreted the troubled young man into our midst, Livia knew about it, had kept it from me, and now she and I, and perhaps others, were in a deadly amount of trouble.

The king stood, spreading his hands up and out to indicate no action was to be taken. Crassus glowered, but said nothing. He still looked a little pale. "And who might you be?" Deiotarus asked in a voice reserved for royal pronouncements.

Hanno looked up, overwhelmed by the sound and sight of this tall, white-haired man wearing a gold crown, long fur-lined robes and a necklace made of links of metal squares that would have bowed lesser men. Hanno may not have absorbed much in his young life, but as a person of no consequence, he had learned the only lesson of weight: to recognize and respond to authority. Remembrances of the mighty, one in particular—his mother spreading his fingers while his father drew near, opening and closing the sheep shears—were snipped permanently into the softer flesh of his simple mind, in spite of the kindness shown him in the house of Crassus.

Fear and compliance overcame him, closing his eyes even as they opened his mouth. He shifted back and forth on his feet as he spoke, big head rocking, maimed hands ungloved and flailing like unpetaled flowers. "I'm sorry, I didn't know, I'm really sorry because Brenus promised he'd take me for a ride like he did when we were in Rome but then it got dark and he was gone and I thought he went to get a chariot but then he didn't come back so Livia said stay but I didn't because Brenus promised. I'm really sorry are the chariots yours would it be all right if he could take me I know it's dark now but maybe tomorrow?" Hanno opened his eyes and pointed with a thumb. "That's Brenus right there hi Brenus, he has red hair like Livia but Livia's is prettier except not now. Brenus is sitting next to Taog hi Taog but Taog can't take me because he's too big he'd tip the whole thing over."

Octavius was glowing with anger, flailing the Celts with his eyes.

"Well," said the king. "You are a remarkable young man. Tell me your name."

"Hannibal my name is Hannibal. But my secret name is Hanno."

King Deiotarus shielded his mouth, lowered his voice and said to Crassus, "You never miss an opportunity, do you?" Crassus' look of incomprehension held more impatience than query. "The grotesque's name," the king supplied. "Someone's idea of a cruel joke?" Before Crassus could deny that he had anything to do with it, that it was, in fact, his wife's generosity that had given the boy life and a home, Deiotarus had turned his attention back to Hanno, who was practically dancing on the floor before the king. "I am afraid, young Hannibal, though I would be happy to permit it, the decision does not rest with me."

The king looked to Crassus, and Hanno followed his eyes. He saw *dominus* and me for the first time. "Father Jupiter! Master!" Off like an arrow he ran around the high table and into the unyielding grip of Octavius.

The legate lost control. "Concealing non-military personnel," he shouted. "Amongst the legion? I could have you all executed for this!"

Crassus caught his host's wry expression and knew he had no choice but to interject, "Easy, commander." He held up a hand while he drank more water. "The blame here lies with me. It was I who invited the boy to come along. It slipped my mind to have him added to the roster."

A very ugly scene was thus averted, or at least postponed. Octavius fairly brimmed with contradiction, but knew better than to voice it in this, of all places, or anywhere, until he had calmed down. Crassus motioned for him to release Hanno, who spilled immediately into *dominus'* arms. A slender arm shot out in my direction, beckoning, but I dared not move. Crassus untangled himself, uncomfortable under the amused scrutiny of his host, and Hanno jumped up to spring into my arms. Would I be whipped or worse for returning his hug? I had a son whom I hoped to see again one day, and a wife standing not twenty feet before me. My hands had no choice but to remain fixed to my sides while Hanno pressed his forehead to my chest and locked his arms around me. The lie of my immobility was unbearable. It was matched only by the horror that he was here, now, with us, instead of safe at home.

Crassus commanded Livia to remove Hanno. She padded behind the dais, mumbling apologies until she stood before me. All the while she cooed to him and pried his arms free, I forced my sight to remain fixed on the front of the hall. Hanno was under no such constraint. He looked up at me as Livia pulled him away and said, "Master, come watch me tomorrow. If you're feeling better."

King Deiotarus turned in his seat to wonder at another member of the Crassus menagerie. Thankfully, there was no time for further interrogation, for *dominus* got to his feet. He made curt thanks, then made his excuses, cutting the evening short. A shame, really, for among the several diversions Deiotarus had prepared for us were trained, performing dogs, which I very much would liked to have witnessed, but *dominus* waved me ahead to wait at the three steps at the end of the platform. In case a shoulder were required to steady him.

Just as Crassus reached the end of the high table, King Deiotarus said, "Father Jupiter, eh? That's one even Pompeius Magnus has not discovered."

"Do you not worry, your highness," Crassus answered, knocking my arm aside as I was trying to pin his cloak with its *fibula*, "that you have left the construction of this mighty fortress to the twelfth hour? It would be a shame for you to miss its completion." The chatter in the hall fell as fast as a traitor thrown from the Tarpeian Rock. My master, as fine a diplomat as had ever been bred by his city, had uttered an inexcusable insult to his host, under the man's own roof. My hands hovered in mid-air. It was an affront that made no sense, for King Deiotarus looked little older than my own age, and I was ten years younger than Crassus. However, upon reflection, mention Pompeius in a positive light, regardless of the subject, and you are apt to find yourself left alone in the dark.

Into the silence, the king laughed. "General," he said, "are *you* not marching off to war at an equally late hour? What a pity it would be were you unable to visit me when I am done with Blucium, and Parthia is done with you."

My face burned as our party walked briskly down the center aisle and out into the night. What had Brenus and Taog done? What had Livia done? The light rain still fell. We pulled our cloaks up over our heads and made for camp. When the other legates had said their brief good nights, I approached *dominus*, thinking to help him wrestle with his daemons and perhaps discover how many I would be facing on the morrow. He read my mind. "Don't! Go to your woman and see to that boy. I will not send him back, but do not trouble me with him. We will write Tertulla tomorrow and put her mind at rest. Better he march with us than be a trial to her."

What? Should I be happy to have that poor young man with us, as if Hanno could somehow even the scales for our removal from our own son? One of many responses that came to mind, those that would not see me flogged, required me to thank my master. I turned and walked into the wet night without saying a word.

CHAPTER XXVI

55 – 54 BCE - WINTER, ON THE MARCH

Year of the consulship of
Gnaeus Pompeius Magnus and Marcus Licinius Crassus

Livia had only just discovered that day that the two Celts had smuggled Hanno on board their *trireme* by claiming he was their servant, when in fact it was they who worshipped him. It had not been difficult to spirit him away: all Brenus had to do was tell the boy they were taking him to see Livia and master and Father Jupiter. Livia, once she had exhausted herself verbally stripping the woad, skin and flesh from their bones, had been watching him for the Celts while they went off to the king's dinner. He had spied a chariot and bolted, running through the rain to search them out with the news.

What good would it do now to lecture Brenus about the danger in which he had placed the boy? Hanno was here and there was nothing either of us could do to see him safely home. They thought he would have a place of honor, but Romans know nothing of Lugos. For weeks, Hanno had been sleeping beside their tent, under the guy ropes; spurned even by the slave assigned to the eight-man *contubernium* whose "preferred" place was at the front of the tent by the flaps. I remember that spot well.

369

That poor man had no reason to be proud, but how could I begrudge him, when that place was all he could call his own? And not even that. Pride costs nothing, yet it is especially precious when it can be "purchased" at someone else's expense.

Though it must have been written two month's earlier, Tertulla's letter found us not long after the incident.

> Husband, I am furious at what those reprehensible Celts have done. If the journey were not so treacherous, I would have you send Hannibal back to me at once. Promise me you will keep him safe. I know he is happier on this adventure with Father Jupiter than he could ever be stuck at home with me tending the gardens. I would rather be with Father Jupiter as well.
>
> Eternally, Tertulla

I asked for and received permission from the general to allow Hanno to share my quarters. Up until that moment, I had been feeling powerless. I realized I had always been powerless. Away from home, from the accounts and the estate, I had control over nothing. Lucius Curio now kept his fingers on the pulse of that elegant creature. It no longer belonged to me. And I realized, like that plot of ground outside the legionaries tent, it never had.

It took the arrival of an innocent like Hanno to restore my sense of purpose. At least I could get him out of the rain. At least I could see he was well fed. At least I was able to give him a hug whenever he needed one. Or the reverse.

Outside Rome, here in the world, I was an insignificant man with a couple of interesting metal plaques. The thought of it made me tired. Knowing that

Livia and now the boy were close by, sharing the same fate as mine made me both tired and frightened. I did not know what to do. There was nothing that could be done. Not by me. Action was denied me. Thought was my only refuge.

•••

After our brief visit with the "old" king, we continued down amongst the bitter Lycaonians, whose country Pompeius had cracked apart and gifted to its neighbors after the war with Pontus. We came then into Cappadocia. To the south, the green hills of the Taurus Mountains shoved up against each other, row after row, till the blank sky froze them grey, then white. There was a trick I had learned as a child, a game I played by myself given the many hours of opportunity, and I employed it now. I could choose any place within my field of vision and in my mind, swap places with it, visualizing with what I supposed was uncanny accuracy what it would look like to gaze back from that other spot toward the place where I stood. Perhaps I should have been a painter. As I say, I did this now. Instead of looking up at the peaks from the valley below where I rode on Apollo near the head of the column, I placed my mind's eye on a snow-brushed mountaintop and reversed the view. What did I see from such a height? Did encompassing the full majesty of the army take my breath away, a snake of red and gold stretching the length of the valley floor? No, from such a distance, we were barely visible, save for a thin plume of smoke that might have marked our passing, or might merely have been the smoke from a farmer burning brush, or dust from a caravan's passing. One couldn't really say.

Half an hour after the scouts had begun the day's march, and sounds of breaking camp came through the command tent, the vapor of our breathing mingled above the day's map as we gathered around the general's table for the morning staff meeting. It was still dark outside. Servants passed around cups of hot water and small chunks of bacon. After Cassius finished the supplies report, Vargunteius innocently remarked that at this pace, we could be washing our underwear in Ctesiphon by the end of Aprilis.

The quip earned a few laughs, but silence from the general. He appeared to be making up his mind about whether or not to speak, and then he did. He told us that while we would engage the enemy after a short rest in Antioch, we would not be pushing on to Ctesiphon this fighting season. He offered no explanation to soothe the stunned looks of his legates and would brook no argument. He would say only that his reasons were sound, and that once we arrived in Syria, all would be made clear. He assured us that when the facts were known, his reasoning would be readily accepted. Cassius asked him why then, was it necessary to wait? Why not tell them now? Well, Crassus told him, expecting a laugh, you never know, I might wish to change my mind between here and there. No one thought he was funny.

I had no warning that *dominus* was about to make this mad miscalculation, and had I known, I would have done my best to talk him out of it. His error lay not in remaining in Syria but in allowing his officers two months to fret about it amongst themselves with no logic to underpin their general's pronouncement. There was no need for him to say anything, unless it was to watch himself assert his own dominance. Why, in a *world* dominated by Romans, who in turn look to the smallest handful of men to govern themselves, Marcus Licinius Crassus among those exalted few, why he of all people felt the need to assert his dominance, I cannot tell you.

Nevertheless, by his own hand, *dominus* had brought the axe down twice upon the floor upon which his own commanders stood. The first blow had been insisting that we sail into the storms of the Adriatic. Then, to rush into winter seas only to be told there had been no need for haste? One error in judgment compounded the other, and quietly, like cobras testing the lid of the basket, the susurrations of doubt began. Words like "confidence," "leadership" and "ability" were, for the first time, whispered with hesitation and anxiety in dark corners by troubled men of character. The floor had been sound, but hairline cracks were widening.

Through this fracture I, fool that I was and grant you still am, would try to slip, and save us all. I was *dominus'* scribe; there was no need to practice forgery. His seal was readily available. Two more requirements need only be met: in the letter which I intended to alter, Crassus must not reread the contents of what he always signed with a personal flourish, and *domina* must obey, as she always had, the command of her lord and master.

No, I fooled myself, there must be still more than this. For this pie to be swallowed and digested, it must be fully baked. With those two measures, the dish was as yet underdone; left as is, I'd be caught and I'd be cooked. To succeed, there was a third essential to which *domina* was not nearly so accustomed, in fact, if she complied, it would prove a first for both her and her slave: she must also obey me.

It had been clear from their parting, now that the venture was close upon them, that Tertulla was having serious doubts about the scope and breadth of their vengeance upon Caesar. If she knew she would be parted from *dominus* a year more than planned, perhaps that knowledge would be wedge enough to pry her husband loose from his strategy. If there was anyone alive who could turn Crassus aside from this madness, it was his wife. This, I prayed, would tip the scales toward peace. Save for Livia, I had never met a more determined woman than the wife of Crassus.

In nuce, in a nutshell, this is what I intended. Without his permission, in addition to his own dictation, I would add into the body of my lord's next missive this news that *dominus* would tarry for a full year in Syria before even thinking of taking his war to the Parthian capital. If Tertulla were having doubts, this would be the time for her to press them upon her husband. Then I would hold my breath as Crassus signed the letter, a composition of both his words and mine.

Still, further nudging was necessary, for *domina's* entreaties must be of a nature so sincere, so contrary to their initial plan to ruin Caesar that even Crassus must pay heed. In the next sealed mail packet leaving for Rome, I added my own letter to Tertulla, knowing that by doing so, my life was now as much in her hands as it had always been in my lord's.

My lady, you know what it means for me to write to you directly without *dominus'* knowledge or permission. I have served the Crassus family with honor for three decades, and with this letter I continue my service, even if it means my life.

I write to you so that you may know what we here have witnessed: the journey to Syria has taken its toll on all of us, but on none more so than the general. It grieves me to tell you he has made command errors which have cost unnecessary lives and a dangerous loss of confidence by his legates. His health has deteriorated. He is not the man you last embraced in Rome. I fear not only for the man, but for our mission.

Your husband's greatest strength has always been his political skill. Let him wage war against Caesar in the senate. There, he has allies in both parties; there, he is armed with the backing of the people. You and I both know that on that battlefield, he will be victorious. Here, we are on unsure, dangerous ground.

If you value my life, you will destroy this letter and speak of it to no one, especially *dominus*. If you value you husband's life, you will do what no other can accomplish — write him and turn him aside from this madness. Convince him to return home.

But if, in your next letters there is only encouragement for the Parthian campaign, I shall know I have failed to dissuade you from your original course and will, as I always have, do my best to keep *dominus* safe.

Faithfully, Alexander

If I knew my lady, and none other than her husband knew her better, she would begin a literary campaign, within the confines I had set, to bring her husband home. In six or seven months we would see if this tree would bear fruit, and if Crassus would eat of it. For the time being I, along with all the general's commanders, would be left to wonder why he would arrive at his destination and not pursue his goal.

People, I have observed, are the most unpredictable of creatures. A contrivance of the kind such as I have just described often runs afoul of unanticipated outcomes. Could I rely on my lady to react as I hoped she would? Were there other possibilities I had not even imagined that might sprout from such a seed? My fervent hope was that all would go as planned. I had decided that this was an opportunity I had no choice but to exploit, and was worth the risk. You may be wondering if I communicated this scheme to Livia. Fairly certain that my wife was more predictable than most, no, I did not.

•••

The army tramped down through Tarsus and across the plain of Cilicia, a Roman province which thirteen years earlier had provided a haven for bandits plaguing Roman shipping. Pompeius, approaching the height of his popularity (with the people if not the aristocratic senate), was given command of five hundred ships, thanks in great part to the support of a certain Tribune of the Plebs, one Aulus Gabinius, the man Crassus was on his way to replace as governor of Syria. In less than a year Pompeius had extinguished the piratical flame. As we made our way around the eastern tip of the Middle Sea, Crassus' only grumbled comment about his rival's victory was that "the field had already been plowed and planted by Lucullus and Vatia; all Pompeius had to do was harvest yet another triumph."

We turned south to march down the coast of what the men boasted of as the Roman Sea. The air was moist, oppressive and drained of color. Mountains pressed us up against the still, grey waters. To the southwest, across this filmy, disturbingly quiet void lay unseen Cyprus. The sound of our passing seemed a sacrilege. We slept fitfully that night on the shore, tucked up under the looming hills. The dawn brought no change in the weather, which seemed like no weather at all. There was little conversation as the skirmishers walked their mounts through the camp gates, their horses breathing twin plumes of damp sky. Soon, our fortifications would be abandoned to the impatient gulls.

Before midday we came upon a break in the mountains. We had found the Syrian Gates, and as we climbed up through the narrow, misty pass, I thought of my namesake, the brash Macedonian who three hundred years ago had stood with his back against this same pass to block the hordes of Darius. Now Crassus sought to reenact Alexandros' victory at Issus; would my master face descendants of those luckless Persians, and would they share the same fate? The clouds dropped low and the mountains leaned in to get a better look at Roman arrogance as it passed.

Having arrived in the friendly Roman province of Syria, Crassus had sent the entire vanguard to the rear so that he could command the very head of the column. Behind him rode the eagle standard bearer of Legion I. After the *aquilifer* came three horn blowers, then Cassius, his four clerks and Octavius, legate of Legion I. Behind them rode Crassus' personal bodyguard, a *cohort* of over four hundred handpicked soldiers, including many *evocati*, retired soldiers who had served with Crassus against Spartacus and who had answered his personal invitation to join him on this expedition. These included Malchus and Betto, though I could not see them.

Dominus either did not know or did not care how he had split both my attention and my devotion by forcing Livia to join the expedition. Though I rode at the spear point of one of Rome's greatest armies, the nose of my horse a flared nostril away from the tail of the general's mount, though I was likely never again to pass through this exotic and storied land, every other thought rested

377

miles behind us where Livia walked beside the mules carrying the medical tents and supplies.

Advancing briskly south once we had negotiated the pass, we rode through a wide, fertile valley. Farms sloped up gentle hills on our right, blocking the sea from view. In the distance, a small mountain called Silpios rose sharply on our left. Now I could barely contain my elation, for I knew that Antioch lay at the foot of that peak. Our journey was coming to an end. The marching legions felt it as well: you could sense the excitement building all down the line. We followed a bright, green river, hidden by waxy, flowering plants and twisted trees that bent to protect its shyness. As if to guard our curious eyes, when we could catch a glimpse of it, the sun threw blinding, silver spears at us from its surface. We made excellent time on a new, wide stone road; evidence of Rome's recent influence. Palm trees of a variety I had never seen played a high, percussive song as the breeze passed through their fronds. Hundreds of natives intent on their daily tasks parted to let us pass, and though they stared, they did not look afraid. In fact, as we neared the city, many of the locals began to cheer. I was soon to learn that our approach was not the cause of this unexpected good will, but rather that our arrival marked the departure of another.

Peoples unknown to even the great sink of humanity that was Rome paraded on either side of our column. Merchants led both camels and mules laden with what fabulous commerce I could only imagine. Strange headdresses adorned both men and women, although woven baskets filled with merchandise were favored by the women, each offering unique, as far as I could see, to the seller. I must admit their posture was flawless. Attire, outlandish and colorful as the birds overhead, was on display. The unintelligible chatter of the throng was just as raucous. On the crowded river, sleek feluccas with sloping, graceful sails avoided smaller craft whose hulls, so fully laden, bowed to kiss the water line. I hardly knew where to look first, it was all so marvelous.

•••

At last, eighteen hundred land and sea miles and nine vials of bruise liniment from Rome, we could count days, not months, until we would arrive at the free capital of Roman Syria, *Antiochia ad Orontem*, Antioch on the Orontes. Here we would install its new governor and ever my master, Marcus Licinius Crassus. If only this had marked the end of our journey.

Was it I who had stood upon the lurching deck of *Scourge of Ctesiphon* watching the storm's inevitable approach? Could I have been the one standing on the very ground where Alexandros of Macedon had tutored the young Aristotle? I could swear these memories belonged to someone else, for *this* head was stuffed with a lifetime of day after miserable day on the march with these odiferous Romans.

Truth to tell, the journey had taken only four and a half months, but I am trying to make a point.

CHAPTER XXVII

55 – 54 BCE - WINTER, ON THE MARCH

Year of the consulship of
Gnaeus Pompeius Magnus and Marcus Licinius Crassus

At the sound of the scream, I jumped from my bedroll, ducked through my tent flaps and rushed to the command tent. As I ran, I heard Flavius Betto cry, "Bona Dea! What was that?!" from within his own tent just behind my own. Why couldn't he be more like these stalwarts here? The guards let me pass unimpeded, doing their best to look as if they had heard nothing unusual. Then I remembered Hanno. I raced back, thrust my head through the opening and saw with relief that he was snoring softly, mouth agape. Back I went to the command tent, skirting the huge map table to throw aside the heavy drapes that hid my master's bed. The proconsul was sitting up in his camp bed. (Do not be fooled — the name may be evocative of simplicity itself, but accommodation for the general's rest had required its own ox cart to haul it from Italy.) His gray hair was mashed flat on one side and sticking straight up on the other.

"Bad dream," Crassus replied to my questioning look. He mopped his brow and added, "Yes, the same one."

"They'll be here any moment. I'll tell them it was I who cried out."

"You're a good man, Alexander. We'll dine in Antioch soon, and have a proper rest."

Crassus rose, and though the dream still clung to him like a grasping lover, managed to bid a fond good morning to his water slave, then waited patiently while he emptied and refilled the wash stand basin. While other nobles barely noticed the existence of their slaves, Crassus had a well-earned reputation for being courteous and gracious to all, regardless of their station. It was one of the qualities which he had used to good effect to win high office. And when he got there, the senate was frequently reluctant to oppose him because of his popularity with the people. I could never tell whether he was motivated by guile or genuine regard for the masses he represented, but I should like to think it was the latter.

Another slave, rudely roused by a swift kick as I flew to meet any who might have heard Crassus' outburst, ran yawning to fetch the day's clean uniform. I ignored the fact that I was as yet still barefoot in an unbelted tunic. When I returned, having placated a concerned Octavius and Petronius, a curious Antoninus and a skittish Ignatius in their turn, the general had donned tunic and sandals and sat before a small, spare field table waiting for the arrival of the barber. The rest of his armor was laid out neatly on the sleeping couch.

"You look worn out, *dominus*."

"Keep that to yourself," he said, looking up at me with a thin and fleeting smile. "It's just the aftertaste of that dream. It always leaves me drained. I could manage it better if it were a normal dream, but this wretched nightmare is not some flight of nocturnal fancy. It is nothing more than a reenactment. My dreams, Alexander, will take no pity on me."

Dominus reminded me of when I was a boy. Several times I dreamt that I could fly, but I was so immersed inside the wonder of this vision that I could not step outside myself to recognize that I was dreaming. It was not that I believed that what was happening was real. It *was* real. I ran down the dirt lane that ran from our farmhouse to the road and leapt into the air. My outstretched body dipped back toward the ground but I pushed with my mind and up I went. I swept over field and village and into the heart of the great city, past the Altar of the Twelve Gods, around the Temple of Hephaistos, back along the Panathenaic Way and up to the Acropolis. A hundred feet in the air I looked down at death smiling back up at me from that great height. But I could not fall! I banked into a cloud and felt the cool damp upon my face. I chased a hawk but my talent was crude. At last, it was time to meander back home. My feet made twin tori of dust that rose in the evening sun as I landed gently in our lane. When I woke to discover that this exhilaration, this ecstasy was a lie, I wept. Tears dampened my pillow and I shut my eyes tight, trying in vain to return to a place far more wondrous than the waking world.

Unlike my remembered fantasy, while he slept, some part of Crassus realized that he was dreaming, but that only increased his agony. Each time he walked down that darkened hallway in the hours before dawn, listening as the sounds of his wife and Caesar grew louder, he struggled to change the inevitable, alter what he had seen, be a man, die if he had to, for honor's sake. But the outcome was always the same—his wife raped, his dagger bloodless, while he had watched and done nothing but slip back into the shadows.

•••

Lost in our own thoughts, we stared at the tent rug.

My lord heaved a sigh as the *tonsor* arrived; the forlorn expression on Crassus' face was not lost on the compact, little man, who instantly made note of it. Everyone in the camp knew that their general's days were better than his nights, and this they took to be an ill omen. They waited anxiously for news that Crassus rested peacefully, but my public relations efforts to improve morale on this issue were constantly undercut by an army of attendants who could see the truth for themselves. "*Salve*, proconsul!" The barber hurried to unroll the tools of his trade from his leather kit. Every part of him—calves, thighs, arms, torso, was short, fat and cherubic. Though he was middle aged, his hair having all but abandoned him except for a semi-circle about his ears and the back of his head, he still gave one the overall impression of a pudgy baby.

"Why is it, Tulio," Crassus wondered idly, "that so many *tonsores* I have met over the years are either bald or balding?" As he said this, he removed a gold ribbon from about his neck and laid it and its painted ceramic pendant carefully on the pedestal table before him.

"General, with respect," said Tulio in an affable and only slightly obsequious tone, "how many professions allow someone such as myself to approach important personages such as yourself with shears and razors." With his scissors, he snipped the air rapidly several times for emphasis. "Worrying is the natural state for such a...with your permission...talented tradesman like me. No, my lord, if you see a barber with a full head of hair, it is likely he services the plebs."

"I see your point." Under his breath, Crassus added, "No wonder Caesar suffers the daily plucking of his facial hairs with tweezers."

"Pardon, General?"

"Nothing. Just musing on the paranoia of my fellow senators."

"Governor, forgive me, but may I ask why you wear a portrait of the noble Caesar?" Tulio tilted his chin toward the ribboned medallion.

"Why, Tulio, Caesar is my inspiration." I pined fruitlessly for my lord's sarcasm to be a little less obvious. Still, it might pass high enough and quickly enough over the barber's shortened stature and attention span. Lamentably, Crassus continued. "I've worn this portrait every day for the last two years. I gaze upon it whenever my resolve flags or my spirit weakens. It gives me strength."

"He is indeed a great man, a Roman without peer," the barber said appreciatively. Then quickly added, "As are you, General, as are you!" His brow furrowed and he continued nervously, "But of course, two cannot be precisely without peer, therefore you must be more without peer than Caesar."

Crassus laughed. "Calm yourself, Tulio, before you burst a blood vessel. Today, my friend, so far from Rome's laurels and triumphs, you and I are but soldiers. Let each of us do what we came here to do, and leave to others the task of judging our efforts. For now, I wish for nothing more than a little trim and a fine shave." To me he said, "Alexander, sit with me while Tulio worries away another hair or two from the several left on his pate." The little barber looked up from his kit and smiled broadly and with relief; then, as was their odd custom, he bowed his head and tapped his glowing, tanned scalp. Crassus reached over and gave it a quick rub for luck.

I pulled up a camp chair and sat opposite my master. "Will you take wine?" I asked.

"Water only. And perhaps a little bread and fruit." Two attendants ran off to the kitchens before I could utter a word. "Alexander, I can't believe it's been five months. We must write to her today. Do not let me forget."

"I'll fetch the writing table." I started to rise.

"No, stay awhile. It can wait till after the staff meeting. Talk with me." I sat with *dominus* and watched Tulio trim an already perfect haircut. We sat in silence, listening to the conversation between scissors and razor. If there were words to be said, they were private monologs. The food and drink, when it arrived, went untouched.

Crassus' face relaxed into that state that only a barber's ministrations can summon. *Dominus'* grey eyes remained fixed on some distant point, hardly blinking. For once, the normally loquacious *tonsor* sensed the mood and concentrated on his work.

"Tulio, another excellent performance." In a hand-held metal mirror he confirmed with satisfaction that not one nick marred his clean-shaven face. "You may leave us now," he said, tossing him a silver *denarius*. The barber thanked him profusely.

"Is it so wrong," Crassus asked me as the little man gathered his tools, "for love to set great events in motion? Did not Menelaus do as much for Helen?"

While I was crafting a response that might somehow cast a benign light on the countless tragedies of the Trojan

War, Tulio jumped in. "No, General, not wrong at all. Great love may be proved by deeds both great and small."

What prattle is this, you ignorant, rotund sycophant? I wanted to ask him how his affirmation of my master's hopes would sit with him were they to be abruptly interrupted by the razor point of a Parthian arrow piercing his pale, hairless breast? Would Tulio regurgitate such nonsense if he knew that on this misadventure, we were all of us slaves, not to love, but to vengeance? I thought about it and came to the conclusion that yes, he probably would.

When Tulio the fawner had departed, Crassus stood up, toweled off his face and continued in a subdued voice. "I must tell you something, Alexander. If Caesar returns to Rome before me, Tertulla will make her way to Siphnos. He will not think to look for her in Greece. I have sent word to Nicias. She will be safe there. Should the gods send you home without me, follow her there; look after her." I started to protest, but Crassus raised his hand. "As I left her, I kissed her hands, and folded her fingers about a bronze key hung on a gold necklace. The key opens a strongbox hidden behind the *lararium*. In it are fifty talents of silver and certified copies of my will and all the deeds to all our properties. She will have those with her. My will is recorded with the Vestals; everything is documented and registered. Hopefully, none of these precautions will be necessary. When all goes well, she will be waiting for me at the *Capena Gate* upon our return, the same one through which I departed."

"Then I will pray we both find her safe on Roman soil."

Crassus grasped my arm in the Roman fashion. "If the fates allow, this war will knit together what Caesar has tried to tear apart."

"Syria is beautiful, *dominus*. It is not too late to summon *domina* to attend you while you serve out your proconsulship without ever having to cross the Euphrates."

Instead of releasing my forearm, Crassus squeezed till his fingertips turned white and red. "Quiet! Enough! Again, Alexander, you presume too much." His grip relaxed only after he was sure he had left his marks upon me.

"*Dominus*," I said, taking a step back and bowing my head. "May the gods grant us all safe passage back to our families."

"If you cannot give me counsel within the boundaries I have set, you are no more use to me than Tulio. Less. At least whenever *he* leaves the room," he said, the metal in his voice softening, "I feel better. And look better as well."

"Think of me, *dominus*, as the little hairs that Tulio leaves behind that prick and itch throughout the day to remind you not only of your stately appearance but of your responsibilities to Rome and family."

"Oh, I do, Alexander, you may rely on it. Those hairs are nothing, however, that a good brushing wouldn't remove."

CHAPTER XXVIII

54 BCE - SPRING, ANTIOCH

Year of the consulship of
Lucius Domitius Ahenobarbus and Appius Claudius Pulcher

T hree days after we passed through the Gates, on the 4th of Martius, we came upon the northernmost city gate. There was a lovely hill overlooking the spot, shaded by several sinewy-limbed arbutus. Their smooth, muddy-orange branches spread like outstretched arms. Just below them, we passed several Roman work crews repairing the ten-foot tall defensive wall that stretched across the narrowing valley. The triple-arched gateway and river bridge were in good repair, but in many places stones from the original walls and watchtowers had tumbled. The old Seleucid monarchs may have been at the mercy of the ground-shaking gods, but those chthonian deities were no match for Roman engineering.

Further on we were met by a most curious sight. A single cavalry commander and two natives rode up meet to us. The Roman looked to be about thirty years of age. "Governor Gabinius bids you welcome to Antioch, proconsul Crassus," he said formally as he and his dusky companions turned alongside our officers and rode with us. The general made no signal to alter our pace—a column stretching twenty miles was not about to stop for such an informal greeting. The stranger's voice was deep and rich; he might have been a stage performer. He had the looks for it, with black, curly hair and a full beard in the Greek style. He continued, "Allow me to present Abgarus II, king of Osrhoene, client state of Armenia and ally of Rome."

The road ahead had been cleared of traffic. Lining the curb on each side were several hundred turbaned horsemen, each facing his counterpart across the road. As Crassus reached the first pair they raised their curved sabres; when he had passed the swords were sheathed and they sat at attention, their right fist on their breast in Roman salute. This was repeated hundreds of times, creating the illusion of a slow wave of blades rising and falling with our passage.

Crassus, in as foul a mood as ever I had seen him said, "I know neither of you."

The officer, clearly shocked, said, "King Abgarus has made a peace with Pompeius Magnus that has lasted for years. Osrhoene is as good a friend to Rome as any of our provinces."

Crassus flinched at the name of Pompeius; he could travel to the ends of the empire and still not escape him.

Every place *dominus* set his foot, Pompeius had walked before. "It has been my experience that the further one travels from Rome, the more the bonds of friendship tend to loosen. Sir, I have no reason to doubt your good will. In fact, when I spoke thus, I had in mind my own countrymen." Crassus turned to the bearded Roman. "Now who did you say you were?"

"Marcus Antonius."

"You must forgive me. My memory lapses frequently in my dotage," he said with unrestrained sarcasm. "It is, after all, a common enough name." If my master knew how close the fates of *this* Marcus Antonius and Julius Caesar were to become entangled, it was a name he would never forget. After Antioch, however, their paths were not to cross again. "You must be," he continued, "a hero of the Syrian province to represent all of Antioch on this historic day, the only Roman to receive us upon our arrival. Or perhaps the son of the good Gabinius?"

"I am neither," answered the soldier. "Though some may think me so."

"What, a hero or a relative?"

This seemed to stump the burly soldier, for he paused to exhibit behavior which had all the trappings of thought, though I doubt it contained much of the substance. This was followed by a low, guttural sound which the man had apparently learned to substitute for cogitation. Though I do not often leap to conclusions, I landed firmly on one now: the man was as thick as his beard.

"Marcus Antonius," Crassus repeated thoughtfully. "Not the son of Creticus?" Antonius nodded. "Never was a praetor more incompetent. But your grandfather was a statesman, and a fine orator. Let us hope, for your sake, the inheritance of your family's qualities has skipped a generation."

That was unkind. Defensive and clearly stung, the commander responded, "I fought with general Gabinius against Aristobulus in Judea. I also attended the governor in Egypt and—"

"I am not interested in your exploits. But I am curious to know if it is the habit of your general to welcome a senator and consul bearing the dust of two thousand miles upon his shoulders with but a single countryman and a few choreographed natives?"

The young Roman glanced at his comrades to gage the impact of the insult. The king's face, whose participation in this embarrassingly paltry reception argued against the legitimacy of his title, remained bland, and the other was clearly a servant; no help for the Roman in that quarter. A flash of anger illuminated Antonius's face long enough for me to recognize it as an emotion with which he was most comfortably intimate. We often find ourselves at ease with that with which we are most familiar, regardless of whether or not the trait serves us well in the end. Is that not yet another example of how we enslave ourselves? I never realized there were so many forms of the condition, my own being but the most obvious.

I gave Antonius credit for stuffing his nature back into its bottle and muffling his reply with discretion. "Humble apologies, general. Governor Gabinius would have been here himself, indeed he would have sent a *cohort* to meet you, but everyone, including the governor, is preparing for tomorrow's games in your honor."

"He is governor no longer, and whether he knows it or not has been out of office since the day he refused to receive the officer I sent ahead of me over a month ago. Is

Gabinius wielding a broom or lending a hand in the kitchen?" Those of Crassus' commanders who could hear him snickered, but Antonius remained quiet, though his color brightened.

"The fort and fields are prepared for your men and livestock," he said. "Shall I familiarize your second-in-command with how things are done in Antioch?"

"Do that." Marcus Antonius wheeled his horse about and dropped back to ride beside Octavius. We rode on at a brisk walk, letting the column fall further behind.

The king spoke in perfect Latin. His tone was even and without rancor. "With your permission, general," he said evenly, "I would be honored to escort you to the palace."

Everything I had seen since we began our approach to the city was a marvel. I was bedazzled by each new sight, including Abgarus. I do not know who was more finely caparisoned: the prince or his horse. The man, who looked to be in his mid-fifties, wore a formal headdress of multi-colored fabric, twisted and intertwined in such a way that I could not help but be reminded of a very expensive pile of laundry. As I said, he was dark-skinned, but not as black as some of the merchants I had seen on our approach to the city. His most striking feature was the hair above his lip: it was greased and twisted to points extending far beyond his face. He wore a black tunic and baggy leggings gathered at the ankles. His waist was covered with a very wide sash of woven fabric—dark greens and deep reds on a field the color of sand. A single curved and bejeweled dagger was thrust through a leather belt adorned with heavy, silver buckles. Its sheath and hilt looked to be fashioned entirely of gold. His long, many-hued coat partially obscured an open vest of some fine, green fabric shot with silver thread. Several tasseled pouches and bags were slung around his neck.

The king's attendant was another matter entirely. He was curiously unkempt for such a position of honor. Distastefully so. Perhaps it was the custom for an Aramean prince to be accompanied by one so plain of attire as to catapult his own resplendency to even greater heights by comparison. The young man wore light, flowing robes of no distinguishable color; his blouse and leggings were homespun. His head was uncovered and unkempt; every now and again he would sweep a hand through dark, unruly curls. His face had not seen a razor in several days. About his neck, a white head scarf was loosely wrapped, its tasseled ends falling unevenly. As far as I could tell, he was unarmed. His eyebrows, set close to dark brown eyes, implied a serious disposition I suspected was unwarranted. When at rest, his mouth lay straight across his face until at one end it curled in the suggestion of a smile. His only adornment was a length of exquisitely woven multi-colored fabric that tied a knot of his hair at the back of his neck. At the time I remember thinking he did not look like any Eastern native I had ever seen, but then my limited experience did not qualify me as a reliable judge. Whatever his heritage, there were ladies in Rome who would forfeit fortunes to make his secret acquaintance. The lad looked to be no more than twenty or twenty-one.

"Forgive my rudeness, King Abgarus," Crassus replied. "We are tired and ill-humored, but my perturbation with my hosts should not have descended upon your shoulders."

The king leaned in his saddle toward Crassus, careful with so many watchful eyes to keep both hands on his

393

reins. He lowered his voice and said, "An inexcusable affront. In Ourha the entire palace would be turned out to bid you welcome."

Crassus removed his plumed helm and wiped his brow. "To be honest, Abgarus, all that matters is that we have arrived, and to these stiff old muscles, it makes no difference whether one or ten thousand line the way. Do not misunderstand me, I do appreciate and thank you for the precision display of your guard."

"My swords are your swords. General, Abgarus is the name taken by all who sit on the throne of Osrhoene. You would honor me by dispensing with the formality of title and use my given name, Ariamnes."

Crassus said, "Highness, I do not wish to create insult where none is meant, but let us rely on and take comfort in formality until time and experience build friendship and trust. In Rome, the *praenomen* is reserved for family or intimate friends, not to be given lightly. In time, let us hope that we both earn that privilege."

"As you wish, my general," the king said coolly. "My people are more quick to recognize a friend. But it is no matter. I shall, of course, respect your wishes."

We rode in silence for a while more, then Crassus said, "Would it be against custom to ask who this handsome young man is by your side?"

"Not at all. May I present my cousin, Melyaket puhr Karach. He is visiting from afar and traveling under my protection, having recently endured a family tragedy."

"My condolences for your loss, Melyaket son of Karach," Crassus said sympathetically.

"You are kind, my lord. However, while the tragedy was real, the family was not my own."

"How do you mean?"

"The retelling, Governor Crassus, would be as tiresome for you as the reliving of it would be painful for me. To make quick work of it, there were people who wanted something of mine that I did not want them to have. Regrettably, lives were lost."

"More than one?" Crassus asked.

"A few."

"Indeed! And you are here under the good king's protection presumably because you left more of them alive than you slew."

"More than a few."

"And now they search you out. You see the price of not being thorough. Your people could learn a thing or two from Marius or Sulla."

"Unfortunately, great general, my enemies are rarely gathered in one place, out in the open, all at the same time."

Crassus laughed. "I like this man. And also that such a cunning warrior rides beside me unarmed. You are unarmed, are you not?" At these words, Cassius jerked his reins and interposed himself between Crassus and Abgarus. In an instant, three more mounted legionaries had crowded round Melyaket, their swords drawn.

"Jupiter's knees, Longinus," Crassus exclaimed. "I was in jest. Leave the fellow be."

Cassius replied, "With respect, general, I cannot afford your sense of humor. A perfect and ironic time for treachery to strike—just as we are about to enter the city."

"Nonsense. If you want to rise as a politician, Cassius, and what young officer does not, you've got to think like a chef. Look at this fellow. He simply does not have the right ingredients for the meal you suggest. Combine cleverness, youth and a quick wit and try as you might you will never prepare a dish of suicide. You don't want to kill yourself, do you, Melyaket? There, you see, Cassius? Trust me, I've been mixing recipes of men in the senate for thirty years." *Dominus* ordered the guards back into rank and the march continued. "Tell me this, son. How did you dispatch these enemies?"

"As quickly as I could," the young man answered. "I apologize, general, I know what you are asking…"

"I understand. Let others boast on your behalf. Otherwise the glory is diminished. What are your weapons of choice?"

"I am trained in many, but some have said I have a gift with the bow."

"I will require a demonstration."

King Abgarus asked, "If I may, general, what weapon do you prefer?"

Crassus took no more than a moment to answer. "Overwhelming odds." He glanced back at the column that disappeared in a haze beyond the last bend in the road. He turned back to Melyaket and added, "I think you will enjoy meeting my son when he arrives."

"I look forward to meeting the renowned Publius Crassus."

Dominus furrowed his brow but made no comment. "Well, Melyaket puhr Karach," he said, "I hope your cause was just."

"If it were not," said King Abgarus, "he would not be riding at my side."

Cassius said to the king, "Regrettably, majesty, I am unable to risk the life of my general upon the word of a…new friend." The *quaestor* shifted to face Melyaket. "Tell me, my clever, funny friend, exactly where is this place from which you found it necessary to flee?"

"My village rests at the base of the southern flank of the Jebel Sinjar, my lord."

"Sinjar? That's Parthian territory, is it not."

Abgarus shrugged, "Parthian, Armenian, Mygdonian. Even Osrhoene has at one time raised its banners in that barren dirt. There is nothing there worth owning, I promise you. Apologies, Melyaket, but you know I speak truth."

"Noble king," Melyaket said with a wink, "you will never see the riches hidden there, for unlike me, you have never called Sinjar 'home.'"

Cassius used a tone of voice which made those who heard it cower and those at whom it was directed blurt truth from fear. "To which nation do you swear allegiance, boy?"

Melyaket neither cowered nor blurted, though his eyebrows creased in thought before he spoke. "There is a brook that tumbles down the mountain above our village. Its spring is a sacred place. The women beat our clothes against the flat rocks of the stream's banks. As the water passes beneath an overhang of rock shaped like the palm of a hand, there is a deep pool where the water rests, cold and clear, before refreshed, it continues its rush down the hill. If the day is sunny and warm and the echoes of laughter and splashing cannot be heard from this place, we know a child must be in trouble. Before it reaches the village, this playful stream hides from us, diving beneath the earth, but we catch it again by the bucketful in the well that sits in the center of the square. It is surrounded by three olive trees so old no one remembers who planted them, but we know what feeds them.

"We do not own that stream, sir, though we have built our homes about it, and our lives depend upon it. So if you asked them, the villagers of Sinjar would gladly swear allegiance to that water."

"You are impertinent," Cassius Longinus said, "or woefully ignorant."

Melyaket answered, "If you permit me, sir, ignorance suits me far better."

"That I doubt," said Longinus.

Legate Ignatius of Legion V spoke up, having been handed one of the general staff's maps by a centurion. "The Parthians claim everything east of the Euphrates. The Jebel Sinjar is an insignificant range of mountains at its northwest border; nothing else in any direction for miles save empty desert. Nevertheless, King Orodes would most definitely insist it belongs to him."

"Then it's settled," Melyaket said. "I'm a Parthian."

"General, this is too much," Cassius said, pleading, "a Parthian in our midst?"

"Calm yourself, Cassius. I don't think this young man can be much of a threat to seven legions."

"He could easily be a spy."

Vargunteius, a commander I took to be of more temperate demeanor said, "Look about us, Cassius. I wager one in twenty are Parthians. Who among this throng does not know why we are here?"

"Worthy king," Crassus asked Abgarus, "when was the last time Roman legions were seen massed in Syria?"

Ariamnes twisted the shiny ornaments of hair above his lips in thought. "Let me see…"

"Petronius, have we had any word of a defense being mounted against us?"

The commander looked to Crassus. "Whether ten or ten thousand," said *dominus*, "does the sea serpent flinch from the number of minnows that appear out of the murk? The beast swims where it will. Speak freely, Petronius."

The legate of Legion II said, "None. Many of the towns across the Euphrates have been populated by the seed of Alexander. These Macedonian and Greek settlements will most likely welcome us as liberators."

"Alexander, you've been very quiet. Let's hear what you have to say." Most of the legates leaned in to listen, though one or two were smiling. Cassius turned away.

"Through Armenia, Osrhoene is a sworn ally of Rome. Its king is therefore held by that bond. I cannot speak for the Parthian."

"There, you see," Crassus said. "If Alexander says it, it is so."

"Alexander said nothing of the Parthian," Cassius said.

"If I may ask," King Abgarus inquired, "what post does Alexander hold in your staff?"

"He is my closest personal advisor, and has held the position for over thirty years. No strategic decision regarding my affairs is made without his counsel. Why do you ask?"

The king said, "Is he not a slave?"

"How is that relevant? Is that not a horse you are riding? Whether the animal belongs to you or is borrowed from another, are you still not upon its back? Does it still not function exactly as a horse?"

How comforting, master, to find that though the years have greyed your hair and stolen from your once stately height, your penchant for hurling spears of unstudied disregard continues still, undulled and unabated.

"General," Cassius persisted, "the matter of the Parthian."

Crassus laughed. "Longinus, I heartily approve of your caution. But reason it out. Let us assume the man is a spy. Let us say the next ear in which he whispers is that of Orodes himself. The only thing this spy could tell his master is, 'I have seen the Romans. Save yourselves.'"

Dominus turned in his saddle to look over Abgarus so he could face Melyaket eye to eye. "Melyaket puhr Karach, you have nothing to fear from Rome. When Parthia has become our easternmost province, life in your little village of, what was it? Shingar?"

"Sinjar."

"Life in Sinjar will change not one jot. We are here to negotiate a peace. The skirmishes that have scarred our frontiers need not continue. If your king will but swear allegiance to Rome, Parthia will continue as it always has. So, if you are a spy, be certain when you depart to relay that message to your master." His tone and smile were avuncular.

"I would do so, my lord, were I ever to see him, but I doubt he would believe me."

"Why is that?"

"Two reasons. If a man walks into a room where another is sitting and demands his chair, how can he trust that life will continue as it always has if he must give up his seat? At best, the chair the man owned will no longer be his and at worst, the man will be left standing."

Cassius almost whined with ardency, "General, let me take him into custody, I beg of you."

"With apologies, great general," Melyaket said, glancing at Cassius with a twitch of an eyebrow that said *I am no threat to you* and *you are no match for me*, "some version of that very thought is in the mind of every person who has seen the dust raised by this column, a cloud surely visible from here to Aleppo. It is no trick to imagine what everyone across the Euphrates, even the king, is thinking."

"Even so, we prefer peace. Let us hear the second reason."

"The second lies within the first. The king is fond of his gold."

"You seem to know much about the mind of King Orodes."

"He is a king. Is this not true of all kings?"

Everyone laughed, with the exception of Cassius, who was already planning to post two guards on this Melyaket wherever he went; four when he was near the person of the general.

•••

We had come into a very large, tree-lined plaza with six roads radiating out like the spokes of a wheel. At its "hub" rose a massive fountain: a charioteer road half-immersed marble waves, water spraying from the nostrils of his four flying mounts. The city sprawled before us, spreading out from the banks of the river, crawling westward as far as it could up the steep flank of the mountain to our left. The road we traveled continued south through the plaza; off in the distance rose gently sloping hills and the misty outlines of a high-walled garrison. The circle that defined the plaza was not quite complete, sliced through by parks and gardens that honored the banks of the Orontes. Just ahead and to the right, a gently arcing bridge crossed the river to an island so large I did not recognize it as such. We turned to ride to its apex, then Crassus bid us halt. We turned and looked back, watching as Marcus Antonius and Octavius passed at the head of endless ranks of men eager to shed their gear in the fort beyond the palace.

"Your highness, I would be honored," said the general to the king, "if you would accompany me to the palace." He turned to Cassius. "Go follow Octavius. Let him know I'll be laying on a feast for them after these games. And pass the word, once they've been billeted, three days leave. After that, drilling as usual. Alexander—with me." As always, the cream of the *evocati*, fifty of Crassus' most trusted legionaries accompanied us over the wide bridge. I looked behind me and caught a glimpse of Malchus and Betto. I did not wave, that would be unseemly, but big Malchus gave me a wide grin. Betto looked too uncomfortable on his mount to smile at anything or anyone.

•••

Yes, reader, I could have told you earlier that this Melyaket puhr Karach was the very same irritatingly attentive old ruffian to whom I had introduced you many scrolls ago. Are not my gnarled joints tired and stiff enough? Have you no responsibility whatsoever? You might have rummaged through these ramblings to see for yourself. One might also ask, how many Melyakets does one meet in a lifetime?

The truth is, I was not paying much attention to either Crassus or anyone else. The marvel of Antioch was unfurled before me; my eyes and mind were filled with little else. Here there were great works of art, a theater, temples to Athena and Ares that not even the Romans dared disturb. Somewhere hidden among these graceful, paved streets there was even a library which had stood for almost two hundred years. Antiochus III had enticed the epic Greek poet, Euphorion of Chalcis to be its first librarian. I ached to find it, and hoped that Crassus might give Livia and me leave to spend a few hours amid its wonders.

A nagging consternation was finally resolved as we crossed the pillared bridge. Something was missing. As we approached the tall, open gates on the far side, I realized what had been troubling me. There was no smell! No. Better. Antioch was fragrant! Here the scent of flowers and baking bread were not smothered to a barely recognizable ache by the stench of sewage clogging the Tiber or by orphaned clumps of filth and excrement simmering to eye-watering perfection in the summer sun. This was not Rome. Antioch was healthy, or appeared to at least make the effort to care for all its people in a way that at home was restricted to the noble and the wealthy.

We completed our crossing of the bridge and passed beneath a high, stone archway decorated with lapis blue tile and exquisite mosaics. We had entered the Regia, the palace of the kings of the Seleucid dynasty, now surrendered, first to Armenia, then to the rule of Rome. For the past ten years the Regia had served as the residence of the Republic's governors; now it belonged to my master.

CHAPTER XXIX

54 BCE - SPRING, ANTIOCH

Year of the consulship of
Lucius Domitius Ahenobarbus and Appius Claudius Pulcher

"**G**eneral, the proconsul is waiting for you in the gallery. Which is *this* way." The little man who had met us at the blue and gold double doors of the governor's private residence within the palace appeared to be a shorter, squatter version of me, if you added makeup, jewelry, pursed lips and painted toenails. By which I mean to say I believe our escort was to Aulus Gabinius what I was to Marcus Crassus. *Dominus*, followed by his retinue of a dozen legionaries and as many personal attendants and baggage haulers, had turned right down a wide, columned hall lined with tall, glazed urns filled with potted plants whose vines draped themselves almost to the ground. On the marbled floor, the soldiers' *caligae* sounded like an invasion. A water boy stood wide-eyed with his back to the wall as we passed.

"What's down this way?" Crassus asked as the out-of-breath servant shuffled to catch up. We were approaching a dead end and another set of deep blue double doors, these carved with receding squares inlaid with silver.

"Those are the governor's private quarters."

"Are they indeed? Then we've come to the right place, haven't we?"

"But proconsul Gabinius awaits my lord in the gallery...my lord."

"What is your name, man?"

"Mercurius, my lord."

Crassus said good-naturedly, "the proconsul, Mercurius, stands before you. Is that clear?" Gabinius' man whimpered. "Mercurius," Crassus mused. "I had an *ornator* by that name, oh...it must be twenty years ago at least. Nice fellow, but slow as sludge. What ever happened to him, Alexander?"

"You had me sell him, *dominus*."

"Did I?" It would be pointless to add that Mercurius' new master was less forgiving than *dominus* and his *medicus* less talented than ours. The wounds from the lash had festered and the poor man had died from his lack of alacrity.

"Tell your master," Crassus was saying, "that I will rest awhile in my quarters before meeting him in the gallery, say in two hours time. For a man as busy as he, I am certain the time will fly on Pegasus' wings. Until then, I do not wish to be disturbed. Is that clear, Mercurius?"

The man looked like he was being ground between two blocks of the Great Pyramid of Giza. He mumbled his assent and shuffled off to perform his unenviable duty. Crassus turned one of the hanging brass rings and unlatched the door. It swung open and he peered inside.

405

"This is for one person?" we heard him say, his voice muffled by thick wood. He pushed the door wide and motioned the attendants inside behind two soldiers. As our people went in, several young men, women and boys came skittering out. "Centurion," he said to Vel Corto, "post your guard here. Admit no one."

Three stone steps led down to a wide floor of the same sand-colored tiles. Long narrow rugs woven in patterns of gold, red and blue crisscrossed throughout the room, matching the half-columns that rose to the painted twelve-foot ceilings. The tables, walls and floor were littered with all manner of decoration. Nothing simple, not a clean line in sight, only keepsakes to which the word ornate could cling with comfort. We stood on a platform, fifteen feet on a side. Straight ahead, steps led down to the open bed chamber; to the right one descended to the baths, separated from the main room by painted screens. Close by, a tall tripod topped by a burning dish of incense sent curls of cedar smoke toward the ceiling. Crassus wrinkled his nose and I motioned for an assistant to take the bronze platter away and douse it.

I inspected this Syrian bed. It was raised off the ground, not much higher than a sleeping *lectus*, but much wider, with a thick layer of matting. It was held aloft by a golden frame, the sleeper guarded on each side by twin winged Assyrian bulls. A pale blue curtain no thicker than a cobweb dropped from the ceiling to surround the entire piece. I was not sure of its purpose, for I did not think it would give a mosquito more than a moment's pause. The bath was a sunken oval whose far wall contained a diamond-latticed window so wide it required the support of three gilt columns. The view of the river and the city beyond was stunning.

"This room is obscene. I shall need a potion or at the very least a mask in order to sleep here."

"I will have it 'simplified' after the ex-proconsul departs." Sending the attendants below to begin unpacking and preparing a bath, I asked *dominus* to sit for a moment on a couch near the double doors.

"I lied," I said quietly. Crassus began unlacing his boots. A servant ran up the steps but *dominus* waved him off.

"I thought as much." I waited. *Dominus* continued. "You never gave me a direct answer to my question as to whether or not you agreed with Cassius' concerns. That is unlike you, at least when we are not alone."

"As I recall, you never *asked* a direct question."

"I attend, eager as ever."

"I don't trust either one of them, the Osrhoene king or the young Parthian."

"We are agreed." I raised an eyebrow. "My father once told me, 'if you arrive for a meeting with a man you do not trust, and the man you do not trust does not arrive, do not trust the man who first arrives at the meeting."

"He told you no such thing."

"Not precisely, no, but they were words to that effect. Go ahead, explain yourself."

"What of Marcus Antonius? He was among the 'first to arrive.'"

"Pff. He is a Roman through and through. I can smell it on him."

"Agreed. The first reason I don't trust either one of the others is something you said earlier today. Something about the bonds of friendship loosening with distance. Armenia and Parthia have been at odds for ages, and Osrhoene sits between them and wonders, I am a dwarf caught between giants, and my 'friend' is far away. If I were Abgarus, I would not be motivated by friendship, but fear. Be cautious, my lord."

"Agreed. And of the bowman?"

I pursed my lips. "With him it is strange. He is, there is something about him…"

"He is too likeable."

"Yes! He is like a fragrant bowl of steaming soup you are compelled to taste knowing your tongue will burn. And his presence at our arrival was completely inappropriate. But there is more to distrust regarding the Aramean king. When you asked him when a Roman army was last seen in Syria, he hesitated."

"Maybe he was traveling when Gabinius began his own invasion of Parthia."

"It was less than three years ago! What reason could he have to hesitate?" *If Pompeius hadn't called his dog off to (illegally) put Cleopatra's father back on Egypt's throne – with a bone of thanks from Ptolemy, a fortune of 10,000 talents of silver – Gabinius might have conquered Parthia and Livia and I would be safe at home with our son. I had as much reason to be as disaffected with Magnus my master.*

"Abgarus might have a hundred legitimate reasons. I see nothing there. However, here is how I shall play the Parthian. I shall take him into my confidence while at the same time removing you from it."

"*Dominus!*"

"Patience. I shall keep the lad close. As I befriend him, I shall confide in him that I have reason to mistrust you." *My facial muscles felt as if they had begun to dance.* "I will ask him, while he is able, to keep watch on you and report back to me. He should decline the offer outright, for he has no business with us."

"If he accepts," I said, my pitch and inflection straining for normal, "we have indication, if not evidence."

"And if he makes frequent excuse to go and return, there can be but one reason."

"He reports to his Parthian overlords."

"Then, if we so choose," said Crassus as he stood and smiled, it appeared in equal measure from his deceit as much as from the joy of wiggling his once again bare toes, "we may feed him a soup of our own choosing."

•••

The man's hair was in ringlets that fell to the back of his neck and halfway down his forehead. Each one was crimped with a narrow gold band. A fringed purple headband was tied tight at the top of his head. His face was rouged, but exertion had caused the paint to run. His matching robe was barely tied, beneath which his lean body was naked. Mercurius sat behind a rosewood table tucked diagonally up against the far corner of the room. He wrote furiously, his pen dipping in and out of the well, his eyes flicking from one piece of parchment to the next. Several players stood idly against the wall, fingering their instruments. Marcus Antonius sat on the edge of the long table. Draped over the back of his uniform, its paws tied beneath his neck, was a lion's skin. The head, I am pleased to say, was not in evidence, but I am certain Antonius knew its whereabouts.

With a dozen bewildered legionaries behind us, we had entered the grand gallery of the Regia, unwilling players upon a bizarre and foreign stage. Crassus was dressed in all his polished military finery save for his helmet, which was tucked under his arm. The hall was magnificent. Columns painted green and black were spaced every twenty feet and rose almost that high to the beamed ceiling. Birdsong vanquished the echoes of our footsteps on the polished tiles as we drew to a halt. The entire length of the gallery was open—through the columns we could see a covered portico and from there a quadrangle planted with rows of trees whose white, starry flowers perfumed the air. Green, misshapen globes, some having turned bright yellow, hung so large and plentiful they made of their branches two-color rainbows. Later I learned the thick-skinned, tart fruit was called citron, what the Hebrews call an *etrog*, and the Persians know as a *limun*.

"You must forgive my appearance," said Aulus Gabinius, Roman statesman, general, tribune of the plebs, propraetor and proconsul.

"Why must I?" asked Crassus.

Gabinius tilted his head to the side. The gold in his ringlets made a pretty sound. "I should think professional courtesy." Marcus Antonius hopped off the desk and offered his pelt to Gabinius. As this would have been useful only had he donned the garment backwards, the ex-governor declined.

"Professional courtesy would be the last thing to raise between us, I should think," *dominus* said pointedly. He looked around him. "What has been going on here?"

"When I could not access my rooms, I took my exercise." Crassus waited, uncomprehending. "I dance. To music."

"You *are* the same Aulus Gabinius who suppressed the recent revolt in Judea?"

"Who welcomes you to Antioch."

"Our welcome, Gabinius, was notable only due to your absence. I trust you're packed?"

"With your permission," he said, bowing deeply, "I shall leave for Rome directly after the games. You and I have much to discuss. About Syria. About Parthia?"

"I will not deny the people their games, but you will be gone and on your way back to Rome before the last team has been unharnessed, bandaged and brushed."

•••

People had been streaming across all five bridges onto the Regia's island since sunrise. The racing track had been completed thirteen years earlier, built so that the governor and his guests could take a short stroll through his gardens, under guard of course, and enter the broad red and black arch of the Proconsul's Gate into the arena. Every one of the 80,000 seats in the hippodrome was occupied, though defended might be a more appropriate word. The Circus Maximus may have taken twice as many Romans to its bosom, but these clumps of blue and green flag-waving Antiochenes expressed an even greater joy to be held there. The track itself was an oblong almost 1,500 feet long by 220 feet wide. Down its center ran an 850 foot long by 24 foot wide *spina* only a few feet tall around which the chariots ran. Bronze statues of rearing horses reared thirty feet in the air at both ends, and in the center a red granite obelisk, forty feet tall and just delivered from Alexandria lay on its side waiting to be erected. I cocked my head, but the gold-painted hieroglyphics engraved up and down its spine made as much sense to me either way. Feeling for a moment like a schoolboy, I half-wished that the Egyptians had covered their gift with execrations and scatological humor at the Romans' expense.

We had just taken our seats in the governor's box; the noise became so loud at our arrival it precluded conversation. I took note that at our approach the volume of cheers increased in equal proportion to the number of boos. Somewhere high above us, Livia must be laboring mightily to restrain Hanno from leaping into the aisle to tumble twenty rows to the railing for a better view. After gaining *dominus'* permission, the only way we had agreed we would allow the sixteen-year-old to attend was if we tethered the two of them together. What with the unbridled—I beg your pardon—enthusiasm of the crowd, I was relieved that Malchus and Betto had graciously agreed to be their escorts.

For this special occasion, Crassus looked particularly resplendent, wearing a laurel wreath upon his brow and a gold-bordered purple cloak over a double tunic of black and gold. I was wearing my best tunic, which was simple and black with no ornamentation, but I was very fond of it. Marcus Antonius, Octavius, Petronius and Cassius joined *dominus* and Gabinius in the box, and Melyaket had been included at Crassus' insistence, but King Abgarus was curiously absent. Cassius was miserable, as usual, and *dominus* had thought it best to leave him out of his plans for the Parthian to keep his reactions natural. They were very 'natural' this morning. Mercurius and I sat behind our masters among the wine and food servers. Luckily for the generals we were outside the *pomerium*, for the heat of this climate and the strict tradition of the toga would have undone many a noble. Lucky for all, Gabinius, though ostentatious, was at least fully clothed.

Gabinius stood to give the signal for start of the games, but as soon as the masses saw him, whether green or blue, a throat-swelling of disapproval rose all around us. Crassus shouted up at him, "It would seem you've stolen one *denarius* too many from this province, Aulus."

Unfazed, Gabinius made an exaggerated show of pointing to the new governor of Syria sitting next to him, motioning for him to stand. When Crassus rose, the cheering grew louder than the noise from any triumph. It was clear that *dominus* was deeply moved. There was no speech he could give that would be heard, but he greeted every corner of the stadium with broad smiles and raised arms. Every time he turned, that section of the hippodrome went wild. Was it this sound he had been waiting for all his life? I hoped it would never end.

And then he ruined it.

"They don't know me," he shouted, taking his seat. "They simply have had quite enough of you."

Gabinius flicked a hand and horns draped with the red and black of Antioch were raised on either side of us. Their fanfare announced the parade of charioteers. From the red granite arches of the starting gate at the south end of the track came five blue team chariots and five green. Four matched beauties pulled what could only be called an insane driver, for in any contest of speed, power, inertia or stress, the horses were likely to win out over the frailty of the two-wheeled platform on which he balanced.

Gabinius stood. Mingled with the cheering for their favorite drivers, several dozen knights in the best seats above us started booing again. "Let's take a walk through the shops in the colonnade," he said, ignoring them. "We'll be able to talk there. The chariots parade twice around. It will take the cleanup crew half an hour to rid the track of garlands and curse tablets, not to mention the odd fish head and sow's nose."

"That's why the teams are all drifting toward the center island," Mercurius added helpfully.

413

"After that there's the procession of the gods. If we're lucky, no one will miss us."

Everyone rose. Crassus said, "Melyaket, I'm afraid I must ask you to stay here with Cassius Longinus. I've given it some thought, and well, we mustn't take chances, must we?"

"I completely understand. It's an honor to be invited here today. May the legate and I share a cup of wine while we wait?"

"I insist," *dominus* said, staring meaningfully at Cassius, who was wrestling with looking both disappointed and gratified simultaneously. "Get to know each other. We shan't be long. The races cannot start without the dropping of an *orarium*, and I've already seen how this crowd reacts when they are angry."

We stood and I looked up behind me to scan the upper reaches of the stadium for a glimpse of my friends and wife. I could not find them, and decorum prevented me from waving madly. Besides, everyone else was already doing that.

•••

"Shall I buy a flag?" Crassus asked after we had made our way down beneath the stands. He reached for a pendant of green to the amazement of the stall's owner, but froze at the shout of alarm from Mercurius, who almost leapt from his painted slippers.

"Apologies, proconsul," the little man said, "but that would be unwise, unless you were to buy equal amounts of both colors."

"Even if one or two of the good citizens of Antioch are color-blind, none of us are likely to leave the hippodrome alive," said Gabinius. "Best leave the flags, and the betting, for the true fans."

"Green is favored by the local Aramean population," Mercurius explained. "Blue by the more conservative Greeks and Romans. Should they ever grow too far out of balance, we shall have to introduce more colors."

"Let me give you some practical advice about your administration," Gabinius said as we continued our stroll. Crassus, ever the politician, made certain to smile and notice everyone he passed. Now and again he would even stop to chat with a mother and child or a shopkeeper. Most of the signage everywhere we looked was trilingual: Aramean, Greek and Latin, yet *dominus* quickly found that the language with which he was most successful was Greek.

"Truly, Aulus," he said, reverting to Latin, "anything you might teach me about governing a province would be a lesson in negatives—what *not* to do. There is only one subject upon which you may instruct me, and it does not lay within the confines of Syria."

"I can and will tell you much about my experience in Parthia," said the departing governor. "Don't underestimate them, my friend, and don't ever let them catch you out in the open. But first, there are things you should know about what is available to you here in your new home."

"How can you treat your own troubles with such indifference? Do you not know that you are being tried for treason *in absentia*? Cicero practically foams at the mouth in expectation of your return."

"I am always being tried for something, aren't I? That's what bribes are for, Marcus. You practically invented the practice, did you not?" My master bridled at the inference, or perhaps at its being spoken aloud. "Between my money and your friends, I have every hope

415

of acquittal from every vicious charge, whatever they may be."

"What do you mean, 'my friends?'"

"Pompeius has promised to speak up for me, even to bend Tully's arm if need be. And Caesar, well, Caesar." Gabinius laughed aloud, then suggested we turn about and return to our seats.

"What about Julius?" Crassus said as evenly as he could. We began retracing our steps.

"I've accepted a posting with him," Marcus Antonius said. "I'll travel with Aulus as far as Rome, then on to Gaul."

"Don't forget your lion skin," Crassus said.

"I know!" Marcus Antonius said. "No more balmy Judean winters for me."

"What was this about Caesar?" Crassus pressed.

"You know how he loves to wriggle beneath the *peplos* of any noble's wife who'll let him?"

"What?!" Crassus shouted.

"General," Petronius whispered, putting a hand on his arm.

"Calm down, man," said Gabinius. "All Rome knows about his insatiable Cyclops."

"Haul yourself out of the gutter, sir."

"Please, Rome *is* the gutter. Or can't you see it from the Palatine? Come now, Marcus. This is a marvelous story. I knew putting Ptolemy back on the throne without the senate's blessing would put me in the deep end of the pool, but what can you do when Pompeius asks and Egypt loads so much silver in my ship it lists? Gabinius must answer.

"As it happens, your friend Caesar proved my savior. You've never met my wife, Lollia. Strange that she and your wife have never socialized." *Not so strange.* "She's as stunning as the statue of Diana in her Aventine temple, and just as cold. She's even more beautiful than I am."

Gabinius stopped and balanced gracefully on one leg, bringing his raised heel to rest across his other knee. Mercurius hurried over, lifted his master's painted toe and removed a pebble caught between sandal and foot. Crassus asked, "Does this have a point?"

We carried on. "Of course. Lollia and I share a mutual hatred of each other, so I was delighted to return from the senate early one afternoon to find her splayed across the dining room *lectus* with Julius between her thighs."

"Outrageous. What did you do?"

"Just that — appear outraged. I sent Lollia to the baths. Then, after some fine tragedian acting and wringing of hands, promised to avoid a scandal if, in return, Caesar would swear that should my case ever be tried, he would write on my behalf. Which he has. Illicit sex, Marcus, drives at least half the decisions of the modern world, wouldn't you agree?"

"What a bankrupt and reprehensible philosophy."

"Yet Pompeius now awaits to appear in court on Caesar's behalf with a letter stating that not only should I not be on trial, the senate should confer upon me a *supplicatio*, thanking me for bringing Egypt back into the fold, and for all my victories in Judea. I may have a statue in the forum before this is done. All thanks to Caesar and that magnificent shrew. A victory all around, don't you think?"

"If you hate your wife so much, why not just leave her?"

"Why leave her, when I can leave her in misery?"

"I think I've heard quite enough." We had arrived at the steps which would take us back up to the governor's box. "Octavius, walk with me back to the Regia. I'm feeling tired."

"*Dominus*, I'll come with you." Crassus' eyes were already somewhere else, more than likely Luca.

"No, Alexander, you stay and watch the races. I'll be fine."

"Marcus," Gabinius said, "We need to discuss Parthian tactics and weaponry."

"Tell it to my legates. I'm done with you. Alexander, wait. Take this." Crassus unbuckled his long purple cloak and fastened it about my shoulders. He laid the wreath on my head and stuffed the handkerchief in my hand and my slave plaque down my tunic. With little enthusiasm he said, "Something little Felix can tell his grandchildren about someday."

"You're joking," Gabinius said.

"I never joke in front of people I despise."

"Despise me all you like, but hear me out if you seek to finish what I began across the Euphrates." Gabinius saw with rising panic that this public arcade beneath the vaulted columns of his stadium was likely to be his final audience with Crassus. He took hold of the new governor's arm. Crassus recoiled. "Listen to me!" As *dominus* was stepping away, I leaned in, straining to hear whatever it was this man who'd actually faced the enemy we planned to engage was trying to tell us. But the crowds were thickening, their holiday babble amplifying off the bottoms of the concrete seats rising above our heads, and I could not comprehend every word. Two phrases were all that came through clearly: "Armenia's mountains" and "using the rivers."

Crassus may have understood more, for he answered, "Why would I take advice from Pompeius' torch bearer, a man who dances naked and lets loose a viper like Julius Caesar beneath the bed sheets of his own wife? Why should I listen to anything a man like that has to say about anything?"

"Because he's right, you stubborn fool." But Gabinius was already shouting at the back of his replacement.

Aulus Gabinius left the following morning for Rome. His advice regarding the Parthians was never heeded or even heard. The senate tried him on three counts of treason. He was acquitted on two, but convicted for extortion, with special reference to the ten thousand talents of silver he had accepted from a province that was outside his governorship. His property was confiscated and, like Cicero before him, he was sentenced to the worst fate a Roman citizen could suffer and still live: exile. Five years later, however, Julius Caesar called him back to fight in the civil wars, but Gabinius would raise no hand against his old patron, Pompeius. He died of illness two years after returning from exile.

CHAPTER XXX

54 BCE - SPRING, ANTIOCH

Year of the consulship of
Lucius Domitius Ahenobarbus and Appius Claudius Pulcher

I was shaking badly as we made our way back up to our seats. Mercurius had to give me a little push from behind on the final step. The waiting crowd exploded into a roar when they saw the purple of my cloak. It was hard to say whose jaw dropped further, Cassius' or Melyaket's, but it was Marcus Antonius, following me up the steps who was first to laugh. "I know!" he said. "Can you believe it?"

Gabinius cornered Cassius Longinus and Petronius, insisting that the two legates meet him in the gallery after the evening meal. There were things he needed to impart to *someone* of intelligence before he left for Rome, or the army would be ill-prepared to meet Parthia's defenses.

"What do I do now?" I asked, still standing. Apparently, I was doing it, for the horn blowers played another fanfare and two drivers came onto the field, this time riding in two-horse rigs. They pulled up to the starting line and waited for the signal.

"Hold up that handkerchief, you idiot," Gabinius hissed. I did that.

"Now *drop* it!"

When I let it flutter out of my hand, four flag bearers on both sides of the track lowered their poles and the first race began. Each heat of this first contest was two laps, then another pair raced till their were five finalists. These five then raced against each other to discover the winner. By the start of the final race of this first contest, I was becoming quite proficient at raising and releasing my handkerchief with aplomb. Following this first event, there would be two more races, a three-horse contest, and the wild and most dangerous finale, where the drivers would ride chariots pulled by four horses.

While we watched, Mercurius pointed out a charioteer with bright red hair. His name was Varro. He was eighteen, slave to the largest stable owner in the city, and if he won the grand prize today, he'd have enough to buy his freedom. He rode for the greens, but today he was everybody's favorite. In Aramaic, they called him The One Who Sings.

"Do you ride?" I asked Melyaket. The race was very close. Three greens and two blues were all within a chariot's width of each with only one lap to go.

"Oh yes. Every day, if I can. My people practically give birth on horseback. And you?"

"The same. We build our schools, write treatises, prepare complex medications, all mounted."

"I see."

"Forgive me, Melyaket puhr Karach. I am very nervous."

"I can imagine. Just Melyaket, please."

"Do you own slaves, Melyaket?"

"There are none in my village. But I have seem them in Hatra. They are always from someplace else."

"Then we are all slave fodder to someone."

"Yes, I suppose we are," Melyaket said. Ten horses, five teams, made the final turn and came down the long, straight run to the finish line as if they were chained together. Everyone was on their feet, including us. You could hear the cracks of the whips above the thunder of the wheels. But one whip rested in its holder. As the riders told their teams that this was the moment to reach for that last ounce of speed, we saw him, the boy Varro, leaning over the lip of his chariot. Of course, no sound came to us above the din, but the melody was not intended for our ears. Varro's team and one other, driven by one who rode for the blues pulled away from the pack in the final seconds of the race. In the end, I could not see who had crossed the finish line first.

"Aieee!" Melyaket cried. "The red-haired boy has won! I have never seen such a thing in my life!"

"You're quite young, aren't you," Gabinius said.

The judges agreed with Melyaket.

"What happens now?" I shouted.

Gabinius said, "You give him this ribbon and purse." The ex-governor shoved the correct prizes into my hands. People were streaming onto the dirt track.

"Me?"

"Oh, here, take this." Gabinius took a thick gold chain from around his neck and slipped it over my head. "Curse Crassus. You've got to wear something besides that wreath to look the part. No one has gotten a good eyeful of your master. The box is far enough away from everyone else. I'll handle the guards and servants. Just act imperious, if that's possible, or at least noble."

"I'm going to be sick." Mercurius overturned a lead-lined copper pot, dumping its former contents of minted figs and dates on the serving table. He ran up to our seats and placed the vessel by my feet.

"Stand up straight," said Marcus Antonius.

"Alexander, you can do this," ever-earnest Petronius said, gripping the band of iron that was my shoulder.

"Find someone else."

"There is no one else," Gabinius snapped.

It occurred to me that Livia might recognize me in this absurd costume as I performed this humiliating pantomime. I bent over and filled half the fruit bowl with my insides.

"This is a disaster," Cassius said.

Mercurius stepped between us. "May I have a go, *dominus*? Alexander," he whispered to me, "just pretend that you are the *dominus* and he is the slave. I do it all the time. Imagine it is he who has to clip your cuticles, clean between your toes, wipe your ass, remember all your friends' names, and never get so much as a well-meant hug, not even during Saturnalia."

I shook my head, breathing hard through my mouth.

"Then imagine you're going to have him executed in the morning," Gabinius said. "That ought to strike the right tone."

The crowd had completely surrounded Varro's chariot as he carefully directed his frothing team toward our box. Grooms muscled their way in and began wiping the two blacks down. I thought my legs might give way. If I did not find a device to latch onto and quickly, this deception would fool no one.

Varro's eyes were the blue of the high mountain lakes north of Brixia. He fought for solemnity as he approached, but was unable to keep the smile from chipping flakes of dried dust and sweat from his grimy face. I studied his expression—he barely knew where he was, yet he was completely immersed in this moment of good fortune. Then I had it. All I had to do was run down the lane and leap into the air, just as in my dream. I walked down the center of our aisle, past the tables piled with food and drink and stood with both hands on the railing.

"That was quite a performance, young man." My voice was authoritative and controlled.

"Thank you, my lord."

"You are Varro, correct?"

"Yes, my lord."

"Varro, wait one moment longer please." Near the *spina*, the driver who had placed second was leading his team off the track. I called to a guard to summon the man to me. He was bearded, filthy and dejected, but he was wearing blue. His name was Galeno. When he arrived, bewildered and awestruck, I reached over the railing to grab his hand; habit appropriated his muscles and obliged him to stretch up to give it to me. I congratulated him on a race well run. Now the entire stadium had more equal reason to cheer, and they did, wildly. I wished him luck in the final race and sent him on his way. He had deserved at least that much.

"Apologies, Varro." The boy's dusty red hair came to the top of the railing. I was confident I could do this with no more than a sprained ankle at worst. "I have kept you and your magnificent beasts waiting long enough. Their legs will stiffen and cramp. Shall we let them walk off their win?" Before anyone could react, I hopped up on the broad bronze railing, swung my legs over the side and dropped down the few feet to the hippodrome floor. My sandals made two small clouds of dust in the midday sun (shades of my flying dream yet again). I held up my hand and Varro took it. When I stepped up to stand beside him on the platform of his chariot I draped the winner's ribbon about his neck and displayed the bulging purse to the crowd before placing it in his hands. I told him to put the reins in his left hand, then took his right and held it aloft.

There was pandemonium from the moment we began our slow ride around the stadium. It was not precisely like flying; the ride was far less smooth, the path of our flight more predetermined than haphazard, but the adulation of 80,000 people whose cheers were meant for the two of us, even if mostly for the boy, was as uplifting as any sustained gust blown by the *Anemoi*. "I know why you do this!" I shouted as we rounded the final turn. "I will do it till it kills me!" came his reply, and I believed him. Every time he raced, he lived a waking flying dream of his very own.

By the time we had completed the entire circuit, steps had been placed beneath the governor's box to allow me to reclaim my seat with dignity. I shook Varro's hand and wished him luck, then with surprising reluctance, stepped down off the back of his chariot.

Hands reached for me and assisted me back to guarded safety. "Mercurius, do you think I might have a cup of watered wine to still these trembling hands? And some bread and a little cheese?"

"Of course, my lord," he said without thinking.

Marcus Antonius clapped me on the back as he was taking a swig of his own. I'm fairly sure he was about to give me a compliment before he started choking.

425

"That was quite clever, Alexander," Cassius said. "I estimate your master will be able to show his face at a public event in this city in oh, about a year."

"I'm not so sure," Gabinius said, picking a date up off the floor, wiping it on Mercurius' outstretched sleeve and putting it in his mouth. "They're about the same height. Crassus has a bit more hair, but the wreath covers much. You'd be surprised what people will accept once you insist two or three times running that they have seen what you tell them they have seen."

Red-faced, Antonius managed to nod his head and rasp out, "Bravely done!"

Melyaket leaned over to me. "That was a wonder. How long did you say you've been owned by Marcus Crassus?"

"Since I was nineteen."

"Three years younger than I am now," the Parthian said, his voice solemn. "Are you very angry?"

I looked at him, but did not answer right away. "I am rarely very angry at anyone for very long."

"Perhaps you should be."

"Perhaps you should be older."

"Perhaps I shall be."

"May your gods keep you safe until then."

"And hopefully a little longer."

"Yes, for quite a bit longer beyond that, if they are kind."

The Parthian youth ran his fingers through his hair; it fell immediately back to the places from which he had swept it. "This has been most enlightening. A day I shall long remember."

"You're leaving?"

"I have a prior engagement."

I leaned closer and tucked my head down to elude the ever-suspicious ears of Cassius Longinus. "Will you be free at the dinner hour?" I asked under my breath.

Melyaket raised an eyebrow. "Why?" he whispered. "Are you a worshipper of Mithras?"

"No! Certainly not," I said, raising my voice. I collected myself and resumed my surreptitious composure. "My master would like you to meet with him privately in his quarters."

"For what purpose?" Melyaket asked suspiciously.

"He does not confide in me," I lied.

The Parthian raised his voice to a normal speaking level, which in this venue was tantamount to boisterous. "Well then, I'll give that some thought."

"I look forward to our next meeting," I said. "I am intrigued to learn more about a village that thrives without slaves."

"Come see for yourself. You would be an honored guest. May the rest of your day prove less taxing."

"Till next we meet, then," I said, bowing my head slightly. Crassus was right. The youth was too likeable.

The moment Melyaket threw his white neck scarf over his shoulder and disappeared up the steps leading to the exit, two of Cassius' men followed him out. "If that man isn't a spy for Orodes," the *quaestor* said to Gabinius, "I'll eat those gold crimps in your hair."

"Touch them and it will be your last meal."

"And I thought you were a man who understood metaphor, governor." Cassius turned on me. "What were the two of you whispering about, eh?"

Have I mentioned that I have never been blessed with an excess of imagination? After stumbling blindly about for something creative to say, out came this: "I...I asked if he might be free for dinner."

Gabinius said, "I admire your taste."

The *quaestor* was not as complimentary. "The man is under suspicion. I don't give a fig for your personal proclivities, but I suggest in this case you confine your affections to your healer. "It's not his fault," Cassius said, turning to the others, "the blame is ours. If we don't set a high moral standard, why should they bother to emulate us? The long-term consequences are dire, mark my words."

"Don't be such a prig," Gabinius said.

"And a bore," added Antonius. Petronius, ever-tactful, was silent.

Oh, the unintended consequences of perfidy!

"Back to business. Governor, while you were talking to Crassus, I asked the Parthian about Abgarus. He had no idea, of course, why the king wasn't here today. Do you? How long have you known this Melyaket?"

"I met him the same day you did. As for Abgarus, he told me he had business outside the city."

"You see. Neither of them is to be trusted. Did you hear the Parthian mention Hatra? That is their main western military outpost. A training facility the size of Praeneste."

"I wouldn't know anything about that." Gabinius stood to a spattering of boos. "Seeing as I am *persona non grata* in this city, I think I'll take my own quiet departure. Best of luck to you all. Come, Mercurius. We're leaving."

"If it's all the same with you, governor," Marcus Antonius said, "I've got some silver riding on the final—"

"As you wish. Join me later."

As the painted *atriensis* hurried to gather his master's belongings, I put a hand on his shoulder and thanked him for his help. "Better times," I said. He smiled weakly, then jumped as Gabinius shouted for him from the top of the steps. He hurried to follow, and that was the last I saw of the little fellow.

Looking at all the extra space in the governor's box, I suddenly had an inspiration. "Guard," I said to one of several lining the periphery of our accommodations, "up about twenty rows, you'll find a red-haired *medicus* with a young man wearing brown gloves. They're sitting with two legionaries in tunics, one very large. I don't think it's a party you're likely to miss. If you have difficulty, call out for Malchus or Betto. Bring them all down to me, if you'd be so kind."

Five minutes later there came a happy squealing from above us. We looked to see the guard leading Livia, unfettered, followed by Betto wincing at every piercing cry that came from behind him. Hanno was too excited to walk down the stadium steps without doing himself or others injury, so Malchus had scooped him up into the cradling logs of his forearms. The boy was sitting cross-legged, facing forward, waving his arms at everyone, pointing at whatever drew his attention, which bordered on the infinite, and occasionally reaching back with his gloved hands to hug the back of Malchus' neck or pat a drum beat on the top of his head. Every few steps, Hanno would crane his head back and kiss Malchus on the cheek. This would set both of them laughing, which increased both the frequency of the act's occurrence and the level of Betto's irritation.

When they were admitted into the booth, with thousands of eyes upon us, I could do no more than greet them formally, which was especially painful for Livia and me, though I am not certain I wished to embrace her considering the expression of suppressed amusement she wore upon her face. There was, to be sure, one exception, and before introductions could be made all around, Hanno had me in his usual, and I must admit, very welcome clutches. To keep him safe, we put him back in the capacious lap of Drusus Malchus, who didn't seem to mind at all. Betto busied himself with the display of food near the railing, where he and Marcus Antonius exchanged pleasantries, or so he told me later.

Before the next event, the drivers walked to a recessed area filled with screaming young women and not-so-young women waving scarves and tokens for their favorites to wear. The drivers took the ones they fancied, and later, when the day was done, took the ones they fancied.

On his way back to the *carceres*, the starting end of the track, Varro glanced at the governor's box and noticed two gloved hands wildly waving at him. This was partially commonplace: everyone was waving and everyone was wild. But the young charioteer did now have a special relationship with the ersatz proconsul, that is me, and so veered in our direction.

"He's coming! He's coming!" frothed Hanno, bouncing in the tight restraint of Malchus' grip.

"Drusus," Betto observed coolly from below, "you look like a horse breaking a rider." A flailing arm sent a glass cup into the air but I caught and set it down out of harm's way.

"Left-handed," Malchus said, impressed. "'Guess all that extra work you and Betto did up in the Circus Flaminius paid off."

"I could give him something," Livia said, reaching for her kit.

"No," I said. "We're not giving Hanno any of your Egyptian opium. He may never be this close to a chariot race again. Let him enjoy it."

"My lord governor, why such pessimism?" my wife said with joyful sarcasm. "You may yet preside over many more races."

A withering glance was all I had time to give her, for Varro had arrived. The newcomers crowded about the railing.

"You're the winner your name is Varro!" a delighted Hanno said.

"I am."

"My name is Hannibal, but my secret name is Hanno. This is my master and his secret name is—"

"Varro needs to get ready for the next race, Hannibal," Livia said, introducing herself as the boy's doctor.

"An honor to meet you, Hannibal. Shall I tell you a secret?"

Hanno drew in his breath. "What *is* it?" he whispered, leaning over the railing as far as Malchus would allow.

"As of today, he is my master, too."

This sent Hanno into the rapture of one of his smiles, and Varro was too close not to be infected. "Tell me, Hannibal, do you have something to give me for luck, for the next race?"

Malchus almost lost his grip on the boy as Hanno's level of thrilled excitement spun into frantic indecision.

Betto, his mouth full of grapes, said, "Give him a glove."

Malchus whipped around to glare at his thoughtless friend, but it was too late. Hanno insisted, and as Livia untied the laces, she explained about an 'accident,' but nothing could prepare the charioteer. The look on Varro's face when he saw the mutilated hand froze not only his own features, but everyone else's who could see the horror in the young man's eyes. And then it was gone, most of it.

"That's pretty awful," Varro said.

"Yeah, it is," Hanno agreed. "I have two of them they look just the same. You can see—"

"I had a little brother who died when he lost just one of his fingers. He got a fever and he never got better."

"I'm sorry I didn't know I'm really really sorry."

"Of course you didn't know," Varro said, looking up at the boy looking down upon his new hero. "But if you'd let me, I can't think of anything better than this glove to take with me for luck."

Ten charioteers began the next race, this time driving three-horse teams on larger, stronger chariots five times around the *spina*. I won't keep you in suspense. Varro won. The One Who Sings walked up the steps at the railing and made a solemn and grateful ceremony of returning Hanno's lucky talisman. Livia held the glove while Varro grasped the boy's bare hand in both of his and told him how he was sure that when he sang of its owner to his horses, they practically grew wings. After a short moment, Hanno withdrew his hand and as was his usual custom when he had no words, pressed his head onto the charioteer's chest and let his arms do the talking for him.

Because of the more spacious accommodations in the larger chariot, this time when the new governor of Antioch drove round the track with the red-headed boy who, with this new purse, was only 150,000 *sesterces* shy of buying his freedom, they had company. I venture to say that for that third boy, his deformities hidden by kind distance from the crowd, his brown-gloved hands extended in victory, his smile evidence of a delight unmarred by a single grain of impurity, this had been the happiest moment in his life.

I cannot write more about that circuit or the look in my wife's eyes when it was done. I simply do not have the words. Now mark me. I am not one for sentimentality. Do not expect it of me often.

•••

Two of the participants that ended in that touching moment, however, did not make it across the finish line. And one of the spectators had to be dragged first to the center of the field, then carried off it. No one died, but perhaps there were one or two that wished they had.

It may be a lesson for other fields of endeavor that those who lag behind find themselves not only in the exponential difficulty of gaining the lead, but also in the most danger. Certainly the physics of a race track lends itself to such a theory. As any equestrian well knows, running to the inside of the track means there is less track to run. Therefore, horses, riders and chariots all tend to congregate close to the *spina*. How is one, then, to break free of the mob? The inside track is jealously guarded; but to outdistance the leaders by hurling yourself around the outside circumference means having to run both faster and farther then everyone else, making the task that much more difficult.

Two contestants, one of each color, found themselves in just such a predicament. Mid-way through the fourth lap, they were forced to the outside as they came out of the turn on the far side of the track. From our seats we did not have a good view of what happened, which is the only good thing I can say about the incident. Remember, we were sitting at the finish line halfway down the length of the hippodrome. We were therefore looking across the near track, the *spina and* the supine obelisk resting on its back, in addition to the width of the far track. Above all this the car of a chariot came briefly sailing in a most distressing arc. It was upside down, its pole broken, its driver nowhere in sight. The sound of the crash followed instantaneously, accompanied by gouts of screams and billows of dust.

Careening round the turn to our left raced the remaining six teams, Varro among them. Though we told Hanno that his new friend was safe, he would not leave his chair; for the remainder of the race he sat with his face buried in his gloved hands.

The wreckage—human, equine, wooden and iron was barely removed in time. Two of the six horses survived; the rest were put down. The charioteers lived, but would never race again. It was almost enough to make one believe in the gods: neither driver had been killed and each raced for different stables. Had either of those conditions not been met, a riot might easily have ensued. Even the horses were slaughtered equally between the greens and the blues.

As for the overzealous devotee of the greens who, whether to impress his girlfriend or win a bet, had thrown a nail-encrusted curse tablet onto the track, to his great and everlasting misfortune, he had neither good aim nor good luck. He been seen and seized. Because of this malefactor, the final race of the day, the most grueling and the most demanding, the contest Antiochenes had been thinking of as they packed their baskets of fruit, bread, cheese and wine in the dark that morning, would have to be postponed a while longer while the track and justice were restored.

I had not noticed them before, but beneath the bronze legs of the giant outward-facing horses that reared at each end of the *spina* were two seven-foot iron posts set five feet apart. The southern set of these were still awash in full sunlight, and to them the officers of the hippodrome had the hapless man chained, one arm to each post. He faced inward, toward the verdigris flanks of the great horse. There was just enough room at the tapered tip of the *spina* for the bare-chested *lorarius* to stretch and get his footing for the work ahead. Not once so far in the day's events had the crowd ever grown as quiet as during those seconds as when the slave prepared to give the criminal twenty of his best. It was critical to their enjoyment of this moment that they strain to hear the whisper of the whip as it descended, the crack as it bit into flesh, the scream of the prisoner as muscle and nerves that were never meant to be disturbed were violently aggrieved.

The distance from us was not so great that Hanno could not both see and hear. He sat now between Livia and myself. At the instant of the first strike, his eyes widened and he put his hand up to my cheek, turning it toward him. "Master, master can you make him stop, can you?" I shook my head. "Then you must look away," he implored, "look at Livia look at me here I am look at me. It's all right it will be over soon look at me till it's over, master." I needed no more encouragement. Livia, Hanno and I sat with heads bowed until it was over.

But what of the thousands on the opposite side of the hippodrome? Never fear. They were not to be denied. The perpetrator was unchained and assisted to the floor of the track. Feet trailing wavy patterns behind him in the dirt, arms draped over the shoulders of two guards, he was dragged the length of the *spina* to the unused iron posts waiting for him at the other end of the stadium. On that side, only the grand head of the horse remained in golden sunlight. There, the second half of the punishment was administered.

The man, whose name is irrelevant, had been a citizen. Had he been a slave, he would have been executed. Since before this day he was not a slave, he became one. The auction was postponed until the two injured charioteers were well enough to bid. They were both veterans of the Antioch hippodrome, and therefore were both exceedingly wealthy. I am told that on the day of his sale, the auctioneer noted record attendance, but only two bidders when his lot number was called. It is said that a private, shared accommodation was reached.

The last race was the most grueling. Eight contenders at the reins of *quadrigae*, chariots drawn by teams of four horses, raced ten laps around the track. From the very beginning, it was a two-man contest between Varro and Galeno. Long before it happened, Varro realized they were going to lap their opponents. He intentionally "lost" the fight with Galeno for the inside, pretending something had gotten into his eye, letting the blue charioteer veer left. With only a little more than one circuit left in the race, Varro's blacks and Galeno's snow white teams came upon a wall of impenetrable dust and thunder.

Varro was on the outside, the only way to pass, but he faced another difficulty I had not thought to mention earlier. The pilot horse, the one used to steer the others, is always positioned to the left, since races are run in a circle from the right hand to the left. Varro held the reins for this animal separately in his left hand. The leads for the others, the power horses, were wrapped about his waist. It was a delicate matter to nudge these other three to go against their natural instincts when the slightest misstep at such speed meant instant disaster. But that is what he did, knowing that some chance of breaking through was better than no chance at all.

Leaning over the top of his car, The One Who Sings asked his four blacks to lift them all beyond the dust and noise and take them into the clear air waiting for them before the finish line. He did not see until his team had done what he had asked of them that Galeno, too, had accomplished the impossible. Nearest to the *spina* had been a blue driver, a green, and then another blue. Galeno, as Varro had known he would be, was bogged down behind them. Sensing what was about to happen, another green dropped back and boxed Galeno in. One could almost hear his curses. The blue charioteer in lane three broke this deadlock by pulling ahead into the second lane as they made the turn into the final run to the finish line. What this clever driver did then was slow his team, forcing both greens back and creating a gap for Galeno to slip through.

Varro was ahead, but he was on the outside. Galeno came up fast. Marcus Antonius had ripped the cushion off a chair and was punching it to the rhythm of his profanity. Petronius, I was somewhat shocked to see, had joined Livia, Hanno and myself and was jumping up and down and cheering for Varro.

•••

"I won't allow *that* in my chariot," Galeno said.

I shrugged. "Your blue fans will be disappointed. I imagine they would like to see you take your victory lap with your governor."

437

Andrew Levkoff

"And I don't think they'll like it if you refuse, seeing as how you've already done it twice with Varro." The bearded wretch smiled at me. So, the sweaty charioteer had beaten the lofty politician. I longed to tell him he could feel proud having bested an impostor, and a slave at that.

Livia stood behind Hanno, both arms around him, not in restraint but pure affection. "I don't want to go I don't. I went twice already with Varro."

"You don't have to, love."

"One time with Varro would be better than five, no ten times with Not Varro."

As before, I congratulated the second place finisher. As I shook his hand, it was as if Varro could read my mind. Before I could say a word he said, "My lord, free or not, I will still race for the greens."

I wished him good health and good fortune, then turned away to step up into the winner's chariot. Slipping the ribbon over Galeno's head, I gave him his purse. I even took his hand and held it aloft. I had to let the charioteer have his way or it would seem I was favoring the greens. However, I did take an inordinate amount of satisfaction from the less than deafening roar as we made our circuit around the stadium.

CHAPTER XXXI

54 BCE - SPRING, ANTIOCH

Year of the consulship of
Lucius Domitius Ahenobarbus and Appius Claudius Pulcher

"Is it my imagination, or are you spending every idle hour devising new and unique ways to torment me?" Crassus adjusted the laurel wreath upon its pedestal bust and flicked a bit of stadium dirt from one of its leaves. *Dominus* had had the governor's suite emptied of any piece of furniture he considered extraneous, and now the cavernous rooms echoed.

"I was under the impression I had you to thank for my triumph, *dominus*."

"You went too far, Alexander. And you go too far now."

"Forgive me, *dominus*. I was rash."

"Have I not been kind? Have I not been generous? Does Livia not now share your bed in the Regia rather than a cot in one of the hovels at the fort town?"

"Yes, *dominus*."

"If the crowd had suspected, or had not been so well-pleased…"

"You are a hero of Antioch. Yet, I apologize for creating the precedent."

"I suppose I shall have to keep you close at hand at least until those two charioteers retire. Who knows when you might need to portray Marcus Crassus again."

"I shouldn't worry. The odds are high they will both die an early and horrific death." *May Varro outlive us all.* "How was your meeting with Melyaket?"

"Pleasing. Truthfully, your stunt in the hippodrome was well-timed. It was the talk of the city, and I used it to our advantage in my meeting with him. I confessed to him that it pained me to see you take such liberties. You were one of my most trusted servants, and it made me feel old and tired to see you take advantage of our friendship. I also told him something of the truth: that you were fighting me every step of the way on this war. I told him how much Parthia stood to gain from a partnership with Rome, and how I feared you were speaking out against it. He asked how it could be that a slave could have such freedom. I told him of the Latin schools you had started, the medical clinics, the trade schools; that there were only a handful of men in Rome who had ever held such responsibility. That nobles, senators with influence and power, would seek your advice, and while I loved you, I was beginning to fear you."

"You lied."

"Somewhat, yes."

"And he believed this?"

"After your chariot rides round the hippodrome, it's just possible. Who knows? He is so forthcoming, I begin to doubt our suspicions."

"Yet you asked him to observe me?"

"He said he could think of at least three people who would be most displeased to learn of the arrangement: King Orodes, Cassius Longinus, and you. Before he could decline outright, I offered him silver, more than he could carry. He refused the money."

"I am not surprised."

"Is that so? And why is that?"

"I cannot tell you. Something about his agreeing to take money for betraying his people seems...out of character."

"Then I suppose," said Crassus, sitting on his bed and letting a servant remove his shoes, "you will think it out of character when I tell you he accepted the assignment."

"No, I do not, though I cannot for the life of me tell you why."

"Then I shall tell you," he said, a hint of exultation in his voice. "I think he'd like to prove me wrong about my assessment of you. From what I could gather, he finds the idea of a creation like you fascinating."

Ah. I had overlooked the obvious. I waited for him to explain.

"Your talents versus your condition, obviously."

I was in no mood for this game tonight. "Did you learn anything of your adversary?"

"*Our* adversary. No. Truth to tell, I forgot to ask. But that will come. The man is a puzzlement. He is brash and confident, like my youngest. But unlike Publius, he doesn't strike me as reckless. There's a sureness about him, a confidence, almost a glow." *Dominus* made a sound in the back of his throat and kicked a shoe over the shoulder of his *ornator*. "I don't know what I'm saying. It's late; I truly am tired. Let's write a short note to Tertulla, then retire."

•••

A week later, Crassus sent me out into the city to meet with several camel merchants to discuss availability and terms for the purchase of two thousand of these improbable beasts. Have you ever allowed your nostrils to be stung by the bouquet of one these creatures? Allow me to advise you. Should you require transport over desert sands, and are left with the choice between your own two feet and a camel, walk. Die of thirst if you must, but walk.

This, of course, was *dominus* being clever. If Melyaket had indeed taken up the engagement to observe my activities, and should he truly be the eyes and ears of Orodes, passing on this information should set the Parthian king's head spinning. If he did not burst out laughing. A far more plausible suggestion would have been to have me bargain for horses, but I was overruled. I prayed that Cassius would not get wind of my morning's work, for if it were legitimate, as *quaestor*, a purchase of this size would have been his responsibility. The height from which he looked down upon me was great enough as it was.

When I returned, I discovered that Crassus had also just arrived from his morning at the garrison. He told me he was tired and wished to lie down. I should rouse him in two hours. Hanno was with Betto and Malchus or Brenus and Taog and having the time of his life; Livia would not see me during the day—it interfered with her credibility. Never mind, I knew just how to use this time to my advantage. I went straight to the old city on the lower slopes of Mount Silpios and there, beyond a colonnaded street, found a public park and a shaded bench. From my satchel I removed some correspondence, several wax tablets and a stilus, then began to practice. I was almost as meticulous as she, so with time and repetition I was confident I could master her style. After half an hour or so, the city life around me faded until nothing remained but the craft of forming each letter.

"What beautiful handwriting," a voice said softly in my left ear.

"Pan's hoof!" I yelped as I leapt from my seat and spun around. Two of the tablets fell to the ground, ruined.

Behind the bench stood a desert nomad, his headdress, robes, boots, everything was dyed in shades of black or deepest grey. His scarf, protection against the sandstorms which plagued the deep desert was drawn unnecessarily across his lower face. He spoke to me in lightly accented Latin. "May I join you?"

I picked up the tablets and sat back down, angry at having my senses childishly jolted. "How do you know I am not being watched by Cassius?" All right, they weren't ruined. A little scraping, a little fresh wax and they'd be fine. But still.

"Because I am the one who has been watching." Melyaket moved to the front of the bench. When he sat, his robes rose on an errant breeze like dark wings, then settled about him.

"The *quaestor* would have us both arrested if he saw us talking together."

"Do you remember the white robes I was wearing the day we met? Cassius' men are chasing those, but they are worn by Hami, not me."

"Who is Hami?"

"My best friend. I hope that some day the two of you will meet." He let the face cloth drop. "I've had an interesting request. Your general has asked me to spy on you."

I blinked, trying to think which features my face should be displaying—surprise, anger, disbelief. What I manufactured was something like a concerned grimace. "Did you accept?"

"Naturally! How could I resist?"

"Why would he do this?" I asked, giving an atrocious performance of someone trying to sound hurt. "Furthermore, why would you come straight to me with the information?!" That was said with genuine and quite believable frustration.

"He claims he does not trust you. But of course we both know that can't possibly be true."

"How do you know it isn't true?" *Was I arguing in favor of my disloyalty?*

"You are a terrible actor, Alexandros, but not when it comes to your master; then, you have in every instance acted in his best interest."

"You know nothing of me, or of Marcus Crassus."

"You asked me why I came to you. The faster we end this game the sooner we may begin to help each other. Your master is trying to flush me out. He used your genuine misgivings about the invasion to entice me to watch you on his behalf. That and quite a lot of money. If I am I spy, through you he will feed me information to confound his enemy. By the way, I hope the camels were not your idea."

I could feel his eyes seeking mine. My fingers played with the leather bindings of my satchel. I jutted my lower lip and pressed down upon it from above, making any shape that would not be construed as a smile. Melyaket persisted. "Can you picture it? A legionary. On a camel." I did picture it, and then I looked at him, and we both burst out laughing.

It took a moment for us to collect ourselves. "I *told* him it should have been horses," I said, which was a mistake, because it sent us back to that place where laughter lives in spite of reason.

The second attempt at composure was successful. Melyaket removed his headdress and ran his fingers through his hair. He wiped his eyes and steadied his breathing. We sat a moment doing no more than watching the elegant passage of commerce on the street beyond the colonnade. "How have you done it, Alexandros? So many years. What hatred you must have felt for him. I can't even imagine. I don't feel it there now. Frustration, yes, and sometimes anger, too. But no matter how many thousands he brings across the Euphrates, I know that Marcus Crassus is at heart a good man."

"How can you possibly know that? You are too young to know anything."

"You must learn to stop talking about the difference in our ages. Even your own philosophers know that it is not how long you look but what you see that discovers truth, and despite my youth, I have seen much. No, don't bother to ask, just trust a stranger a little while longer.

"Let me tell what I know. I know when politics drew their real father away for days, sometimes months at a time, little Marcus and Publius turned to you and never found you lacking. I know that before you departed, Crassus hadn't a clue what amounts resided in all his treasuries, because he trusted you to guard each balance down to the last *sestercius*. I know that the arrival of Lucius Curio stung like the crack of the *lorum*."

"Who is telling you these things? Is *dominus* revealing such intimacies to you?"

"I am a spy, am I not? Let me share one last discovery. I know you are practicing a woman's handwriting."

"That was nothing," I said offhandedly, glancing at the tablets.

"More than this, I know that when Chanina, one of the servant girls who cleans the Regia, takes the refuse to be burned, she sometimes finds crumpled letters; once in a while, after she has been through your quarters, she will discover two notes almost identical in every detail. A letter, copied, then the original and the copy, both discarded, neither sent. Most unusual."

"I know her. A sweet child. Why would I not have her arrested the minute I return?

"Why not arrest me? Sympathy? Empathy? Caution, perhaps?"

"Melyaket, what game are you playing at?"

"I could ask the same of you," he said, nodding toward the folded tablets in my lap.

"None that is of your concern." I slid the wooden frames back inside my satchel. "Tell me how you come to know these things."

"By looking in your eyes. I see a man who is far from home, a man more worried for the safety of those dear to him than for his own fate."

"What sane man would not want to protect those he loves?"

Melyaket laughed. "Many men. Men like Orodes and many who follow Crassus. Men who are not like us."

"Not Crassus himself?"

"Marcus Crassus is beset by demons."

That this man, hardly more than a boy, should pluck such private truths about my master and me seemingly from the air suddenly made me angry. "I know who *I* am," I said, "and what I am doing here; but you, I see no reason to trust a man who betrays first his own people and then the enemy who subverts him."

"I would *never* betray my people," he said, his sensibilities pricked. "You think those schemers in Seleucia and Ctesiphon are my people? Parthia is even less an empire than the one your Roman masters have stitched together with their swords and politics. The 200 families who live on a mountainside village out there at the desert's edge are my people," he said, pointing east. "They know nothing of Parthia. Yet this war will come even to them.

"Now, Alexandros, do this. Take one insignificant Sinjar and sprinkle ten thousand of these about the wastes and valleys of a land so vast it rivals whatever part of the world Rome lays claim to. That is Parthia—a kingdom of cook fires separated by hundreds of miles of nothing."

"Then Parthia is doomed. You have seen the army of Crassus."

"It is unstoppable, invincible."

"Is that what you tell your king?"

"No, as a matter of fact, that is what I tell a man called Salar. Yes, Alexandros, I *am* a spy. You will not believe me, and that is acceptable, but in spite of that truth, here is another: I am not here for Orodes, or Crassus, or any man. I am here for almost the same reason as you."

"I am here because I am a slave and I have no choice but to be where my master drags me."

"You are here to try to prevent this war."

"You have an odd notion of the power granted to slaves. Tell me, spy, if what you say were true, how do our reasons differ?"

"You want to stop the war. I know it is too late for that. Crassus is here. He is not going home. But the sooner he is gone the better."

"Then why not assassinate him?" I asked him, testing. I felt the sheath of my knife pressing against my hip.

"Because I'm not a fool. Rome is an eagle with many heads. And I like this old bird."

I relaxed. "So you spy on us while deceiving my master."

"I will hurt neither of you. I swear it. As for my other duties, what is it that Cassius Longinus thinks I can tell the men in Hatra? They know your numbers; they know your intentions. I *have* been watching you, Alexandros, even before your master invented his little deception. And what I have seen is a good man, a decent man in a hard circumstance. My surprise came when I beheld yet another. I saw Marcus Crassus through your eyes, Alexandros; the way you care for him, chide him, protect him. A man with reason to hate does not do this. I have seen how he is with you as well. He respects you, seeks your opinion, even your companionship. You should hear how he speaks of you. There is a bond there beyond master and servant." He pointed at me, a kind accuser. "You have made a place for him in your heart, and a man like you could not do that for anyone who did not deserve such an honor."

"You are impudent," I said, but my voice cracked.

"How it must hurt to see him falter. He is a great man, but I can see that once he was greater still. A man such as this deserves an old age with dignity and honor, a graceful decline with grandchildren and great-grandchildren at his feet. Let us find a way to help him rediscover what it is he does not realize he has lost."

"What do you want?"

"Me? I want to go home to my people, to my village. But for the time being, fate has brought the two of us together, here, now. It is up to us what we do next. I must gain your trust, I know that. Here is a coin that may buy it: you are right not to trust King Abgarus. Osrhoene fears everyone—Armenia to the north, Rome to the west, Parthia to the south and east. Abgarus will bend toward whoever he thinks has advantage, and whoever blinds his eye with the brightest glint of gold. Did you see how richly he was dressed and how his horse was caparisoned? Gifts from Orodes. Crassus trusts you. He will be more likely to believe that I am here for your cause if he hears it from you, not me."

"You are here for *our* cause?"

"You asked what I want, Alexandros. I want the one thing that will cost the least amount of lives in the days ahead. Your army is invincible. I want it far from Sinjar. I want to help your master win this war."

•••

After more weeks of drilling and marching and training, at the start of Aprilis, Crassus assembled the army. He explained to his legates and centurions that the main settlements most likely to welcome our advance were not to be found along the main river but were spread along the length of a gentler tributary several days' march east. Our mission was to garrison these towns, destroy any resistance met along the way and create a base of operations from which we could learn more about the land and the people. Cassius asked once again why not fight on to the capital. *Dominus* agreed with his *quaestor* that it could easily be done—so feeble was the resistance he expected to encounter, it would take only a matter of weeks before the war was over and the spoils were oppressing the ox carts. But he had made a promise he would not break. "I will not enter Ctesiphon," he told his commanders, "without my son at my side. And Publius will not reach Antioch before November."

Octavius, never one to foment conflict, cleared his throat. "General, your oath is sacrosanct, but once we cross the Euphrates, Orodes will see this as an act of invasion, and if he hasn't already, he surely will begin preparing his defenses. If we let this fighting season go by while we wait for your son to arrive, the Parthians will have a whole year to prepare to meet us on the field."

Petronius scratched his beard, an eyebrow raising like a gull's wing over his blue eye. "Could we not take Seleucia, Ctesiphon's sister city across the Tigris, saving the actual surrender of Orodes for the arrival of Publius?"

"That would work," Crassus laughed, "but my son made it clear that he actually wished to participate in the battle. And you must remember, gentlemen, Publius brings with him 1,000 Gallic horse; having seen them at close quarters I can tell you they will outweigh by far anything Orodes can cobble together by the time we cross the Euphrates when we head east for the second time next spring. Is that not right, Alexander?"

"Gentlemen, the day I witnessed their arrival in Rome, I promise you many a *subligaculum* required an extra washing."

"Not yours, though, right Alexander," said Vargunteius with a heaping of sarcasm.

"Vargunteius, you know I never wear them. I thought we agreed that would remain our little secret."

As we were leaving the command tent, the legate who'd bitten off more than he could chew gripped me around the shoulder, knocked heads with me and said, "Nicely played, ya' bastard."

Marching northwest from the city, eight days later we arrived at Zeugma, a lovely little trading town where the wide, teal waters of the Euphrates, so broad and still that it seemed more meandering lake than river, were pinched narrow enough for a crossing. King Abgarus of Osrhoene had accompanied us with his escort of 300 cavalrymen. Like our own complement of 3,000 outriders, they ranged up and down our lines, providing scouting and flanking support. I saw little of the bejeweled, turbaned monarch with his twin waxed swords of hair quivering above his lip as he rode; he tended to stay toward the rear of the column. Crassus dismissed my repeated misgivings about Abgarus as irrelevant; he agreed the man was duplicitous, but as impotent as our enemy.

In Zeugma, Crassus shored up the existing bridge that had stood since Alexandros' himself had crossed the ancient river on his travels East. Now it must withstand the passage of the greatest army that land had seen since those days. We marched east for three days across green valleys and fertile farmland until we came to the Balissos, a tributary of the great waterway. There, the garrison town of Carrhae welcomed us. There also, the King of Osrhoene begged permission to return to his capital. Ourha was only two days' ride north, and Abgarus had pressing business at home, so he said. Crassus thanked the king over and over for his loyalty and assured him that his continued fealty would be well-rewarded.

To the north, the land sloped upwards into the mountains of Armenia. Here, then, at Carrhae, we stood at the border between those northern states allied with Roman and the great Parthian Empire. We turned south along the Balissos and began the war that for Crassus would begin and end not far from the very spot where he sat astride Eurysaces.

CHAPTER XXXII

54 BCE - SUMMER, MESOPOTAMIA

Year of the consulship of
Lucius Domitius Ahenobarbus and Appius Claudius Pulcher

I t was Quintilis and we had received no communication from Tertulla since crossing the Euphrates.

•••

They threw the bodies over the city walls. One hundred legionaries from the first *century* of the first *cohort* of Legion V, executed in the style favored by the ancient Greeks: shot to death by a volley from Scythian archers. Except for the fact that the arrows were Parthian, it was an accurate reenactment. The town's headman, Apollonius, was fond of irony.

•••

Having sent word to the Romans that he, too wished to rebel against the onerous Parthian yoke, but that his beloved city of Zenodotium had too few citizens to man the siege walls, Apollonius laid what he thought was a clever trap. Disappointed that the invaders had sent so

453

few, he opened the gates and took what he could get. He had performed this seemingly insane act of defiance because he had assurances from the envoy of King Orodes that the royal armies would within hours be sweeping up from the south to repel these insolent Romans. In retrospect, Apollonius must have marveled at the speed with which the emissary and his party had galloped down the river road back to the capital. It was an irony he might have appreciated, were he not at the heart of it. No help was forthcoming.

A month earlier, Silaces, satrap of northwestern Parthia, his arm bandaged, his pride eviscerated, his future uncertain, kneeled before Orodes in his court. Silaces had been the first Parthian commander to engage the Romans when Crassus crossed at Zeugma, and his resistance had been demolished. But Orodes was magnanimous in his forgiveness. He asked many questions about the invaders, complimented Silaces on his survival, and wondered how he might devise his own.

The Parthian king needed to take the measure of this man Crassus. And then he thought of that strutting little tyrant Apollonius. Let us see, he thought, if with this Roman, we are dealing with reason or ruthlessness. And in the meantime, Orodes gave orders for the nobles to gather their men at arms and prepare for war. To the cavalry stationed at Hatra, more than halfway between the palace and the invaders, he gave orders to remain close by that formidable citadel, and to redouble its recruiting efforts.

Crassus, having reassembled his legions after the brief engagement with Silaces, was systematically marching south down the Balissos, installing *cohort* after *cohort* in all the major Parthian towns: Dabana, Ichnae, Callinieum,

Nicephorium. When news of the betrayal reached him, he unleashed Legions IV, V and VI to swarm over Zenodotium like hornets from an overturned nest.

Melyaket and I arrived with the general to find the retribution well underway. *Dominus* had been polite but unimpressed with the Parthian's offer of assistance, reminding the young man that treachery was a spy's stock in trade. His trust would have to be earned with more 'proof' than what Crassus himself had already surmised, that King Abgarus was an unknown quantity. In the meantime, the general instead invited Melyaket to learn how discipline, training and technique made a Roman army indomitable, giving him free passage to roam among us as he pleased, with equal freedom to come and go so that he could convince his masters of the futility of anything but a negotiated surrender. Even Cassius had to admit that when it came to Rome's legions, an informed adversary was a pliant adversary.

The first spectacle to insist on our unwilling attention was the sight of our men hauling the executed Romans to a growing pyre where they were being stacked with military precision. Several soldiers were stripping the armor off the dead, leaving them barefoot, but decent in their tunics. Their weapons, possessions, tags and any medals were carefully inventoried and carted off by Cassius' people. Other legionaries were coming out of Zenodotium carrying ladders, for while each and every one of them were experts at building ramparts, they had no wish to trample upon their fallen brothers.

There were twice as many Romans here now as there were ever civilians of this small walled city. Crassus sat atop his horse on a small rise overlooking the town. He stood by as every shop, home and plaza was stripped of anything of value. Shrieks, shouts and laughter rose on the flame-lit smoke that was visible in the eastern quarter of the town. Ox cart drivers cracked their whips, following legionaries door-to-door to fill their loads and withdraw before the grey stench unnerved their beasts. Men who resisted were killed, men and women too old to work were killed, any child who couldn't stand on its own was killed. Women and girls were raped in situ.

I moved Apollo so that I could speak into my master's ear, but found I was frantic, almost shouting. "*Dominus!* There is no one down there named Caesar!"

"Hold you tongue, Alexander, and close your eyes, if you cannot see this for what it is." He was sitting tall and rigid, his arms locked across his muscled chest piece, his helmet obscuring most of his face.

"I am looking, *dominus*. But I cannot see the enemy."

"Understand, Alexander. This is what *latrunculi* looks like when it is played off the board."

"General Crassus," Melyaket said. "Please have your commanders look at this."

"He should not be here," Cassius said. Ignoring the general's orders to give Melyaket free rein, he pointed and two mounted legionaries interposed themselves between the Parthian and the general.

"Where did you get that?" Crassus asked. *Dominus* inspected the broken shaft and bloody, three-pronged point, then passed it to his legates. While we talked, Crassus wiped his hand on Eurysaces ebony neck.

"I pulled it from one of your legionaries," Melyaket said. "Compare it to your own arrows. Your shafts are thinner, the heads lighter, less sharp."

"True," said Ignatius, his disdain evident, "but your archers will never get close enough for them to do any good. These are too heavy to have any range." His other legates agreed.

"They are not my archers, but you are wrong, gentlemen. Parthian bows are better than yours. I will demonstrate," he said, patting a wide leather case slung by his side, "at your convenience."

"Later, Melyaket," Crassus said. "We are engaged now."

Even Petronius had an edge to his voice. "Do you see what has happened here, son?"

"Yes, commander. And I see what is happening here now."

"I can stand no more of this," Cassius said. "Alexander, if you do not remove this enemy from my sight, he can stay and join this one here." The *quaestor* pointed down the hill.

I expected thunder and lightning from my lord, for Crassus hated to be contradicted in public, but the general merely said, "Perhaps you'd better do as Longinus says, Alexander. It's not a good time for Melyaket to be here."

As we coaxed our horses away from the officers, Apollonius was being dragged up the hill to be presented to Crassus. A woman, his wife most likely, stumbled after him, wailing. Whatever courage or arrogance that had once filled that rough hewn face had leaked away, leaving wide-eyed panic and terror that confounded his muscles and chalked his once-ruddy cheeks. Soon, his head would be on a pole planted above his burning city's gates, but worse would come before the end. The woman, if she lived, would be sold with what was left of her people— 2,500 men, women and children to be sent back along the lines, their old life gone, their new one hardly deserving of the name. If I stayed long enough in this place, I would be able to watch the reenactment of my beginning as a slave pass before my eyes, including all the appropriate props and participants: innocents, victims, chains, carts and cages. And Zenodotium was one town, one small engagement.

Orodes would learn what he wanted to know, and his fear would grow. Crassus had allowed his men a display of ruthlessness, a tactic this Parthian king would find quite reasonable.

Melyaket and I urged our horses down the hillside to the pleading song of Apollonius' widow-to-be and made our way past the growing tower of dead legionaries. Just as we were about to pass the bridge that led to the city, we saw Betto and Malchus carrying out one of our own.

"We volunteered," Betto said to my questioning look. Their rank absolved them from this bitter duty.

"Hold a moment," I said. "I know this man." The corpse, his vine stick still neatly tucked inside his belt, was that of the embittered Lucius Vinicius who had chided me on the ramparts when I had met Ludovicus. "This man was *primus pilus* for Legion V. I heard he volunteered for this assignment."

"More fool he," Betto said as they lowered the corpse to the ground.

"Give it a rest," said Malchus.

"He felt he'd been passed over and wanted any job that might lead to promotion. Poor man."

"That's a bad death, that is," said Malchus. "A death without honor." There were four broken shafts protruding from Vinicius' stomach and chest.

"Look behind you," said Betto. "If I were him, if I were *any* of these boys, while their executioners were pulling back their bowstrings, I'd be praying for vengeance, and right now they're getting their wish ten times over."

"Did you hear," Malchus said, "there's talk of acclaiming the general *imperator*.

"I still don't believe it," Betto said. "This wasn't even a battle."

"Who knows," Malchus said. "Maybe some of the legates passed the word down the line to have the men talk it up, you know, to boost the general's confidence."

"*Dominus* needs no confidence boosting," I said.

"Alexander," Malchus said, "it *has* been a while since he's been in the field."

How embarrassing, to be offered this grand accolade for a 'victory' as paltry and as vicious as this. "I sincerely hope he rejects it."

He didn't.

Betto said, "We saw your friends while we were inside."

"You don't need to tell me. Herclides and Palaemon."

"They're a disgrace," said Betto. "I won't say what we saw them doing; it's an embarrassment to the uniform."

"We should have dealt with them when we had the chance," said Malchus. "The least they deserve is exile."

"Or an unfortunate accident," said Betto.

"Couldn't you stop them?" I asked.

Malchus looked shame-faced. "They weren't the only ones," he said quietly.

"At least we're not tent-mates," Betto said, "Now, could we get a move on, please? A little respect for the departed?"

He reached down and made ready to lift the dead centurion up under his arms. "By the way, who's the native? I like his baggy trousers."

I introduced Melyaket to my companions and moved on quickly before Betto said something everyone would regret. We rode north along the river until the sounds of anguish and vengeance were only a memory, but one that wouldn't let me be for weeks. We let the horses graze and sat near the bank by bulrushes taller than a man. "You cannot stay," I said, tossing a stone into waters of molten silver. "After today, no one could guarantee your safety, not even Crassus."

"It may be so."

"You shall miss our talks. You could have learned much."

Melyaket laughed. "I regret I did not have the opportunity to meet your wife."

"I never told you...ah yes, I forgot, you're a spy."

"Men speak of her hair with reverence."

"She will be pleased to hear that all her years of training have earned her such high regard.

Melyaket shrugged. "It's true — good healers are rare, but a color such as that red in this part of the world, what can one say, it borders on the miraculous."

I was about to say that I had never disclosed that Livia was a healer, but caught myself in time. We shared some water and bread; I apologized for the horrors we had witnessed.

"You've lived too long among these Romans," Melyaket said. "You're not one of them. They won't *let* you be one of them. As I told you at the races, you should feel, not responsible."

I stared at this young, handsome warrior with the soft, smiling eyes. "I withdraw the advice I gave you then. You're quite old enough. No more aging for you."

"Shh! Be still," he whispered. Crouching low, Melyaket crawled to his horse and without a sound removed a wide, leather case, then slid back to me. It held two compartments, one filled with arrows; from the other, he quietly withdrew a bow unlike any I had ever seen. It had far too many curves. As he strung it, he said, "Keep watch across the river, just north of us. Think you can reach the far bank with a stone?"

"Unless you know Palaemon or Herclides by sight, I trust we are not going to kill anyone."

"I'm ready," Melyaket said, nocking an arrow. "Aim for that clump of reeds just beyond the bend. Stand up very slowly." I did as I was told. The stone sailed across the river but fell just short of the other side, making a modest splash just shy of my intended target.

"Ta'us! They're running! Quick, up there." We scrambled up the small incline and scanned the far side of the river, lined with waving grass and reeds, a mirror likeness of our own bank. But for Melyaket's agitation, the bucolic spot seemed as tranquil and lovely as a garden.

Of a sudden, the Parthian raised his bow and loosed an arrow in a high arc across the river, at what I had no idea. Before the missile had reached its zenith, he stood ready to fire again. An instant later there was a great commotion on the other side. Half a dozen abnormally large birds flew into view just above the grass. "You'll never hit one," I said. "They're flying away from us." But Melyaket had already loosed his arrow.

Without waiting to see where it landed, he gathered his things and urged me to do the same. We rode across the river; surprisingly deep for the summer, it rose to our horses' bellies.

Melyaket had wasted neither arrow. "We call them *mescejn,* flying feast," he said as we dismounted on the opposite bank. The birds were of mammoth proportions; a marriage between goose and vulture, but twice as large, and with their white, tan and brown markings, twice as beautiful.

"I should say so! They must weigh forty pounds apiece. What marksmanship!"

"The gods allowed us some luck today, seeing that we part company." Melyaket tied them together and slung them over Apollo. "A gift for your general."

"I have nothing for you," I said.

"I am giving you nothing."

"Oh, I believe I'll manage at least one supper of table scraps from your generosity."

"Eat well, then. If it makes you happy to give something in return, convince your general to do as I have told you: hug the mountains, follow the river, avoid the open plain." (In the weeks and months that followed, in every meeting of the commanders where heads were bent, not in prayer, but in concentration over the map of Mesopotamia, I repeated the advice of Melyaket puhr Karach. The greatest irony of these discussions of the invasion of King Orodes' empire was that the legate who voiced the loudest support of the young Parthian's strategies was Cassius Longinus himself.)

Melyaket promised he would return when he could. He told me he would not forsake his charge. I asked him to explain, but his reply was a grin and a scratch for Apollo behind his ear. We shook hands and parted as friends.

CHAPTER XXXIII

54 BCE - FALL, ANTIOCH

Year of the consulship of
Lucius Domitius Ahenobarbus and Appius Claudius Pulcher

C rassus garrisoned half a dozen towns in Parthian territory with seven thousand legionaries and a thousand cavalry. In September, we headed west and crossed back over the Euphrates to return to Antioch. In the Regia, two welcome sights awaited us: a packet of letters from Rome, and Publius, arrived early from Gaul. The celebration that night was raucous, overstuffed with meats, wines, braggarts and Celts. Hanno was so upset with Publius for not bringing any chariots with him, he stayed in our room and wouldn't come out all night. Livia managed to get him to drink some poppy juice with honey and water to settle him down. He slept well into the next morning, just before his unwitting participation in my destruction.

For the occasion, Livia had piled up her red hair, held high with threads of gold, and she wore a pale green tunic cut of some sheer fabric to whose maker I would always be indebted. At the first opportunity, she and I slipped

463

away to seek out the locked correspondence box on the moonlit gallery table where the heady scent of citron still lingered. We both hoped to hear news of Felix, but more than that, I prayed there might be some plea from lady Tertulla begging her husband to relent from his present course.

"Are you sure this is all right?" she whispered.

"I've missed you," I said, searching for the hem at the back of her tunic with my left hand while I fumbled for the key with my right. "Of course it's all right. It's my key." The noise from the banquet hall was a distant echo.

"Then I guess it's all right," she said, and her legs parted ever so slightly. I dropped the key.

Over the next few moments, from a distance, one would have thought that we were simply two people standing still very close to each other. One would have been mistaken. Out of breath, eyeing the cool expanse of inlaid stone, I said, "A cluttered table is the emblem of a busy mind."

"Or a cluttered mind," Livia said.

"Either way, there's plenty of room for us." Livia had hopped up on the polished surface before I could assist her; in one smooth motion she lay back, bent her elbows, rested her head on her hands, and wrapped her legs about my thighs. There was nowhere else for me to go, and nowhere else I preferred to be. I took hold of her hips and found her. In my haste, she gasped, but nodded fiercely thereafter. Our eyes stayed locked upon one another, even as the slow frenzy of our bodies pulled at us to lose ourselves. We held on, each seeing the other, not letting go, until finally at the end, as rhythm became spasm, I fell into her arms.

"I still miss you," I murmured into the damp, disheveled hair that had fallen about her ear.

She turned and kissed my neck. "I still want you."

"Again?"

"No, there's no time. But let me say it here, while we are still one, while the moonlight carries the scent of the garden to our senses. I love you, Andros, with all my strength."

I lifted my head to see her face transformed by the night: green eyes — black pearls, pale cheeks — living marble. "I live for you, little fox."

"Don't. Don't cry, Alexandros. What will Publius say when we return to the party?"

"He will say," I said, collecting myself, "'Praise Jupiter, for Venus, abducted from our midst, is returned. Here, too, comes Momus, god of mockery and satire. The light and dark that had fled our celebration are now restored to us that we may see.'"

"You know," Livia said, sliding us off the table and rearranging her clothes, "he probably would say something like that. But be careful, Andros. Momus' sharp tongue got him banned from Olympus."

"As long as we leave together, I am ready for exile."

Hunting for the key, I asked, "How goes it with Musclena?"

"Still an ass. Still limping. It hasn't helped that when the army camps in Antioch, I sleep with you here in the Regia."

"Does the man expect you to stay in the slums of the fort town?"

"Of course he does. And I wouldn't mind, either, except that you're here. Nebta and Khety send their love, by the way. Don't worry, I take my satisfaction where I can find it. Somehow, my treatments for headache and toothache have made it into the general log book. Here it is!"

We put everything aside save the letters from our lady, of which there were many. I braved Livia's temper to scan each of them myself for word of Felix, for I and I alone was privileged to read *dominus'* personal mail. And then there was always the possibility that my death warrant was among the sealed pieces of parchment. What would I do if I found it? But then I realized if Tertulla had read my letters to her (I had written more than once) and called me 'traitor,' she would have sent word secretly and separately to *dominus*, instructing the courier that her note be hand delivered to her husband and her husband alone. I would not know that I was doomed until they came for me.

Felix, Crassus was informed, was healthy and happy. Here were a few dim pictures of our son viewed through a window that was barely older than when we had left him. Tertulla's latest letter to *dominus* was dated Martius, when Felix was six months old. He would be almost a year old now. Was he standing? Walking? Did he have his mother's eyes? It was cruel beyond measuring to experience his first months secondhand. I was halfway through recounting how Eirene had taken him in a basket to his first festival when Livia stopped me. "I don't want to know, Andros. As long as he is healthy. I'm sorry. We were stupid to be in such a hurry to torture ourselves." She kissed me and walked quickly to the entrance of the gallery before turning back to me, her smile weak and forced. "I'll let them know you'll be back shortly."

I understood and agreed with my wife's sentiment. But I still had work to do amongst these letters. If there was a positive reply to the note I had sent over six months ago, it would be in the form of a plea to Crassus to return home. But if I found encouragement for his invasion plans, I would know I had failed to convince her. I scanned every letter, and there were dozens. Yet there was no definitive signal either way. My frustration peaked when I realized that it was entirely possible that Tertulla's reply to my letter might still be in a courier's pack on its way here, that I had not allowed enough time for my correspondence to reach her and for her response to return to Antioch. No matter, for in short order, I was to discover that I had no time to wait for my lady's reply. I had to act, and hope that when my intervention was discovered, reason would prevail.

•••

Crassus had drunk too much wine, such was his joy at seeing his son returned to him. Later, I knocked gently on one of the towering doors to his private quarters to see if he had any last needs before retiring. When I entered, I found father and son together, drinking not wine, but citron flavored water.

"Alexander! Come, join us," Publius said. He was still wearing his military finery, including a chest's worth of gold *phalerae*, nine all told. They reclined on couches by the bathing pool. "Pour yourself a cup of this marvelous drink. There's honey there if you find it too tart. Father and I were just discussing our departure date." Publius had thrown his sword belt on the floor, but his father, already in night clothes, had withdrawn the weapon from its scabbard, hefting it for weight and balance. I stood between them, feeling inexplicably ill at ease.

"A gift from Culhwch," the young Crassus said. "Longer than a gladius, better reach. I've had them made

467

for all my troopers. But Father, if things go the way I've planned, there'll be no need for you to draw a sword. You and Alexander may sit, relax, and count the treasure at your ease."

"The way *you've* planned! Publius, you forget your place." *So, there it is — a clash of hubris in the air.*

"Is it not my place to serve you? Will I not do this best by using that *spatha* you hold in your hands to sever the head of whatever Parthian general they send against us?"

"I have seven legates, Publius, all accomplished commanders. Now, I have eight."

Laughter is not always a welcome sound, as Publius was now proving. "Accomplished, I don't doubt it. Within the last decade? Please. There is not a commander south of the Alps with as much fresh experience in the field."

"I'll say good night, then," I said.

"Stay," Publius commanded. "Tell Father, since wine does cloud the vision, that while it is true that all eight of his commanders have been in the field, only one of them has been conquering the enemies of Rome. The rest have been planting grain. Is it not so, old friend?"

I shuffled my feet and glanced longingly at the door. "Is there anything else you require?"

"Alexander, you have grown useless in my absence."

"Let him be, Publius. Would you have him set father against son?"

"I'd have him tell the truth. Father, *imperator*, I did not race all this way from Gaul, driving a thousand Celtic men and their mounts past limits of which even *they* were ignorant, arriving two months earlier than planned just to put the horses out to graze. Let us go to war!"

"No, my headstrong son. You are right, it is too early for winter quarters, but it is too late in the year to start a campaign. The rains will be here within a month, two at the outside. I will not risk it, especially when there are other conquests more readily at hand."

"The men could march double-time."

"The men are not ready," Crassus said. "Alexander, did you not teach Publius the importance of listening? I'm sure his mother did. Have we written Tertulla today, Alexander? I find myself missing her most acutely."

My head was swimming. "We have not, *dominus*, no, not today. Perhaps tomorrow. She will want to hear every detail of Publius' arrival."

"Well?" Crassus asked.

"Well...?"

"Did you teach Publius to listen?"

I sighed. "Your son knows a good commander must listen, after which he needs to be heard, *dominus*."

"I can only give you half my thanks, Alexander," said Publius.

"Am I not commander here?" Crassus asked. "Now both of you, pay attention. Alexander, prepare yourself: you will take umbrage with this stratagem." Crassus turned to his son and said, "You should have seen the color drain from his face at Zenodotium.

"You better than anyone know how much this war will cost, Alexander, and what an extra year encamped in Antioch will mean, provisioning the army and auxiliaries, to say nothing of feed for the animals. We need money. So I have mapped out the perfect solution while we wait for the spring campaign." *Dominus* looked pointedly at his son. "It is a three-pronged strategy that will not only restock the treasury, it will keep the *cohorts* occupied and sharp until we unleash you, Publius, on your next conquest.

Andrew Levkoff

"First, we levy contingents from every sizable Syrian town, from Antioch to the Judean border. We don't need more auxiliaries, so at the first cry of hardship, we will reluctantly accept a fair equivalent of silver as compensation for each village's lack of patriotism.

"Step two. We march south and pay a visit to the good people of Hierapolis."

"*Dominus*, no," I said, horrified.

"I know this city," Publius said, his eyes widening to sapphires. "You don't intend —"

"I do. There sits the Temple of Atargatis, and we shall have it."

"Now there is a plum worth picking. Father, I did not believe you had it in you."

"Nor did I. *Dominus*, it is sacrilege, madness."

Crassus sighed and pinched the bridge between his eyes. "Why must you continually urinate on the flame of our ambition. You have become short-sighted, Alexander, and frankly, tiresome."

"I am unhappy," Publius said, "to see my father vexed by you. Is this how things have changed in my absence? Why should we care, in any case?" Publius asked, nodding to a servant for more citron water to be poured. "What is Atargatis to us?"

"Publius, you are changed if you can no longer reason it out. Atargatis, Astarte, Inanna, Ishtar, Isis, Artemis; these are all one goddess known by many names."

"There is nothing wrong with my reason, or my memory. Though I do not recall such impertinence from you."

Publius rose off his couch and wrested the sword from his father, who said, "Proof, then, that you were not paying attention."

"Of course I am changed, tutor," Publius continued, ignoring Crassus. "Who do you think it was who set me on this path? Are you not proud of your handiwork? I am a Roman." He held the sword out in front of him, balanced on his open palms. "This is who I am."

"I did not teach you the sword. I taught you philosophy, mathematics, honor, integrity. Have you forgotten those?" I said, my voice rising.

Publius had the great sword half-sheathed, but stopped. He turned his head to me. "Have you, tutor, forgotten your place?"

"So you are reconciled, then, to a few more less strenuous months on the west bank of the Euphrates?" Crassus asked of his son, as if none of this altercation was in progress.

Publius shoved the sword home and stood. "I have heard, now that we speak of it, that the doors to the temple are fifteen high and covered in hammered gold. The statue of the goddess is molded of solid gold and studded with precious stones."

"My lord, we do not need the money," I pleaded.

"Do not forget the pilgrims," *dominus* said, "who trek hundreds of miles to lay an unending stream of rare artifacts and offerings at her feet."

"I'm beginning to like this plan," said Publius, clearly enjoying my distress.

"It is settled. We will go to Hierapolis. I say we do need the funds, and the army needs the discipline of the engagement," Crassus said.

"We do *not* need the money," I insisted, "and will prove it, if you let me. Are you speaking, *dominus*, of the discipline the men displayed at Zenodotium," I said.

"Mind your tongue," Publius snapped.

My tongue, it seemed, had a mind of its own. "Millions of our subjects worship Atargatis," I protested, "millions more again whom Rome would conquer. She is the Great Mother, goddess of fertility, creativity and destruction. The moon is her sign, as powerful as the sun. Do this, and plant a forest's worth of rebellious seeds."

"Let them grow," said Crassus. "Winning this war is everything. All else is vapor."

"Why do you bother, Father. We have been too kind to this one for too long. Remember what you once told me: after forty, they become intractable. Alexander, your time is past."

Crassus said, "Now, I won't have talk like that, Publius. Alexander understands. He knows we don't begrudge these children their bedtime stories. Let Atargatis rule the night, so long as the people know that Rome rules the day."

Though I was reeling from what this newly minted stranger had just spat at me, I said what needed to be said. I had never done otherwise. "*Dominus*, Syria is your province to govern with a just and even hand. Have you forgotten the reception Gabinius received at the hippodrome the day before he departed Antioch? They will *hate* you for this, my lord. Is this the legacy you seek, to be reviled, like Pompeius on the day of the elephants?"

Publius was before me in an instant. As his hand came across my face, he spoke in measured, disciplinary tones. "Know your place."

"That's enough," the elder Crassus said. "Alexander and I have played this game for over thirty years. You have been away at war. He and I like to wage our own every now and again, don't we, Alexander?"

"May I have permission to speak without being struck?" I asked.

Crassus nodded, but Publius said, "That depends on what comes out of your mouth."

I rubbed my burning cheek. "My lord, what will men say when they hear the name of Marcus Licinius Crassus a hundred years hence, a thousand?"

Publius looked at his father, and *dominus* considered, then spoke. "Alexander, I do not care, for I shall not be there to hear it. You know my purpose. I am steadfast in it."

"Good for you, Father. Now tell us," Publius said, not without a little malice, directed straight at me, "the third part of this exercise."

"Perhaps it is better if I do not hear it," I said. "I beg permission to withdraw." In my mind's eye, I heard the arrhythmic echo of Sulla's axes thunking into Plato's sacred olive groves for his siege engines, the buzz of the stone balls from his catapults and the screams of the vanquished as the bloodletting began. It was the year I had become a slave, and the year Athens was raped. The Romans had violated the sanctuaries at Delphi, Olympia and Epidaurus. On the day I was taken they had tramped into the *Agora* and seized statues, paintings and dedicatory shields that had graced the *Stoa* of *Zeus Eleutherios*.

It is all happening again, and I ride with the looters.

"You must hear it," said Crassus, "for I want to give this gift to you. I know how you value the study of foreign cultures, anthropology, sociology and, you know, things of that nature." *Who is this man now talking? Who is it who listened?* "You must put the rest of it out of your mind, Alexander. I command it. I want you at my side when we step inside a place where only one other Roman has ever set foot. We will enter their Holy of Holies, but unlike politic Pompeius Magnus, we cannot afford to be merely sightseers."

Publius shrugged without understanding, but I felt my knees begin to buckle. "Tell me you will not do this thing," I said, water rising to weigh upon my lower eyelids.

"I tell you we will. After Hierapolis, we continue south into Judea, and Jerusalem."

CHAPTER XXXIV

54 BCE - FALL, ANTIOCH

Year of the consulship of
Lucius Domitius Ahenobarbus and Appius Claudius Pulcher

I don't remember leaving, or walking the short distance to my rooms, or even writing the first draft of the letter. I must have moved with ghostly quiet, for thank *Somnus*, both Livia and Hanno were still sleeping soundly when the rising sun slipped a sliver of red through the drapes and across the table where my head lay on ink-stained hands. I rose stiffly, gingerly lifted the final copy from the table and crept from the room.

The gallery was chilly at this hour. The citrons in the courtyard watched my treason in bitter stillness as I unlocked the letter box, rolled my forgery, sealed it, waited for the wax to dry, then broke the seal and swept the debris into a pouch. After tucking the letter I had written in Tertulla's hand back amongst the rest of the correspondence, I closed and locked the box. What a stroke of luck, you might say, not only that my lord and lady's seals were identical, but that that they used the exact same color of wax. You may thank me for this romantic notion. In retrospect, my fortunes would have fared far better had a more random selection of utensils forced me to think twice about my pernicious meddling.

While I shivered at my task, shaking only a little from the cold itself, I could not stop thinking about the changes that had come over both my masters. War had hardened Publius, as it must. He and I were lovesick when last we met, between the distractions of lady Cornelia and Livia, neither one of us could have been the keenest judges in contests of discerning character. His cruelty and arrogance were hidden from me, and to be honest, I was blinded by and eternally grateful for his bravery, or to be more precise, his sense of timing.

Throughout the previous evening's nightmare conversation, *dominus* appeared and disappeared, confident and commanding one moment, lost and uncertain the next. The wise Crassus would never dream of sacking the temples of Hierapolis or Jerusalem. He had never committed an act so foolhardy in all his long career. It was as if some daemon had possessed him, and I knew that monster's name. I had half a mind to steal the portrait of Caesar he wore around his neck and crush it underfoot. His grey eyes went in and out of focus, sharp, then dim. I believe that when that faraway look came upon him, his thoughts were of Tertulla. But you who read this understand it served my purpose to think so.

Marcus Crassus' love for Tertulla was a great an unsullied thing, once. Theirs was a marriage celebrated throughout Rome as the paragon of partnerships, a bond unbroken for thirty-four years. If they could but look at each other through the eyes of their youth, there had to be a chance they would see the tragedy of this misadventure.

I was there through all those years; I saw them newly wed, helped them build their homes, raise their children. No one knew the playful spirit and happy, stubborn intelligence of my lady from those days better than I—no one except her husband. I remember the banter between them the nights Crassus left with our fire brigade to make cheap purchase of some burning apartment building. The heat in their bedroom as lady Tertulla tried to coax her young spouse back to bed was enough to require the brigade's expertise. It was embarrassing. But it was wonderful.

As *atriensis*, half my time was spent reviewing or turning away applications; every servant in Rome wanted to be a part of the *familia* of the house of Crassus. That, more than anything else I might remember, may be the greatest monument to the quality of the bond between this man and this woman.

Had so few months passed since Caesar had come between them? Khronos, the master deceiver, made those two-and-a-half years feel like the thirty that had come before. Time is the most unfair of gods, stealing from us a joyous hour in a moment, but over the same span, allowing us to languish in our misery for what seems like an age.

Time was taking its toll on Crassus, devouring him from the inside out. He woke from sleep haggard and ill-rested, plagued by the incessant chatter of his constant nighttime companions, Guilt, Shame, and Vengeance. More each day, *dominus* paid heed to those voices and would hear no other. They were his advisors now, urging him to bring this plan of destruction to light ever since Luca. Now here we were; he had made his nightmares a reality, not just for himself, but for tens of thousands who must also heed the madness of his daemons.

Was I the only one left who could still remember that better time, now locked away in a place neither *dominus* nor *domina* could reach? That is why you need a steadfast, reliable *atriensis*, one with long years of experience, one who knows all the secrets of the familia. Because, like a good *atriensis*, I believed I had the key.

Why should I care, you ask, especially now? I had a love as great as theirs once was. She was here, now; I had but to return to my bedroom to hold her in my arms, warm and gentled by sleep. And what of Livia? How could I take this chance and risk losing her all over again, this time for good? Livia the woman and Livia the wife would never understand why I, with only the thinnest sliver of success, would gamble everything. I had to trust that, should all be lost, Livia the slave would understand.

There was more. I had a son whose face even now began to grow indistinct in my mind, who if I saw today I might not recognize, and if I failed and perished, I would never know. Yet if I died, half the condition would be met that would set him free. And though I would never, ever wish for Livia's death to complete the bargain, in my own idyllic image of a world without me, I prayed for compassion, prayed that Livia would return to Felix and that my lord and lady would give them their lives. What else could I do?

Finally, what of the changes that had come over me? Had I lost my mind? Had I grown as callous as Crassus in my willfulness? Would that I had been as mindful as that, for I might have been able to see alternative paths. No, it was something else that drove me now, a singular motivation that rudely shouldered all others aside — if

Crassus was gone, what had become of Alexandros? I could not allow the man I had grown to revere and respect to disappear, for without him, I too would fade away.

It was too late for second thoughts. I harkened back to Menander, who commanded, "Let the die be cast." As I walked back through the brightening halls of the Regia I said to the playwright's ghost, "It is thrown."

•••

It was a beautiful morning for my undoing. As quietly as I could, I had drawn the curtains opposite my work table and opened the doors leading out to the small balcony overlooking the island, the river and the city beyond. The sun had tired of painting the bellies of the eastern clouds, deciding instead to punch through them with rays of yellow-gold. Up there, where infinity had meaning, it looked so peaceful. I wondered with some longing what it might feel like to ride those celestial beams in silence, save for the rushing of the wind, to go wherever the starry morn would take me, to let go of thought and will. And just at the moment when Livia wrapped her arms about me from behind, I realized that once, long ago, I had been cordially invited at the point of a sword to do just that here on earth. But it was hardly the same thing.

She kissed my neck and I turned from the sunrise to her parted lips. With her tongue, she pushed the leaves of macerated mint into my mouth and snaked them about in such a way that my hands pressed lower to the small of her back, then lower still.

"No." She pulled away from me, hips first. "I must leave early for the fort. Andros! You look awful," she said. "Did you get any sleep at all?"

"Not very much, *vulpecula*. Come back here." She shook her head, walking quickly to the *lectus* where she'd thrown her healer's tunic. "I was restless," I said, watching her pull her night tunic over her head. "Guests arriving, lots to do. Don't trouble yourself about me. Go patch up a broken legionary. I'll be fine."

"Who said I was worried about you? Can you take Hanno today? Octavius has half the army training, the other half on parade."

"He and I will have a grand time in the palace. If he ever wakes up."

He did, about an hour later. Hanno insisted on getting himself dressed, and I donned my finest inner and outer tunics, black over white, since today was the day a procession of princely visitors would arrive to make obeisance to the new Roman governor and place before him their grievances, mostly remnants from Gabinius' prior mis-administration. Indoors, I had no need for my steel slave plaque, or any markings for that matter, but I decided to wear my single *phalera*, the gold disk Crassus had given me before our departure from Rome. This, in addition, as always, to the simple necklace hidden beneath my tunic on which hung a single, worn scallop shell, a charm I never removed.

Hanno and I ate a light meal of fruit and bread, then we went to check on *dominus*. He was dressing in his senatorial toga for the occasion, and none too happy about it, as the day promised to be warm. Father Jupiter was in no mood for a hug, from either one of us, so after receiving a list of letters I was to compose, written in a scrawl only I could decipher, we returned to our quarters. I pushed the doors to the balcony wide open to feel the light breeze that every now and then would talk to the curtains who, respectful of my concentration, whispered their reply against the stone floor. Nothing sets the mood for a productive day's work like a fresh pot of ink, a full tin of reed pens, a new roll of parchment sheets, and my cherished Nile River parchment weights (a gift from Livia when she'd first returned from Egypt). Behind me, Hanno sat cross-legged on the floor playing his favorite game of catch, tossing a balled up piece of parchment back and forth, trying to snag it with the articulated fingers of his gloves.

It occurred to me investigate. "Hanno, where did you get your ball?"

"I caught it! You saw it I bet you did."

"I did. You are much better at that game than I ever would be."

"I know," he said seriously and somewhat sad. "You are not a good catcher like me."

"That is true. I am a fairly accomplished thrower, however."

Hanno's eyes lit with remembrance. "You are, master you are! Better be careful not to catch what you throw!" He thought that was very funny. He thought that was very funny for a very long time. I wondered where Livia had left the poppy juice. At last I discovered that Hanno had rummaged around in the waste bin and found the incomplete draft of my forgery from the previous night. I convinced him to exchange it for a fresh piece of crumpled parchment. I would have burned the evidence then and there but for Hanno's skittishness around open flames. Chanina would be along any moment; I'd ask her to burn it outside.

What I did not know was that while my back was turned, lost in the concentration of my work, Hanno, having decided the unsullied sphere was not formed into a shape to his liking, had abandoned it and retrieved his original plaything. It was not long afterwards that I heard a faint, familiar and vaguely disquieting sound, like the popping of small insects underfoot. And immediately following that came the sound of parchment dropping to the floor.

"What's the matter, Hanno, bored already?" I asked. "What are you doing?" He had crawled under my table. "Come out from there. You know I cannot concentrate with you fidgeting at my feet."

I heard that snapping sound again and turned to see Lucius Curio standing there, a dusty brown traveling cloak on his shoulders, a dusty, evil smile on his face. He was contentedly and meticulously cracking every last one of the slightly knotted knuckles on his long, delicate fingers.

"Charming room," he said. "Splendid view."

"Curio?"

"For pity's sake, do not ask me why I am here."

"What?"

"You know very well why, so off you go, I'm certain my lady will be most anxious to have words with you." Curio tried bending a forefinger, but it was already spent. Disappointment pinched his face, then he brightened. "I believe *dominus* and *domina* said they were going to spend some private time together—you can understand his surprise at seeing her. And then *dominus* said something about wanting to show lady Tertulla the strange trees in, I believe it's called the gallery?"

The letter box. "Hanno, come out from there right this instant," I said, reaching out for him with a trembling hand. "We have to go." It was either the urgency or the terror in my voice that convinced him to obey.

"I think I shall enjoy this very much," Curio was saying as we lurched past him. He walked slowly down the entrance steps and around the painted columns. His voice followed me down the open doorway. "Yes, this will do nicely."

We careened into the gallery and barely kept our footing. Hanno's silence as we righted ourselves was more frightening than any protest. He clung to me, and I to him, but even from the far end of the long room I could tell it was empty. Completely empty. The box was gone.

When he and I limped back to our unoccupied quarters, Chanina was just coming into the room to clean. She greeted me pleasantly, but all I could do was nod. The waste bin was empty, and one other item on the floor caught my attention, caught it by my throat and pressed till my breath wheezed, a tiny bellows in the back of my throat.

"Master, what's wrong?" Hanno asked, finally voicing his fear. He squeezed my hand with his glove mechanism. "Master!"

"Hanno, can you find Arba in the stables and spend some time helping him?"

"Yes I can but I don't want to leave you."

For the boy's sake, I summoned the remembrance of that man who used to be Alexandros, made him turn to Hanno and speak in soothing tones. "Thank you for worrying about me, but I am going to be fine, have no fear. Look, the sun is shining! Go have adventures today, don't stay here, stuck in this dreary old palace with piles of boring old documents." Hanno started to protest, but I raised a finger. "Ah, you haven't said good morning to Bustan, have you? I know he would be delighted to feel your brush on his mane." Hanno hesitated; he was not the fool I thought him to be when first we met. He understood I needed to be alone. But there was a price to pay. As compensation, he insisted on an extra-long, extra-hard hug. I didn't mind it at all. No, not at all.

After he had limped away, I turned back into the room. Leaning against a column for support, for some moments I stared at the solitary piece of crumpled parchment that had never felt the kiss of ink or the light scratch of a pen, and wondered how this day would end.

•••

Dominus was in the Great Hall receiving the Aramean princes when lady Tertulla summoned me. I was led to a curving balcony on the western side of the Regia that looked out across a sloping patchwork valley of farms. In the distance, the forests of the Amanos Mountains were dressing in their fall colors. On the other side of the long arm of those peaks stretched the great Middle Sea, and home.

Tertulla was alone, occupying one of two couches. She motioned for me to sit. I did and studied her. My lady wore her favorite pale blue *peplos*, draped by a sea green *stola*. Her hair was as I remembered it: short and curled in ringlets. She had not succumbed to the growing fashion of wearing outlandish dyes or wigs. One could not improve upon that starless black, now streaked here and there with comets of silver. She saw me looking at the tiny lines that had grown about her eyes.

"You may lay claim to at least a few of those," she said.

"I meant no harm, my lady." My voice was dry and cracked, but there was no refreshment on the small table between us. "But I must tell you —"

"You have done no harm, Alexander. Whatever happens, know that I shall always be indebted to you. Your letters to me were not acts of betrayal. We know you love us, as we love you. But *dominus* and I made our choice long ago; did you think your writing alone could cause a reversal of heart? I could not dissuade him in Rome; as his wife, the only path left open to me was to encourage him. I knew we were wrong then. I know we are wrong now. And when it is over, I will live the rest of my days knowing the terrible mistake we made." *Domina* reached across to take my hand, then released it. "Sweet Alexander, I did not come to Antioch to change my husband's mind."

"My lady?"

"*Dominus* is as you described him. Even the mighty Crassus cannot conduct three wars at once: against the Parthians, his age and his memories. My poor love is tired. Why should his wife not be near? There is nothing on the Palatine for me now; the Regia is as good a home and better. If I must wait for Marcus, I would be in a place where he can find me if he needs me. You know me, Alexander: I am a stubborn woman. I would travel twice as far to steal even a few more days with my husband."

"I thought I could convince you to write him to bring him home. I had no thought that you yourself would make the journey. I have ruined everything."

"Don't talk nonsense. I will keep your secret."

I woke up, suddenly realizing that time had collapsed into something squat and hard and finite. There was little of it left to say what I must. "Listen to me, *domina*. They will come for me soon. I forged a letter in your hand."

"What?!"

"Please! I assumed you would remain in Rome. I thought to convince *dominus* in your voice that he should call off this war and return to the city and the family that needed him more than the deserts of the East."

Tertulla considered. "The letter sounds innocent enough, though I would have had a lesser man flogged."

I shook my head. "*Domina*, I will not be flogged. You must not protect me. You must deny any knowledge of — "

"Why should I not help you? Were you not trying to save my husband?"

"*Domina*, I tell you, you must not defend me."

"I will not betray you. I will claim the letter as my own."

"You cannot. There was a copy. Curio has taken it from my quarters, here in the Regia. As soon as he brings it to *dominus*, I am undone."

Domina stood. "I will see to this!"

The ring of marching footsteps approached, and two legionaries appeared at the entrance to the balcony. One of them looked vaguely familiar, but his name escapes me. You would think I would remember it, since he spoke the words that ended my thirty-three years of bondage. "Forgive me, mistress. Alexander, slave of Marcus Crassus, you are under arrest. Come with us."

As I stood to accompany the guards, lady Tertulla said, "Do not lose faith. I will speak with *dominus*."

"*Domina*, tell Livia what has happened. I beg of you, keep her and Hanno safe. And if you love us, free our son."

The soldiers each grabbed an arm and marched me off.

Domina then said something I wish she had kept to herself. "I have him here. Felix is in Antioch."

CHAPTER XXXV

54 BCE - FALL, ANTIOCH

Year of the consulship of
Lucius Domitius Ahenobarbus and Appius Claudius Pulcher

C urio was no fool. Had he taken the balled up forgery to *dominus*, he'd have run the risk that the matter might be handled discretely and quietly by the *familia*. No one likes a scandal. Well, no one likes a scandal without lurid details and horrifying public consequences, and that was just the kind of exhibition Lucius Curio had in mind. It must be said that once having decided to discredit me and insure his place in the house of Crassus, Curio set about it with a zeal and dedication I would otherwise have found enviable in a domestic. He had not only brought the letter to Publius Crassus instead of *dominus*, but had suggested to him the venue for its public airing which would have the most salient political impact.

The Great Hall of the Regia was built to impress. It was a rectangular space the size of a small forum, supported by a double row of gilt columns painted lapis blue that divided its length into thirds. The floor and walls were of a green marble one could easily mistake for semi-precious malachite. All along the top of every wall, seven feet above each flickering wall sconce and eighteen feet above the cowed visitor's shoes, deep rectangular cuts two feet high and four feet long let in light and air. Between the sconces hung giant murals of larger-than-life immortals performing heroic deeds to add to one's feeling of intimidation. To walk awestruck from the entrance to the dais required an athletic one hundred paces, all the while under the scrutiny of men who, from their elevated perspective, you might rightly assume were your betters.

The dais itself was thirty feet wide, three steps above the common fray. There was no throne; Romans had long ago stopped believing in kings, though they never seemed to stop talking about them. As in the senate, however, there was a curule chair, in which Marcus Licinius Crassus sat, soggy yet resplendent in his *toga praetexta*. On either side of him sat his officers and behind them the city magistrates, a group of twenty well-dressed and serious men. For added theatrics or solemnity, take your pick, Crassus had arranged for the seven legionary gold and silver eagles to be temporarily removed from their altars at the garrison to be planted on a raised platform behind the dignitaries, displayed amongst seventy purple standards, their numbers threaded in gold, picked from among the army's highest ranking centuries.

Just below the dais, on either side of the center aisle, pillowed benches were reserved for family members and other privileged friends and guests. This is where I would have sat had I not been bracketed by two soldiers awaiting my turn for justice. In my place, absentmindedly at work on his fingers, sitting painfully upright was Lucius, as anxious, apparently, about this moment as I. My lady

Tertulla sat on the bench opposite, staring at her son up on the dais. Either he refused to look at her, or it did not occur to him to look her way. The mother was steadfast; it was the man turned soldier who had changed.

The morning hours had been reserved for a reception of visiting dignitaries, sheikhs, tax collectors, and other local luminaries. The boredom of forced smiles, a heavy toga and a too short break for the midday meal had been enough to sour Crassus' mood and shrivel his temper. Now, more than half of those same distinguished gentlemen were lined up once again for the afternoon session, during which time the proconsul would begrudgingly hear complaints and settle disputes.

The room was full. Beside the *century* of legionaries placed like lethal ornaments every few paces, the outside aisles formed by the two rows of columns were filled with Antiochenes wanting to catch another glimpse of their new governor, the man who had caused such a stir at the hippodrome. (How surprised would they be to know they were looking in the wrong place.) The center aisle was reserved for supplicants seeking consideration, visiting dignitaries, and others awaiting the impartial justice of the court.

The late afternoon sun was slicing through the western windows as the grand personage of Alchaudonius, king of the Rhambaean nomads was announced by the resident majordomo, a white-bearded ancient whose staff was of far greater utility keeping this relic of the Regia vertical than it was for announcing newcomers. Alchaudonius, in flowery peroration, claimed that during the time Gabinius had abandoned his province to dally in Egypt, he had been attacked by a litany of thieves, robbers and pirates. He begged, no, he demanded justice and restitution! His highness was at least the tenth to do so. My mindfulness of his troubles, or the paucity of the judgment he received was less than enthusiastic, for I was next in line.

"What cruel sport is this?!" Crassus leapt from his seat when the good king's entourage parted and there I stood before my lord and master, feeling alone and foolish. *Dominus* would have tripped on his toga had not Octavius and Petronius risen to catch him. The hall, which had maintained a steady buzz of noise had gone utterly still, for Curio's entertainment had now begun.

Publius rose from his place to the left of Octavius. "Proconsul Crassus, I bring charges of treason against this slave."

"Impossible." Crassus sat back down. I could see he was trying to work out if he was being made the butt of an enormously inappropriate joke.

"May I present my evidence?" Publius asked.

"If you are serious, this is not a matter to be heard at this time." One look at Publius' hard expression and *dominus*' voice became unsure. "I will hear your evidence in my quarters." A murmur of doubt swept the crowd.

"Eminence, for ten years the good people of Antioch have been waiting for the justice of Rome. They have been waiting for Crassus." A cheer went up. "Let the governor show he is a just man. Let him prove to the people that he believes in the rule of law, that it applies in his own home, even as it applies in the streets of Antioch!" *Publius' tongue was as skillful as his lance.* "Show all of Syria, here in this hall of justice, that Rome is just, that Gabinius is truly gone, and that under Crassus, a new regime has begun!"

When he could be heard again, Crassus held out his hand. "Show me the evidence." *Dominus* looked down at me as if to ask what ridiculous insanity was afoot. I could not meet his eye.

Publius stepped across the dais and handed his father the letter that I had only hours before slipped into the correspondence box. Crassus took a moment to read it. He looked up and shrugged, shaking the humid air out of a fold in his toga before readjusting it. "A letter from my wife. I have never seen it before."

"It is newly arrived," Publius said.

Crassus asked, "Alexander, have you seen this?"

"Yes, *dominus*," I answered, but the words withered at the back of my throat. I bit my tongue, swallowed and tried again. "Yes, *dominus*. I have seen it. I have read it. And it was I who wrote it."

"You are mistaken," Crassus chided, ignoring the muttering building all around him, especially from his commanders. "While the sentiments expressed are upsetting and contradictory to my purpose, there is nothing treasonous here. Its contents are private; a letter from my spouse, nothing more."

Publius said, "With respect, proconsul, ask Lady Tertulla to confirm the authenticity of this document."

"Legate, do you not think me capable of recognizing my own wife's handwriting?"

"Sir, please."

"Go on then, but I am warning you, commander, neither the good people of Antioch nor I will stand to have our time wasted much longer."

Publius started across the dais and down the steps. I looked at my mistress, and saw anything but resolve. I could not let her lie for me. "*Dominus*, my lady ..."

"Legionary," Publius barked, "silence the prisoner." One guard tightened his grip on me and the other brought his fist across my cheek and jaw. I did not completely lose consciousness, but I did require help standing for the next few moments. In addition to the startling amount of astonishing pain, it was a curious thing to see a bolt of lightning strike *inside* my head.

"…is my handwriting," lady Tertulla was saying as I came to myself.

Publius was struck dumb, but not Curio. He leapt to his feet and shouted, "That's not true!"

Crassus snapped, "If I hear another disrespectful word from you, your back shall pay the price for your tongue's insolence."

"Abject apologies, proconsul."

"Now what part do you have to play in all of this?" Crassus asked with exasperation.

Curio looked to Publius. *Dominus'* son said, "It was the freedman who brought this unfortunate deceit to my attention, proconsul. He discovered a draft of this letter," he said, holding up the original, "crumpled on the floor of the accused."

"That does not surprise me," lady Tertulla announced, "since that is where I must have dropped it accidentally when I first arrived in Antioch. Thank you, Curio, for retrieving it for me."

"Mother…," Publius started, "lady Tertulla, do you mean for us to believe that you have been carrying a crumpled copy of a letter you wrote over six months ago, on your person with you all the way from Rome?"

"That is exactly what I mean to tell you."

"One moment, please." Octavius leaned over to Crassus and said in a voice I barely heard, "General, hadn't we better clear the room? This is not state business."

"No need," Crassus replied. "Publius is right: a just man must act with consistency, whether at home or in public. Let them see I do not fear scrutiny. In any case, this will all be over shortly." In a louder voice, he said, "Continue, legate."

"Lady Tertulla, what would possess you to do such a thing?" There was clear disbelief in Publius' voice. A sneer of contempt curled across Lucius Curio's lips.

"The minute I let the original out of my hands," lady Tertulla answered, "I regretted my negativity, and my attempt to dissuade the proconsul from some of his...strategic goals. I had no idea when the courier might arrive, but remembered, thank Minerva, the discarded draft. I recovered it and intended to show it to the proconsul at the earliest opportunity, whether or not the original had been delivered. I would have done, but your haste in accusing an innocent man has robbed me of my private confession."

The two outside aisles of the Great Hall had been filled all the way to the entrance when the afternoon session had begun. Now, the same number of people pressed themselves into half the space, ears and necks craning. In the entire center aisle there remained only myself and my two guardians.

While Crassus was doling out admonishments, I was thinking. "This all strikes me as highly inconclusive," he said. "Legate Crassus, you and your informant have acted with imprudence and haste. I charge you to be sure of your facts before you waste the court's time." Crassus motioned for the forgery to be handed over to him. "Lady Tertulla, you and I shall have a further conversation regarding the contents of this letter."

What I was thinking was this:

Rome stole your life from you — for 32 years you have lived a life without choice.

I have a wife.

In this moment, you are free. You chose this path. Now walk it.

I have a son.

Tertulla wants to save my life, but not my freedom.

I love and I am loved; I have friends, and a life that may justly be called my own.

If you let yourself be rescued, every day you will awaken not only a slave, but a coward.

"*Dominus*!" I called, wincing at the pain in my jaw. "I can prove that the letter is a forgery and that I am its author."

Crassus looked down at me with anger and disbelief. "Do you accuse the lady Tertulla of lying?"

"She is trying to protect me, and for that I thank her and beg you to forgive her."

"I am not saying I will accept your proof, but I ask you this: why would you do such a thing, when it could mean your life?"

"Because, *dominus*, the life you speak of does not belong to me. It is yours. Watch now, as I take it back. I declare, Marcus Crassus, that you are wrong, that what you plan here is wrong, that every greatness you have taken a lifetime to achieve will turn to dust if you cannot remember the humane statesman you once were. Be that man again. Leave Hierapolis in peace. Leave Jerusalem in peace. Leave Parthia in peace."

"Treason," Publius said. The crowd stirred.

The old majordomo banged his staff for silence. "Nothing has changed, Alexander," Crassus said quietly. "Your life still belongs to me."

"You are wrong, *dominus*. Look about you. There are too many witnesses. You must follow the law. This time, you must finish it. Now here is my proof. You hold the letter in your hand. Ask your lady to recite any part of it."

Domina's eyes begged me to stop. She turned to her husband and said, "That is an unfair question. The letter was written months ago." Even *dominus* could hear her voice tighten with the tension of a lie.

"Forgive me, *domina*," I said, "but in truth, the letter was written yesterday." I began to quote. "'Rome has need of you—'"

"Stop!" Crassus shouted. "I forbid it!"

"Let him speak!" someone called from the crowd. The cry was echoed and repeated till it swelled throughout the Great Hall. Crassus looked at his legates but all were thin-lipped and stone-faced. My own face, at least one side of it, felt as if it were being filled with concrete. The striking of the majordomo's staff reverberated in my head.

"You are mad," Crassus said to me as if we were the only two in the hall.

"They say, *dominus*," I said when I knew that he could hear me, "that over as many years as I have served you, it is not unusual for the slave to exhibit the personality of the master."

"Impudence!" Publius snorted. He raised his hand.

"Do not touch him!" Crassus roared, and his son's men backed away. "Go on then, madman, move your piece on the board. But the game is mine."

"Before I do this thing," I said in a quiet voice, shaking free of the guards, "since I may not be given the chance afterwards, allow me to say that, in spite of certain difficulties between us, a few disagreements here and there, it has been an honor, Marcus Licinius Crassus, to

495

serve you." Then, as loud as my bruised face and terrified heart would allow, I said, pointing to the parchment in his hand, "Follow along, if you like. 'Rome has need of you, the signs are strong for your return. The Tiber has overflowed its banks, drowning crops and causing much wreckage in the city. The people blame the manner of your departure and the curse of Ateius. I, too, have dreamed of a great river, not of water, but of sand.' Shall I go on?"

"There," Publius said, "he proves his own guilt."

Petronius, his eyebrows furrowed, said, "This is no proof, Alexander." I've always been fond of Petronius. "Lucius Curio says he found a draft of the letter in your room. It is possible for you to have read the letter and committed it to memory."

"You are a good man, Petronius," I said, "and I wish you and every legionary in the army of Crassus a safe and speedy return home. What folly it would be for me, however, to find the note, and instead of returning it immediately to its owner, which you know I would do, to read it, commit it to memory, crumple it up once more and drop it onto the floor of my room. Additionally, I think you will find that the crumpled draft is incomplete. The excerpt I recited can only be found on the final letter."

There was some additional bickering, several more well-meant attempts to undo what was perceived as my self-sacrifice, but in the end there could be no doubt, and with a crowd that smelled and demanded blood, Crassus was forced to give it to them.

He rose and walked to the edge of the dais. "Alexander, slave of house Crassus," he said, in a tone that disturbed me almost as much as the words themselves. He spoke as if this were merely another intellectual game played between us, where as usual, I was outmatched. "I find you guilty of forgery, manifest theft of the identity of a Roman citizen, with intent to subvert another citizen. According to the *Law of the Twelve Tables*, the penalty is death.

"So that all present may know that Rome is a fair and equitable administrator, even within its own house, I pronounce sentence upon you. Tomorrow, two hours before the setting of the sun, you will be taken to the hill outside the northern gates of the city. There you will be crucified."

Publius rose to address the crowd, who having received the portion of Roman justice for which they hungered, now found themselves a little queasy at the thought of having to swallow it. "Below your feet let a sign be posted: 'Roman Law Prevails in Antioch.' Let no man remove the body upon pain of taking its place. All must know that fairness has returned to Syria."

My legs, having decided they preferred the Great Hall to any place I might now be taken, had ceased to function. My old arrow wounds chose this time to twinge and trip me up. I was trying to cooperate, trying to be the model condemned prisoner, but Publius' guards were forced to practically hoist me off the ground with each step. We had therefore traveled only as far as Curio's place on the bench when he stood up. "Before we conclude these proceedings, may I make a brief statement?" The way Lucius said it, with his upturned chin and pursed lips, he made it sound more like a demand than a request.

Crassus told him to be brief. "I have noted," my replacement began in high nasal form, "the reticence of these good officers to find negative intention harbored in the bosom of the accused. I would like to set their minds at ease by submitting a further piece of evidence proving the

497

prisoner's attempt to subvert my lady Tertulla many months before the general's arrival in Antioch."

Publius said incredulously, "How many times would you like to see the man executed?"

"I act solely to assuage the peace of mind of those who may have any lingering doubts." Curio handed Publius a piece of parchment, who in turn handed it to his father.

Crassus held the letter at his side, making no attempt to read it. "Did you write this letter...curse my memory...Curio!"

"Yes, *dominus*, Lucius Curio. I am your *atriensis*." The strength in my legs was returning, and I was becoming vaguely aware of my surroundings, enough so that my bruised face registered a half smile.

"Yes, I know full well *what* you are. Answer me."

"No, I am not it's author. It was written by the condemned."

"And to whom was the letter written?"

"Why, your lady, general. It makes most foul accusations, it undermines your authority. If you would just read it."

"I have no intention of reading my wife's private correspondence. Octavius, return this property to lady Tertulla." The legate took it, face down, crossed down the steps and handed it to *domina* who put it quickly out of sight. Had I been more aware of my surroundings, I would have taken note of how unshaken my lady was by the revelation that my letter to her had gone missing. Crassus continued. "How and when did you come by this note?"

Curio said, "I found it on her reading table approximately two weeks before we departed for Syria."

"Did you ask your lady's permission to remove this letter from her things?" Curio's brow frumpled, but for once he said nothing. "Then you stole it, is that what you are saying?"

"No! I...my intent was to reveal this supposed hero of the household for the traitor he is."

"Did you discuss the matter with lady Tertulla? I cannot hear you. No? Why was that?"

"Well, it was..., I did not want to — "

"Let me help you," Crassus said. "Not only are you a thief, you wish to impugn the character of one of Rome's most respected matrons in a deceitful plot against her *paterfamilias*."

Long before Crassus finished speaking, Curio had begun to cry. His broad nose leaked, he sniffled loudly and his, "That was never my intent," was barely intelligible.

"Did you not think a lady of your mistress' character would bring the matter to me at the earliest opportunity? You are a thief, sir, and untrustworthy. Normally, I would have you flogged and put you back into service, but frankly, I cannot endure the sight of you. You will join the man you are so happy to condemn in custody."

Crassus flicked a finger and nodded at the guards, who took hold of the former *atriensis*. He was standing within reach of me. There were so many things I could have said to him, but I decided to let *dominus* speak for me. "Lucius Curio, freedman of house Crassus, I find you guilty of manifest theft from a Roman citizen. According to the *Law of the Twelve Tables*, the penalty is scourging and enslavement. I pronounce this sentence upon you."

"For pity's sake!" Curio cried.

"Tomorrow morning, you shall be taken to the fort courtyard to receive your thirty lashes. Normally, your duty would then be to the house from which you had stolen, but lady Tertulla has told me she cannot abide that habit of yours, the thing you do with your knuckles. There are many fine houses in Antioch; I'm sure several will come to bid on you at the local market, which is where you will be sold at the next auction."

Till that moment, I had never seen a man faint without some physical provocation. I wondered if it was typical for the eyes to roll up in the head as Curio's had done just prior to collapsing.

"Octavius," *dominus* continued, "as to Alexander. I want no nails, no scourging, no bloodletting of any kind. No beatings. He is to be bound with ropes. His legs are not to be broken. And a foot rest is to be provided."

The legate of Legion I gathered his courage, made more audacious by his youthful appearance and said, "General, the men are fond of Alexander. These measures you require will prolong his agony. It will take hours, perhaps days for him to die. I cannot deny the severity of his crimes, but ask only that you consider his past service. Let me to help him on his way with a quick thrust of a spear. I know I speak for many when I beg you to show leniency. Allow me to give the man a faster, less painful death."

"Take my arm," Crassus replied. They grasped each other's forearms and shook once. The commander saw the paternal smile on his general's face and took hope. "Gaius Octavius," Crassus said, lowering his voice, "do not question my orders in public. I have my reasons. Now do as I have asked."

The legate bowed his head and said, "Yes, general."

Down on the floor of the Great Hall, Lucius Curio had recovered and was now on his knees blubbering up at Publius Crassus. "*Dominus*, I beg of you. I acted for the good of the house. Will you not intercede on my behalf?"

The youngest son of Marcus Crassus was standing in a shaft of the day's late golden sunlight. It illuminated his gilt, muscled breastplate and made his arms and face glow with reflected light. The hero of Aquitania looked down at the red-faced, sniffling, puffy-eyed servant and said, "No, Curio, I don't believe I shall."

CHAPTER XXXVI

54 BCE - FALL, ANTIOCH

Year of the consulship of
Lucius Domitius Ahenobarbus and Appius Claudius Pulcher

"That's it. We're not waiting any longer," the *optio* said, the stiff arc of horsehair on his helmet brushing the air as he shook his head. "Bind his hands."

"Due respect, sir," Malchus said, "in these foreign parts, how can we be sure if it's two hours till sunset? Maybe there's three left. Who can say?"

"I can say," said the *optio*. "And I'm saying it now. Malchus, don't make this any harder than it already is. Just do your job."

"Sir." Malchus left the road and walked back up to where I lay. He shook his head and bent to his task.

Betto was already crying. "*Furina's* feces, Alexander."

"I'm glad it's you, Flavius," I told him. "I'd rather it be you than a stranger. I am sorry for the distress this is causing you."

"No. It has to be us. We'll see you off right."

"Don't stretch his arm out too far," Malchus called from the other side. He smeared his nose across his forearm. "Bind it wide, but not too tight."

"Stop telling me how to do this," Betto yelled across my prone, almost naked body. "Cerberus' four balls," he muttered, "you'd think I'd never done this before."

"Cerberus only has two balls," Malchus said.

"So you keep telling me." Betto paused to wipe his eyes with the back of his hand. "Why don't you go down there, bring 'em back and prove it to me?"

"Because," I interrupted, "even if Malchus could somehow demonstrate that the testicles were taken from the beast, it would still only prove the dog has two."

"Oh," Betto sniffed, "we've done this one before, have we?"

"Once or twice," I said. "You'd accuse him of deliberately leaving the other two behind."

I was on the cross, on the ground, my head aligned up the gentle slope of the hill, my feet pointing down toward the base of the fifteen-foot post that rested at the edge of the road into Antioch. Betto was tying my right wrist to the beam already notched and tied to the vertical post. If I let my bare legs fall on either side of the rough-hewn wood, I could feel grass and earth on my calves and the heels of my feet. Above me, the arbutus swayed, a shifting canopy of shade. The trees' smooth orange bark was peeling back like parchment, exposing next year's pale green arms. Behind my head, further up the hill, the Etruscan from my friends' *contubernium* was digging the four-foot hole for the post. Their remaining tent-mates were on the road, joined by another dozen soldiers holding back the crowd. Cavalrymen were stationed at either end to make sure no one flanked the human barrier.

503

"Can you push off from the foot rest easy enough?" Malchus asked. "On your toes, your legs should be able to take most of the weight off your arms."

"That arrow wound in his right thigh's going to make itself known."

"Shut up, Flavius," Malchus said.

"It hardly ever gives me any trouble," I said helpfully.

"It will, lad. Sooner or later."

Malchus glared at his friend, an exchange I had looked upon with fondness countless times over the course of our friendship.

"Oh. Sorry," Betto said. "Let's not tie his legs; he'll just get rope burn when he pushes himself up to get a breath."

"Must you, Flavius? I am barely managing my terror as it is."

"*Merda*! Curse me for an ignorant ass!"

"Done," I said, trying and failing to make him smile.

Malchus said, "No curse required."

"Where is Livia?" I asked. "She is coming, isn't she?"

"She'll be here," Malchus said, casting a worried look at Betto. "Don't worry. We won't hoist you up till she has a chance to, you know, say goodbye." He glanced behind him down the hill. I craned my neck and saw the officer pacing on the empty road between his men and the Antiochenes who had gathered to witness the execution.

"Could I have some water, please?"

Betto tilted my head up and put his flask to my lips. When he did, I could see the city, a bit of the river, even the Regia. I wondered what Crassus was doing at this moment. Was he standing on a balcony, looking this way? Or now that I was free of him, had he already put me out of his mind? As Betto was about to let my head back down, I saw a flash of red hair in the crowd. "Wait! I think I see her!"

"Sir!" Malchus shouted to the *optio*. "There she is! The *medicus*."

The officer walked briskly up to his men. "Make a path for that woman! Let her through!"

Betto found a large, smooth stone and placed it gently under my head. Then he and the rest of the legionaries moved off down the hill. Betto and Malchus touched Livia's shoulders lightly as they passed. She was wearing her belted healer's tunic, stained from work. I wondered if she had been the one to treat Curio's wounds. Cradled in her arms was a small child. In two days, Felix would be a year old.

She knelt in the space made where the two pieces of wood were joined. "Here is your son," she said. She put Felix down in the tight triangle of ground between us. He giggled and picked at the bark on the unplaned side of the beam. I spoke to him softly and finally got his attention. He put both hands on my face, squeezed my cheeks and laughed. I smiled, my mouth and chest tight. Something I would not be able to control began to well up inside me. Thankfully, at that moment he turned, held his arms in the air and Livia picked him up.

"He has your looks," I said.

"He'll most likely have my temper as well."

"One of your finest features. That and your whistling. How is Hanno?"

"Oblivious. Soon he'll be destroyed, like the rest of us."

"You'll see to him, though."

"He was surviving before he met you. I expect he'll do as well when you've gone." She inhaled deeply and blew the air out slowly. "I came out here with half a hundred questions to which I already knew the answers. There's no point to any of it, is there?" Her voice constricted with her breathing. "You've killed yourself, Andros. And murdered me."

"I'm hoping you'll forgive me."

"No. I never shall."

"I know. I understand."

"I understand, too, I do. I know why you did what you did. But you had no right."

"Little fox, I had no choice."

"You *always* have a choice, you stupid man! Who gave you the right to act as one? You were not one. We were the three of us. You had no right." Her voice trailed off, but she refused to allow any tears to fall.

"What if *you* were given the chance, Livia, to do something you knew was just and good? Something that would make right at least a little of the wrong."

"I would never leave you; I would never leave our son."

"Even if it meant your freedom?"

"Death is not freedom, Alexandros. It's just death."

Livia put Felix down on the ground beyond the beam above my right arm. He sat, crossing his chubby legs, happily bubbling to himself as the patch of ground before him became a new unexplored universe. She wasn't tired of holding him. She wanted her hands free.

"I swear to the ancient gods," she said, unleashing the storm that had to come, "you are so ignorant I could kill you myself." On the last word she pounded my chest with her fists. "Look at you! Where is your philosophy now? What good can come of this, tell me that. You are a selfish, thoughtless man. How could you do this to yourself? I really, really want to hate you, Andros, truly I do."

"I don't blame you."

"Be quiet! So what if you did the right thing? How will the world change except that it will lose a little of its brightness when you have gone? For pity's sake, Andros, even the soldiers who bind you cry for you. Gods, you are the most distressing of idiots! Did you never stop to consider that there are things you could have done while alive, but absolutely nothing you can do now, except die?"

"You make a valid point."

Livia made a noise deep in her throat. "You are stupefying, you and your logic. Now we both will suffer, but you are so selfish, you do not even see that I will suffer for a lifetime longer than you. Take that with you on your journey."

"I had to try."

"No, Alexandros, you really did not. But you are a man of principle, aren't you? A man of ideals. And it is clear that this absurd gesture of yours means more to you than life, more to you than me, or your son, or our life together." Livia's hands went to her face. When she removed them, they were wet with angry tears. "I swore I wouldn't do this."

There was no time. I could see the officer motioning to Malchus. "Will you kiss me?" I asked.

"I won't stay to watch this. I won't."

"Of course. You must leave. It will be agony to watch you go."

"Listen to me." She leaned in close. "These two tiny vials are glass, filled with a concentrate of opium. When I leave I will put one between each cheek and gum. When you are ready, bite down hard on the vials. It's not enough to kill you, but you'll be unconscious when…it happens."

"I'm afraid, Livia."

She put her arms around my neck. She was suddenly my Livia again, and now I was losing her. "What will I do tomorrow," she said, kissing my cheeks and eyelids, "when I wake and remember that you are no longer in the world?"

"Carry the memory of us with you. I will carry the scent of your hair with me."

"Don't be afraid to tell me. I won't be angry. I need to hear it. Please."

"Thank you," I said, weeping. "I didn't think you wanted me to say it. Livia, how I have loved you. When Sulla's archer shot me all those years ago and I almost died, you were the first sight that met my eyes at my rebirth. When I close them at the end, my last thought will be of you."

"I wanted so much more for us."

"Malchus!" the *optio* called.

From the road, I heard my friend ask, "Can he not be untied so they may have one final embrace?"

"Look at the sun. We'll be lucky if we're all not whipped for this."

Livia held my face in her hands and kissed my lips, a fleeting eternity of touch that would never come again. "If I did not have our child," she said, pulling away from me, "I would follow you."

"Then I must hope that after I am judged, after you have lived your life, I may find you on the fields of Elysium."

She laughed as she cried. "And all this time I thought you were one of the most intelligent men I had ever known. Goodbye, my sweet *pelargós*."

"Goodbye, love."

Livia slipped the thin vials into my mouth, took Felix into her arms, rose and walked down the hill.

•••

With the help of the *optio*, who held my legs steady on the foot rest, Malchus and Betto dragged me back past the waiting hole so that the foot of the post fell over the top of the opening, but not into it. Another legionary took Malchus' place on the left side of the beam. Drusus came behind me, squatted, wrapped a saddle blanket around the post, slid his arms around between the wood and the backs of my thighs and with the other legionaries helping marginally, shoved, heaved and tilted the cross up till it dropped into the hold of its own weight. That was jarring, I can tell you, even with several arms supporting me to cushion the blow. Once upright, Malchus and Betto held the cross vertical while other legionaries tamped earth and stones into the remaining space to secure it.

My first reaction once the *optio* released my calves so that my weight was borne entirely by my arms tied at the wrists was to recognize that this was a death by degrees. Which is to say, it wasn't that bad, not at first. To alleviate the pain in my shoulders and sides from hanging limp, I could use my chest and arm muscles to pull myself higher. It was almost like exercise. When I relaxed, my sides stretched, my shoulders bunched and it became a little more difficult to breathe, but I could manage. I put my feet on the rest, now three feet above the ground, and let my knees swing to the side. Betto came up to me and readjusted my *subligaculum*, making sure it was fit snugly about my loins. I nodded my thanks.

He stepped back beside Malchus and the *optio* pronounced the work complete. Till sunset, the full guard would remain to discourage gawkers. Nights would be taken in four-hour shifts by a squad of four soldiers. Malchus and Betto would not be among them. The officer was assigning them duties elsewhere.

"Take your leave now," he said. "You won't see this fellow again. I'm doing you a favor, believe me."

Betto asked, "What's the ladder for?"

"General's orders. Once a shift, the condemned is allowed half a cup of water."

"You're joking?" said Betto. Malchus slapped him on the back of his shoulder.

"No, I mean, really? It's generous and all, but is it a kindness, prolonging the inevitable?"

The *optio* asked me, "Are you thirsty?" I shook my head. "Right. Then I'll be off. You men be quick about it. Son, your friend Betto's got a point. If it was up to me, I'd turn it down when it's offered to you. This is the kind of thing you want to get over as quick as possible, and you're already at a disadvantage with no wounds or broken bones. But suit yourself." Before I could begin to thank him he had turned and marched off.

Malchus reached out and held the back of my calf. He looked up and said, "We've shared a better, longer road than most."

"'Been a good friend," I said, the pinched strangeness in my voice hopefully excusable.

Betto said, "See, he doesn't want to talk. We'll go."

"Keep my knives, Betto."

"I will," he said, tugging at the sleeve of Malchus' tunic. "We won't forget you, Alexander."

•••

Across the valley, the sun was sitting on top of the coast range, forcing me to close my eyes. Down below, I could hear the crowd slowly seeping away. After all, it was time for the evening meal, there were chores to complete, and frankly, not much to be seen here, just a middle-aged man tied to a pole in his underthings. Hardly a show worth the lingering. To be sure, the entertainment was free, but it was also living proof that you got what you paid for. It was not long before the legionaries had no one to hold back; the cavalry clopped off toward the fort, the detachment gathered their gear and followed suit, and the first four legionaries on watch set about making camp down by the road. They offered me water. I declined.

I tried squinting one eye partially open. The sun had sunk halfway below the rim of the Amanos, and a trick of the light had turned the Orontes into a coruscating ribbon rushing through the valley. Crassus had chosen a lovely spot for my drawn-out demise. While I watched, the sun, having tired of the day, lowered itself till it was no more than a god's fingernail above the ridge. Then it dropped into the sea, splashing bolts of color skyward. In the city, lamps already lit now became visible, a gathering of fireflies that welcomed the first stars.

It was about an hour (or so it seemed) into my execution that I began to feel my first real discomfort. The fatigue in my arms was becoming noticeable; my shoulders ached and I had to let myself hang for a long while to avoid getting a cramp in my left chest muscle. I had used the foot rest for little more than a place to keep my body weight from pulling even further on my arms, but now I realized my breathing had become shallow and I was having difficulty exhaling. I pushed up till I was on the balls of my feet and blew out a long breath. My head cleared almost instantly.

While I was thus elevated, I considered the vials still present in my mouth. I was looking down a dark spiral of increasing pain; every moment I persisted was as good as I was ever going to feel ever again. The next moment would be worse, and the one after that, more distasteful still. There would be no rest from this exertion, no hiatus where I could gather myself to begin again. I could not scratch the infernal itch on my cheek, nor alleviate the growing agony at the top of my shoulders. My legs began to tire and I let myself hang from my arms once again.

Imagine this if you can: while I hang upon the cross, do not let every hurt I describe fade from your memory as you put each scroll aside. Rather, try to let each description of an insult to my body compound and layer upon the next, building into a glorious fanfare of pain. While it may not be an entirely accurate representation of my sentence of execution, it will pull you much closer to the awful experience than these scribblings could possibly achieve without assistance. If that is your wish.

I had never wanted to sink my teeth into any succulent, steaming roast boar as much as I desired to slice my gums and tongue apart on the bitter contents of those glass vials. But I could not do it. I let myself hang for as long as I could, then minutes later as my breath grew shallow, I pulled myself up again. Livia had provided the antidote to my ordeal, but I could not take it yet. I could not allow any suspicion to fall upon her. I could not die too soon. I had to be strong. Not my worst quality, but certainly not my finest.

I had to think.

It was dark. The men below were seated around a campfire, talking, eating, drinking, ignoring me. Were they the same legionaries that began the first watch? My mouth was paste. I should have taken the water. Too late. They were too far away and I did not want to waste a painful breath or worse, risk expelling a vial by calling out.

To protect Livia, I had to survive until morning. I swore to myself I would not crack the vials till I could see the sun ignite the highest peaks of the Amanos Mountains.

•••

You cannot know what it was like, and I am fully aware that you do not want to know. But this thing was done to me and done by me — to know my story, and the story of my master, you must be strong and hear me out. To communicate the torment of this cruelty, to give you even the smallest inkling of the madness of a Roman hanging, I must crawl inside myself and speak of those hours as I have remembered them for each of the thousands of days since I said my farewells to the world, to everything and everyone in it that I loved. And when I am done, when I have described this abomination to you, you must ask yourself who it is you condemn more, the man who passed judgment, or the man who brought the sentence upon himself.

•••

Gods my breath does not come easy.

How many hours? Eleven? Twelve? It has to be less than twelve. Two more guard changes after this. Pins and needles shooting through my fingers. Making fists only makes it worse.

513

Tired. Sagging. Lift up. Pull up. Breathe out.

Must be a full moon rising behind me. The ground is turning ghost blue. My tongue rolls over the vials like a lover. It is difficult, very difficult—not to keep from biting down on them, but to keep from swallowing them whole. My arms burn. My insides ache. I am soaked with sweat.

What are they doing down there? Laughing, gambling. Good for them.

Breathe. Take one more step toward dying.

I must devise a regimen of exercise. Hang with feet draped on foot rest. Count to twenty. Up on the balls of your feet. Pull up with your arms. Exhale. Take five normal breaths. Let them laugh at you. Shake the stiffness from arms and neck as best as you can. Repeat. Repeat. Repeat...

Something crumples in my right thigh. There is a twisting, grabbing pain clawing at my leg! A cramp, its black heart the muscle torn by Sulla's archer. A wound received on the first day of my employment with the house of Crassus come to haunt me on my last.

My left leg will have to do the work of two. Will have to...

Hours or only moments have passed; it could be either. My breathing is so shallow I am panting like a bird. I must rise up to breathe freely—grip the ropes with the tips of my fingers, pull down with my forearms and ignore the rope burns, contract the spent shoulder muscles one more time and push up on the ball of my left foot. There. I look at the darkened city beyond the curling smoke of the spent campfire around which three legionaries sleep; the fourth sits with his back to me, poking at the embers with a stick. A few seconds is all I can stand, then down I slump as slowly as I can, my torso twisting back into its contorted lassitude — constricting my lungs with the weight of my body while my muscles cramp and my shoulders scream.

I am puzzled by a question that hangs before my closing eyes, prying them open long enough to wonder why I am asking it.

Why did Crassus condemn me to this torture, to the one form of Roman execution that is not instantaneous?

•••

I am still crucified, but the cross is on the Via Appia just outside Capua. As far as the eye can see other crosses line the way, two facing each other every hundred feet. They are all skeletons, or mostly so. I had been to the city several times on errands for *dominus*, but it had never looked as dingy and drained of color as this. The sky presses low and dark; clouds move swiftly past, escaping the sight and the stink. The crows don't seem to mind, though. Several sit on the beam above my outstretched arms, what is left of them, picking every now and then at a remnant with lackluster enthusiasm. The wind whistles low and tuneless through our bones. Thunder rumbles in the distance. There is no pain, so either I have died or I am dreaming. I think about it a moment, but can not decide, considering the landscape before my — whatever I am using for eyes, which possibility I hope to be true.

The corpse directly opposite me picks up its head and speaks. It has to raise its voice to be heard over the wind and the width of the wide road between us. "Why would you serve a man like that?" it asks.

I recognize him at once. "Your body was never found. You should not be hanging here."

Spartacus laughs. "Name one who does deserves this death. Not you, surely. Not me. Yet here we are. You found me. You have succeeded where others have failed."

"I shall count it, then, among my very few accomplishments. What do you mean, 'a man like that?' You no nothing of Marcus Crassus."

"I know enough. I know he killed 70,000 innocent people. I know you are defending him this very moment, even after he has had you killed."

"Innocent? Who among us is innocent? Not all of us are as handy with a *gladius* as you. You did the best you could. We both failed."

"You compare yourself to me?"

"Never. I led no uprising. You used a sword. I wrote letters."

"You could have poisoned him in his sleep."

"No. I would have saved him from himself had I been able."

"Then you're a fool, and deserve your fate."

"I could not kill a man I once thought of as my friend, if only to myself."

"That's right, because between the two of you, you would have been the only one to think it. Look what your 'friend' did to my people." He turns his head from side to side. "All I wanted to do was lead them to freedom. And he slaughtered us."

"Blame Crassus if you must. But if not Crassus, then Pompeius, and if not Pompeius, then Caesar, or a dozen other generals, as many as it would take. *Rome* would have kept coming until the task was done. Rome was wrong, Crassus was wrong, but until you have spent thirty-two years with the man, lived his life with him, become closer than any brother, do not be so quick to condemn him."

"And be sure to wash between his toes when he demands it."

"I was his slave, and that is my misfortune. But Crassus was a great man, once. Now he has become misguided. I mourn for him."

"She is beautiful," Spartacus says. "You made the wrong choice."

I had been looking off into the hills, but as the dead gladiator makes that pronouncement, I turn toward him again to say, "Why do you — " He is gone. Squawking and complaining, the crows are flapping away in fear of his replacement. In the middle of the Via Appia stands Marcus Crassus astride Eurysaces, his giant black mount snorting and pawing at the paving stones with impatience, anxious to be moving away from this place. The general wears the armor and weapons lady Tertulla had given him before his departure from Rome.

"Who were you talking to?" he asks.

"The slave, Spartacus."

"Hmph. A shame. I would have enjoyed a word with him."

"I am almost certain it would not have been mutually relished." We appraise each other in silence. Eurysaces stamps his hoof. "Well," I say, "you finally got me where you wanted me."

"You put yourself up there, not I." Crassus looks behind me as if searching for something. I cannot afford such luxury of movement.

"You are a cruel, heartless, hate-filled shell of a man."

"Alexander!"

"What perversity to kill me thus. Whatever there was between us is gone."

"It saddens me to hear you say so."

"Where has noble Crassus gone? Do you remember that man? Gods, but you were a paragon! In the beginning, after I stopped hating you, it wasn't long before I actually began to revere you. How could that be? You were decent, a man of character—I was baffled."

"It is always disorienting when one begins service in a new house." Crassus rises in his saddle and peers off into the distance.

"Am I keeping you from something?"

"Of course not. Do continue."

"'Service.' At this point in our lives can we not call it what it is?"

"All right. Slavery. You were my slave. What of it? You had money, power, respect, comfort, even love. How many free men can claim as much?"

"That is true. You make a fine argument for the condition. If only every slave had the opportunity to rise as high as I; if only every master could be as kind as you.

"A slave, even a slave like me, has but one choice: obey, or die. Either way, whoever that man was before—vanishes. He becomes something new. But what? For me, in order to survive as another man's property, the only way I could make sense of it and remain sane was to take my identity from you. Don't you see, Marcus, I have always been defined by you—it was your essential goodness that allowed me to live in this abhorrent state."

"Deliriousness," Crassus admonishes, "is no excuse for familiarity."

I ignored him—what more could he do to me? "I became a reflection of you—instantaneous justification for living one day to the next. I had become a slave, but the man I served was honorable. I could be just and noble because Crassus was just and noble. I could become wealthy, fall in love, start a family, all because my world existed inside the universe of Crassus, and Crassus was good."

"So you have reconciled yourself to this," he said, pointing at the endless geometry of crosses curving into the distance.

"You did what you had to do. But even that foul necessity is not as heinous as what you are about to do now."

"Why is that?"

"You believed your war against Spartacus was for the good of Rome. You don't give a fig for Rome now—you will instigate this war with Parthia, risk tens of thousands of lives, disrupt hundreds of thousands of families who will pay the price for generations—for spite, for the lost virility you think you should have found on that night, for the chance to take your vengeance upon one man. You have lost your way, Crassus. If you are lost, then I am lost."

"You are taking this very personally."

"I thought there might yet be some hope of redemption, because *domina* still stood by your side. Do this, and you will no longer be deserving of a woman like the lady Tertulla. You were a man of honor, a statesman. Now look at you. Do you know what you have become? A Roman. How disappointing."

"I, too," Crassus said, nodding ever so slightly, "have very much enjoyed your company over the years, but that is not why I have come. Prepare yourself. As for the rest, I do what I must, but I did what I could."

"I do not understand."

"Breathe. Take one more step toward living."

"What?"

"Wake up. It is almost time."

•••

A spasm in my stomach jerks me forward, cracking my shoulders and setting the muscles of my chest on fire. My feet fly off the foot rest; all my weight is being carried by my arms. I am flailing about like a torn sail. I inhale in short gasps but I cannot seem to let it out. My left ankle slams into the foot rest but I am grateful for that little agony, a beacon to guide me up and onto the flat surface. There—I push off on the ball of my left foot, my arms almost useless.

My chest cavity releases my lungs from its grip and I am free to exhale. I have no idea how long I have hung in this place, or what guards amuse themselves below. My left thigh burns and I know my calf will cramp at any moment. I need not worry, for the foot rest fails before I do, splitting in half and setting my body free to be wrenched back by my arms. This is more than I can bear, but my body goes on struggling without me. Down the hill a voice says, "That's it for him, then." My knees bend, my feet and back press upon the post, pushing, pushing up against the rough wood. Two things, however, are now as clear as the tear that hangs on my eyelash, refusing to fall: the first is that I can no longer feel the glass vials in my mouth; the second is that I will never last to see the sunrise.

•••

There are some predicaments from which the mind, once it has been exercised in misuse, even though it bring all its powers of reason and logic to bear on the thorny snare that entangled it in the first place, simply cannot escape. Cause will have its effect.

EPILOG

19 BCE - WINTER, SIPHNOS, GREECE

Year of the consulship of
Quintus Lucretius Vespillo and Gaius Sentius Saturninus

Y ou will not be surprised to learn that I did not perish upon that cruel wood, and may have some interest in the circumstances leading up to my rescue and consequent escape. I have but a hazy memory of the former, and none at all of the latter — I must combine my own memory's etchings with the version accorded me by my savior.

I suffered greatly that night, but to my unending shame, I made Livia suffer more. Looking back to that wretched time with the perspective of another thirty-seven years, I see a fool blinded by his own pompous, self-justifying rhetoric, a sagacious and perceptive shade by the name of Spartacus, and a lord of Rome who paused in the making of the means of his own destruction to help a man he would, but could not call "friend."

I shall tell you what I can, but first I require a brief nap, for in this heat, my thoughts, rather than marching in orderly fashion like the line of ants that now stream in single file along the terrace wall with blind determination, are like a rabble of copper butterflies startled from a field of campanula, flying this way and that, with no…

•••

The thwack of the ladder against the back of the crossbeam brings me out of my semi-conscious stupor with a thrill of agony. Instinct and pools of strength kept secret even from myself push and pull me up to work at the air with my crumpled bellows, my cheeks inflating each time I send a befouled breath out into the darkness. It is the last deep of the night, that hour when dawn's nearness may be smelled and heard, but not seen. Behind me, a legionary takes each complaining step with caution, either to minimize the jarring of his movements, or (could it be?!) to guard against spilling his precious charge. I peel my tongue from the roof of my mouth in preparation to receive the balm of water which he carries. This time there will be no brave declination. I shall take what is offered. I have no wish to extend my misery, though that will surely be the result. I am beyond caring. It is the sensation I crave — the slippery invasion of liquid, its coolness, the oppositeness of the hardening concrete which has become the interior of my mouth. I anticipate the wetness on my lips, the drops that will fall to run down my broken chest, the clean taste of life that my body must have, that it demands, overriding any argument my shriveled mind might make to refuse it. In my delirium, I believe that I can smell it.

"Thannuh," I rasp as the soldier reaches the top of the beam, but the sounds I emit are unintelligible.

He laughs. "You sound like me now. Worse."

I want to say that I do not understand, but what comes out instead is, "Wahr."

"Water? Is that what you want?" The dim face that leers down at me over the top of the beam is a nightmare of exposed teeth and gums; I remember that the rest is a scarred ruin left by the pox. It is a face made for the night. Palaemon reaches down and holds a camp cup in front of my own exhausted features. He moves the rim just below my lips. Then he stops.

"Ah'ff phulled guard duty for you. Phretty funny, don't you think? "

While he's talking, my stomach muscles cramp involuntarily and I buckle. My forehead knocks the cup and water spills to the ground. As if he's talking to a child Palaemon says, "Aleckthander! See what youff done!" He looks at what little is left in the brass cup, then drinks it. He makes an exaggerated sound of satisfaction, then sets the cup on top of the beam behind my head.

"You din't really think you were getting any, did you?" My disappointment is so severe that a tear rolls down into my mouth. It is hot and salty and might as well have been burning oil. I slump back down, too exhausted to even attempt to keep my knees bent and my feet flat against the post. My breath is shallow and labored; strange, animal sounds that must be mine scrape and wheeze to its rhythm.

A moment ago I glimpsed a thought that brought me comfort, but now it is gone. As Palaemon rambles on, it comes again, clear and cool among the red, throbbing clutter—I will be dead very soon.

"Ah came uffere for something else. Ffeelus says there's some chance we might get killed in this war. You will be gone for certain, but if Ah don't surfife, Ah don't want to meet up with you in Hades. Effryone knows about your skill with a knife, so Ffeelus says if Ah'm so worried aboudit Ah should make sure you can't take reffenge on me once Ah get to the underworld.

"Ah'm just going to take your thumb is all. 'Probly won't hurt any worse than anything else. You might not even feel it."

I am vaguely aware the man above me is saying something about my hand. I say, "Hanno?"

"You're far gone, you are," he says. "Still, you might scream. Thass why Ah brought this." He reaches down out of sight and comes back with a rag which he balls up and forces into my mouth. He whispers conspiratorially, nodding toward the other guards. "Ah din't menshun this to them."

With one hand, Palaemon flattens my own right hand against the face of the beam. I grunt with the additional insult, but it is almost as if someone else's thumb is being pulled away from the rest of his hand, high and taut. There is a flash of polished iron as Palaemon draws his dagger, holding it above the beam while he decides on the best place to draw the blade. "Wha d'you think, should be chust like cutting a chicken wing."

He knocks loudly on the beam, then is silent.

•••

A little after sunrise, Palaemon's watch was relieved. I had neither witnessed the break of day, nor, as the evening had progressed, did I expect to be extant for its arrival. At some point during the night I had come to the conclusion that I would never gaze upon the chariots of Helios again. This one example that life was subject to certain limitations ranked as minor compared to a thousand other shocks of loss. I was more than reconciled to my fate.

The tale of the attack spread like quicksilver throughout Antioch, eventually, some weeks later, even reaching my own ears. Every school child could repeat the grisly details to his comrades; every adult whispered to each other of the reprisals to come. But they didn't.

The legionaries who walked, then ran to the charming hill just outside the northern gates of the city came upon a scene of carnage. About their small campsite, one soldier lay beneath his cloak, his throat slashed. A second had been shot in the side. He had fallen and rolled over the campfire and apparently had been put out of his misery by a second arrow. His legs and midsection were still smoking. A third man was some distance away from the others, but he too, had died of knife and arrow wounds.

The furious Romans looked up the hill, blinded as the sun rose behind it. Shielding their eyes against the light, they saw an empty cross, but one that was not completely unoccupied. A brass camp cup, the split foot rest and an iron *pugio* lay on the dewy ground, but Palaemon still claimed his place atop the ladder, his chin resting on the beam, his arms hanging over the cross. The back of his neck was securely fastened to the wood by the smooth shaft of a Parthian arrow.

My thumb was not among the detritus. Still attached to my unconscious body, it and I were already many miles east of Antioch.

When Crassus was informed of the murders by Antoninus, he thanked the legate but gave no orders for a counterstrike. It was no coincidence that the general had requested the worst soldiers from among each of the legions to be picked for this particular guard duty. (Velus Herclides had been called but, preferring the warmth of his tent, had bribed his way off the list.)

Before retiring to his quarters where his wife awaited him, Crassus sent word for the *medicus*, Livia, to attend him. His bunions had immediate need of the palliative relief only her pungent, brown balm could bestow.

•••

"I told you I would not forsake my charge." The rag was moist against my lips, the voice familiar. Eyes closed, I listened politely (something deep within told me this was the correct behavior), but I was far more intent on wresting what drops I could from the damp cloth. I could not feel my body, only a great thirst. He spoke again. "We will remain here till you are fit for travel. Sleep, my friend. You have suffered greatly." I considered opening my eyes to see where "here" was, but drifted away before I could lift a single eyelash.

•••

It was a thin soup, most of which made rivulets down either side of my chin, but it was warm, and it was good. I was swaddled from the neck down in long strips of muslin. My wrists had been medicated and bandaged as was my right heel—apparently one of the nails which had split rather than secured the foot rest had caught my foot while I dangled. I was propped up against a palm whose fronds chattered overhead. Before me, two horses drank from the pool of an oasis; a makeshift sling hung from a boxthorn bush. Somewhere in my mind I knew I must still be wracked with pain, but that Alexandros was far from the one thinking and feeling—his pain barely mattered. Drugged, thank the gods.

"Do you remember," Melyaket said, taking a sip from the bowl himself, "when we were by the river hunting the *mescejn*? I told you then. Marcus Crassus bid me watch over you, and so I have. Though not very well, I'm afraid."

Crassus. Very bad memories began blooming like the sewers backing up when the Tiber overflowed its banks. I grunted — the distant Alexandros had begun walking closer at a frighteningly brisk pace.

"See what you've done," said another voice, deeper than Melyaket's. "Let him be."

"Here," Melyaket said, forcing a bitter liquid into my mouth. "Your healer is not the only one who knows how to extract juice from the poppy."

I had many questions, but I also wanted very much for that other Alexandros to go away.

•••

"Eight days!" I cried. "Where is Livia?" My swaddling had been removed and I was dressed as they were, in plain tunic and belted baggy pants. I could sit up on my own, even walk to the water and back to my place by the palm.

"Surrounded by seven Roman legions," Melyaket said, "the safest place she can be. They'll march from Antioch before the last almond flowers have fallen."

"He's very poetic, isn't he," Hami said, eating a dried plum. Hami was as tall as I, but broad and powerfully built. His head was completely shaved. Like Melyaket, he looked to be in his early twenties.

"Rhapsodical," I replied, "but what does he mean, and where are they going?"

"Hierapolis, end of Aprilis," Hami said.

"I must go to her."

"Go that way," Hami said. He spit a seed westward.

"Alexandros," Melyaket said, "you are in no condition to travel, least of all back there. Think about it."

I did think about it, and realized I had something else to say. "Thank you."

"I should have been there sooner." Gently, he rested a hand on my bruised shoulder. "I only expected one or two guards."

Hami smiled and said, "Sorry you had to wait, but coming to me for help was the first smart thing this one's done since we left Sinjar."

Melyaket bowed gracefully toward his friend, then said to me, "As if he would recognize 'smart.' I have something for you." He ran to his horse and returned with a scroll and a red purse tied with gold threads. He held them out to me, but I took the letter from him first.

> *Pelargós*,
> You are alive. Don't scold me for restating the obvious — that has been the only thought in my head since *dominus* summoned me. He told me you were taken from the cross by a Parthian raiding party. I don't know why you were saved or by whom, but whoever they are, I will kiss their feet in gratitude when we meet.
> The gulf that separates us now is as wide as death from life. *Dominus* will not release me, and you cannot return: if I die in the war, Crassus will free Felix. Like you, I must discover how to become a living ghost, then we will find a way for the three of us to be together again. We will cross this divide, I swear. Look for me.
> Livia

"I don't understand. How did you come by this?" I asked.

"The same way I got this." Melyaket opened the pouch and dropped my heavy gold *phalera* and its purple ribbon into my hand. Almost in shock, I ran my thumb over the etched likenesses of Crassus and myself; turned it over and saw the enigmatic riddle which still meant nothing to me.

"*Dominus*?" I asked incredulously.

"General Crassus said for me to tell you, 'guard it well, you might have need of it.'"

"Let me see that," Hami said, grabbing it out of my hands. "Look at this—'Alexandros, beloved of Crassus. Harm him, harm me.' What a hypocrite!"

"Did he give you my slave disk?" I asked Melyaket.

"He gave me only what you see."

Hami said, "Why are you still calling him *dominus*? You're with us now, Alexandros. You're *free!* Mithra's bloody bull! I saw with my own eyes what they did to you, what *he* did to you. How can you speak of Crassus with anything but hatred?"

"Hami," said Melyaket. He sounded exasperated. "How many times do I have to go through this? Crucifixion was the only way the general could save Alexandros' life."

Suddenly, a dream flitted across my consciousness—a man on a skittish horse.

"So he was doing Alexandros a favor?" Hami said. "I suppose that Roman who was about to slice off his thumb was doing him a favor, too."

"I understand," I said. "Melyaket is right, Hami. My crimes were punishable by death in any number of ways. Crassus could have had me beheaded or had a sword thrust down my spine. He could have ordered a scourging and nails for the crucifixion, but he didn't. He wanted me to survive, to give you as much time as possible to rescue me." *How the solution must have satisfied him—vicious and kind in the same, clever stroke. Too harsh a parting, Crassus, too harsh.*

•••

Cut from the umbilicus of Marcus Crassus after 32 years, I was newborn, dressed in foreign garb, among new friends, heading to a new destiny. The general and his son, men I no longer knew, would soon march on Hierapolis and Jerusalem. I grieved for the Marcus Licinius Crassus of my younger days, the student of Aristotle, the orator, the rhetorician, the kind father, the adoring husband. That man was gone, yet enough of him remained to enlist the aid of Melyaket to engineer my escape. It was regrettable that my master's magnanimity first required me to weep, cursing death for a coward. Though I have made lukewarm attempts at the urging of others, I have never been able to bring myself to despise him.

As a slave, I had always complained that I existed in a world without choice. It was a fine excuse to wash my hands of life. What were self-responsibility and self-reliance to me? I was allowed no self—Crassus set the limits of my world, and I was safe within them. I had never had to fight for anything—now I had never felt so powerless, or more alone.

Somewhere across the desert, Livia carried on without me. Melyaket, Hami and I would make our way to the fortress at Hatra. When we got there, I would be on the wrong side of the Euphrates.

•••

I have fallen asleep yet again. Another exasperating interruption from the completion of my work. I smell the sea and feel a stripe of hot sun lying across my bald dome. I don't remember putting this pillow beneath my head. I hate being coddled. I sit up and roll the kinks from my neck. Citrus and bergamot perfume the warm, unruffled air. But here's a welcome surprise! She has placed a fresh bowl of figs and a cup of honeyed wine on the table, an island oasis amidst the unruly seas of my scrolls.

Livia knows how I crave figs.

###

AFTERWORD

When reading historical fiction, I am constantly asking myself the question, "Which category does this piece of information fall into, historical fact, or poetic license?" So if you are also trying to separate fact from historical fiction, here are some of those answers. If any reader has more to add, please let me know.

Seneca, Pliny the Elder and Cassius Dio all assert that the killing of the elephants commemorating the inauguration of Pompey's theater was conducted in the Circus, and although not specified, this is most likely the Circus Maximus, not the venue more convenient to the theater, the Circus Flaminius. I have chosen to place the final day's massacre within the theater itself, in order to make the carnage more intimate.

There is no evidence that Cicero took the stage with the actor, Aesopus, at the dedication of Pompey's theater.

Little is known of Gaius Cassius Longinus' early life. Since his first recorded military action was acting as *quaestor* in Crassus' invasion of Parthia, it is probable he must have had some prior military experience. I have placed him with Caesar in Gaul to make it plausible for Publius Crassus to know and trust his abilities.

There is nothing in the historical record that I am aware of that confirms that Tertulla ever made the trip to Syria. In addition, the old palace known as the Regia in Antioch, built by the Seleucids, was most likely located in the old town, not on the island as I have placed it. The Imperial Palace, said to have begun construction by Gallienus (253-268 CE) completed by Diocletian, was the structure actually built there. Either way, in 526 CE and again in 528, two severe earthquakes flattened the palace, and the area was abandoned.

Julius Caesar did have an affair with Aulus Gabinius' wife, Lollia, though whether or not he was aware of it is unknown.

While nailed curse tablets were known to thrown on the tracks during chariot races, the scourging depicted at the hippodrome in Antioch is not based on any factual account.

It is probable that Publius Crassus did not arrive in Syria before November of 54 BCE. I had him appear in Antioch two months earlier because I did not want the brunt of Alexandros' sentence to fall on Marcus Crassus alone.

Thank you very much for reading the second installment of the trilogy! I would love to hear from you - please visit me at www.andrewlevkoff.com.

Andrew Levkoff
Phoenix, November, 2012

A brief Timeline follows the Acknowledgments and the Glossary.

ACKNOWLEDGMENTS

To my family, who both encourages and puts up with my passion. Never has "enabler" had a more positive connotation.

To Laura, who gives me such a hard time; and to Kevin, who doesn't.

To Margie, who taught me when to dash and when to slow down.

To my grandfather, Sammy. Little Pop could fake any accent like a native. When I was around him, I was having too much fun to realize he was teaching me the true lessons of love.

To my grandmother, Gert. Gigi taught me that life without fine art is less fine.

To Mr. Peter O'Toole, whose use of the English language makes one appreciate why it is so damned complicated and convoluted. Music is what he utters. Hear him, and you'll know why they call them *pipes* and vocal *chords*. If you doubt it, listen to him speak extemporaneously, off the cuff. The Bard weeps in heaven for never having heard him on the boards. I hope this little book finds you in good health, and if not, may there be a good bottle within easy reach.

A final word of thanks to Stephany, who wielded all the right tools whenever they were needed: mirror, window and sieve.

• • •

Every effort has been made to trace the copyright holders of all photographs used in this book. In the event that any have been inadvertently overlooked, please contact me so that the situation can be rectified in future editions.

GLOSSARY

<u>Aediles</u> Municipal magistrates and record keepers. They organized and sponsored public games, maintained temples and public buildings.

<u>Agora</u> Greek. The public square. It was the heart of an ancient Greek city, socially, athletically, artistically and politically. The Agora of Athens is known as the birthplace of democracy.

<u>Amphorae</u> (s. amphora) Storage vessels, usually large, to contain liquids. The three shown at right are from the Archaeological Museum of Rhodes.

<u>Ampullae</u> Jugs or bottles, usually clay.

<u>Anemoi</u> Greek wind gods.

<u>As</u> Roman coin worth one-quarter of one sestercius.

<u>Atriensis</u> Chief slave or majordomo of a Roman household.

<u>Aureus</u> Gold Roman coin worth 400 as, 100 sesterces, 25 denarii.

<u>Balnea</u> (*pl.* balneae). A public bath complex, usually less elaborate than the more magnificent *thermae* of the Empire. The layout of the baths to the right comes from Pompeii. The ritual of bathing was an integral part of Roman society, its significance going far beyond our concept of simply taking a bath. The baths were for exercise, politics, socializing and of course, soaking in a nice hot tub. Separate

Plan of the Old Baths at Pompeii. (Overbeck.)

facilities for men and women, changing rooms, pools both heated and unheated, atriums and even ancient versions of a sauna and a steam room might be included. Learn more at http://en.wikipedia.org/wiki/Thermae.

<u>Bulla aurea</u> A small, roundish ornament of gold, worn around their necks by wealthy Roman children, a talisman to protect against evil. When they reached the age of 17 they traded it and the toga praetexta for the toga virilis. If the grown man should ever be honored with a military triumph, he would wear the bulla once again, to protect against envy.

<u>Calidarium</u> Roman hot bath.

<u>Caligae</u> Roman military hobnailed boots. Their open design gave them the look of sandals, but they were much sturdier.

<u>Capena Gate</u> The gate through which the Appian Way enters the city of Rome.

<u>Catilina</u> Lucius Sergius Catilina, accused of leading a revolt to overthrow the Republic in 63-62 BCE. Catiline, as he is known to us, wanted to achieve power by offering

debt relief to the plebeians. His bid for the consulship failed twice. In the fall of 63 BCE, Crassus received a bundle of letters, left anonymously, which warned of plots to kill many aristocratic senators. Crassus took the letters to Cicero. Some say Cicero wrote the letters himself. Cicero vehemently denounced Catiline in the senate, who volunteered to go into exile, where he raised a small army. The rebellion was put down in 62 BCE and Catiline was killed. Cicero was hailed as the savior of the Republic, but later would face exile himself for his summary execution without trial of some of the conspirators. The subject, motives and actual facts of the Catiline Conspiracy are complicated and muddy. This brief summation barely skims the surface, for the scope of this novel is focused elsewhere. More study is recommended.

Century A Roman military unit composed of ten contuberniums, or 80 legionaries. Each century had its own standard and could act as an independent fighting unit. It was led by a centurion, assisted by the second-in-command, the optio.

Cohort A Roman military unit composed of six centuries for a total (at full strength) of 480 men.

Columba Dove.

Comitia The legislative assembly of the Republic. for more information, see http://en.wikipedia.org/wiki/Roman_assemblies.

Comitium The center of all political activity in Rome. In this 19th century drawing, the forum is in the foreground; the *comitium* is behind the fence. The *rostra, curia* and many of the ancient symbols of the city are within its bounds. The illustration below depicts how the area looked after the restructuring and rebuilding begun by Julius Caesar and completed by Augustus.

<u>Compluvium</u>   An opening in the roof of a Roman atrium which let in light and air. Rainwater would fall to be collected in a pool below called an impluvium

<u>Consuls</u>   Similar to co-presidents, they were joint heads of the Roman state and were elected

<u>Conscript fathers</u>   Roman senators were originally called "fathers." When new members joined their ranks, they were known as "patres et conscripti." The term evolved into Patres conscripti.

<u>Contubernium</u> The basic eight-man unit of the Roman army of the first century BCE. Also the term used for an intimate relationship between two slaves, who were not allowed to marry.

<u>Cubiculum</u>   Small room in a Roman house or villa, used as work spaces, meeting rooms or bedrooms.

<u>Culina</u> Kitchen.

<u>Curia</u>   Where the senate met in the *Comitium;* during Crassus' time, Sulla had destroyed the old *Curia Hostilia,* which had stood for centuries, and replaced it with the *Curia Cornelia* to accommodate Sulla's doubling of the number of senators from 300 to 600.

<u>Cursus honorum</u>   The progression of offices each magistrate had to climb on his way up the Roman political ladder.

<u>Curule Magistrates</u> the highest dignitaries of the state, distinguished from all others by enjoying the privilege of sitting on ivory chairs when engaged in their public functions.

<u>Decimation</u> A punishment for cowardice in the legions. One of every ten men in a century or cohort or any military unit is selected at random and beaten to death by his fellow soldiers.

<u>Decurion</u> A Roman cavalry officer.

<u>Denarius</u> Silver Roman coin worth four sesterces.

<u>Domina</u> Mistress of a Roman household.

<u>Dominus</u> Master of a household.

<u>Domus</u> A Roman house. For more information, go to these links:

penelope.uchicago.edu/Thayer/E/Roman/Texts/secondary/SMIGRA*/Domus

roman-empire.net/society/soc-house.html

mariamilani.com/ancient_rome/ancient_roman_homes

Even the richest estates usually followed some variation of the pictured layout, though the rooms were larger, more ornate, more plentiful, often with the additions of private baths and exercise rooms.

<u>Familia</u> The family members, including servants and slaves, of a Roman household.

<u>Fasces</u> The fasces was the symbol of power and authority in ancient Rome. Made of wooden rods, perhaps birch, surrounding an axe, bound together with red leather. The fasces was carried by a lictor, the guardian for curule magistrates who held imperium. The rods symbolized the power of scourging, and the axe the power of capital punishment. When inside the pomerium, the lictors removed the axes from the fasces to symbolize that a citizen could not be executed without a trial, and that within the city, the power over life and death resided with the people's assemblies, not magistrates with imperium. Upon entering the Comitia Centuriata (where the people elected the magistrates), the lictors would lower the fasces as a demonstration that the powers of the consuls derive from the people. (Image courtesy: http://www.friesian.com/rome.htm)

<u>Fibula</u> Clasp or brooch.

<u>Fortuna</u> Goddess of Luck.

<u>Forum</u> If the *comitium* was the center of all political life in Rome, then the forum was its heart. Encompassing the *comitium*, over the centuries, it included many temples, basilicas, shops and plazas. In the 80's, Sulla raised the entire plaza almost a meter and covered it with black marble paving stones.

<u>Frigidarium</u> The bathing pool in Roman baths left unheated, often used after exercise and warmer pools had opened the pores.

<u>Furina</u> Goddess of thieves.

<u>Garum</u> Aromatic fish sauce.

<u>Gladius</u> Short sword, plural: gladii.

<u>Imperator</u> General who has won a great victory.

<u>Imperium</u> the power of magistrates to command armies and (within limits) to coerce citizens.

<u>Impluvium</u> A shallow pool, usually to be found in the atrium, that captured rainwater from an opening in the roof (the compluvium).

<u>Insulae</u> Apartment houses. Singular — insula.

<u>Lacerna</u> A cloak fastened on the right shoulder by a buckle (fibula).

<u>Lares Domestici</u> Minor Roman deities whose function was to guard and oversee all that transpired in the home.

<u>Lararium</u> Household shrine usually found in the Atrium.

<u>Latrunculi</u> A popular Roman board game, similar to the Japanese game of Go. Learn more at http://www.aerobiologicalengineering.com/wxk116/Roman/BoardGames/latruncu.html.

<u>Latifundium</u> Large Roman farming estate.

<u>Laudatio Funebris</u> Eulogy.

<u>Laverna</u> Roman goddess of cheats, thieves and pickpockets, perhaps evolved from the Etruscan goddess, Furina, protector of thieves.

<u>Law of the Twelve Tables</u> The foundation of the Roman constitution, written in the middle of the fifth century BCE. It established basic rights for citizens, the result of the class war between the patricians and the plebeians. The original documents were lost when the Gauls destroyed Rome in 390 BCE.

<u>Lectus</u> Couch, bed. Romans ate reclining. Sitting in chairs around a dining table during the late Republic was unknown. A slightly larger version of the dining *lectus* was used for sleeping, although, as always, the rich tended to larger, more ostentatious sizes, materials and trappings.

Legate   Commander of a legion; one with authority delegated by a consul or magistrate.

Legion The Roman legion of the post-Marian era toward the end of the Republic was ideally composed of 10 cohorts, 6 six centuries of 80 men in each cohort. There were 10 contuberniums per century, each with eight men. Therefore, each cohort contained 480 soldiers. *However*, legions rarely fought at the full strength of 4,800 fighting men. For example, Caesar often fought in Gaul with legions totaling only approximately 3,500 men. I have guestimated that Crassus was understaffed at the outset, with seven legions of 30,000 soldiers. Due to the catastrophe of the crossing from Brundisium to Dyrrachium, I have reduced the army's strength to 28,000 legionaries, 4,000 light infantry, and 4,000 cavalry (including Publius' contribution of 1,000 Gallic horse).

Liburna   A faster and more maneuverable warship than the trireme, it was powered by only one level of rowers sitting below-deck. It could transport about a century (80 legionaries). Picture courtesy of easypedia.gr.

Lictor   A bodyguard for high-ranking Roman magistrates. The more powerful the office, the more lictors were assigned to you. Each consul was accompanied in every public appearance by twelve lictors; praetors – six abroad, two within Rome; proconsuls and propraetors – six; curule aediles – 2; vestal virgins – 1; dictator - 24.

<u>Lorarius</u> A slave whose job it was to punish other slaves by flogging; also, in the arena, a person who encouraged reluctant animals or humans with a whip.

<u>Lorica</u> Armor.

<u>Lorum</u> A short leather whip, often with two leather strips, thirty inches long, knotted at the ends.

<u>Magus</u> Sorcerer, magician.

<u>Malaria</u> The Romans called malaria the "rage of the Dog Star," since the disease was most prevalent during the *caniculares dies*, the dog days of summer, when Sirius disappeared in the brightness of the sun.

<u>Medicus</u> A Roman physician. While doctors in the military were surprisingly adept at healing wounds, performing surgery, even using antiseptic techniques, the local physician was typically regarded as a charlatan and a quack. Knowledge of the healing arts was expected of each pater familias, and doctors were not generally trusted. This attitude continued until the advent of Galen of Pergamon, arguably the most famous physician of the second century CE, made the practice of medicine respectable.

<u>Merda</u> Excrement.

<u>Ministratore</u> Servant, waiter.

<u>Mithra</u> (also Mithras) The central god of Mithraism, an ancient Persian cult possibly having its origins in Zoroastrianism, which gained widespread popularity throughout the Roman Empire into the 4th century CE.

<u>Mundus</u> A round pit, possibly located on the Palatine Hill, which served as an opening to the underworld. (It may also have been were the precious seed-corn for the planting of grain was stored). On three days of the year,

August 24, October 5 and November 8, the cover of the mundus was removed and spirits were allowed to roam free about the city. On these days, public business was forbidden, no battles were to be fought and no marriages were to take place.

Nobiles   A mix of old patrician families and wealthy plebs who had amassed most of the power in the Republic, generally applied to those who had served as consul. Their wealth came from land ownership, because commercial enterprise or trade of any kind was beneath a nobile, and sometimes illegal. A man like Crassus, therefore, used intermediaries to manage his vast holdings and business ventures.

Optimates   Conservative, aristocratic senators who wished to limit the power of the popular assemblies in favor of the senate. They were opposed by the *populares*, of which Julius Caesar was the most famous. Men like Pompeius and Cicero switched back and forth between factions. Marcus Crassus sided with the optimate Sulla until his death, but thereafter, his business interests were better served by being a purported voice of the people. The truth is, most senators backed whichever party could give them more personal wealth and power. The people's needs had to be met only to the extent that it kept them in power.

Optio   Junior officer, assistant to a centurion.

Orarium   A small, linen handkerchief for wiping the face.

Ornator   Slave who adorned or dressed his master; f. *ornatrix* (who concentrated more on her hair.

Otium   The Roman concept of leisure, ideally occupied by pursuits of philosophy, art and music in a natural setting.

<u>Palla</u> Cloak. Usually a rectangular piece of fabric worn for modesty over the stola and/or tunic.

<u>Palaestra</u> A large central courtyard devoted to exercise and games, usually adjacent to a balnea or thermae, sometimes including a pool.

<u>Paludamentum</u> The official cloak worn by a Roman commander in the field.

<u>Paterfamilias</u> Head of the household: the father.

<u>Peculium</u> Money or property acquired by slaves in the course of conducting business on behalf of their master. While technically any such gains belonged to the slave's owner, the master might allow these sums to be considered the slave's property, and might even allow these assets to be used to purchase the slave's freedom.

<u>Patria potestas</u> In Roman family law, the male head of the family held absolute power over the lives of his wife and children, even their descendants, as long as he lived. It was even within his right to administer capital punishment, if he saw fit. Under the law, all possessions accrued by his offspring, or given as gifts by the father, were still the legal property of the father.

<u>Pelargós</u> Greek. A stork.

<u>Peplos</u> Long sleeveless tunic worn by Roman women. Illustration courtesy of vroma.org.

Peristyle A spacious courtyard within a Roman home, open to the sky, framed by a covered colonnade. The picture above was taken by Carlo Brogi in 1896 of a reconstructed peristyle in Pompeii.

Phalera A sculpted disc worn on the breastplate made from bronze, silver or gold denoting valor or victory in battle

Pilum Roman throwing spear; plural: pila.

Plebeians Free, non-citizens of Rome, also called plebs.

Pomerium The spiritual limits of the city of Rome, marked by cippi, small pedestals used as boundary posts.

Pontifex Maximus Supreme supervisor of all things religious, and of matters of worship both public and private. Guardian of the ancient customs. The Pontifex was not subject to any court of law or punishment. The pontifex maximus was elected for life.

Populares Aristocrats, like the optimates, but favoring stronger representation of the people in the popular assemblies and tribunes of the plebs who wielded power to veto senate rulings.

Praetor Chief law officer and deputy to the consuls.

<u>Primus Pilus</u> The most senior, decorated and experienced centurion of a legion, given command of the double-strength first century of the first cohort, which would mean 160 legionaries at full strength.

<u>Pteruges</u> Leather strips protruding from under the cuirass that offered some protection for the shoulders and thighs.

<u>Pugio</u> Dagger.

<u>Quaestor</u> An officer in charge of military and civic treasury, as well as record-keeping.

<u>Quaestorium</u> In the late Republic, a Roman military camp's supply tent, as well as the quarters of the quaestor. During the Empire, the quaestorium came to be used to store booty and high-ranking prisoners.

<u>Quintilis</u> The seventh month of the pre-Julian Roman calendar, i.e. July.

<u>Quinquereme</u> A large Roman warship with five rowers to a side on three levels.

<u>Raeda</u> 4-wheeled carriage, usually pulled by two, sometimes four horses.

<u>Rage of the Dog Star</u> See malaria

<u>Rostra</u> The large, raised platform in the *Comitium* where consuls and other magistrates spoke to the Roman people.

<u>Sagum</u> Military cloak.

<u>Salve</u> Good Day! Good Morning! Also used in bidding farewell, as was *vale*. *Ave* is a less formal usage and "would seem to be more a morning greeting or a simple expression of goodwill" (http://catholicforum.fisheaters.com/index.php?topic=26 67068.0;wap2).

<u>Salutatio</u>   A time-honored tradition of the patron-client relationship. At the start of each day, the patron would don his toga, open the doors to his home and give audience to all the men dependent on him for council, favors and money. In return, the clients might be asked to perform certain services, such as drumming up political support or gathering information.

<u>Scutum</u>   Roman shield. During the late Republic, the shield had evolved into a convex rectangle of several plies of wood, approximately 4 feet tall by 2-1/2 feet wide. The center held an iron boss, used both offensively and defensively. This shield, or some variation of it, was at least as important a part of a legionary's kit as his weapons (a foot soldier's armor was far from invulnerable). It weighed anywhere from 12 to 22 pounds. Unless on parade or in battle, the shield was kept dry in a goatskin or leather bag.

<u>Serapeum</u>   It is said that the Royal Library of Alexandria, the greatest collection of books in the known world, was accidentally destroyed by Julius Caesar during his war with Pompey. The surviving scrolls were moved the temple of Serapis, or the Serapeum.

<u>Sestercius</u>   Brass Roman coin worth one quarter of a silver denarius; plural: sesterces. 100 sesterces equaled 1 gold aureus.

Sherwal   Baggy trousers tied at the ankles. The garment originated in Persia but is still worn today by Kurds and other peoples of the Levant and Middle East.

Sixth hour   The Roman sixth hour of the day was always noon; The sixth hour of the night was always midnight.

Sol Invictus Latin: another name for Mithra

Somnus Roman god of sleep.

Stoa Greek. An open, columned, covered portico or walkway, sometimes storied.

Stola   Long sleeveless tunic worn by women over other tunics; a symbol of marriage.

Strigil In the Roman baths, after oil has been applied, this curved metal tool was used to scrape dirt and sweat from the body.

Subligaculum   Underwear worn by either men or women, usually a wrapped loin cloth.

Tablinum Room usually between atrium and peristyle where guests were received and records kept.

Tepidarium The warm bath where Romans soaked after the steam or hot bath, then cleaned themselves before venturing into the frigidarium, or cold pool. It did not always have a pool, but did keep its occupants warm with heated walls and flooring.

Theater of Pompeius A derivative work of a 3D, Computer generated image of the Theatre of Pompey by the model maker, Lasha Tskhondia. The temple of Venus Victrix is at the lower left, the Portico is at

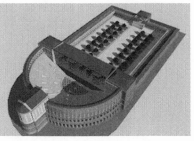

the upper right. Below, an early 19th century lithograph by A. Schill depicting, from the left, the stage building, the stage itself (front curtain removed), the semi-circle of the orchestra, seating and the temple of Venus Victrix.

DAS THEATER DES POMPEJUS MIT DEM TEMPEL DER VENUS VICTRIX. Von Ad. Schill.

Toga praetexta The toga of the curule magistrate, off-white, with a 2- to 3-inch wide purple border along one side. Also worn by boys until the age of sixteen or seventeen, and by men engaged in sacred rites.

Tonsor Barber.

Triclinium The dining room in a Roman house, its name derived from the fact that three wide couches, each accommodating up to three diners, comprised the seating. A table in the center held food and the fourth side was left open for servants to move in and out of the dining area. A diagram and pictures may be found on my blog at http://www.andrewlevkoff.com/blog/files/meals.php.

Trierarch Captain of a Trireme.

Trigon A ball game with three players who stood at the points of a triangle about 20 feet apart. The ball, small and hard, perhaps like our baseball, was thrown to one or the other players (feints were encouraged), and points were scored for left-hand catches, hitting the other player and batting the ball without actually catching it. Slaves were on hand to keep score and fetch lost balls.

<u>Trireme</u>   Originally Greek, then Roman galley. Approximately 120 feet long, they were powered by 170 rowers on three levels. Picture courtesy of Zvezda Models.

<u>Triumph</u>   The crowning achievement of a Roman imperator, or general. City-wide celebration of a great victory awarded to the returning victor. In Republican Rome, only the senate could grant a triumph. As the parade marched through the city, according to Tertullian, a slave would stand behind the general in his chariot, holding a bejeweled wreath over his head and whispering over and over to remember that the imperator was only human.

<u>Typhoid fever</u>   We do not know what the Romans called this disease, but have inferred that it might be named after the red spots that often appear on the victims' chest and abdomen.

<u>Urukku steel</u>   The first true steel, believed to be manufactured in what is now modern-day India between 500 and 300 BCE. Also known as wootz steel. Pounding

heated urukku steel formed what was known by the Middle Ages as Damascus steel (made by this process since about 330 BCE), characterized by its swirling patterns of color, strength and flexibility. Although Romans knew of it, for unknown reasons they never attempted to manufacture it in any quantity.

<u>Venatio</u> Literally, the hunt, but in reality, a slaughter. Wild beasts were brought into the arena and either killed by the least respected class of gladiators, called *bestiarii*, or used as a form of execution of criminals. If the ancient historians are correct, by the end of the empire, literally tens of thousands of lions, elephants, panthers, bears, leopards, bulls, hippopotami, crocodiles, giraffes, rhinoceroses and other exotic animals were butchered.

<u>Virtus</u> The Roman god of military strength and bravery, as embodied in the manly characteristics of valor, courage, toughness and the stoic bearing of adversity. These qualities of virtus defined much of ancient Roman society. When depicting qualities associated more with ancient Greeks than Romans, such as virtuousness and moral fortitude, Virtus is sometimes depicted as female.

<u>Vulpecula</u> A little fox.

<u>Zeus Eleutherios</u> Zeus the Liberator. A temple in the form of a stoa was constructed to honor the god at the end of the 5th century BCE.

•••

TIMELINE – all years BCE, Before the Common Era

115	Born: Marcus Licinius Crassus Dives
106	Born: Gnaeus Pompeius Magnus, Marcus Tullius Cicero
105	Born: Alexandros of Elateia
100	Born: Gaius Julius Caesar, Tertulla, wife of Marcus Crassus
93	Born: Livia, daughter of Sabina
89-85	First War with Mithridates, King of Pontus
88	Sulla marches on Rome to oust Marius and Cinna
87	Crassus' father and brother murdered by Marius supporters
86	Athens sacked by Sulla; Alexandros taken as a slave
86	Born? Cassius Longinus
85	Born? Marcus, Crassus' eldest son (debated)
84	Born? Eran Spahbodh Rustaham Suren-Pahlav; Cinna murdered by his own troops
83-82	Sulla's 2nd march on Rome; both Pompeius and Crassus fight for Sulla against Marius
83	Born: Marcus Antonius
82	Born: Publius, Crassus' youngest son (debated)
82-81	Lucius Cornelius Sulla dictator of Rome
79	Sulla retires to his estate to write his memoirs
78	Death of Sulla (60)
76	Born: Melyaket puhr Karach
73	Crassus elected praetor
73-31	War of Spartacus, which Crassus wins, but for which Pompeius takes credit
70	Crassus and Pompeius elected as consuls

66 Pompeius given unprecedented authority to defeat the Cilician pirates

66-64 Pompeius participates in the victory of the Third Mithridatic War and makes Pontus a Roman province in 64 BCE

65 Crassus elected censor

63 Born: Octavian, the future Augustus Caesar; Pompeius establishes Roman supremacy over Coele-Syria (including Judea) and Phoenicia; Pompeius defiles, but does not steal gold from temple in Jerusalem; Caesar appointed pontifex maximus

61 Pompeius celebrates his third triumph on his 45th birthday

60 Caesar elected consul

59 Caesar, Pompeius & Crassus form what historians will call the first triumvirate; Caesar marries Calpurnia; Pompeius marries Julia, Caesar's daughter

58? Publius accompanies Caesar to Gaul

56 The conference at Luca-deal to make Pompeius governor of Spain, Crassus governor of Syria & Caesar commander in Gaul for another 5-year term is struck; Gabinius aborts his invasion of Parthia to re-install Ptolemy on the throne of Egypt

55 Pompeius inaugurates his theater; Pompeius and Crassus serve their second term as consuls; in November, Crassus departs for Syria

49 Caesar crosses the Rubicon, civil war ensues

44 Gaius Julius Caesar assassinated.

BIBLIOGRAPHY

Balsdon, J.P.V.D. *Life and Leisure in Ancient Rome*. McGraw-Hill, 1969.

Burns, Thomas S. *Rome and the Barbarians, 100 B.C. – 400 A.D.* Johns Hopkins University Press, 2003, p.114.

Cassius Dio. *Roman History, Book XXIX*. Loeb Classical Library Edition, 1914.

Carcopino, Jerome, Cicero: The Secrets of His Correspondence, Volume 1. Greenwood Press, 1969, pp. 208-209.

Ferrero, Guglielmo. *The Greatness & Decline of Rome, Vol. II, Julius Caesar*. G. P. Putnam's Sons, 1907, p. 91, Chapter VI.

Ginzel, E. A. *Steel in Ancient Greece and Rome*. http://www.tf.uni-kiel.de/matwis/amat/def_en/articles/steel_greece_rome/steel_in_ancient_greece_an.html. 1995.

de Jongh, Brian. *The Companion Guide to Greece*. Companion Guides, 2000, p.191.

Libanius_Redux, http://libaniusredux.blogspot.com/, Antiochepedia = Musings Upon Ancient Antioch

Matyszak, Philip. *Legionary, The Roman Soldier's (Unofficial) Manual*. Thames & Hudson, 2009.

Mitchell, Stephen. *Blucium and Peium: The Galatian Forts of King Deiotarus*, British Institute at Ankara, 1974.

Plutarch. *The Parallel Lives, Comparison of Nicias and Crassus*. Loeb Classical Library, 196.

Plutarch. *The Life of Crassus*. Loeb Classical Library, 196.

Rawlinson, George, M. A. *The Sixth Great Oriental Monarchy or the Geography, History and Antiquities of Partha*, Dodd, Mead & Company, 1890.

Seager, Robin. *Pompey the Great*. Wiley-Blackwell, 2002.

Ward, Allen Mason. *Marcus Crassus and the Late Roman Republic*. University of Missouri Press, 1977.

ABOUT THE AUTHOR

Andrew Levkoff grew up on Long Island, New York, got a BA in English from Stanford, then put that hard-earned degree to dubious use in the family packaging business. After a decade of trying to convince himself to think 'inside' the box (lots of them), he fled to Vermont where for eight years he attempted to regain his sanity by chopping wood and shoveling snow off his roof.

Since 2005 he has been taking the cure out West, where his skin has darkened to a rich shade of pallid. Andrew lives in Phoenix with his wife, Stephany and their daughter, Allison, crowded into close proximity by hundreds of mineral specimens Stephany and he have collected while rockhounding. "They're just a bunch of rocks," says Allison. Ouch.

Since its publication in the fall of 2011, *The Other Alexander,* the first installment of *The Bow of Heaven* series, has been read by lovers of historical fiction worldwide.

www.andrewlevkoff.com

Made in the USA
Charleston, SC
15 January 2013